FIRE & ICE

A Last Resort Novel

By

NATHAN BIRR

Published by BEACON BOOKS, LLC

Cover Images Copyright ©
SeanPavonePhoto/iStock/Thinkstock
panic_attack/iStock/Thinkstock
Amir Kaljikovic/Shutterstock.com

ISBN: 978-0-9981813-6-3 (hc)
ISBN: 978-0-9981813-7-0 (sc)

www.nathanbirr.com

To my wife, Sierra . . .

Thank you for always being there.

Chapter One

It wasn't supposed to be like this, Rachel Taylor thought as she looked out the window of the Boeing 737. After a long, cold winter and a raw, rainy spring, she had anticipated being welcomed to Myrtle Beach by tropical sunshine and heat, not more rain. She was supposed to see sun-kissed palm fronds fluttering against the late afternoon's deep blue sky, not wind-whipped and rain-battered gargoyles gyrating in the dark. Her first glimpse of the Atlantic Ocean in years was to be of a magnificent body of blue, not of an indistinguishable black mass identifiable only by the lack of any orange lights dotting its surface.

As the wheels thudded to the runway, Rachel looked over at her husband of ten years—minus a few weeks—Jake. He hated flying, not because of any fear of heights or a particular phobia, but because it reminded him of the death of his parents nearly fifteen years ago. They'd gone down in a small plane crash—coincidentally on a rainy, windy night like this one. He had chosen to cope with that hatred of flying by sleeping most of the way from Chicago, leaving Rachel to browse a travel book she'd brought along. An actual travel book, not TripAdvisor or Wikipedia.

His caramel brown eyes jarred open, and Rachel took his hand, offering him an anchor in the present. Jake smiled in response, then leaned slightly forward to look past her. "Paradise, huh?"

"Hardly," she said, rolling her head back to look out the window. As they screamed down the runway, they might as well have been in Chicago or back

1

home in Omaha for all she could see. In addition to the darkness and rain, a fog hung over the airport like a cloak. She'd checked the forecast a dozen times in the last week, and it called for abundant sunshine and highs in the mid to upper 80s most days. With a sigh, she accepted the lack of fanfare accompanying their arrival and banked on things being better tomorrow.

They had left their suburban home at 7:00 a.m., arriving at Omaha's Eppley Airfield at 7:45, a good hour and a quarter before their scheduled departure. Scheduled, as it was delayed ninety minutes—spent sitting on a cramped Airbus and not in the terminal where they could at least get up and move around—while an issue with the plane's communications system was resolved. Then they hovered over the Illinois-Wisconsin border as heavy rain and midday thunderstorms delayed their landing in Chicago by another hour. The net result of the two delays was that they stepped off the Jetway into the terminal at O'Hare International four minutes before their connecting flight departed. They dashed to their next gate—of course in a different concourse—disregarding full bladders and rumbling stomachs, and arrived literally as their plane was pushing away from the gate. So they spent four hours wandering around O'Hare, waiting for the next flight, which fortunately had room for standby passengers. The only benefit, and one Rachel hadn't cared about at the time, was that the airline upgraded them to first class for free, meaning they got to deplane first. Now, after a day in "the tube," Rachel was as glad as she was sure Jake also was to leave planes and airports behind.

Jake was the type who could pack for two weeks in a single, standard-sized duffel. Rachel, on the other hand, had two large suitcases full of clothes and shoes; a small hardside case for cosmetics and toiletries; a tote bag full of books and magazines, brochures on various Myrtle Beach establishments, a neck pillow, her camera, and other miscellaneous travel items; her laptop case; and her purse. So when the jet finally docked at its gate after what seemed like far too much taxiing for a relatively small airport, they quickly unbuckled their seatbelts and began retrieving items from under the seats and in the overhead compartment.

A pretty and petite flight attendant came to "help" Jake with his bag in the overhead compartment. At just shy of six feet, Jake didn't need help from a five-six—if that—peroxide blonde, but Rachel was used to it. Maybe not in the league of Ryan Gosling or Chris Pine, Jake had what she termed "natural good looks," and drew plenty of glances and flirts from other women. If Jake noticed, he didn't let on, and he'd never given Rachel any reason to doubt his fidelity. Which is why, instead of a crooked scowl, she plastered a smile on her face as they filed past the pretty, petite, peroxide blonde and off the airplane.

Carry-ons over each arm and her laptop case in one hand, Jake reached over and quickly massaged Rachel's neck before draping his arm over her shoulders. "You hungry?" he asked as they emerged from the Jetway to the terminal at Myrtle Beach International Airport. He spoke with a typical Nebraska drawl, one he denied having, as did all Nebraskans. Rachel—a former Long Islander—could still hear it, but had long ago stopped minding.

"Oddly, no," she answered. They'd had lunch in Chicago—if you could call overpriced airport fast food "lunch"—and then a snack before their flight departed. And, of course, four mustard-flavored pretzels in the air. "Right now," she said, "I just want to get to the condo and crash."

"I thought you wanted to make a break for the beach right away. This way."

Rachel sighed and followed Jake under a sign with an arrow and the words, "Baggage Claim." Making a break for the beach had been her plan. She'd gotten through a hectic last week of work by closing her eyes and picturing settling her feet into the warm sand and letting the saltwater rush ashore and caress her ankles. But the sand would be cool and her ankles wet from the rain before the waves ever reached them.

"How about something to drink at least?" Jake asked as they descended the escalator.

"Does something seem off to you here?" Rachel asked.

"Off?"

"I don't know," she said, surveying the airport. "I feel like we walked into a ghost town."

"After O'Hare, what wouldn't be? Plus it's dark."

"I don't know," she repeated as they stepped off the escalator.

Jake nudged her and turned the gesture into a point toward a sign advertising Boardwalk Café. "Coffee?"

He'd already passed a Caribou Coffee, which Rachel considered remarkable, so she could understand his preoccupation with java. "I could use a tea," she said, mumbling a "hot" at the end of it. Hot drinks on a tropical vacation—this was so messed up.

3

"We should have time before our luggage comes," he said, steering her toward the café.

Rachel pulled from under his arm. "No chance. I can see it now, we wait in line behind a dozen people or their cash register malfunctions, and by the time we get to the baggage claim, our luggage is lost forever in lost and found. You go get us something to drink. I'll wait for the luggage."

"You sure? You don't mind being left alone in this ghost town?"

She leveled a narrowed eye at him.

"I'm sure you're just feeling off because of how crazy the trip was."

The frown turned into a smirk. "Go," she said, giving him a slight push. She watched him for a fraction of a second, as she liked to do, just observing little things like his gait or the way he subconsciously did a little snap-and-pop thing with his hands or whistled as he walked. She also wondered if he knew his attempts to reassure her usually worked—even if she didn't really need that much reassurance.

The light by the baggage claim wasn't blinking yet, so she dug into her tote and withdrew her camera, a Canon EOS Rebel T5i. Knowing he would mock her for it later, she snapped a few quick pictures of him with the airport as a backdrop. Some women kept a journal; Rachel documented via photograph, enabling her to capture those quirky, spontaneous moments that were often some of the fondest to remember.

Smiling genuinely at last, Rachel returned the camera to her bag. Then she turned toward the baggage claim, determined not to let the airlines mess with her vacation any further.

Jake set his assortment of bags on the floor as he approached the counter at the Boardwalk Café. It was a spiffy little place, delineated by a rope fence resembling a dock railing, and decorated with other nautical knickknacks. The café's décor was the sort of thing that often went unnoticed by Jake, but maybe Rachel was wearing off on him. Or maybe having no responsibility for two weeks was freeing up his mind to be more observant. Perhaps that could also explain why he'd noticed the guy across the aisle and a row back checking out Rachel several times during the flight—like when she bent over to reach into her bag. Jake wasn't the jealous type—not that Rachel wasn't worth being jealous over—but he'd almost asked the guy, a soap-opera stiff with puffy black hair, if his eyes were stuck.

"How can I help you?" the cashier at the Boardwalk Café asked, and Jake pushed leering hunks from his mind.

"Large black coffee and a medium hot tea."

The cashier processed Jake's payment and stepped back to fill the drinks. Jake looked around, fiddling with the zipper on his Nebraska Cornhuskers jacket. It was one of those things, a tic you could almost call it, but he was constantly fussing with zippers on his jackets, coats, and sweaters. Rachel said it had to be OCD. He shrugged it off; it was hardly an impairment—at least until he started doing it with pants zippers too. But he had noticed she tended to buy him clothes with buttons instead of zippers.

"Excuse me, my friend," a man said as he lightly brushed Jake's elbow, reminding him that it was still sore from when he'd banged it in the plane's lavatory somewhere over the Appalachians. He really hated airplanes.

"No worries," Jake said, casting a quick glance at the man—a few inches shorter than him, similarly "mussed" dark hair, what might be categorized as a swarthy complexion. Yep, he was definitely more observant without work occupying his mind.

"Can you tell me where the restrooms are?" the man asked, leaning over the counter to speak to the cashier.

"Just ahead on your right," he answered, turning and gesturing over his shoulder, toward the baggage claim.

The man thanked him and headed off, and Jake watched him go and looked for Rachel until the cashier placed two drinks on the counter. Jake hoisted his bags back onto his shoulder and lifted them both with one hand.

"You need a carrier?"

"Nope, thanks."

Shifting the drinks so they rested in the palm of one hand, Jake mused for a moment that Rachel, a one-time waitress, would be impressed. He spent another moment wondering why, after several years of dating and a decade of marriage, he still cared if she was impressed by something so trivial. He hadn't spotted her a moment ago when his gaze followed the man toward the baggage claim, so shrugging such thoughts away, Jake set out to find his wife.

🌴　　　🌴　　　🌴

This trip, according to him, had been inspired by her.

A few months prior, as they had been preparing for bed—which, in her case, meant rubbing an assortment of cold creams, liniments, lotions, and ointments on her face, hands, arms, and feet; and, in his, laying out clothes for the morning—she'd rather flatly said, "Our marriage is kind of blah."

He rolled his belt into a circle so it wouldn't flop all over, ultimately knocking socks and underwear onto the floor before falling there itself. "Meaning?"

"There's just no spark."

"I bought you those silk pajamas last Christmas."

"And they were lovely," she said, looking up as she fluffed her pillow, "but I kept sliding out of bed."

"Hmm."

She removed a collection of decorative pillows, setting them on an armchair, then pulled back the covers. "Don't worry, this isn't the start of an 'I'm about to leave you' or 'I'm seeing someone' talk. But you have to admit, we're in something of a rut."

He furrowed his brow and shifted his mouth to the side, wearing an expression he'd practiced when he didn't know what else to say. It conveyed that he was at least trying to think of something to say, whether he was or wasn't.

"We go to work every day," she said, "we have dinner out on Friday's, movie nights on Sunday, you golf or watch football with the boys on Saturdays, I have small group on Wednesday nights. We come and go, we have our routine, we make scheduled time for each other, but it's such a . . ."

"Rut."

"Yes. We're more like roommates than a happily married couple."

"You're not happy?"

"Happy's the wrong word," she said as she got into bed. Not wearing silk pajamas, she didn't slide out. "But it isn't like it used to be, where coming home to each other was the highlight of our day. It's just the next . . . stage."

He made the face again as he sat on the bed, this time truly thinking.

"It's late," she said. "Something to think about." She leaned in, pursing her lips, and he gave her a kiss. "I do love you," she said.

"You have to say that."

"I don't have to mean it."

He nodded. "I love you too."

She turned off the light by the side of the bed. Ten seconds later, it came back on.

"What?" he asked.

"You had that look on your face."

"Which look?"

"The one where you act like you're trying to think of something to say, but unbeknownst to you, you actually are thinking of something to say."

"It's nothing."

Rachel made no move to turn out the lights.

"Seriously, Babe. It's nothing." He reached over to kiss her cheek, then settled under the covers.

Accepting his answer—or, more likely, that she wouldn't get anything more from him—she turned off the light.

"I just have to cancel an order for a matching silk robe to go with those pajamas."

Chapter Two

One of Rachel's two monster suitcases already stood beside her when Jake found her, clustered with fifty or sixty other people around baggage claim carousel number three. He admired her from the backside as he approached— her dark brown hair with a touch of natural wave, kept in a loose ponytail that reached to the middle of her back, lay over a three-quarter-sleeve white Henley accompanied by designer blue jeans. Quite a contrast to his T-shirt, wind pants, and the old Huskers jacket he'd donned on a crisp, cool morning back in Omaha. He looked like a basketball player at pre-game warmups, so she'd said when they left the house. She looked, as always, like a department store model. It was a compliment, even if he didn't pay it to her verbally.

"Here, Hon," he said, handing her both drinks. He wedged his way forward to search for her other suitcase and his Creighton University duffel bag. Hers came first, weighing in at just under a ton. Actually, at forty-nine and one-quarter pounds, thanks to some quick rearranging at the Eppley check-in counter to avoid an extra fee. He'd asked Rachel why she needed *so* many clothes, even for a two-week vacation. She'd answered that she wanted to look good. He'd countered by saying that it could be done with far fewer clothes, if she caught his drift. She'd caught it all right, and returned it with a playful slap to the arm.

Among the first to have all their bags—perhaps a perk of first class and perhaps not—they quickly headed for the exit. Rachel routinely expressed amazement at the ease with which Jake always knew where to go. One of the few secrets he kept from her was that it wasn't anything innate but rather his well-hidden roving eyes and planning ahead that made it look so effortless.

With the customary swoosh, the double set of glass doors opened and the Taylors, burdened with luggage, stepped out into the tropical, South Carolina air. It did not smell of salt, but rather diesel, and the first waft of breeze on Jake's skin was cool, not warm.

"So this is how Bugs Bunny felt when he popped up in a snowdrift instead of Pismo Beach."

"Normally I love your boyhood cartoon references," Rachel said, "but let's get a move on."

The rental car agencies were across the street from the terminal. They waited for a few cars and a shuttle, then crossed under a canopy that protected them from the elements. A raven-haired woman was the sole associate at the rental desk, and when Jake gave her his name, she pecked it into the computer and promptly bit down on her lip.

"Um, we have it in the system that you were to pick the car up by five."

"Our flight was delayed."

If Raven Hair bit her lip any harder, blood was going to squirt out. "Unfortunately, since you weren't here at that time, we couldn't hold the reservation."

Ignoring flashes from an old episode of *Seinfeld*, Jake glanced at Rachel. Her jade eyes conveyed fatigue and frustration. And a little of here-we-go-again.

"Are you telling me you gave our car to someone else?" Jake asked the woman behind the desk.

He was wrong, blood didn't come out. But her lip turned white. "I'm afraid so. It's a busy time of year, and when you didn't arrive by the scheduled time and corresponding grace period—" The phone rang. "—we assigned it to another customer, a walk-in. Excuse me." She picked up the phone and cheerily offered a canned greeting.

Jake looked to Rachel again, who gave an exasperated sigh. He felt for her hand in an effort to soothe her, but just as his arrived, she raised hers and crossed her arms over her chest.

"I'm sorry," Raven Hair said as she returned the phone to its cradle.

"Is there something else available?" Jake asked.

"Let me check . . ." she said with a total absence of conviction. A pained expression accompanied renewed lip biting. "I'm afraid not. It's late, and on a weekend . . ."

"You're telling me there's no car for us," Jake said evenly. "Not even a Chevy?"

"No, sir. I'm sorry. The soonest we can have something available would be tomorrow morning."

Jake turned to Rachel. She sighed again and swiped a strand of hair behind her ear.

"What about another agency?" he asked.

"I can make a few calls for you. Just one moment please," she added as another line rang. She answered with the same greeting, took a reservation over the phone—a five-minute process—then proceeded to place calls to several other rental agencies. Jake watched for steam to come from his wife's ears, but she appeared too tired to be angry.

Raven Hair hung up the phone. "Hertz and Enterprise both have available vehicles, but unfortunately, because you didn't give twenty-four hours' notice, we would still have to bill you for your rental with us."

"For real?" Rachel asked.

"Yes, ma'am, it's policy."

Rachel shook her head.

"Even though you didn't have a car for us?" Jake asked.

"We did have a car at the appointed time," Raven Hair answered meekly. "I'm very sorry, and I do feel bad about this. We will provide you with the first vehicle that becomes available if you choose. Otherwise I can book something from one of the other agencies."

"I'm not paying twice," Jake said.

"Then I can arrange for our shuttle to take you to your hotel, assuming it's within our service radius. Unfortunately, that's all I can do."

Jake looked again to Rachel, who gave him her "whatever" shrug.

"Fine," he said to the agent. After checking where they were staying and announcing, with a grand smile, that it was within their shuttle's courtesy range, she reached for a walkie-talkie.

"It's almost like someone doesn't want us to be here," Rachel muttered to Jake as Raven Hair called for the shuttle.

"What, you mean like God?"

10

"Or the other guy."

"Come morning, when the sun's out, all will be right with the world."

"It had better be."

Jake wrapped an arm around Rachel's shoulder and began humming "Holiday Road," the theme song from *National Lampoon's Vacation*.

The borders of Myrtle Beach, Rachel knew from her guidebook, were somewhat vague. Sure, Myrtle Beach had official city limits like any other municipality, but for practical purposes, North Myrtle Beach ran into Myrtle Beach, which ran into Surfside Beach and Garden City without a whole lot of delineation. But the "hub" of Myrtle Beach consisted of the recently constructed "Boardwalk and Promenade," a 1.2-mile-long oceanfront walkway that ran between the beach and an assortment of hotels, condominiums, shops, and restaurants that lined Ocean Boulevard. The hotels and condos continued north of the Boardwalk for another twelve to fifteen blocks, and it was this stretch from approximately 2nd Avenue North to 30th Avenue that constituted—at least in Rachel's mind—Myrtle Beach proper. Their condominium was at the north end of that strip (technically northeast, as the coast ran at almost a forty-five-degree angle to true north). Myrtle Beach International was south of Myrtle Beach proper by a mile or two, and also a mile inland, so their condo was just a few miles from it as the crow flies. But as the shuttle drove, it took a quarter of an hour, on top of a twenty-minute wait for the shuttle to pick them up in the first place.

They didn't even catch a glimpse of the ocean—black, amorphous blob that it was. Fog and drizzle took away all the charm of palm trees, and only the preponderance of beachwear shops and typical resort-town strip malls indicated they were anywhere of note as opposed to, well, Nebraska. Rachel didn't even remove her camera from her bag.

The shuttle dropped them at the lobby of their condo, a twenty-story, peach-colored high-rise off Ocean Boulevard, less than a hundred feet from the beach. The location had been a key selling point. The shuttle driver, a friendly, stocky guy named Orlando, offered to help them with their bags, but ever independent, Jake declined, and he and Rachel lugged their suitcases inside. They had reserved through the condo, paying a little extra—because she was worth it, Jake had said—for a ground-level suite that opened directly to beach access. The idea had been incredibly appealing to Rachel when she'd pictured sunshine instead of drizzle.

The suite was spacious, with a full kitchen, a cozy living room with beach views, and a private master bedroom with a fireplace. (Who'd have thought that would come in handy?) It was up-to-date, cutely decorated with an abundance of beach-themed curios and beautiful paintings, and full of amenities—flat screen TV, DVD and Blu-ray players, PS4, Keurig coffee (or tea) maker with a full complement of K-cups, every imaginable kitchen utensil or implement, plenty of bath and beach towels, and an in-unit washer/dryer combo that had caught Rachel's eye on the condo's website.

"We made it," Jake said, dropping the luggage off his shoulders at the door to the bedroom. Rachel did likewise and allowed herself to be enveloped in a warm hug. At five-eight, she was just "short" enough for him to kiss her head without straining, which he did before easing her back so that she faced him. "What would you say to a quick walk on the beach?"

"Jake, it's raining."

He shrugged. "It's drizzling. And you've been looking forward to dropping your bags and dashing onto the beach for weeks."

"That was with a daytime arrival and tropical weather in mind, not Omaha in November."

"It's still the beach, still our first night."

"And it's still raining."

He shrugged again. "So you get a little wet," he said, brushing some hair off her forehead. "When we get back, I'll draw you a nice hot bath and take care of dinner."

"I hadn't even thought about dinner," she said, shrugging back from his grasp. "So what, ordering pizza?"

"That hurts a little, but yes. We'll veg, relax, and tomorrow when the sun comes out, the tropical vacation begins in earnest."

She hesitated. He pulled a face, a puppy-dog pleading that was just this side of pathetic. It worked half the time.

"Okay," Rachel conceded. "Just let me put on something warmer."

"What every guy wants to hear before heading to the beach with his girl."

She stuck out her tongue and turned toward the bedroom, getting a tiny pat on the rear as she did.

This trip, according to her, had been his idea.

She'd returned home from work one Friday, dropped her heels in the entryway, thrown her purse on the counter, and padded to the refrigerator. Friday nights they dined out, but after a full day of work, she was starving and needed a little snack. Besides, Jake never made reservations earlier than eight.

Rachel stopped cold when she saw a fully set dinner table: fine china, crystal goblets, and more silverware—actual polished-silver silverware—than was necessary. Two long-stem candles stood in the middle of the table on either side of the centerpiece of fresh flowers.

"Hon?" she called.

Jake appeared from down the hallway, wearing the tuxedo he'd bought for their wedding. "You're just in time. My lobster bisque is almost ready."

"What lobster bis—Jake, what's going on?" She looked from the bare stove back to him in his tux. "What are you wearing?"

"I think you have a few minutes to change," he said. "I laid something out for you on the bed."

She narrowed her eyes. "Jake Taylor, what are you up to?"

"Patience, my dear, patience."

At his repeated urging, she retreated to the bedroom where she found a floral sundress—one of his favorites—laid across the comforter. It was also one of her favorites, fitting her perfectly and comfortable enough to wear all day. She quickly changed, brushed out her hair, freshened up for a few minutes, and returned to the kitchen.

"You look beautiful," Jake said.

"Thank you, but it's a little cold outside for a sundress."

"Are you cold? I set the heat to seventy-five."

"I'm fine. What is going on? Why are we dressed like this?"

"After the first course." He nodded at the table and pulled out her chair for her. He retreated to the kitchen and returned with two steaming bowls of creamy liquid.

"You didn't?"

"I had some help from Bonefish Grill. There's bread too," he said, ducking back into the kitchen. Rachel reached for a goblet of water, too stunned to process any rational thought as to what he was after. Jake wasn't completely inept in the romance department, but his idea of wooing Rachel was to spring for dessert after dinner or suggest a chick flick instead of the newest iteration of *Mission: Impossible.*

Jake returned, and Rachel ladled the first spoonful of lobster bisque. He just smirked, looking downright debonair in the tuxedo she hadn't seen in a decade. It brought back a flood of happy memories, along with serious questions as to whether or not she'd fit into her wedding dress—or anything from that long ago.

He made the usual small talk as they ate, asking about her day, plans for the weekend, etcetera. Usually, she had to force such conversation on him, and it was all he could do to muster the appearance of enthusiasm. Tonight, she found him hanging on every word. If this was just a ploy for sex . . .

When they finished their bisque and bread, he cleared away their dishes. He puttered in the kitchen for a moment before announcing dinner would need just another minute.

"What are we having?" she asked, sniffing but failing to catch the aroma.

"Wild Mahi Mahi with jasmine rice and French green beans."

"Sounds delicious."

He reached for a folder on the counter and slid it to her.

"What's this?"

He simply nodded at the folder. She opened it to find a pair of airline tickets.

"Myrtle Beach?" she asked.

"We leave a month from tomorrow."

Her eyebrows shot up. "Hon . . . I can't possibly. I've got wor—"

"I spoke to Beth. You have over a month of unused vacation time. I swore her to secrecy and talked her into giving you two weeks off."

"You did what?"

He didn't reply, staring at her with flame-licked brown eyes.

"What are we going to do in Myrtle Beach for two weeks?"

"Keep looking," he said with another nod at the folder. "We have a beachfront condo. You can watch the waves roll in, have breakfast on the patio, read under an umbrella." He flicked his eyebrows up. "I can always reorder that silk robe."

She rolled her eyes.

"You said we were in a rut," he said, a serious look taking over his face.

"And you think this is the fix?"

"A surprise vacation won't prematurely pop us out of a rut. But it's a start. And I did some thinking," he said while she flipped through several brochures from the folder—the condo, shopping, attractions, lots of seafood. "You were right when you said we were more like roommates. So we're going to spend two weeks together, just the two of us, doing everything together. Call it placing kindling in a fireplace. It won't burn through the night, but it will get a smoldering fire going again."

She looked at him, a smile breaking out on her face. "You're not just doing this for the golf?"

"They have golf in Myrtle Beach?" he deadpanned.

"Two weeks in Myrtle Beach? In a month? I'll need to do some shopping."

"I've cleared my calendar for tomorrow. Why else do you think I asked about your plans? We'll hit the mall, that boutique downtown you like, and we'll buy everything you need. Money is no object for this trip."

Her smile couldn't be contained. "I like the way you're talking. I just hope my husband won't mind."

Chapter Three

Jake was torn. He enjoyed walking arm-in-arm with Rachel down a mostly deserted beach, feeling her beside him, her arm around his waist. But she looked so darn cute—with her hair bundled behind her head, a little damp, strands blowing everywhere, and with the tails of a loose purple-and-white striped sweater trailing in the breeze, her jeans cuffed to mid-calf as she walked barefoot across the sand—that he wanted to hang back a few paces and watch her. It was not something he admitted to his buddies or even his brothers, but every once in a while, Rachel still took his breath away. Actually, more often than that. She was in her mid-thirties now instead of her mid-twenties, and it showed in little ways. But not half as much as she feared it did, and not in a way that diminished her intrinsic beauty and appeal. Thinking of that, he gave her a quick squeeze and decided to keep walking arm-in-arm. Besides, it was kind of cool. Normally warm blooded, having grown up in the Midwest, he was glad he'd thought to bring his jacket on the walk, even if he'd done so less for himself and more in case Rachel needed it.

They'd exited their condo onto a spacious deck with chaise lounges and a four-place table and chairs with umbrella. Their building was a typical high-rise, with ground-level projections that extended at forty-five-degree angles toward the beach. Containing several suites each, these "feet" of the building formed an enclave between them that was home to the condo's pool, public deck, and tiki bar. The Taylor's suite was at the end of the southern projection and situated such that their deck looked not at the pool area but at the seagrass-covered dunes that formed a barrier between the beach and the building. Two wooden footbridges, one just south of their condo and one a couple dozen yards north, provided access through the dunes and grass to the beach.

The breeze was off the ocean, meaning neither direction was into or with the wind. For no particular reason, Jake and Rachel had opted to go south and had strolled mostly in silence for ten minutes. Up ahead, the lights along the Boardwalk—most prominently those on the neon-clad, nineteen story SkyWheel—reminded them that they weren't alone on a deserted beach. So did the row of high-rises to their right and the beams of flashlights swirling back and forth across the sand. Crabbers, Jake realized.

At a secluded spot on the beach, Rachel suddenly stopped. She reached up and gave Jake a slow, soft kiss. When she stepped back, her eyes sparkled, he knew despite the lack of light. They always sparkled when she kissed him.

"What was that for?" he asked.

"This," she said, taking his hand and pulling him farther along the beach.

"This the walk or this the vacation?"

She shook his hand as a way of brushing off his corniness.

"So'd I finally get it right?" he asked a few minutes later.

"Don't say that."

"Why not? It's true."

"Yes."

"Yes it's true, or yes I got it right?"

"You got it right. This is the perfect vacation. Well, in theory. So far it's pretty dreary and abysmal, but that's not on you. The idea is perfect."

"Good," he said, giving her hand a squeeze. He couldn't help but think that his "missing the mark" was one of the reasons their marriage had become, in her words, blah. It wasn't like he was totally out of tune with her—just the opposite, she often assured him. But his gestures of love and kindness always seemed a little . . . off.

"I'm glad you didn't give up," she said. "After my birthday last year, I wasn't sure you'd ever try again."

He'd thrown her a surprise birthday party, at thirty-four instead of a benchmark like thirty-five, so she definitely wouldn't suspect it. The surprise wasn't so much the problem as the when, on a Friday night and after a hectic week of work. And he'd invited a couple from church that Rachel couldn't stand, couldn't seem to get along with. To top it off, his present to her had been singing lessons. Rachel loved to sing and knew she wasn't very good at it. The truth was, she was terrible, and Jake had thought lessons would be something she'd appreciate. They hadn't been perceived that way, despite his best explanations.

"Well, going for another surprise made me nervous," he admitted. "It's just frustrating, because I am trying."

"I know," she said.

"And I don't mean that to blame you. It's just . . ."

"We're on different wavelengths," she finished.

"X and Y chromosome."

"I don't know. I think it's more than that."

"Then what?"

She stopped, folding her arms over her. Jake didn't know if she was cold or creating distance from him. She opened her mouth twice but closed it without speaking.

"Come on, Rach, I can take it."

"I think you sometimes get so consumed with an idea that you forget to fully think it through. You don't always consider how a thoughtful gesture to you might seem totally different to me."

"Like the singing lessons."

"Uh-huh. Or that time you invited Mom to come stay with us."

"You had just said how much you missed her."

"Yes, but that doesn't mean I wanted her staying with us for two weeks, looking over my shoulder while I cooked or cleaned, making sure everything was up to her standards . . . I also said how she and I don't do well in long spurts in close proximity."

Jake winced, remembering what had been a rough fortnight with Rachel's mom in the house. It had been another week after that before Rachel had kissed him and meant it.

"Or the time you lined our bed with rose petals and cinnamon candles and forgot that I'm allergic to cinnamon."

"Yeah, that kind of got messy. All the sneezing . . ."

She reached for both of his hands, holding her palms against his. "But I don't want you to stop trying." Her fingers were like the legs of a spider, tiptoeing across his hand.

Jake opened his mouth to reply but shut it.

"Out with it, Taylor."

"I feel dumb even saying it, it's so typical. You should give me more hints."

"I do give you hints. Like the time I left that Target circular open on the coffee table for a week leading up to my birthday after telling you how much I wanted a new kitchen stand mixer. Or how I repeatedly complained about the living room furniture not matching."

"Which is why you seemed less than thrilled by that devotional book on contentment."

She continued to play with his hands. "I mean, I hate to have to come right out and tell you 'Do this nice thing for me' or 'Buy me this specific present.'"

"I don't want that either."

She leaned into him. "Small potatoes," she said at last. "And we'll work on it. I'll be more creative in leaving clues without beating you over the head."

"And I'll try to be more Sherlock and less Watson."

She shivered.

"Ready to head back?" he asked.

"Yes."

"See, I can read signals just fine."

"Elementary, Sherlock."

"So what's the itinerary for this trip?" Rachel asked as they walked side-by-side back toward the condo. They had discussed a lot of options while looking at websites and visitors' brochures over the last few weeks but had yet to set anything in stone.

Jake shrugged. "Let's just see how it goes."

Rachel took a few slow steps. "I meant, is there any plan besides all the touristy stuff we talked about?"

"You mean . . ."

"No, I do not mean that," Rachel said with a demure smile. "I mean, you said this trip was about rekindling our marriage."

"I did say that."

"So any plans for that, other than spending two weeks together?"

He took a few steps. "Not especially."

"Because if that's all we do, I'm afraid this will be a really nice trip, and by the middle of summer, we'll be back to the same old Jake and Rachel."

"We could move to Myrtle Beach."

She gave him a playful glare.

"I hear you," he said.

"To that end, I've been thinking."

"Have you?"

"We should use this time to really talk things out. We're on a romantic getaway, with no distractions. We both want things to get better, want to work on it. I think it's the perfect, safe environment to have conversations we might not otherwise."

Jake said nothing. Rachel's heart pounded inside her, exposing nerves she hadn't realized were there. The fact that they were, regarding something as unassuming as talking to her husband about discussing their marriage, spoke volumes.

"It opens a dialogue," she said, still selling. "Fuel to that kindling you mentioned."

"This isn't just you looking for an excuse to dump on me, is it?"

"It's not, Jake, I prom—"

He winked to show he'd been kidding as he said, "Then okay."

"Okay you'll go along with it to appease me or okay you actually think it's a good idea?"

"It's a good idea. Just nothing scripted, no talking points. I don't want this to turn into marriage self-counseling. We're not coming home to write a book about marriage retreats where we pose like Chip and Joanna on the cover."

"What's wrong with Chip and Joanna?"

"Nothing. You know the books I mean. Flowery script, heart-warming encouragement, chicken soupy stuff."

"No book about it," she said, resisting an eye roll. "Just sincerity."

He nodded.

"But nothing's off limits."

He nodded again, this time looking at her. "Fair enough."

The only sound for several minutes was the rhythmic washing of waves on the sand. Rachel cast her eyes to where white trails of foam distinguished themselves from the darkness. Even in the darkness, even with the drizzle, it was soothing.

"Okay, so you're the one who brought this up originally," Jake said. "Why is our marriage blah?"

She turned to him. "I really didn't mean it to be that harsh."

"No, I get it, and you're right. But what's at the root of it?"

"It's not a lack of love," she said after a moment. "I know I still love you and I know you still love me."

"I hear a 'but' coming."

She sighed. "Sometimes I wonder if we're still *in* love."

He slowed.

"I'm not saying we never have any feelings, but we seem to be missing the excitement, the heart palpitating, body tingling sort of feeling. Like it used to be."

He nodded and trudged. "I can see that, at least some of the time."

"Yeah, some of the time."

"You know, that's probably only natural."

"Sure. But I still miss it."

He was silent for a dozen paces. Then a dozen more. He was mulling, she could tell by the way he held his jaw.

"I think we've just gotten into a pattern," he finally said. "A rut, so to speak. Same house, same jobs, same entertainment, if you can call dinner and a movie entertainment. And we're completely used to each other. There's no mystery anymore. On the one hand, that all makes us incredibly functional. On the other hand, it leaves us—"

"Functional," Rachel said.

"Yeah."

"Not exactly the greatest descriptor of a married couple."

"No."

As had become the pattern, they took a few steps, thinking. Rachel pondered "mystery" for a little while. She'd long ago heard that a woman was supposed to possess mystery and even had read a Christian bestseller about the importance of maintaining some mystery for her husband. She still had no idea what that meant, unless it was being a dingbat who lost her keys and couldn't remember to make dinner or purposefully keeping secrets or going out of the way to be "mysterious." She put those thoughts aside, figuring it would make good pillow talk after one of Jake's thriller movies made it hard to sleep.

"You're right, I think," she said after a few more steps in the cool sand. "But it's more than just being stuck in a routine. That's part of life. But it's almost . . . It's almost like we've settled for 'stale.'"

Jake nodded.

"And that's the scariest part for me, that we've sort of accepted that this is the way it is."

"Except we're here," Jake said. "We're trying to fix it."

"We are," she said, reaching for his hand.

"Is there more?" he asked, rubbing his thumb over hers.

"I don't know. It's kind of hard to define. It's something I sense, something I feel. I know that isn't helpful, you need specifics. You're a left-brainer." She stared into his eyes. "Let me think on it. Try to come up with some concrete examples."

"Okay."

"And you do the same. Don't shrug it off."

"I'm not."

"I mean, don't just accept that it's routine. I think if you look deeply, you'll see it's more than that."

"I'm stale, and you're blah."

She punched him under the ribs.

"I'll think about it," he said.

She pulled him close. "I love you, Jake," she said by way of thanks.

"I love you too. Now, no more thinking tonight. You take a bath, I'll order some pizza, and then give you a good back massage."

"Mmm, now you're talking."

The rain had been spitting off and on, but it intensified into a steady drizzle, and they quickened their pace. Still holding her hand, Jake led Rachel up onto the deck, then spun her around and pulled her toward him as he leaned against the deck railing.

"What—"

He interrupted her with a kiss.

She backed away. "Jake, the rain's really starting to come dow—"

He kissed her again. "You liked *The Notebook*, right?"

"It's cold," she complained as he kissed her a third time. Then he stopped.

"What?" she asked.

He gently moved her to the side.

"Jake, what's going on?" she asked as she turned around, wiping a wet clump of hair from her forehead. She followed his eyes to the sliding glass door of their suite, which was slightly ajar.

"Did you close the door?" he asked.

"Yeah. Tight."

"You're sure?"

"Positive."

"Wait here," he said.

"Jake?"

He approached the door and slid it open, slipping into the darkness. She saw the light come on through the sheer curtains, then waited, shivering in the rain.

A minute passed, then Jake stuck his head out the door. "Come on in."

Rachel took his offered hand as she entered the condo. She stopped suddenly. The entire suite was a mess. Couch cushions and pillows on the floor, drawers and cupboard doors open, plants tipped over, and the contents of their suitcases strewn throughout the living room and into the bedroom.

Rachel felt her jaw drop and her hands reflexively rose to her face, tenting over her nose and mouth. "Jake," she said through her hands. She lowered them. "Jake, what happened?"

"I don't know, Babe. I don't know."

Chapter Four

"Have you identified anything missing?" Detective Robinson asked. He looked more like a former surfer than the stereotypical TV detective with a beer belly, graying or fading hair, and a cheap suit. He'd arrived five minutes ago, fifteen minutes after the first officers. He and his partner, a quiet Latina woman with short, spiky hair, had taken Jake and Rachel's statements. They were still shaken, having had their condo ransacked, but at least had calmed down. Rachel had initially shaken physically for five minutes, from either the cold or shock, and Jake had been worried. But she had regained her standard poise while talking to the detectives.

"Not that we've found," Jake answered. "We haven't had time to go through everything in detail yet, but we didn't notice anything."

"Were you traveling with any valuables, anything that might present a target?"

"We have a fair amount of cash," Jake said, "but we're here for two weeks, so considering that, I wouldn't say it's an unusually high amount."

"My jewelry," Rachel said with a shrug. "But it's all pretty standard."

"Anything from back home that might suggest someone would do this? Any problems with a boss or coworker, maybe a family member with whom there's bad blood?"

"No, nothing," Jake said. Rachel shook her head in agreement.

"Anything suspicious happen on your trip, once you got here? Anyone approach you in the lobby, did you see anyone lurking about as if surveilling you?"

Jake shook his head, even as he remembered the guy ogling Rachel on the plane. Checking out a good-looking woman in an airplane was a long way from tracking her down and breaking into her condo.

"Even if it wasn't suspicious, anything out of the ordinary?"

"Not that I can think of," Jake said.

"Other than our flights being delayed and them not having our rental car reservation," Rachel said. "No, nothing."

"Afraid there's nothing out of the ordinary about either of those," Robinson said. His half smile quickly faded. "This may seem like an odd question, but what were you folks wearing when you arrived?"

"You're looking at it," Jake said.

"I had on a shirt instead of this sweater," Rachel said.

"I ask because what you wear can make you a target, for example, if you're flaunting your wealth."

"Not exactly," Jake said, tugging on his jacket.

"No," the detective said with a tight smile. He closed his notebook. "We'll finish dusting for prints, see if there's anything obvious in the way of some piece of evidence left behind, and then go from there. It's not incredibly likely. And since he appears to have come in off the beach, the condo's security cams aren't likely to have anything, but we'll check to be sure."

"Thank you."

"I'll tell you, we get the occasional break-in, what with all the tourists. Usually, it's money or jewelry taken, but since you're not missing either of those, I'll admit it's a head-scratcher. Could be someone looking for drugs, but nothing missing on that front either. We'll see what we find here, see if there's any report of anyone breaking into other condos or hotels in the vicinity. It could be someone looking for something specific. Other than that, if you do notice something missing, if you notice something that maybe isn't missing but was tampered with, or spot anything suspicious—no matter how small— give me a call at this number," he said, providing Jake with a business card. "Anytime, night or day."

"Thank you, Detective."

He nodded, offered a handshake to both Jake and Rachel—as did his silent partner—and then went to talk to the officers processing the scene.

Jake turned to Rachel, read the look in her eyes, and opened his arms. She fell against his chest, and he held her tight, taking a brief moment to note that he'd successfully read another signal.

When Rachel had packed sleepwear Saturday, she'd been thinking of tropical romance, not vegging with pizza after their condo had been broken into. So she didn't have her comfy flannel pajamas along. Despite a long, hot bath, she was still cold from a walk in the rain, and perhaps more accurately, from what they had come home to. She still couldn't believe it.

The police had stayed until quarter to eleven, at which time the condo manager—who had come from his home across town after hearing what had happened—had offered Jake and Rachel a vacant "honeymoon" suite on the penultimate floor of the building, at no additional charge. He'd explained that a block of condos was actually owned by an agency for the specific purpose of renting them to tourists, and he'd made the necessary arrangements with the agency and contacted the owner from whom they had originally rented. Not interested in the details and citing the ways in which a nineteenth-floor condo was safer than one with beach access, Rachel had beat Jake in agreeing.

They had bundled up their things and ridden the elevator to the nineteenth floor, where the manager had shown them a room remarkably similar to their first one. The bedroom was larger, and opened to a balcony (instead of a deck), as did the living room. The décor, while distinct, was similar, and every amenity that had been included with their first condo was present here. A few upgrades were also thrown in—notably a whirlpool tub. After she and Jake thanked the manager profusely and assured him they had all they needed, Rachel had double-checked all the locks, left a pizza order of sausage and red peppers with Jake, and practically jumped into the tub.

Having soaked for a while, Rachel now toweled off and put on her comfiest pair of cotton pants and a black sweatshirt with an Iowa Hawkeyes logo emblazoned in yellow on the front, which she'd brought along just in case of a cool, rainy day. A gift from Jake a few years back, it was a size too big, but that's what made it cozy. Knowing that Jake liked her barefoot, she padded out into the living room.

The smell of pizza greeted her. Jake stood by the kitchen counter, a square, white box in his hands. "Just arrived," he said, setting it down and searching for plates. Content to be served, Rachel plopped onto the couch.

"What a day," she said, resting her head on her hand, her arm on the back of the couch.

"I went through most of our stuff while you were in there," Jake said.

"Find everything?"

"Near as I can tell. I tried putting it away, but I'm sure you'll need to rearrange it tomorrow."

He'd found plates, and carried two to the coffee table, each with a generous slice of pizza. Rachel had lost track of time—11:45!—and not noticed how hungry she was until she saw the pizza. She picked up her plate, cradling it for warmth, and waited for Jake.

"Fork?" he asked.

"No, just a napkin."

He returned with two, along with glasses of ice water. "Promised you five-star dining, didn't I?"

"After this day, it's perfect," she said, leaning forward for a quick kiss.

They ate mostly in silence, mulling what had happened and thinking through Detective Robinson's questions. Try as they might, neither could remember anything even vaguely suspicious from the time they'd left home that morning nor could they conceive of a reason for someone to break into their suite and ransack their possessions.

"Wrong room?" Jake guessed. They had finished eating, and she lay against his shoulder while he stroked her head.

"I suppose that's possible."

"Or maybe it's like Detective Robinson said, they were looking for something specific."

"Still, you go to the trouble of breaking in, you might as well take the cash if nothing else."

"True."

More silence.

"You ready for bed?" Jake asked.

"Yes."

"One condition."

She sat up and looked at him. "What?"

"Absolutely no alarm clock."

Rachel made short work of her evening routine, especially since she had no idea where Jake had put most of her stuff. She at least found her toothbrush, and was rinsing her mouth when Jake entered the bathroom.

"Rach, any idea what this is?"

She spat and wiped her mouth on a hand towel. She looked at his hand, which held something tiny.

"What is it?" she asked, reaching for it.

"Kind of what I asked you, Babe," he said, handing it to her.

She palmed the object, then teased it with her finger. Made of hard plastic or dull metal, it was maybe one centimeter by two, one end rounded, the other tapered. It was solid white except for silver trim on the square end.

"It's a USB drive, isn't it?"

"Not like any I've ever seen, but it might fit into a port."

"Looks like the dingle you get with a mouse or keyb—What'd I say?"

"Dongle, not dingle."

"It's late. Where'd you find this *dongle*?" she asked, brushing past him.

"It was in my jacket pocket."

"You didn't bring it home from work, did you?"

"I don't wear this jacket to work, and we don't have anything like this. I've never seen anything like this."

She shrugged. "Well, I have no idea."

He set it on the bedroom dresser. "A problem for tomorrow," he said and ducked into the bathroom.

Rachel exchanged her cotton pants for a pair of polyester shorts and the sweatshirt for a plain T-shirt, and quickly dove under the covers, passing on digging around for any of her lotions or creams. One night without them wouldn't kill her. Jake was only a few minutes and turned out the lights before crawling into bed.

"You don't think it has anything to do with the break-in, do you?" she asked as he adjusted his pillow underneath him.

"I don't know. I'll see if it plugs into your laptop tomorrow. Maybe that will give us a clue."

"Maybe."

"Don't worry, Hon. I'm sure it's nothing. Even if somebody broke in looking for it, they didn't find it, so they'll look elsewhere."

"I hope so."

They kissed good night, as was customary.

Rachel dropped her head back onto the pillow. "You locked the door, right?"

"Locked and bolted."

She sighed, and before she could mutter a comment about this being a lousy way to start a vacation, Jake had reached for and found her hand under the sheet, giving it a quick squeeze and then holding on tight.

Chapter Five

Jake was shocked to see light streaming through the drapes when he awoke. He was even more shocked to see Rachel still asleep beside him and, technically, on him, her arm draped across his chest. He'd expected her to be up and reading on the deck most mornings, a pot of coffee brewed for him by the time he got up. That was how it worked Saturdays back home.

He wiggled out from under her arm and stood. She stirred, turned over, but didn't wake up. Grabbing yesterday's clothes, he quickly dressed and trudged out to the kitchen, where he set about making a pot of coffee. While it brewed, he checked out the balcony.

The brightness momentarily blinded him, and he squinted against the onslaught. From down at the pool and beach, playful shrieks rose to the nineteenth floor, and he quickly slid the door shut behind him, lest they wake Rachel. He leaned on the railing, surprised at the warmth. He hadn't checked the time, but the sun was low enough that he knew it wasn't *that* late. And yet, the air was the warmest he'd felt since the previous summer.

Jake studied the brilliant blue water, the sky a few shades lighter and void of clouds, and traced the shoreline north and south. The Grand Strand, as it was called, stretched for some sixty miles, from Little River in the north to Winyah Bay in the south. From his vantage point, it looked as if the entire length of beach was lined with hotels and condos. He listened to the gulls squawking, the shouts from the pool, and the drone of a distant airplane approaching from the south. He waited long enough to read the banner behind the single-engine craft. It touted a pirate-themed dining experience. He'd have to check with Rachel.

He ducked back inside and filled a mug with coffee. He took it back into the bedroom and sat in a chair beside the dresser, watching her sleep. He often did so on the rare occasions when he woke before her, on nights when he came to bed after her, or when she took an afternoon nap on the sofa. Something about the peaceful, innocent nature of her slumber appealed to him as a provider and protector. This morning it also stirred thankfulness in him. Despite the "blah" nature of their marriage, he knew it wasn't in real jeopardy. He knew they were committed to each other, through thick or thin, and he had trouble imagining a better life partner than Rachel.

His eyes dropped to his coffee, and as they came back up, they panned over the counter and spotted the small object he'd found in his pocket the night before. He'd forgotten about it—even about the break-in—until now, and the reminder shattered his moment of tranquility.

Curiosity got the best of him. He set the mug down and tiptoed to the corner of the room, where he'd stashed Rachel's computer case. As delicately as possible, he lifted her laptop out of the case. As he turned, he bumped another suitcase, and it tipped into the dresser with a thud. Rachel stirred again, turned over, and opened her eyes.

"Jake?"

He had to grin. It was a typical morning question from her. He'd long ago stopped asking who else it would be.

"Sorry."

"What are you doing?" she asked, pushing back on her elbows and sitting up partway.

"Getting your computer. I want to check that whatever it was we found last night."

"Now? It couldn't wait until I was awake?"

"I was sitting here and I thought of it."

"Why didn't you bring your own laptop again?"

"Trying to get away from the things for a while." He tried a change of subject. "It's a beautiful, sunny, hot day."

Rachel turned her head. Just the muted light through the drapes forced her to squint.

"How'd you sleep?" Jake asked.

"Fine, until somebody decided to rearrange our luggage," she said with fake (he thought) anger.

"Sorry, Babe. Tell you what," he said, setting the laptop on the dresser. "This can wait. How about you have a shower, I'll make you some breakfast, and you can eat *al fresco* on the balcony."

"Won't Mrs. Fresco mind?" she said in her "dumb jock" voice. She usually reserved it for making fun of football players doing TV interviews, but every once in a while she used it to imitate Jake. In this case, to mock one of his standard corny lines.

"If I'd have known you'd be this cranky," he said as she pushed back the covers and stood, "I'd have definitely been more careful."

A moment later, his head was engulfed by an Iowa Hawkeyes sweatshirt.

He pulled it down to see her standing beside the bed, arms crossed. "What are you going to make me for breakfast? And if you say leftover pizza, no amount of 'rekindling' will be able to save this marriage."

Thirty minutes later, Rachel felt like a new woman. Showered and dressed in a comfy tank top and shorts—no more baggy sweatshirts for warmth—she sat on their nineteenth-floor balcony, basking in the warm sunlight and nursing a mug of tea that chased away any final vestiges of the previous night's chill. Jake had promised that breakfast was almost ready and that he was just going to hop in the shower for a few minutes.

Ten years of marriage in, she still had no idea how he did it. Granted, his hair was shorter, and he didn't have to shave his legs, but it was a mystery how he could enter the bathroom and emerge five minutes later showered, dressed, and smelling like aftershave. This was the same guy, after all, who took ninety minutes to "manicure" a quarter-acre lawn. Was that the type of mystery she was supposed to have for him, according to those "the wonder of a woman" sort of books?

Rachel breathed in the sea air, catching just a whiff of saltiness. She could feel the humidity on her skin, and although it wasn't a new sensation after a decade in Nebraska, it felt different here. In Omaha, summer humidity was oppressive and sticky. South Carolina's coastal version, at least to her, was like a warm embrace.

The doors slid open, and Jake emerged carrying a large serving tray with two glasses of orange juice, two small plates with buttered toast, and two larger plates covered with stainless steel domes.

"What have we here?" Rachel asked, noting that Jake looked and smelled clean in a blue polo shirt and a pair of matching board shorts. He'd balked when she'd suggested them, said he wasn't a frat boy. She'd said they'd look cute, had given him the faintest of pouts, and the deal had been sealed. And, she noted as he reached for the steel plate cover, she'd been right about the cuteness.

"Eggs benedict with hollandaise sauce," Jake said with a flourish. "Let me tell you, the hollandaise is tricky."

"And what do you know about hollandaise sauce?"

"Well, for starters, if you don't whisk your egg yolks until your arm falls off, it'll never turn out right."

She bit her tongue and shook her head. "I'm not buying it, Jake Taylor. You didn't run to the grocery store while I was in the shower, and I know a condo doesn't have room service, so how'd you pull this off?"

"Forgetting for a moment how insulted I am that you don't even think I could make hollandaise sauce, the condo does have a small bistro off the lobby that serves limited breakfast."

"Aha."

"For a nominal fee, they deliver."

"'The hollandaise is tricky,'" she mimicked.

"Well, it is."

"Jake, you can't even spell hollandaise. How do you know how to make it?"

"Remember a few years ago when I got hooked on the Food Network?"

"It had less to do with making sauces and more to do with Giada De Laurentiis, as I recall."

"Be that as it may, I learned a few things."

"So did I," she said, dipping her fork into the sauce.

"And for the record, H-O-L-L-A-N-D-I-S-E."

Rachel grinned. "You forgot the second A, but this is very thoughtful."

"Better than cold pizza at least."

"And very relaxing. The perfect beginning to our vacation."

"I thought we could use a fresh start."

They savored the few first bites, which were delicious.

"So what should we do today?" Rachel asked.

"For starters, pick up a rental car. I called while you were in the shower."

"You were busy."

"They'll have one for us by ten."

"What's it now?"

"Quarter to."

"Knowing that place, you'd better scoot."

"Right? I also plugged the little doohickey into your computer."

"It fit?"

"Rather well, actually, into the USB port."

"And?" she asked as she downed a bite of eggs.

Jake shook his head. "Nothing. The computer didn't recognize it, no auto-play menu came up, nothing. I tried several ports, tried it both ways—it fit even upside down, by the way—and still nothing."

"So it doesn't interface with a computer?"

"No."

"Then what is it?"

"No idea. I thought I'd stop in at MBPD and show it to Detective Robinson." He shrugged. "Just in case."

"You're sure it isn't some piece of something from around the house or the garage?"

"Not that I recognize."

"Hmm."

"This afternoon," he said, "I thought we could go somewhere, do something."

"I have a better idea," she said.

He leaned forward. "Shoot."

"We have two weeks, plenty of time to see everything and go everywhere. So let's spend the first day at the beach. Relax, unwind, settle in."

He mulled for a bite. "Okay. That works."

"You want me to tag along with you this morning?" she asked.

Jake didn't answer, his face going blank.

"What?" she asked.

"See, this is what I'm talking about with you not giving me signals."

"What do you mean?"

"You ask if I want you to come along. If I say yes, you'll feel obligated and might be bummed because you really wanted to hang out here all day. If I say no, you're going to feel rejected because it's day one and I'm already seeking alone time."

"It was a simple question, Jake."

"So if I simply shrug and say I don't care, that's fine?"

"If that's how you feel."

"Do you want to come?"

She shrugged.

Jake dropped his fork. "Rach, this is nuts. Let me make you a deal."

She took a drink. "Okay."

"We both value honesty, right?"

She nodded.

"Then let's say what we mean and mean what we say. If you ask if I want you to tag along, I'm going to say no because I don't have a burgeoning want for company on a drive to the airport. But that doesn't mean you can't come if you want. If you want to come, ask if you can come. And then if I say no, be offended."

She raised her eyebrows. "You're very philosophical this morning."

"This is where I mess up," he said. "I try to be honest, but I'm missing a signal—a tone, an inflection, a flutter of eyelashes—and you get hurt because of what I say. So I'll try to be in tune with you, but you have to meet me halfway and be straight with me and recognize I'm being straight with you."

Rachel thought for a moment. "Fair enough."

"So, you want to come with me?" he asked as a smirk tugged at the corner of his mouth.

She rolled her eyes and returned to her eggs.

The car rental agency's shuttle arrived at 10:30, twenty-five minutes after Jake called for it. Not bad. Traffic was light on a Monday morning, and they reached the airport in ten minutes. He arrived to find that Raven Hair had come through. Their original reservation had been for a convertible, but Jake wasn't sure since they had missed their reservation time, if the agency would be able to supply another on short notice. So he was pleased to find a shiny red Ford Mustang V6 convertible waiting for him. It had power everything, remote start, cloth bucket seats, leather grip on the steering wheel and gearshift, a chrome-accented instrument panel, Sirius XM radio, GPS, and Ford's proprietary voice-activated technology, SYNC. As they inspected the spotless vehicle, the rental agent went over an assortment of other bells and whistles, and Jake wondered if they had "pimped his ride" to make up for the night before. If so, all was forgiven.

Jake signed all the papers and eagerly got behind the wheel of the Mustang. Back home he drove a twelve-year-old pickup, the best feature of which was power windows. When they worked. The only downside to this car, Jake realized as he pulled out of the lot, was that Rachel would want to drive part of the time. She was an okay driver, for a woman, but Jake didn't want to surrender any time behind the wheel of the Mustang.

Sadly, the streets of Myrtle Beach didn't give much opportunity to let the car go, and Jake determined that his and Rachel's itinerary might have to make room for an evening blast through the Carolina low country. But for now, he concentrated on finding his way to the police station. It was a nondescript brick building several blocks inland, and Jake whipped into the lot just before eleven-thirty.

Detective Robinson was free, and welcomed Jake to his desk in the "bullpen." He asked how their night had gone, informed him that condo security footage had given MBPD nothing, and said that the Taylors' condo appeared to be the only one broken into that night. There had been a home invasion out by the airport, but it was unrelated as far as Robinson could tell.

He sat forward. "So what can I do for you, Mr. Taylor?"

Jake reached into his pocket and withdrew the small device. "I found this in my pocket last night," he said and handed it to Robinson. "I have no idea what it is or where it came from, but it was in my jacket, which I was wearing—"

"On your walk, while your place was burglarized," Robinson finished for him.

"Yeah. Not knowing what it is, I have no clue why would want it, but you said to contact you if there was anything out of the ordinary, and . . . this is."

"No, you're right to come." The detective frowned at the device, held between his thumb and forefinger. "Looks like a USB connector for a wireless device. Except it's plastic," he said, tapping it against his thumbnail.

"That's what my wife and I thought. I'm a network engineer back home, but I've never seen anything like it."

Robinson raised his eyes. "You try plugging it into a computer?"

"I did, and it fit pretty well in a USB port." Jake shook his head. "Nothing happened."

"Huh." Robinson looked at it some more. "And you say you've never seen it before?"

"No. Nothing like it."

"Okay. You got a few minutes? I can have the boys in the lab take a look."

"Sure."

Robinson stood. "You want a cup of coffee or something while you wait?"

"No, I'm fine."

"Change your mind, just ask one of the other detectives. I'll be as quick as I can."

"Thanks, Detective."

Jake pulled out his cell phone and resisted the urge to glance at work e-mails. It wasn't an urge born of desire but habit, a reflexive response that was the result of a 24/7 society. He checked the weather forecast instead. The next five days all promised abundant sunshine and a chance of afternoon storms, pretty typical for this time of year in the South.

Noting the time and realizing how long he'd been gone, Jake decided to give Rachel a call. Her phone buzzed three times, then her voice came on. "This is Rachel Taylor. Sorry I missed you. Give me a convenient time to call you back, and I'll do my best."

He thought about leaving her a message but passed. He smiled, thinking of the extra step of politeness even in her voicemail greeting. He almost felt bad spending the next five minutes conniving ways to keep her from getting behind the wheel of the Mustang.

Chapter Six

When Jake left, Rachel rummaged in her bag for the novel she'd started reading a few weeks ago. Something about a private investigator in California, recommended to her by a friend. She'd had trouble getting into it, preferring cozy romances or clever suspense to smart-aleck adventures. But she decided to give it another whirl and took it out to the balcony. She had to admit to herself, she was slowly being drawn into the plot. But sitting nineteen stories above the beach just wasn't working for her. She and Jake were hitting the beach later, so she didn't want to spoil that by going now. And she wasn't *that* drawn into the book. So she traded it for her MP3 player, changed into brightly colored activewear, and donned a new but broken-in pair of ASICS.

About the time she figured Jake was haggling with the dark-haired agent at the rental agency, Rachel took the elevator down to the lobby. Unlike a dozen blocks south, there was no boardwalk between the hotels and condominiums and the beach. Rachel didn't feel like jogging in sand, so she headed toward the street and started north on the sidewalk, cranking up her "mix tape" of aggressive power "anthems." It was an odd assortment of music for a thirty-five-year-old woman to listen to—Katy Perry, Imagine Dragons, Avril Lavigne, Bruno Mars, Rachel Platten, Toby Mac, and Taylor Swift—but it motivated her to run. And what did she care if it was odd? She was the only one who heard it.

A few blocks north of their condo, Ocean Boulevard veered slightly inland. Instead of carving a path through a canyon of high-rises, it was flanked by a variety of beach houses, from small cottages to gated mansions. The properties were lined with oak and palm trees, and views of the ocean were few and far between. A bevy of other joggers or walkers and the steady stream of traffic beside her reminded Rachel that she hadn't drifted back a century to one of those cozy romance novels.

As she ran, keeping about a nine- or ten-minute-mile pace, Rachel's thoughts drifted to her and Jake. She replayed their conversation on the beach from the night before and tried to crystallize her thoughts. The problem was, she didn't think in concrete expressions. She felt emotions, and she couldn't always identify them. She definitely couldn't vocalize them for Jake. She didn't know how to tell him what she felt, even though she knew it and experienced it deeply.

She knew that sounded like nonsense to him. He was analytical, pragmatic. If he couldn't identify or vocalize a feeling, he disregarded it. Even if he could, he would disregard it most of the time. So how did she get him to empathize with what she was feeling, much less match his words and actions to it?

And should he? Was she asking him to meet her ninety percent of the way instead of in the middle? She didn't think so, but she wasn't exactly an unbiased observer either. The more she thought about it and tried to make sense of it, the more confused she became. So she did what she often did on her runs. She prayed.

Rachel's prayers, especially prayers like these, didn't follow the prototypical pattern. They were completely unrecognizable from the Lord's Prayer or some pre-meal ritual. They weren't even necessarily something that could be categorized as Rachel-to-God conversations. They were more like her opening all the floodgates to her thoughts and emotions with a recognition that God was there, was listening, and cared deeply. More than that, understood her *perfectly*. After all, He had made her, had made thoughts and emotions in the first place.

The houses had given way to more condos, and Ocean Boulevard jogged to the right, directly beside the beach. Rachel looked for addresses and saw that she'd made it all the way to the 5400 block north. She paused her music and pulled out her phone. It was only quarter after eleven, but she concluded she'd better head back anyhow. She thought about giving Jake a call, a heads-up to where she was. But then she remembered car rental paperwork and that he was stopping off at the police station. So she passed on calling him, tucked her phone back into her pocket, and started the music again.

Running had always been a way to let off stress for her. More than that, it was something she enjoyed. The physical activity was actually relaxing to her, and it was common for her to run four or five miles around their suburban Omaha neighborhood in the morning before work or in the evening after dinner. So the distance wasn't a problem for her, but the sun and humidity were taking their toll, and by the time she spied the peach of their condo in the distance, she was gassed.

Figuring a change of scenery would fuel the final leg of her run, she cut over to the beach. Her running shoes pounded on the sand, which was packed down by some sort of tractor tire or tread, but still gave added resistance. Her calves burning, Rachel slowed to a walk, pulling her earbuds from her ears and brushing the sweat from her forehead before it could reach her eyes. A few years ago, Jake had bought her a headband as the remedy for just such a problem, but Rachel had refused to wear it, saying it wasn't the '80s and she wasn't working out in one of her mom's Denise Austin videos. Now, as she lamented not bringing a bottle of water along, Rachel wondered if she was too hard on Jake and his gift-giving failures.

She heard heavy breathing and turned to see a young man fall in beside her. "So I'm not the only masochist on this beach, I see," he said with a British accent. Not British, Rachel determined. That was too heavy, reserved for people with no tan and bad teeth who said things like "bloke" and "blimey." It was an English accent, refined, subtle, pleasant to the ear, almost like something out of a Victorian Era film.

Speaking of pleasant, the guy wasn't bad to look at either. He was Jake's height, maybe a fraction taller and a few pounds lighter. A blue sleeveless tee showed off muscular but not bulging arms and was tight enough to reveal that he worked out. His mouth was firm as he smiled thinly—he was English, after all—and his navy blue eyes glinted even though the sun was behind them. His blond hair may or may not have been frosted, and it bore the carefully disheveled look Jake often went for and just missed. His came out just plain disheveled, which was attractive in its own right, but not the same.

Rachel realized it had been a few seconds, and she hoped her deep breathing covered for her. "I underestimated the heat, I think," she said, immediately wondering why she'd cast herself as the helpless female.

"Ah, so you are a tourist then."

"Isn't everybody here?"

"Mostly, yes." He tipped up a water bottle that matched his shirt and eyes—he was a well-coordinated Englishman—and Rachel couldn't help but envy his mouth as it received the cool liquid. He lowered the bottle and eyed her. "You look thirsty."

"I underestimated that too," she said.

"Here. Promise, I haven't licked on it or spit back or anything." His firm lips parted a little farther to reveal a full smile.

"Thank you," Rachel said, squirting a few quick blasts into her mouth. She handed the bottle back, noting the man's perfectly manicured hands.

"My pleasure," he said. "I'm Liam, by the way."

"Rachel."

"It's nice to meet you, Rachel."

It was absurdly prosaic, but his eyes did sparkle as he spoke. And they didn't once drift below hers, say to the cropped spandex top she was wearing.

"So what brings you and your husband to Myrtle Beach?" Liam asked.

Rachel startled slightly.

"Your ring," Liam said. "I noticed it when you took a drink. It's lovely."

"Oh, thanks. Just a getaway," she said.

"Ah. Your first time?"

"Mm-hmm. Yours?"

"No, I've been several times. First when I was just a little boy, too many years ago. Before you were born, I imagine."

Rachel had guessed Liam to be about her age, maybe a few years older, and couldn't tell if he was shooting for self-deprecating humor, making an honest assessment, or flattering her. And she didn't much care. She also hadn't spotted a ring on his finger but kept her curiosity at bay.

"How long are you here for?" he asked.

"Two weeks."

"Wow. Well then, you'll have plenty of time to sample all the delicious food, take in the shows, shop."

"All on the agenda."

"If I may, a recommendation?"

"Please."

"You must try House of Blues. A wonderful mix of food and atmosphere."

"I'm sure Jake will go for it."

"Particularly try the jambalaya. Spectacular."

"I'll give that a whirl," Rachel said with a smile. She gestured with her hand. "This is my building."

"Well, it was nice meeting you, Rachel. Enjoy your stay on the Grand Strand."

"Thanks, Liam. Nice meeting you too."

He smiled and dipped his head slightly before continuing down the beach. Rachel watched him go for just a moment, wondering when was the last time Jake had called her Rachel—not Rach, Hon, Babe, or Sugar Lips—once, let alone twice, in the same conversation. She didn't mind the pet names—liked them, actually (except for Sugar Lips)—but it was nice to hear her full name used.

As she entered the condo lobby, past the pool full of screaming children, she tried to tell herself it had been Liam's English accent that had appealed to her more than the man himself. More than his using her name, his seemingly knowing what she was thinking, or his good looks. She was less than convincing and turned her focus to cooling down with some lemonade—even if it was Crystal Light—when she returned to the room.

She pressed the elevator button, and it dinged almost immediately. It was empty, and she quickly pressed the 19 button. The air conditioning was turning the sweat on her face and arms to a sticky mess, and she couldn't wait to get to the room. But a few floors up, the elevator dinged and paused. Rachel did a double-take as Jake stepped into the elevator.

"Wh—"

No, it wasn't Jake.

"Wh—What floor?" Rachel covered.

"Seventeen," he answered in a voice a touch huskier than Jake's.

She pressed the button and stood back, marveling without staring. He was a pretty good ringer for Jake: same height, same weight, same hair only better styled, same general face shape. But his eyes were a darker shade of brown, the nose was wrong, she realized, and he had shaved, whereas Jake hadn't. Plus, Jake didn't own a Metallica shirt. Still, the resemblance was shocking.

He departed with a nod at the seventeenth floor, and Rachel closed the doors behind him. When she returned to the room, she noted Jake's absence and the time, then quickly mixed a glass of lemonade and took it to the balcony, where the sea breeze completed her cooldown. Having drained the lemonade in minutes, she headed for the shower and tried to forget the men she'd just encountered.

Jake experimented with the Sirius XM radio in the Mustang on the way back to the condo. It was amazing how many stations played music geared for teenage girls—pop, dance, dance-pop. What ever happened to good old rock 'n' roll? He finally found an old-school rock station—currently playing Bon Jovi—which satisfied him. Blasting "I Believe" and letting the salt air whip over and around the windshield felt good, made him feel alive. It also did wonders for the frustration at the break-in the night before.

On the heels of explaining that MBPD's investigation had as much as dead-ended, Detective Robinson had informed Jake that the lab found nothing on the device. It didn't register with their computers, which detected no hidden files, no software code, no virus—nothing. They'd never seen anything like it, had never heard of anything like it. They didn't even bother to pull prints, what with Jake having handled it all morning. Detective Robinson excused him on that, saying that by the time he'd found it in his pocket and examined it—by the time he'd first considered it might be evidence—his prints would have obscured any others. Even if not, it was too small to likely hold enough of a print to run through any databases anyhow.

Detective Robinson had returned the device to Jake, thanked him for coming in, and promised to update him if there were any breaks in the case. He hadn't even been able to muster false enthusiasm, but Jake appreciated the sincerity.

His stomach growling, Jake turned onto Ocean Boulevard. As much as Rachel wanted to veg at the beach all day, he wondered if he could cajole her into a run to a grocery store, just to stock up on a few snack items, if not to a beachside burger joint. Maybe if he let her drive . . .

Thinking of Rachel reminded him again of what they'd discussed last night, before the break-in. He really hated not knowing what she was thinking or what she wanted. Yeah, it was the old cliché that men could never figure out the ways or minds of women. But after a decade of marriage, Jake thought that he should be a little better at it. He didn't know if Rachel was overly complex, but didn't think so from what he knew of other women. (Although he had once caught her reading a book about being more mysterious. What the heck was that about? Was she just trying to make things hard?) Maybe he was just a dunderhead. He didn't really think that was the case either, and lack of explanation for the disconnect bugged him more than anything.

Well, anything except the concealed yet evident frustration it caused Rachel.

With space at a premium, many of the condos and hotels along Ocean Boulevard had parking facilities across the street. The Taylors' was one of them, and Jake waited for a stream of cars before hanging a left into the garage. It was open air, painted the same peach color as the condo. Jake circled the garage twice until he found a parking spot at ground level, feeling very much like Thomas Magnum as he whipped into the stall and killed the motor. Only Magnum never took the time to put the top up after he parked somewhere.

Magnum also, Jake realized as he waited to cross the street, seemed better in tune with the opposite sex.

Chapter Seven

Rachel again felt self-conscious as she and Jake walked onto the beach. Ten minutes ago, the feeling had been in anticipation of Jake's response to her new swimsuit. It was a two-piece "tankini," the top a blue and white floral pattern and the bottom a frilly little skirt. It was the first time he'd seen it (unless he'd found it while unpacking the night before—unlikely), and she'd been unsure what his reaction would be. That was typical because Jake's responses were seldom what she hoped for. He usually made a comment about the color or the style, the same as he might when seeing the item in a catalog or on a mannequin at the store. Rarely did he compliment her in her clothes, and she didn't know if it was because he didn't really like the clothes and sought to deflect by describing their attributes, or if he was just "missing the mark" in an effort to be complimentary, or if she was no longer holding his interest physically. He'd as much as outright told her, numerous times, that the latter wasn't true. Yet she couldn't help but wonder.

So it was with trepidation that she debuted the new swimsuit in their suite. It was one of three she'd purchased specially for the trip, all after hours of solo bargain hunting. Shopping with Jake was bad enough, but when it came to swimwear or—perish the thought—intimates, he became a fish out of water, leaning on racks while trying to look casual, whistling at nothing or singing under his breath with the mall's piped in Fall Out Boy or Five for Fighting, and otherwise behaving weirdly. She'd found it best to leave him at home—or on a bench in the mall—and get his opinion later. It was less hassle to buy something, show it to him at home, and return it if he was less than enthused than it was to bring him along. In this case, she'd waited to get his opinion until they were in Myrtle Beach, a dangerous venture. If he disapproved . . .

Jake whistled.

That was a good sign, she figured. So was the smile just beneath the surface and the twinkle in his eyes. She ducked back into the bedroom to get a few accessories—passing on the California P.I. novel—smiling to herself. *Wait until he sees swimsuit number three!*

Now, ten minutes later, she was self-conscious for a different reason. Myrtle Beach was a family destination, but even so, the little she'd seen from the balcony or while jogging that morning had taught her it wasn't exactly an Amish commune. Most women ran around the beach with the bare—pun intended—minimum of covering. Here she was showing little if any midriff, yet feeling like a prude.

Why? she asked herself. *Why do you care if complete strangers look down on you for not being an exhibitionist?*

She needn't have worried. The beach, crowded in the early afternoon, was home to a little bit of everything. Plenty of young women and girls flaunting all they had. Not a few older women flaunting what they had, albeit tanned like venison jerky. Guys with rock-hard abs and bodybuilder's pecs. Then there was the other end of the spectrum, guys with multiple stomachs hanging over each other, white as snow but for the red crease where skin folded over itself. Women with legs like tree trunks but the modesty of a cabaret dancer. There were guys and gals with shorts and shirts, one sweatshirt, and even a teenage boy in socks and tennis shoes. Nothing was out of place.

Jake and Rachel walked north from their condo to where the crowds thinned a little. They found a patch of beach halfway between the seagrass and where the low tide was beginning to come back in. Jake set out a beach towel while Rachel kicked off her flip-flops. "I'm going to get wet," she said.

He dropped a second towel on the corner of the first. "I'll join you," he said, peeling off the Hawaiian shirt he'd bought on a solo shopping trip of his own and insisted on bringing. (Seriously, he was developing a *Magnum, P.I.* fixation or bromance or something.)

"You think that's safe?" Rachel asked. "You trust all these people not to take our stuff?"

He looked down at their towels, his shirt, and her small bag of magazines, sunscreen, and the like. "More like I trust that no one would want any of our crap. Come on," he added, giving the back of her thigh a light slap.

"Jacob!" she gritted.

"Race you to the water!'

She quickly looked around, feeling the blush creep over her face, hoping no one had seen him slap her rear end. He did it every once in a while in the grocery store, and it was all she could do to keep from hurling a can of peas at his head. But no one seemed to have noticed, so Rachel shrugged it off.

Jake had plowed into the surf as if ready to fight it. Rachel took her time, stopping just short of the ever-fluctuating waterline. The damp, mud-like sand clung to her toes until the first wave swirled over them. It was colder than she'd expected, considering this was the tropics. Sort of. She took a few steps farther, letting the receding water pull the sand around her ankles, burying her feet in the silt.

Jake was chest deep in the water, turned to face her, acting as a breakwater for a wave that split around him. It was higher than the last couple, reaching to Rachel's knees.

"You afraid of sharks or something?" he called.

She slogged toward him. The first wave to hit her waist was chilly, but her body was quickly acclimating to the water. "You maybe don't want to shout the word 'sharks' around here," she said.

"Relax, Babe. Besides, it's jellyfish you really need to worry about."

"Great. Thanks, I'd forgotten about that."

"Hon, relax." He put his hands on her elbows, pulling her toward him. "Look around. This is what we've been waiting for."

She turned her head left and right, biting her lip. The sound of the waves, which reached their room nineteen stories up, could only be described as thunderous from ground zero. Their repetitive motion was mesmerizing, first breaking, then crashing, then sweeping ashore. The sky was dotted with bulky but non-threatening cumulous clouds, tufts that almost felt touchable. When they passed, the brief shade was replaced by marvelously warm sunshine.

Rachel hadn't thought about work all day. Hadn't thought about household chores or the mundane things of everyday life. Her mind was no longer on the break-in or Liam's accent and charm. She wasn't even mad at Jake for his too-public display of affection. She closed her eyes and realized she was *totally* relaxed.

She listened to the waves for a few seconds, then opened her eyes and turned her head to Jake. "You're ri—"

He slid his hands inside her arms and up to her armpits. Then, picking her up with the same ease he would a little child, he lifted her and threw her back into the coming waves. Rachel emitted only a tiny shriek before her body struck the water, meeting an onrushing wave, and she went under.

Fortunately, she got her mouth mostly closed in time. She still inhaled some saltwater, and more went in through her nose. Submerged, she took a moment to get her bearings before floundering to the surface. Her hair, which she had yet to tie behind her, was plastered to her neck and face like saran wrap, and the salt water stung her nose and mouth as she coughed and spat it out.

She turned her eyes to Jake, who laughed and slapped at the water to splash a little more at her. She wished very much to have a can of peas at hand. Not having one, she spat the last of the briny fluid and pawed at her hair with her hand.

Then she lunged forward and tackled her husband.

After a few minutes of flirting and splashing in the ocean, Rachel and Jake tromped back to dry ground. One thing she hated about the beach was how sand clung to wet skin. She brushed it off—mentally—and sat down on their towel.

"Thirsty?" she asked Jake, reaching for bottles of water in her bag. He had talked her into a brief run to the grocery store before heading to the beach, and they'd picked up a few necessities. She had talked him into letting her drive the Mustang back from the store, and had been plotting ways to get behind the wheel again ever since.

"No, I'm good," he said, busily scooping sand with his hands, forming a pillow for himself under the towel. Rachel used the other towel, rolled up, as a headrest, and prostrated herself on the blanket. She sat up briefly, to retrieve a pair of butterfly sunglasses from her bag, then lay down again. She lost track of time, watching the clouds shift and float overhead or attempting to spot the next big swell before it became a foamy, spray-tinged wave. All the while, the warm sun was like a cozy blanket quickly drying her skin.

"So I didn't tell you," Jake said, bursting into her solace, "the cops found nothing on the whatever it was."

"Jake, sometimes your mastery of the English language leaves me speechless," she said without turning his way. She felt a little bad ripping him ever since she'd gone through the *Love & Respect* series with her church study group a few years back. Jake's male ego wasn't exactly fragile, but she knew it was important for her to be sparing with her teasing. After his little stunt heaving her into the waves, however, she figured he deserved it.

He was unfazed. "They said it was empty: no software, hardware, hidden files. In fact, they weren't even sure it was a computer drive. It just happened to fit a USB port."

She lifted her sunglasses and rolled her head his way. "Isn't that quite a coincidence?"

"I don't know. Toddlers can jam all sorts of things into computer ports."

"Either way, it doesn't seem much of a motive to break into our condo."

"No."

"Did Detective Robinson say anything about other leads?"

"No."

She sighed and lowered her shades again. She wasn't sure which would make her feel better, if they just had the misfortune of suffering a random break-in or if someone had targeted them by mistake. At least with the latter, there was an explanation and a reason for it, however misguided. With a random break-in, they were solely at the mercy of the odds.

Rachel closed her eyes, letting the constant waves lull her toward sleep. A child's exuberant exclamation stirred her, and she opened her eyes. Two little boys, no more than four or five, seemed at the same time furious and enchanted as the waves encroached on their rudimentary sandcastle. Rachel watched them attempt to repair and fortify it for several minutes, a smile tugging at the corner of her mouth. When it became apparent that the waves were going to make further rebuilding efforts futile, the boys trudged a little ways up the beach to where their parents presumably were waiting.

Rachel turned her head toward Jake. He was on his stomach, his head rested on his folded hands. She rolled onto her side and tapped his ankle with her foot. "You awake?"

"Kinda hard not to be, what with you walking all over me."

"Please."

He opened his eyes. "What's up?"

She propped her head on her hand. "Do you think part of our trouble is that we don't have kids?"

Jake slowly rotated onto his side, mirroring her posture. To his credit, he didn't deflect the question back onto her. "Yes and no."

She waited for him to go on.

"Kids would no doubt add excitement and variety, definitely keep us busy."

"But?"

"But, anything can become routine after a while. T-ball and dance practice and PTA meetings and Girl Scouts and 4-H all just become another slot on the calendar."

"But they keep growing," Rachel said. "If we'd have gotten pregnant when we first started trying, Jake Junior would be almost seven. Wiffle Ball would have become T-ball would soon become Little League. And dance class turns into ballet and then cheerleading. Even before all that, with learning to walk, learning to talk, teething, potty training, learning to read and write, learning new things at school . . . It's constant change."

He shifted his head in his hand a little. "But doesn't all that just become stuff? Look at your sister's Christmas letter. We chased here, we chased there, we did this, we did that. You even said it this Christmas when you read it, 'Same old, same old.'"

Rachel sighed, dropping her arms and leaning her head on her bicep. Jake reached a hand over to lift hair out of her face and tuck it behind her ear. In the process, he knocked her sunglasses cockeyed.

"Sorry."

She slid them off and readjusted her hair behind her ear. "I see your point, but I can't help but feel that maybe that's part of it, like you said with the rut of work and entertainment and daily life. If we had kids, we'd have so much going on we wouldn't be able to get into a rut."

"You also said we're just functional," Jake said.

"Finishing your thought."

"There's an awful lot of function that goes with kids. Feed 'em, change 'em, bathe 'em, put 'em to bed; no, no, no, no; do this, do that, do this, do that;

breakfast, school, homework, no TV until after homework, supper, rinse, repeat."

"I know."

"But I see your point too," he added a moment later.

Rachel rolled onto her stomach, arms beside her, resting her cheek on the warm blanket so she could look at Jake.

"And adding kids to the equation—adding anything to the equation—isn't going to create more time for us or suddenly forge a bond between us."

"I don't know about that," she said. "Joining together in a venture like parenting might be just the catalyst we need."

Jake scooted closer, until he was touching her. He stroked his fingers through her drying hair. She closed her eyes and relaxed to the hypnotic feeling.

"Have we given up?" he asked quietly.

She rolled back onto her side. He traced his fingers along her cheek, then onto her shoulder, playing with a strand of hair. All the while, his eyes never left hers.

Rachel blinked twice. "I think so. Short of a miracle, anyway. We've tried all we can."

"I'm sure there's always some other drug or treatment, but I hear you."

"And we've talked about those. I . . ."

"Don't feel comfortable with a lot of options, I know. And I get it. I agree, Rach. I just needed to hear you say it."

"I'm sorry."

"No," he said, holding her shoulder. "You never have to be sorry."

She blinked again, but this time she couldn't stop a tear from forming.

He leaned in to kiss her, lingering a little longer than a mere peck. This display of affection in public Rachel didn't mind.

"It's not your fault," he said as she opened her eyes, "and I've never thought that."

"I know you haven't."

"And for the record, miracles happen," he said as a grin started to form on his face. "So we probably should just keep trying. A lot."

She rolled her eyes and gave him a playful shove to the chest that knocked him onto his back before turning over herself.

Chapter Eight

Rachel agreed to let Jake drive if she could pick the music, a fair tradeoff, he concluded. With the sun low in the sky, casting the ocean, palm trees, and towering high-rise buildings in a golden hue, he turned south on Ocean Boulevard, the Beach Boys coursing through the Mustang's speakers.

He looked over and smiled at Rachel as she grooved to the oldies. She wore the pink and purple floral sundress he'd laid out for her the night he'd surprised her with the trip. Her hair was loose with a wide ribbon running over the top of her head. A silver diamond pendant dangled from her neck, matched by earrings that had been a gift for Valentine's Day a few years back—one of the few that hit the mark.

Jake wore white, semi-dressy Dockers and a navy blue shirt. He'd have preferred jeans and a Huskers tee, but for their first dinner out, Rachel had talked him into something a little classier. He'd thought about shaving, but kind of liked the idea of a vacation beard—albeit still just a few days old. It'd stay until Rachel complained.

They had returned from the beach late in the afternoon, taken turns showering, and enjoyed cool drinks on the patio. Over the last week, Rachel had plotted out at least a dozen places they should eat, and he'd let her make the first selection, a place called Beach House Bar & Grill.

The night was young, so first they decided to cruise "the Strip," as Jake had coined the stretch of Ocean Boulevard that paralleled the Boardwalk and

Promenade. Traffic bogged down from about 16th Avenue on, despite the road being two lanes in each direction. Pedestrians filled the sidewalks, many still coming from the beach or water parks, others headed to dinner, and still others doing the walking version of Jake and Rachel's cruising the Strip.

There were numerous crosswalks where foot-travelers had the right of way, but they darted through every gap in traffic as well, adding to the slowdown. Jake didn't mind. He had a pretty girl beside him, appropriate if not awesome music playing, and plenty to watch and observe.

They crawled just past a variety of thrill rides on their right and the SkyWheel on their left. Then came a crowded park with a concert stage backed by the ocean. Thereafter, shops and eateries lined both sides of the street, hawking cheap T-shirts, beachwear, henna tattoos, ice cream and other frozen treats, and every type of greasy food imaginable.

Rachel touched his arm as they sat about ten back at a stoplight. "Thank you for being so understanding before."

"You're welcome," he said, meeting her gaze briefly. His attention was drawn to the building up ahead on her right. "Hey, we should check out Ripley's Believe-it-or-Not."

"Ripley's? You can't be serious?"

"I've always wanted to see what it was like. Ever since that trip to Wisconsin Dells."

"Where I almost fell off the boat, what was it called?"

"A duck, and you didn't almost fall."

"The latch gave way."

"I was holding your hand."

The light turned green, and they inched forward.

"That was a nice trip," she said. "Very romantic, as I recall."

"What were we doing in the Dells anyhow?"

"Not a lot of vacation hotspots in driving distance of Des Moines."

"Was that still when we lived in Des Moines?"

"Our first anniversary. We were still scraping by. It was all we could afford."

"Well, I guess that's why we passed on Ripley's," he said with a glance over his shoulder.

The shops dwindled after they crossed 9th Avenue. Large, undeveloped space filled the next block, and after that, the shops were intermittent before giving way entirely to blocky hotels and condos along the beach and dive motels and hotels on the other side of the road.

Jake drove as far south as the 2nd Avenue Pier, where he turned around. It was the southern terminus of the Boardwalk and Promenade, even though the Strip effectively ended at 9th Avenue.

As they journeyed back, Jake read more of the signs and marquees on the various shops. "We've got to get some saltwater taffy," he commented. "And fudge."

"I was hoping to find a fresh peach stand," Rachel said.

"That would be all right too." He shook his head.

"What?"

He nodded at a three- or four-story glass structure atop a building on her side of the car. Yellow letters on a red marquee announced it as the Gay Dolphin. "It's everywhere, isn't it?"

"What?"

"The gay agenda."

"I don't think it's an ag—" Rachel frowned, then backhanded him in the leg. "It's a gift shop, dummy."

"Dummy, huh?"

"Sorry."

"It's comments like that that get you thrown into the waves."

"I'm sorry, Ja—"

"So it's more of an 'It's the Most Wonderful Time of the Year,' or 'Have Yourself a Merry Little Christmas' gay than what's in the news all the time?" He huffed. "I'm surprised they're still allowed to use the term."

Rachel raised her eyebrows.

"What?" he asked. "It's true."

It took five minutes to make a left turn into the Beach House's small parking lot, what with the constant flow of traffic on the street and pedestrians on the sidewalk. Finally, Jake found a gap and quickly parked. "Think we can leave the top down while we eat?" he asked as he unbuckled his seatbelt.

"Why not?"

Beach House resembled, well, a beach house. A variety of metal signs and placards with cute and clever—and a little crass at times—slogans hung on the seafoam green fence around a deck and patio home to a dozen or so tables, nearly all of them occupied. Surfboards were affixed to the support columns and formed the background for the neon sign hanging on the front of the building, which looked like a beachside shack. A hostess, distinguishable from the patrons only in that she greeted Jake and Rachel, asked if they wanted inside or outside seating. Jake looked to Rachel, who said outside, and the hostess guided them to the sole remaining outdoor spot, a bistro table on the lower level. She placed single-page menus on the table and departed with a smile.

"This is quaint," Jake said as he took his seat.

Rachel hung her purse over the back of her chair and finagled into her high seat. "What?" she asked. The music, modern pop, was loud, coming from a speaker just above them.

"I said it's quaint," he said, leaning forward.

"You mean that?"

"I do." He turned his eyes across the street, just another table and a sidewalk away from them. Beyond it was a parking lot between two high-rises, giving them a view of the ocean through several strands of palm trees. "This feels like the type of place we should eat at while in Myrtle Beach," he added.

For the next few minutes, while Rihanna transitioned to American Authors, Jake and Rachel scoured their menus. When their waiter came, they ordered a fried grouper sandwich and iced tea for her and a shrimp po' boy and lemonade for him. The drinks came in a minute, and Rachel leaned her elbows on the table to sip her tea through a straw.

Jake smiled as he watched her.

"What?" she asked.

He too leaned forward, to be heard over Drake.

"You look like a weight-loss smoothie spokesperson."

"Wow, thanks, Jake."

"The way you sipped your drink, a coy little smile, as if losing weight was the most pleasurable thing on earth."

She nodded.

"Not that you need to lose weight."

"Uh-huh."

"Going to quit digging now."

"Good idea," she said, wrinkling her nose.

His turn to take a sip. The lemonade was crisp and refreshing.

"So can we talk about something else?" she asked.

"Sure. We can try," he said as a muscle car a block away revved its engine.

"I bring it up not to nitpick, but because I've noticed a few instances of it today."

"Uh-oh."

"And this is actually hard to say, because I know it's not a lack of caring, but . . . sometimes I feel like you take me for granted."

Jake sat back. "I take you for granted?"

She nodded.

He shook his head. "How?"

"For example, when you came into the bedroom to get the computer this morning and woke me up. Or on the ride here, twice I tried to talk to you about serious things, and you talk about going to Ripley's and the names of gift shops."

Jake frowned.

"I don't mean to be overly critical, but these are examples I noticed today, and I think it's part of—"

"I was in the bedroom to watch you sleep."

"What?"

Another car revved its engine, this one right in front of the restaurant.

"I was watching you sleep this morning. That's when I got the idea to check the computer."

It was Rachel's turn to frown. "Why?"

"I was curious."

"No, why were you watching me sleep?"

"Because I do that."

"Like, a lot?"

He bobbed his head. "Now and again."

"Why?"

"Because you're cute, Rach."

She swallowed and blushed.

"As for the comments on the way here, I didn't know there was anything more. You thanked me, I moved on."

"You do that a lot. We're having a serious talk, and you bounce to something else right away."

"Okay, so I have ADHD. But that's not taking you for granted, is it?"

"I think it's related. And I don't think it's ADHD. I think it's priorities. And I don't mean to imply you don't value me," she said quickly, "because I know that's not it . . ."

"But?"

She'd paused as their waiter brought their dinners. Jake eyed his po' boy with glee and lifted it to take a massive bite. It did not disappoint.

"See?" Rachel asked.

"Huh?"

"You did it again."

"We're not supposed to eat?"

"No, but we're in the midst of a conversation, and suddenly you're more excited about your sandwich than what I have to say."

"Rach, I mean, taste this."

She pursed her lips.

"Not the time, sorry."

"Like I said, I know that it's not that you don't care about me, but I think sometimes what's on your mind squeezes out what might matter to me. It's not even conscious, I don't think, a lot of the time."

"I'm sorry."

"I know you are. And as I was saying, I don't think you even recognize it, which is why I wanted to make you aware of it."

"I will try to be more aware and more focused."

She nodded and smiled placidly.

He ate another bite of his sandwich, then noted she was just picking at hers, rearranging the lettuce and tomato. "There more?"

"A little. This may seem trivial, but . . ."

"Go ahead."

Rachel leaned an elbow on the table, pulling a strand of her hair. "You seldom compliment me, Jake."

"I whistled at your swimsuit."

"And that was very nice, but it was an exception. I'm not looking for you to go around praising me all the time, but I sometimes wonder if you notice me anymore."

"I do."

"Not just how I look, but things I do. And I'm guilty of it too, Jake. We're so used to each other and our roles that I don't notice that you took out the garbage or mowed the lawn or shoveled snow or started my car in the winter. And you say nothing about me doing dishes, the laundry, making sure you match before you head out the door, or a hundred other things we both do. When was the last time either of us said thank you or good job."

"I don't really notice."

She finally took a bite with a look that said, "Proves my point."

He too took a bite, thought a little as he chewed, then swallowed. "I guess, for me, I see it as my responsibility, so I don't need to be thanked."

"Well, you're about the only person in the world who feels that way," she said with a smile.

"Yeah, maybe."

"Your dad was like that too, wasn't he?"

Jake nodded, his thoughts bittersweet as he remembered his father. Rachel had never met him, but he'd talked about his parents with her so much, she might as well have.

Yet more revving engines distracted both of them, and then a woman with a Mediterranean accent stopped by to take their picture for free. Jake smelled a scam but went along with it anyway. When she was gone and the waiter had refilled their drinks, Rachel leaned in again.

"I know I sound high-maintenance here, but we said we were going to talk this week."

"We did, and you don't."

"Tell me what's on your mind too, Jake. Don't let this become a one-way, what's-wrong-with-him sort of a deal."

"I would if I could only find a flaw."

"Ha."

"That's where we're different, Rach. I see little things and just shake them off. You don't. And that's not a dig. It's just the way we're wired."

"It didn't used to be like this, you know."

"Like what?" he asked, picking up the po' boy again.

"You taking me for granted. When we were dating, I could talk to you for hours about anything, and you'd hang on every word, even during a ball game. You were never distracted when I was around. Never had your head turned by a pretty girl."

"Have I done that?"

"Come on, Jake, we both do."

He nodded.

"It's only natural. We're not twenty-five anymore. And I know you don't mean anything by it, but it does sting a little."

"I'm sorry."

She took his hand. "And so am I."

He took a deep breath. "Who needs therapists?"

"Well, anybody can air grievances."

"And there's a reason, by the way."

"Reason for what?"

"For why I hung on every word back when we were dating."

"What's that?"

"Security."

"Security?"

"That's right. I had to keep you interested in me. Now," he said with a shrug, "we're married. You're stuck with me ever since you signed your life away on the dotted line."

"Cute."

"I'm kidding. The real reason is you're just not that interesting anymore."

She narrowed one eye, then bounced a pickle off his nose.

"You folks up for any dessert?" the waiter asked, appearing at that moment.

Rachel stammered.

"No thanks," Jake said.

"I'll be right back with your check."

Jake waited until he was gone. "I thought of something about you that bugs me."

"What?"

"You have the table manners of a kindergartener. Frankly, you're embarrassing to take out in public."

Rachel lightly kicked him under the table, then put her head down and finished her sandwich. When the waiter brought the check, Jake reached for his wallet, only to find it wasn't there. He looked down, thinking it had fallen out of his pocket, but it wasn't anywhere in sight.

"What's wrong?"

"Uh, we may have to wash some dishes. I can't find my wallet."

"I have my purse," she said. "It's probably on the dresser at the condo."

"I distinctly remember putting it into my pocket," he said, patting the other rear pocket, then both front ones just in case.

"Jake, you look like you're doing the Macarena."

"I'm going to go check the car, see if it fell out there."

"Okay."

Jake hurried back to the parking lot, hoping his wallet had fallen out of his pocket while driving and wishing, if so, that he'd taken the time to put the top up on the Mustang. There was a gap between the Mustang and the nearest car on the driver's side, and Jake tried to remember what sort of vehicle had been parked there. Before he could, he was at the door, and peered over the side. Relief washed over him when he spied his leather wallet practically nestled into the crack between the seat and the backrest. Exhaling, he plucked it out, quickly scanned it to make sure nothing was missing, and tucked it deep into his pocket.

"Nice set of wheels," remarked an accented, female voice.

Jake turned his head and spotted a tall, dark-haired woman standing at the Mustang's rear fender. At first glance, she was attractive, her appearance enhanced by a bikini top and a chiffon skirt cover-up that hung to her ankles. On closer inspection, she was beautiful. Her toned, flawless skin was well tanned, but still much lighter than jet-black hair that fell over her shoulders. Despite the beachwear, it was styled as if she was headed out for a night on the town, yet looked perfectly natural. She ran slender fingers over the Mustang's spoiler while smiling at Jake, as much with almond brown eyes as with two rows of immaculate teeth.

"I bet it's a joy to drive," she said, and he pondered her accent. At first, it sounded English, but now he detected a trace of something else, something sophisticated, like French or Swiss. Maybe even a hint of Spanish. Then again, he was no linguist. He wasn't even sure Switzerland had its own language.

"It is," he answered. "A pity to be locked in the city," he added, wondering why he felt the need to volunteer information and why it had come out in rhyme.

"Is it yours?" she asked.

"Uh, no, a rental," he said, his ego taking a blow.

"Now *that* is a pity," she said with a demure smile and the slightest downturn of her chin. It enabled her to give a very slight flick of her hair as she raised her head, the action sending small quivers through her loosely curled tresses. Jake's eyes were captivated by her hair, which stirred feelings of guilt as he thought about Rachel and her accusation that his head was turned by a pretty girl. But, he reasoned, it was better his eyes be drawn to her hair than be captivated elsewhere.

"Kind of epitomizes vacation," he said in reply, wondering what the heck he meant by the words before they were off his tongue.

"That it does." She offered another smile—more like a widening of a continued smile—and turned to go. Jake snapped out of the vignette and noticed the hubbub of people around them again. He spent a moment wondering why a woman in a bikini and with elegantly styled hair was wandering through the parking lot. He got his answer a moment later when he heard the beep of a key fob and the click of a car door opening. He followed the sound with his eyes and saw the woman get into a black BMW four-door at the other end of the lot. He did his very best not to note the length of her legs as the skirt cover-up parted when she got in, instead turning back toward the sidewalk and Rachel.

"Find anything?" she asked when he returned.

"Uh-huh," he said, pulling enough cash out of his wallet to cover their bill. A moment later, he handed it to the waiter as Rachel finished her tea.

"You want to take a little walk?" she asked as they headed back to the car. "Work off dinner, soak up some ambiance?"

"I've had enough of the Strip for tonight," he said. "I'd rather just head back."

"Okay." She squinted at him. "Everything okay?"

He nodded and pushed any remaining thoughts of the woman in the parking lot out of his head. "Fine."

"Okay," she said again. "Back to the room." She leaned close. "I have another item of clothing that will give you a chance to pay me a compliment."

Chapter Nine

The scene in front of Rachel looked like a painting, one of those classic seascapes with breaking waves framed by wisps of seagrass poking up from the dunes, all beneath a blue sky dotted with tufts of afternoon clouds. It was exactly what she needed after their morning and early afternoon.

Jake had talked her into golfing their second morning in Myrtle Beach, arguing that they had to do it at least once in the Golf Capital of the World. They had golfed once when they were dating, and Rachel had merely walked the last three holes of nine because she'd run out of golf balls. Considering the way she'd sliced, shanked, and seemed to aim for water, Jake had refused to loan her any of his Titleists at $13 per sleeve. They'd agreed it was probably best not to golf together after that.

After nine holes at one of Myrtle Beach's more moderately priced courses, that sentiment had returned. Rachel was actually playing all right while Jake struggled, and she wondered if that was why he seemed out of sorts. He complained that she didn't take his putting woes seriously, replied with one-word answers when she tried to make conversation, objected to her taking pictures of him playing, and wasn't even impressed that she knew to wiggle her buns while addressing the ball like the golfers on TV did.

In fact, he'd been a little out of sorts all morning, since she'd come in off the deck and found him chugging coffee and studying the object he'd found in his jacket Sunday night.

"What doing?" she'd asked.

"Trying to figure out what this thing is."

She came and leaned on his shoulder, looking down at a web page.

"What, did you Google 'little white thing that fits into a USB port'?"

"No, but I should try that," he said with a wink.

"I thought you wanted to go golfing this morning," she said.

"You're okay with that?"

"Would I be wearing this if I wasn't," she said, looking down at her collared sleeveless shirt and knee-length white skirt.

He looked back at her. "Sorry, didn't really notice."

"Exhibit G."

"This thing is just driving me nuts. I'm the computer guy, so I should be able to figure it out."

"Even if MBPD couldn't? No offense, Jake, but their lab techs are probably more advanced than you."

"Maybe so."

"And who says it's even a computer component? Who says it's anything at all?"

He'd sighed and left it at that, at least verbally. But he'd been a little grumpy through the first nine holes. On the back nine, they'd found themselves behind a family (they assumed) of four—a mom, dad, and two kids. The girl was eleven or twelve, and the boy a few years younger. She, like the adults, was white. He was black.

"Have we given up on adoption?" Jake had asked as they waited a hundred or so yards back in the fairway while the foursome putted out.

Rachel's eyes widened. "What brought that up?"

"Them," he said with a nod.

"I know, but the way you phrased it. Have we given up?"

He shrugged. "We've talked about it plenty. Looked at websites a few times, even made a few phone calls. But we've never taken that next step. Never really gotten down to business. Is it still on the table?"

"You always said you wanted your own kids."

"I do. Jason has two girls, Jimmy one. The family name and line is going to die out, and whenever I think about Mom and Dad, that comes to mind more and more."

Rachel nodded.

The family ahead of them cleared the green, and he got out of their cart to hit his shot, one of the better ones of the day.

"Plus, we are getting up there a bit," he said.

"Thirty-five is up there?"

"Figure we'll be fifty-five by the time our kid graduates high school, almost sixty before he's out of college. Losing my parents around that age . . . I don't want that to happen to my kid."

"Just because they died at that age doesn't mean you will."

"I know, but the odds start increasing. It's not a be-all, end-all, but I think it should factor in."

"Adoption is expensive too," Rachel said as they rolled down the fairway. "Not that we couldn't make it work financially, but . . ."

"This is usually where the conversation trails off for six months. Which is why I ask."

She looked at him as he coasted to a stop short of the green. His ball was twenty feet from the flag, hers just short of a greenside bunker. "It kind of seems so," she said.

"We've given up."

"We've closed the door. No . . . we haven't stopped the door from closing by itself. But we haven't locked it yet either."

He nodded.

"Boy, our metaphors need work."

He'd made his putt a few minutes later, for a birdie, which had put him in a good mood and also concluded any meaningful conversation for the rest of the round as he'd concentrated on "grinding" or "scrambling" or something. On the way back to the condo, he'd been unusually chatty—mostly about golf nonsense like sand saves and flop shots and David Feherty impersonations— while Rachel's mind had drifted to adoption. The door was closed. Did that mean it was officially over, as far as kids were concerned? She'd never be a mom? Never find that fulfillment so many women found in motherhood?

"Rach, I'm sorry if I upset you," he'd said out of the blue.

"Upset me. How?"

"Before. It's just that sometimes you don't take seriously the things I do."

"Like golf?"

"For example. Or Nebraska football."

"Just because I cheer when Iowa beats Nebraska?"

"No, because you cheer when Iowa wins but when Iowa loses, you say 'Oh well' and go back about your day."

"Sports don't affect me that much."

"Then why did you dance on the couch when Iowa won last year?"

"Because it's my school. I was excited."

"But you aren't upset when they lose."

"That's because I have a healthy perception of sports."

"It comes off as not taking it seriously, which upsets people who do."

"Like you?"

"And Jason."

"Your brother?"

"There's a reason he doesn't come watch games with us anymore."

"Me?" Rachel asked.

"He says if you don't suffer through the losses, you don't have the right to rejoice in the wins, at least not in front of other suffering people."

"And you agree with that?"

"Yeah, sort of."

"Hmm."

"Same as when I hit a bad shot."

"What, I'm sympathetic?"

"'Ooh, tough one,'" he mimicked, "and then before I've released my follow through, you're on to fudge recipes and trying to figure out which golf movie featured Will Smith and Matt Damon and asking where I want to eat dinner."

"I was trying to interact with my husband."

"And that's fine, but wait at least until the club's back in the bag."

"So I should say nothing when you hit a bad shot, just sit there?"

"Maybe. Like when your parents got divorced, I had nothing to say that made any sense because I couldn't in any way feel what you felt."

"You're comparing my parents' divorce to your golf game?"

"I didn't say they were equal. Just that it's the same principle."

Rachel had huffed and turned her gaze out the window, letting the wind play with loose strands of her hair. The divorce remark didn't bother her too much, as she actually understood what Jake meant. She was more frustrated by the crackdown on any response she made if she didn't feel sentiments as strongly as he did. Definitely something to talk further about, but she wasn't going to let it ruin their vacation.

The day had turned muggy, rivaling August in Omaha. Jake had suggested hitting the beach as soon as they'd returned. After all, why get refreshed in the shower when you could use the Atlantic Ocean? Rachel had agreed, and they had changed into swimwear, grabbed snacks and accessories, and headed down shortly before two o'clock.

On the way back from dinner the night before, they had made a quick stop at an Eagle's Beachwear to purchase a couple of fold-up beach chairs. The beach was, if anything, more crowded than the day before, and they had moseyed southward before finding a place to pitch their chairs and stash their stuff. As they had the day before, they'd started their time at the beach with a quick romp in the ocean. The water—even saltwater—was refreshing, and Rachel had decompressed by backstroking parallel to the beach for a few minutes. When she'd looked up, she had been shocked to see how far she'd drifted and had quickly freestyled back to Jake, who'd been doing his best to body surf.

"We should have picked up some boogie boards," he'd said.

"Next time."

They had spent fifteen minutes in the surf before returning to their beach chairs. Jake had insisted on the "deluxe" model—costing $14.99 instead of $9.99—that reclined and extended a footrest. Rachel left her footrest down, choosing to bury her feet in the warm sand and let her eyes drink in the painting-like panoramic view. She let the frustrations of the morning's conversations with Jake drift away on the breeze and immersed herself totally in the beach.

"I've been thinking," Jake said after a while. Rachel had lost track of time, closing her eyes and listening to the soothing hush of the waves. She raised one eye warily, wondering if he was about to spoil her tranquility again.

"About what you said last night," he continued, "about how things were different at the beginning."

She opened both eyes and turned her head to look at him.

"How I paid more attention to you and so forth."

She nodded.

"Not to make excuses, but isn't that the case in every relationship?"

"Not necessarily."

"Even with kids. When they're first born, you obsess over every little thing, because you have to if they're going to survive. By the time they're teenagers, you just make sure they come home at night and brush their teeth."

Rachel frowned. "I'm not sure, first of all, that you've got a real solid handle on parenting quite yet."

"You know what I mean."

"Maybe. But having to take care of every detail isn't the same as paying attention. I'm not asking you to hold my hand through life, but . . . Jake, we go days—weeks, even—without really talking. Aside from who's cooking dinner and comparing calendars. I tell you about my day and you nod along while watching *The Five*."

"I thought women just needed to talk to hear themselves talk."

"What?"

"It's therapeutic or something. They need to express what's inside of them."

"Well, we don't go around talking to walls. There's something in having a listener at the other end."

"I listen."

"You hear. If I quizzed you on what I said, you'd get an F."

"You don't know that."

"If I quizzed you on what Kimberly Guilfoyle was wearing, on the other hand . . ."

"Rach, that's not fair."

"You opened this can of worms, Buster Brown."

"Who?" He sighed. "Look, I'll grant you things are different than they were when we were lovey-dovey daters. But I think a lot of that is natural. That's all I'm saying."

"And I'm saying, just because it is, doesn't mean we have to go along with the tide. Maybe our marriage should be different—should be the exception to the rule."

He nodded, making that pretending-to-be-thinking face. At least, Rachel thought it was that and not the actual thinking face. It was confirmed when a minute later he reached into the bag between them and took out a Slim Jim. Rachel sighed. She knew she couldn't blame Jake for hunger, but he always seemed to be eating when they needed to talk. Like last night at supper. Or when she wanted to talk about branching out with her own photography business and all he could think about was the plate of "epic super deluxe nachos" he'd made.

"So what is it you really want?" he asked a few minutes later. He'd practically inhaled the Slim Jim, and he washed it down with some bottled water.

"Excuse me?"

"When you feel I'm taking you for granted or not paying attention. What is it that you really want?"

She studied his expression for a moment. "Attention."

"Right, but what's behind that? People want attention for different reasons. I know you, Babe, and you're not one of those people who has to be at the center of attention all the time, who does weird things to get noticed. Like those ear p—"

"Is that what you think this is?"

"No, it's what I think it *isn't*."

She did more studying.

"But when you talk about me not being enraptured by details of your day, is it because of a desire to share everything, to be intimately linked together? Is it because you just need to express things and have another human acknowledge what you say? Or is it something deeper and more profound, a yearning to have some need fulfilled?"

"You make it sound so clinical, Jake."

"I'm analytical. It's what I do."

"And that's part of the problem. I don't need to be analyzed."

"Help me out, Hon. What do you need?"

Rachel sighed. "It's not something I can list out, do A, B, and C. I need you to . . . I need you to be there."

"Be there?"

"Life—even the everyday stuff of work and family—is complicated. I need you to be right there, beside me, through it all."

"Am I not?"

"I mean in terms of experiencing it with me. We're partners, but I'm carrying the load of all that's inside of me. I want you to be there to take up half the load, and I'll take half of yours."

He thought—actually thought, it appeared—for a few minutes. "Okay. So what does that look like? What do I do?"

Rachel sighed again. "Jake."

"What?"

"There's no . . ." Another sigh. "There's no line-item way to go about it."

"Babe, I can't do what I don't know how to do."

She looked for words but couldn't find them. So she sat up.

"What are you doing?"

"I need to take a walk."

"Rach."

"I need to think, okay? Try to figure out what it is I'm trying to express, because clearly, we're not on the same page."

"I'll go with you."

"No. I need some space."

He sat back, doing a pretty good job of hiding the hurt in his eyes. "Okay." He nodded. "Okay."

She pursed her lips and started off down the beach, fighting the lump in her throat. She felt bad, but all she could hear were Jake's words, "I don't know how."

That was exactly the problem. He didn't know how to help her without taking charge. How to be there and be part of it without trying to fix it. He didn't know how to help.

Chapter Ten

Jake watched Rachel leave. "I need some space," was one of those lines she didn't use often, but when she did, it usually meant he had hurt her, and usually in a way he didn't understand. To her credit, she usually came back—usually after an intense run—and was fine.

It struck him as odd, though, that after telling him how she needed him to be there and carry the load and give her attention, her response was to get away and find "some space." He'd learned over the years not to mentally beat her up and to quickly get out of a disparaging thought pattern, so he focused instead on their conversation, trying to understand exactly what Rachel wanted and needed. He was pretty sure he got it more than she thought he did, but without some clue on how he was supposed to respond to her needs, he'd be left floundering in the dark.

"It is you," came a familiar, accented voice. Jake looked up as the woman from the Beach House parking lot sauntered toward him. Sashayed might be a better term. She had a way of walking where each leg swung around and in front of the other, almost as if she was trying to balance on a tightrope. And yet, it was smooth and gracious.

"The Mustang owner," she said with a smile.

"Mustang renter."

"Right." The smile widened.

She looked even taller today, what with Jake sitting. The skimpy, two-piece, black swimsuit added to that appearance as well, especially without any chiffon skirt covering up her long, slender legs. Jake directed his attention to her eyes, a chocolate brown that managed to gleam in the sunlight as her midnight hair swirled around her face in the breeze. He felt the edges of his vision blurring, and as had been the case last night, his surroundings faded into the background in the presence of the woman.

"May I?" she asked, nodding at the empty chair. Rachel's chair.

Jake, rarely ill at ease, was hesitant. It seemed rude to decline, but if Rachel came back and saw another woman in her seat—especially a woman that looked like this—he'd be sleeping on the couch for the rest of the vacation. If not year.

"Um, sure," his tongue said before his brain could stop it.

With another smile—they were perpetual on this woman, but kept changing in radiance and intensity—she sat down. In Rachel's place.

"I'm Gabrielle," she said, extending a hand.

The G, thanks to her accent, was one-half G, one-quarter H, and one-quarter silent altogether. The A had a trace of a short O mixed with it, and the rest of the letters just rolled off her tongue with a flourish. By comparison, "I'm Jake," sounded as exotic as, well, Omaha.

"It's nice to meet you, Jake," Gabrielle said as they shook hands. It hadn't been since the early days with Rachel that a woman's touch sent a shock through him.

"Nice to meet you too."

She turned her head to look out at the ocean. The breeze did wonderful things with the tendrils of shoulder-length hair. Jake felt as if his every look was staring. He hoped Rachel wasn't already stalking back toward him.

Gabrielle lifted some sand with her foot, wiggling it off her toes. The breeze dispersed it. "I just love the ocean," she said. "Ever since I was a little girl."

"Don't get much beach back in Nebraska," Jake said.

"You're a Cornhusker?"

He nodded, impressed that she knew the state's (and the university's athletic teams') nickname.

"Well, there's plenty of beach in Connecticut, but not like this."

Connecticut. That couldn't explain the accent, could it?

"Originally I'm from London," she said with a smile. "Believe me, I've seen that look before."

"Sorry."

"Don't be. London with a touch of Zurich and a kiss of Paris."

"Well technically, Nebraska with a kick in the shins from Chicago."

She smiled some more.

Jake took a mental step back and asked himself why they, two strangers with nothing in common but an affinity for red convertibles, were practically sharing life stories. He had to find a way to work Rachel into the conversation, lest this woman start flirting with him.

Who was he kidding? Her? Flirt with him? Just because he felt like a stammering adolescent around the prettiest girl in school didn't mean she felt the same way. And yet, she had approached him—twice, technically. She had asked to sit down, in Rachel's chair. Unless she thought he had brought an extra chair on the off chance of meeting someone, she had to know it belonged to somebody else. So what did that say about her?

"Your first time in Myrtle Beach?" she asked, now looking directly at him. Her hair caressed her neck, and she gently tugged it back behind her.

"Yeah. You?"

Rachel was right, he sure had a way with words.

"No, I come almost every year. Here or Key West. Nothing makes the stress of life melt away like this," she said, panning her head back toward the ocean.

"I feel the same way about the Rocky Mountains."

Gabrielle's demure smile was almost as beguiling as her choice of swimwear.

"What?" he asked.

"Has anyone ever told you that you have a charming little drawl to your voice?"

"Rachel," he said, relieved for an opportunity to mention her name. "My wife," he added, hoping she wasn't about to return. He'd done nothing wrong, and yet, he couldn't help but feel he was elbow deep in grandma's cookie jar as the kitchen stool started to wobble beneath him.

If Gabrielle was turned off at the mention of his wife or convicted of being in her chair, she didn't show it at all. "That is a coincidence," she said.

"What is?"

"My boyfriend met a woman named Rachel while jogging yesterday."

Jake tried to hide a frown. On one hand, he was relieved Gabrielle had a boyfriend and wasn't coming onto him, blows to his male ego aside. He could also, if Rachel "caught" them, have an innocent explanation for things since there was clearly nothing going on. But he also couldn't help but wonder why Rachel, if it had been her, hadn't mentioned anything to him about meeting another guy.

"Several inches shorter than me," Gabrielle said, "long brown hair, jade green eyes?"

Jake nodded, wondering what kind of man met a woman jogging and made note of the shade of her eyes? The same kind of man who noticed the gleam in the chocolatey brown eyes of a woman on the beach, perhaps?

"That's her," he said. He again worked to conceal a frown. Just what sort of meeting had Rachel had and why had she said nothing to him? Gabrielle's boyfriend had obviously reported back.

"Are you two going to be in the area for a while?" she asked.

"Just arrived Sunday," he said. "Here through the end of next week."

"Wow, you don't mess around."

"Tenth-anniversary trip."

"Congratulations," Gabrielle said, her smile genuine or a politician-worthy fake. She slapped the armrests of the chair. "We should get together, the four of us."

His eyebrows went up.

"I love meeting new people from all over the world, and Liam would like to have another man to converse with."

"Uh, yeah," Jake said as noncommittally as possible."

"I tell you what," Gabrielle said. "There is a little patio bar at our hotel, The Magnolia just behind us," she said, pointing over her shoulder with her thumb. "We're planning on having drinks around five if you want to join us."

Jake nodded.

"Talk to Rachel." Gabrielle smiled again. "No worries if you can't make it."

"I'll check with her," he said.

"If not, maybe we'll run into each other. We're here 'til the weekend." She pushed herself up with ease. "It was nice meeting you, Jake."

"Nice meeting you too, Gabrielle," he said, trying to mimic the way she pronounced it. He was sure he sounded like a total idiot.

She smiled one final time and glided away from him. He tore his eyes from her departing figure and scanned the beach for Rachel. He didn't spot her. He closed his eyes and sighed with relief, a sentiment quickly washed away by guilt at its existence.

"All right, out with it," Rachel said as the elevator doors closed behind them.

"Out with what?"

"You've had a dopey look on your face ever since I got back."

Jake looked at his wife. She'd wrapped a towel around her waist, but her upper body glistened with beads of water. Her hair was damp and crinkly, a contrast to suddenly blazing eyes.

She'd returned five or ten minutes after Gabrielle had departed. Jake hadn't noticed at the time, but the clouds had intensified in the west, and Rachel's arrival had been hailed with a few rumbles of thunder—real thunder. A lifeguard had walked up and down the beach, whistling people out of the water as the sky turned a pale then dark purple-blue. Less than five minutes later, rain had started to fall. Jake and Rachel had quickly folded up their chairs and gathered their belongings. They'd been half-soaked by the time they'd returned to their condo. Throughout, Jake had said nothing about Gabrielle, wondering if he should even mention the offer to meet for drinks. Now, prodded by his wife, he reverted to his "honesty is the best policy" mantra.

"I had a visitor while you were gone."

"A visitor?" Rachel asked, brow furrowed. "Like an angel of the Lord?"

"No, a woman."

Rachel's posture stiffened.

"We ran into each other in the parking lot last night, when I went to get my wallet, and she saw me on the beach and stopped to chat."

Rachel nodded, teeth clinched on her tongue.

"Truth is, she's a beautiful woman, and it was a little awkward. Thus the 'dopey' look."

"You poor thing," Rachel said. "How exactly was being around a beautiful woman awkward?" she asked, pushing herself into him. "You know, compared to . . . normal?"

"You look really hot with your hair all wet and messy," he said, feeling it with his free hand.

"Nice try."

"What?" he asked as the elevator dinged. The doors opened, and Rachel strode out, down the short, carpeted hallway to their room. She punched in the five-digit code that gave them access.

"What?" he asked again, following her into the room.

"Tell me more about this 'beautiful' woman," Rachel said, setting down her chair in the entry. She removed the towel from her waist, blotted herself dry, and wiped residual sand and dirt from her legs and feet.

"Did I say you weren't beautiful?"

"You said it was awkward, as in unusual, as in different."

"Awkward in the sense that I was around *another* beautiful woman, who isn't my wife."

"Um-hmm." She flipped the towel in his direction. "I've been to Christmas parties. Ashley and Courtney are quite beautiful," she said, referring to two of the three women in his department at work. "You're not awkward around them."

"I'm used to them," he said. "And it's different."

Rachel had walked into the kitchen and was pouring herself a glass of sun tea, which she had brewed on the balcony while they golfed. "Different how?" she asked, closing the refrigerator door.

"I don't know. Gabrielle is . . ."

"Gabrielle?"

"I didn't give her the name."

"No, but you didn't have to pronounce it like it's a women's fragrance either."

"It's how she pronounced it. Rach, come on."

She walked onto the balcony. He followed. The rain was still falling steadily, a hissing drumbeat. Down below, the beach was empty, and the blue ocean turned gray and covered with the mist of the passing storm.

"Different how?" Rachel asked, leaning on the railing. The westerly breeze kept her from being in the rain.

"I don't know, it's hard to define. I haven't really thought about it in concrete terms."

"Well come on, Mr. Analytical." She took a drink of tea.

"She's . . . got this sort of exotic, sexy demeanor, and—"

"I don't?" Rachel asked, her arms dropping. She set the tea on the table, her eyes widening.

"No."

They widened further.

"No, I mean, no that's not what I'm saying. You—and Ashley and Courtney—are naturally beautiful. Gabrielle has a sort of . . . glamorous thing going, like it's less her and more her outer appearance, the way she dresses—"

"The way she dresses? And how was this beautiful, sexy, exotic woman dressed on the beach?"

"Uh . . . big flowing muumuu."

"Uh-huh."

"Rach, I'm tripping all over myself," he said, pulling her into an embrace. "You know I think you're beautiful. I'm actually complimenting you more than her."

"Is that so?"

"Rach . . ."

She reached around and smacked him on the butt. "Relax, Taylor, I'm just giving you a hard time," she said as she backed away.

"Really?"

She winked. "Mostly."

He leaned against the railing as she reached for her tea.

"Although the way you keep digging deeper . . ."

"I suppose this is a bad time to mention she wanted to get together for drinks. With us," he added when Rachel's eyebrows shot up again.

"Oh, you mentioned the old ball-and-chain, did you?"

"Well, I had to. She was in your seat."

"You let her sit in my chair?"

"She wants to meet you after her boyfriend gave such a glowing review. Liam, I think she said."

Rachel looked as if she'd walked into a wall. Jake refused to smirk. "Must have been quite a jog, the way he remembered your fiery jade eyes, flowing brown hair." He figured a few embellished adjectives couldn't hurt his cause.

"We talked for two minutes as I was cooling down," Rachel said, covering with a drink of tea. "And he approached me."

"Yeah, well, Gabrielle approached me."

"What'd you tell her?"

"I said I'd have to talk with you. She said they'll be at their hotel bar at five."

"And what's it now?"

"Three-thirty, quarter to four."

"Then I'd better get moving. That's not much time if I'm going to try to compete with someone as glamorous as HA-brielle."

Chapter Eleven

Rachel owned and had brought along a "little black dress," but that felt too prosaic for cocktails. Besides, while she wasn't as jealous as she mischievously came off to Jake, there was a budding rivalry between her and Gabrielle, and she wanted to be anything but ordinary. She looked through her wardrobe three times, finally settling on a formal but fun knee-length patterned skirt with a fuchsia sleeveless drape neck blouse. She had no idea what Gabrielle's hair looked like, but knew hair was one of Jake's main turn-ons, and decided to maximize her appeal by wearing hers down. She spent extra time with the curling iron teasing just enough curl into it; carefully applied appropriate amounts of mascara, blush, and lipstick; and selected the right jewelry to match her outfit.

At ten to five, she emerged from the bedroom with a pair of low-heeled dress sandals in her hand. She waited until Jake looked up, catching his immediate expression and the look in his eyes. In the absence of specific comments, she had come to accept those responses—when she could identify them—as his compliment.

"Rach, you look . . ."

"Yes?"

"'Beautiful' is just going to start something again," he said. Then he stood and walked over to her. He gently tipped her chin up with his finger and gave her a long, soft kiss. She dropped her sandals and embraced him, kissing him back for several wonderful seconds.

She sighed softly as they separated.

"I only kissed Gabby for half as long," he said with a wink.

She whapped him in the side of the head, unable to hold back a smile while at the same time miffed that he, as was so often the case, spoiled the moment with his dorky humor. She sat down in an end chair and started to fasten her sandals. "Are you ready to go?"

"Just gotta pee," he said.

And the last of the magic disappears.

The thunderstorms had long passed, now just distant billows over the ocean. Bright sunshine and warmth, sans the full weight of the day's humidity, had returned. While there was no boardwalk this far north, several of the buildings in the vicinity were connected by a sidewalk that curved around a small patch of palm-dotted grass between the Taylors' condo and the hotel to the south. That same sidewalk fed into the pool deck at Liam and Gabrielle's hotel, a twenty-five-story megalith that was tinged a golden yellow.

Rachel felt overdressed when she saw several dozen people in chaise lounges around the hotel's two kidney-shaped pools. That feeling quickly went away as she and Jake walked up to the poolside bar situated between them and set back into the edge of the grass-covered dunes. The V-shaped bar had seating for a dozen, with a couple bistro tables on either side, all under the shade of a pergola. Sitting at a table in the corner were Liam and, recognizable even without him, Gabrielle.

She was everything Jake had backpedaled into saying, and more. For starters, she was tall, probably six feet. Her black hair had a luminescence as it framed a classically perfect face and eyes like melting chocolate. On an ogre's body, the face would have been beautiful. But Gabrielle was sculpted like a goddess, with long arms and legs that didn't end. She wore an emerald fit-and-flare dress accentuated with lace around the V-neck, a diamond necklace that captured every ray of sunlight, and an assortment of bracelets and bangles that, on Rachel would have felt cluttered, but on Gabrielle were just the right accent. Rachel felt out of her league, a sensation that was incredibly rare.

Jake put his arm around her, a sweet gesture, as they approached the table. Both Liam and Gabrielle stood, and the group made quick introductions, accompanied by handshakes. Rachel had somewhat expected—and sort of hoped for—a haughty look down the nose from Gabrielle. Instead, she flashed pearly white teeth and clasped Rachel's hands as if they were already dear friends.

Liam signaled to the bartender, who came to them. "What'll it be?" Liam asked. "My treat."

"You don't have to do that," Jake said.

"I insist. You were nice enough to cut time out of your schedule to meet us. I'll have a dry martini," he said to the bartender. "Two olives." Gabrielle ordered a mojito, and Jake and Rachel both opted for iced tea.

"Do you not drink?" Liam asked when the bartender was gone.

"No, never have," Jake said.

"Well, Gabs, not only are they a handsome couple, but wonderfully smart."

"There's something of a sordid past in my family," Rachel said, wondering why she was making excuses. The truth was she didn't drink because she simply had no desire to do so, didn't want to risk impairing herself to the least degree. It was the same reason she didn't smoke, didn't use recreational drugs, and didn't engage in a number of other potentially "pleasurable" activities with noted downsides. But why was that so hard to explain to people?

"Did you get off the beach before the rain?" Gabrielle asked, her eyes cutting from Rachel to Jake.

"No, we got soaked."

"Me too," she said with a grin. "At least it was a warm rain."

"So sad I missed out on all that," Liam said.

"Not a beach bum?" Jake asked.

"No, I am unfortunately not here solely for pleasure. Combined holiday and work venture. I had a meeting this afternoon."

"What line of work?"

"I'm a computer programmer. I write security software. High-tech door locks and password algorithms and the like."

"Small world," Rachel said. "Jake's a network engineer."

"Is that so?" Liam asked.

"You like it?" Gabrielle asked.

"I'm good at it."

"That sounds like a no," she said, lightly touching his arm. Rachel took a drink of her tea, which the bartender had just slipped in front of her.

"Not necessarily. It can just be a demanding profession."

"Computers and technology?" Liam said. "Frightfully so. But . . ." He lifted his glass. "I'm done with meetings for the foreseeable future, and none of you came to Myrtle Beach to talk about work." He took a drink. "How long have the two of you been together?" he asked as he set the glass down.

"Ten years," Rachel answered.

"That's good, Jake. She didn't look at you to see if you knew."

"It's our anniversary, so I'd better."

"Oh, congratulations. Today?"

"Not for a few weeks, actually," Rachel said. "Jake surprised me with this getaway."

"Well, Gabby, I feel like a cad," Liam said. "Jake here spirits his wife away on a two-week holiday for their anniversary, and I have to combine business and pleasure."

"And only for one week."

"Quite right."

"How'd you two meet?" Gabrielle asked, turning from her boyfriend.

Jake looked to Rachel, as he always did, to let her tell the story. It was better. His version was: "We were at a football watch party together." The full story was they had both been invited to watch the Nebraska-USC game. The Huskers lost a lopsided affair, and Jake was the only guy at the party who didn't give up and start drinking or playing games or leave. He stuck it out to the bitter end. At first, Rachel found it kind of odd, thinking he was obsessed. She came to realize it was loyalty and not obsession that caused him to stick with his team even when they were getting clobbered, a realization cemented when he shook off the loss and enjoyed the rest of the party. Although they'd been introduced sometime early in the game, Rachel and Jake didn't really "meet" until afterward, when her car wouldn't start. Jake offered to take a look and proposed jumping the battery. Even though she was plenty familiar with the process, she let him take the lead, thanking him when he coaxed her '94 Taurus to life. Then he offered to follow her home, just to make sure she didn't get into any further trouble.

"Mmm, I'd have thought that a little creepy, I'm afraid," Liam said.

"I was afraid she would too," Jake said. He winked at her. "She didn't."

"I could tell he was different than most guys," Rachel said, almost getting choked up at the memory. That sensation faded when she saw Gabrielle pat

Jake's arm and "aw." Rachel opted to change the subject. "What about you two? How'd you meet?"

"Well, I'd like to say I saw her at a party, plucked a few flowers from a bouquet, and captivated her with a brilliant introductory line," Liam said.

"Instead he spilled his drink on my J Kara," Gabrielle said, playing with the straw in her drink.

"And then I put my foot in my mouth by asking her if I could take it off. I, of course, meant take it off her hands and get it dry-cleaned. I think she nearly slugged me."

Rachel covered her mouth as she giggled. Even Jake, who only really laughed when around his brothers or when watching Frank Caliendo bits, was chuckling.

"After that, he wouldn't leave me alone," Gabrielle said. "He sent me flowers by way of apology, called several times, and pleaded with me to meet him for coffee so he could apologize in person. I finally agreed just so he'd quit bothering me."

"I was so nervous, because all this time, I hadn't been able to stop thinking about how she was the most beautiful woman I'd ever seen. We met for drinks, and I didn't order anything because I could hardly swallow."

Gabrielle smiled. "I thought it was just that he was so clumsy he didn't want to risk spilling on me again."

"Yes, well, that too."

Rachel laughed again and tried to ignore the fact that Gabrielle had touched Jake's arm a third time as she laughed along with them all.

🍸   🍸   🍸

Jake was surprised. He was having a good time. He'd expected an Englishman named Liam to have pointy features, yellow teeth, hair slicked and parted like Ted Cruz, and to talk nonstop about Manchester United or Arsenal while using the word "bloody" a lot. Aside from his clipped accent and pale skin, Liam might have been just another guy at the local watering hole.

Even so, Jake couldn't help but notice Liam was a hair taller than he was, and his body a little better toned. His eyes were full of life, enhancing the wry smile that accompanied almost every remark. Jake also couldn't stop glancing at Liam's hair. It looked like that one guy's from One Direction—Liam, maybe?—messy but in an intentional way that looked cool, maybe a touch aloof. It was the look Jake went for but seldom achieved. Like today. His hair looked like he'd combed it with a garden rake while dizzy. And while Jake thought he looked pretty good in a new red, white, and black checkered shirt and name-brand jeans (Rachel had concurred while fiddling with the epaulet on his shoulder in the elevator ride down) he came off like a slob compared to Liam. He wore a pair of chinos and a burgundy dress shirt that was almost shiny. There was nothing fancy about his clothes, but the way he wore them, the way they fit his frame, made him look like a *GQ* model.

To top it all off, Jake couldn't help but notice that Liam finished most of his remarks with a quick glance at Rachel. And she, for all her fussing over his meeting on the beach with Gabrielle, kept smirking in reply. Probably dreaming about diving into those "pools," as she had once described Chris Hemsworth's eyes.

Despite it all, Jake liked the guy. Liam shared Jake's affinity for "guy" movies and history, and they swapped several obscure historical facts related to WWII and the American Revolution with each other, almost in can-you-top-this fashion. Yet not to best each other, but to impress the two women on either side of them.

"Of course, we were actually glad to be rid of you Yanks. Frankly, the Empire would have been too large had we held onto the Colonies." Liam looked at Gabrielle, who had backhanded him in the leg. "What?"

"Sorry," she said, "but he hasn't honed in on my 'you're insulting our companions' warning look yet."

"No apologies necessary," Jake said. "After all, we are enjoying the spoils of victory to this day."

"Touché."

Liam shook his head. "Forgive me, Rachel, but, Jake, is it just me, or does a woman's warning look resemble a woman's 'you've got something on your tie' look resemble a 'let's get out of here, big guy' look?"

"Yes."

"And heaven forbid she should ever start winking or licking her lips or wiggling her nose." He smiled and patted Gabrielle's knee under the glass table. She gave him a look in return that, if Jake was reading it properly, was only teasing in its hostility.

"Well, dear, I'm sure Rachel can attest to the fact that short of taking out an ad on an ESPN program or printing 'I'm too tired' on our foreheads in lipstick, there is no way to subtly tell a man anything."

"I've found a two-by-four over the head works wonders," Rachel said, and they all—even Jake—laughed.

With a glance at his watch, Liam said, "We should be going. We have reservations for six at Aspen Grille. Early, but I promised Gabby we'd take a voyage on the SkyWheel at sunset, and I hear the lines can be quite long."

"Should be a good night for it," Jake said, feeling like a dope. He was a Midwesterner and the son of a farmer, and thus doubly obligated to work the weather into every conversation at least once.

"Yes, well, that's what we thought when we decided to hike up Diamond Head to watch a sunrise a few years ago, and a monsoon hit."

"It rained for fifteen minutes," Gabrielle said with an eye roll, and the group chuckled again.

"Thank you very much for the drinks," Rachel said.

Liam waved it off as he dropped several bills onto the table. "My pleasure. It was lovely getting to meet you both. Jake," he said, extending a hand.

"Likewise, Liam."

Jake watched as he merely shook Rachel's hand, not kissing it or pecking her on the cheek, and he followed suit with Gabrielle.

"Say," Liam said, reaching into his pocket. "I mentioned to Rachel the other day that she must go to House of Blues, over at Barefoot Landing. We're thinking of going tomorrow night." He handed a business card with nothing but a cell number on it to Jake. "We'd love to have you join us. No pressure, but think about it, and give us a call."

"We will," Jake said.

"You two have a good night," Liam said.

"Enjoy the sunset," Rachel called after them.

Gabrielle gave a finger-wriggling wave, sort of at both of them. They headed inside, and Jake drained the last of his iced tea.

"That was fun," he said.

"Was it?"

He looked at Rachel's challenging eyes. "Aside from the five minutes you and he spent comparing names and places in the Hamptons," he said, referring to a conversation that took place after Rachel and Liam both realized the other had grown up, at least partially, on Long Island.

"I thought maybe you meant the way she pawed you every time she laughed."

"I didn't notice."

"Sure you didn't." Rachel finished her tea, and they stood up and headed back toward their condo. "They're nice," she said more conciliatorily, slipping her arm through the crook in Jake's.

"Who?"

She frowned and slowed. "Liam and Gabrielle."

"I thought maybe you meant his eyes."

She lightly slapped the inside of his arm.

"You certainly saw enough of them." He turned and smiled at her to show he was (mostly) joking. "They were nice. There's only one problem."

"You're going to be talking in a lousy he-thinks-it's-English-but-it's-actually-more-like-Australian-with-a-crusty-sea-captain-thrown-in accent the rest of the night?"

Jake grinned. "Aye, indeed I will, love."

Chapter Twelve

Rachel and Jake both slept in late Wednesday, waking to rumbling thunder and steady rain. Neither felt like going out in the elements to get breakfast, so they ate fruit, yogurt, and granola on the balcony.

"Think this is the same storm we saw last night?" Rachel asked, reclining in her chair, her feet propped on Jake's knees.

Last night, after an all-you-can-eat seafood buffet, they'd returned to the condo. Finding the pool area almost desolate, they'd decided to relax in the hot tub and had been treated to a spectacular lightning show in the eastern sky.

"No, that would be long gone. I think it's pretty common for storms to build up over the ocean during the heat of the day. That's probably what we saw."

"Is this more of Jimmy's anybody-can-be-a-weather-guy meteorology?" she asked.

He chugged the rest of his yogurt cup, causing her to shake her head. She dropped her feet and sat up, leaning toward him. "What are we going to do about dinner?"

"With Gabby and Liam?"

"So it's Gabby now, huh?"

He gently stepped on her foot, and she jerked it back.

They'd discussed it last night in the hot tub. On the one hand, they'd hit it off with the couple, and getting out with someone else might be fun. On the other hand, this vacation was supposed to be a getaway, just the two of them, recharging their marital batteries. Spending lots of time with people they found attractive may not be the best way to do that. But back on the first hand, they both felt mature enough to handle it, and neither doubted the other one's commitment.

"Let's do this," Jake said.

Rachel spooned yogurt, listening.

"This day's a wash—"

"Ha, ha."

"Pun not intended. It's a crummy day for anything much, and you did want to do some shopping. So what if we hit Barefoot Landing this afternoon, get the shopping out of your system, and then join them for dinner."

She slowly pulled an empty spoon through her mouth, cleaning it off.

"But we'll pass on any doing anything else with them unless we're both sold on it."

Rachel nodded. "Okay. I can go for that."

They lingered around the condo for the rest of the morning, and Jake called Liam around noon, making plans for dinner at seven. With skies showing signs of clearing, they got in the car and headed north to Barefoot Landing. Situated around Lewis Lake and right beside the Intracoastal Waterway, the shopping center and entertainment venue boasted over one hundred shops and restaurants, a T.I.G.E.R.S. Preservation Station, the Alabama Theater, and Alligator Adventure. Since they had the time (even Rachel felt six hours of shopping might be a little much), they decided to visit Alligator Adventure first.

Traffic was a mess on Kings Highway, three wide yet backed up at every stoplight. The roads were steaming as they quickly dried out under the midday sun, and whenever Rachel and Jake stopped, the breeze was replaced by heavy, muggy air. Rachel was glad, as they finally arrived and parked in a huge lot between the shopping center and Alligator Adventure, that she had chosen a long, cool, rayon sundress for the day. And applied a little extra Secret gel.

While Jake put the top up on the Mustang, she fastened her hair up behind her. Then she followed his eyes over the trees to where House of Blues stood looking like a cross between a haunted mansion and a Pittsburgh steel mill. He took a swig from a bottle of water, then offered it to her. She too gulped from it, then tossed it back into the car and took his hand as they started toward a boardwalk through a murky, mucky swamp covered in algae. It led to the "back" entrance to Alligator Adventure, as well as to House of Blues through a small woods.

They paid the admission fee and were given a brochure showing the various attractions, as well as advising of demonstrations and feeding times. They set out on a self-guided tour, and Rachel slipped her fingers into Jake's, causing him to look down at her.

"Something on your mind?" he asked.

"Are you having second thoughts? About meeting Liam and Gabrielle?"

"I had those already last night."

"You change your mind, we can call them back."

"No," he said. "I was just messing with you last night."

She nodded and let him pull her toward an exhibit. He'd made several comments at dinner and again in the hot tub about Liam being "quite a looker" and debonair and so on. Rachel hadn't been sure if he'd just been teasing or if his joking masked insecurity about her and Liam. And despite his assurance now, she still didn't know. But typical Jake, he changed the subject.

"I didn't know there were alligators in China."

"Are there?"

"That's what the sign says," he said with a nod. He glanced at his watch.

"We're plenty early," Rachel said.

"I know, but they're having a feeding demonstration at two I don't want to miss."

"Why is that such a draw?"

He shrugged, and they moved on. The park was fairly empty, it being the heat of the day and on the heels of a rainstorm. Rachel let Jake lead since this was more his thing than hers. She did wear her camera around her neck but felt like a dorky tourist. Especially since she wasn't using it. She'd thought maybe she could get some really cool "nature shots," but as of yet, she hadn't seen so much as a blink from any of the reptiles. They merely lay—some in the water, some out—motionless. One even had its mouth open as it rested in the grass.

"Look," Jake said, "he breathes like Jason."

She whacked him in the back.

"Wonder what's the difference between gators and crocs?" he said.

"Has something to do with their bite, I think," she said. "Teeth inside the snout or out of it or something like that."

He nodded.

"I think one has better eyesight too."

"Can't they see with their eyelids shut?" he asked.

Rachel shrugged as they approached a pen housing a particularly long specimen. A sign over the exhibit tabbed it as the famed Nile Crocodile, capable of growing to twenty feet. Motionless or not, it was worthy of a few pics.

"Jake, I've been thinking," she said when she lowered her camera.

"About what?" he asked as they passed under a mist fan, a welcome respite. A thin sheen of clouds had moved in, but it did little to block the sun.

"Maybe we should skip dinner tonight."

"Why's that?"

"I don't know. I just . . ."

"Are you concerned about me and Gabrielle?" he asked.

"I'm not concerned."

"Not concerned. So what word should I have said?"

"It's not Gabrielle," she said.

He nodded. They had wandered past a cage of desert turtles, a wolf lair, and several unusual species of bird, including a flock of flamingos. Many of them actually stood on one leg.

"Reptile House?" he asked.

Rachel narrowed her eyes. "If we must."

She was not squeamish. She watched war movies beside Jake without blinking. She'd field-dressed a deer several years back on a hunt in western Nebraska. And it was Jake who had trouble watching Ducky pull out organs during an autopsy on *NCIS*, one of the few TV shows they made time for. But lizards and snakes were not Rachel's thing, and she didn't get the fascination with the slithery, creepy animals.

"So why don't you want to go to dinner?" he asked inattentively while peering back and forth between several cages. Trying to figure out which was the GEICO gecko, if Rachel had to guess.

"I thought maybe you wouldn't want to," she said.

He stood and looked at her. "Why not?"

"Remember what I said the other day about your head being turned by a pretty girl?"

"Yeah."

"And remember what you said that once, about just because you had already made a purchase didn't mean you couldn't still look in the window."

"I wasn't actually saying that so much about me, but—"

"I know, Jake."

He took both of her hands. "Rach, Honey, I'm sorry if I've been window shopping. I don't mean to, and if it's hurt you . . ."

"Jake, remember what else I said the other night?"

"Quite a lot, as I recall."

She squinted at him. He let go of one hand and pulled her by the other toward larger lizards. She ignored them.

"I said we were both guilty of it at times," she said.

"Of window shopping?"

"So to speak."

He tapped the glass.

"I don't think you're supposed to do that."

"I don't see a sign."

"I think it's understood behavior."

He tapped it again, and the two-foot lizard behind the glass flicked its tongue but otherwise remained unmoved.

"Can I have your attention for like two minutes?" Rachel asked.

Jake turned to face her. "Yeah, Babe."

"What I'm trying to say is that I think both of our heads have been turned by Gabrielle and Liam. And I trust you implicitly, Jake. I know I have nothing to worry about. I just wanted you to know that too."

"I do," he said with a nod. Then he gently tugged her around the corner to look at snakes.

"That lacked conviction," she said.

"I know you'd never cheat on me, Rach."

She dropped his hand. "But?"

He sighed. "Come here." He led her out of the Reptile House and found a bench under a palm tree, providing them a reasonable measure of seclusion. He took a deep breath. "Look, it's no secret I'm a Midwest farm boy, and you come from a long line of well-to-do Long Islanders—We even joke about it."

"I left that lifestyle and came to Iowa, remember? I'm just as much a Midwest girl as you are a guy."

"Yes and no."

She frowned.

"Rach, I'm not disparaging you here, but you do have fine tastes. The way you like to dress, the things you buy for around the house, the gifts you give—

We're cut from a different cloth, and you'll always have some of that McGinnis austerity in you. And that's fine, that's who you are. But that's my point."

"What is?"

"Rach, I don't doubt your faithfulness to me, but . . ."

She dropped her chin a little, looking deep into his eyes.

"I'm afraid . . . I guess deep down I'm afraid you'll lose interest in me—that I won't be able to satisfy you anymore."

"Oh, Jake."

"And I'm not even talking physically," he said, looking away at something distant. Anything but remain one-hundred-percent vulnerable. "I'm sure I'll be a strapping specimen into late middle age," he said. "I just see the way my simple way of doing things frustrates you. I know you get tired of jeans and a T-shirt every day, but that's who I am. I wonder sometimes how long it will be until you just grow tired of me."

Rachel didn't care if they were in public. She wrapped her arms around him and hugged his shoulder and chest. "Jake," she said, turning her head up toward his, "I'm never going to get tired of you."

He looked down. "You say that now . . ."

She drew back and looked at him. "I say that because I love you. When I said yes to your wedding proposal, and when I said 'I do,' I knew exactly what I was getting. I knew exactly what I signed up for. I knew we'd clash over trivial stuff like how to decorate our home and what clothes to wear when we go out, all the way up to important stuff like how to deal with families' time demands and how to manage our finances." She shook her head. "And none of those things, none of my preferences and tastes, begin to compare with you. I'd give it all away and wear torn jeans and the same three T-shirts every day if it meant keeping you."

"I think I believe you," he said, looking at her out the side of his eye.

"Jake, if you believe anything I've ever told you, believe this," she said. "You will always be the man I love and want." She cupped her hands around his neck and kissed him passionately, not caring who might have been watching.

After several minutes, they got up and continued around the loop that wound through the park. They saw many more alligators, as well as exotic animals like lemurs and bobcats. They also stopped in the gift shop, where Jake purchased stuffed gators for his nieces. Back outside, they noticed the air seemed juiced for a storm, and the western sky was beginning to darken. They walked along a boardwalk through more fenced in swampland, eyeing several gators in the distance. Beyond them, House of Blues towered above the tree line.

They had once again agreed to go to dinner with Liam and Gabrielle, and for once Rachel wasn't feeling a sense of jealousy toward Gabrielle. Even so, she still struggled to understand Jake's comparison between the two of them. Gabrielle was sexy and exotic on the outside, while Rachel had a natural beauty, he'd said. Even if he'd meant it as a compliment, which Rachel had no doubt he did, it made her wonder if it was possible to have both a natural beauty and a sexy, exotic exterior. If so, was that something she should pursue for Jake? And what would it look like if she did?

He said something, and she stopped.

"What?"

"I said they're not hopping."

"What aren't?"

"The kangaroos," he said, pointing to a pen on their left, where two brown marsupials lay on their sides, legs splayed in front of them. "How boring. You'd think they could at least box on demand or boing around or something."

Having mostly circled the park, they walked out onto a platform extending into the swamp. It was wide, with several levels of wooden bleachers all aimed at the largest pond at the park. Jutting into the pond was a fenced in "dock." The snouts and scaly backs of several gators were visible, floating slowly in the water under or around the dock and basking in the mud at the pond's edge.

"Time?" Rachel asked.

Jake showed her his watch, a multifaceted model with a leather cuff that he thought was cool. It was ten before two, and the platform was filling up with visitors. More interestingly, the number of gators was increasing. They knew it was feeding time.

In a few minutes, a woman in a pink shirt walked out onto the dock, carrying two metal buckets with her. A headset enabled her to communicate via mounted speakers with the crowd of onlookers. As the gators—Rachel counted at least twenty of them—gathered around the dock and jockeyed for position, the woman introduced herself and welcomed everyone, going over the obvious ground rules like not throwing any food to the gators, sticking hands through the fence, or dangling toddlers over it. Then she pulled part of a raw chicken out of the bucket, and the gators started thrashing.

These were not baby gators like at many theme parks. They were full-grown, as long as eighteen feet, the woman said. She tapped the wooden railing of the dock with her palms, and several gators propelled themselves up out of the water by their tails, mouths snapping. She dropped the piece of chicken, and it disappeared in a gulp. Rachel was both fascinated and horrified.

"You may hear a pop," the woman said after dropping and tossing several more pieces of chicken to the gators. She flung one toward a sandbar, and the nearest gator grabbed it with its snout and swam away from two others. "When a gator closes its jaw, it does so with enough force to crush a cinderblock to dust."

Many in the crowd gasped or awed.

"Yet even a child, if he or she were able to get their hands clamped down on a gator's snout when it was closed, would have the strength to hold it shut. Of course, we don't advise trying."

Several of the biggest gators clamored for attention, and Rachel clung to Jake's arm as they pushed halfway out of the water to snap at the potential meal. She hadn't noticed until the lady said something, but now the pop resonated in her ears every time a mouth slammed shut.

After ten minutes, they had seen enough and slipped through the crowd. Gator pops were beginning to be accompanied by rumbles of thunder, and the heretofore absent wind was starting to freshen. That was a golf term Rachel had picked up from Jake. On golf telecasts, the wind didn't blow harder; it freshened.

They exited the park and walked briskly back to the Mustang. They split a bottle of water, then set out to find shelter from the impending storm. The shops at Barefoot Landing were divided into two sections, one on either side of the lake. While many of the stores were housed together, they each had separate entrances, requiring shoppers to step outside to go from store to store.

With the sky in the west a dark purple, and with muffled thunder now constant, Rachel and Jake spent a few minutes identifying the best place to be stranded long-term and set out for the Barefoot General Store at the eastern end of the promenade between the shops.

They arrived dappled with huge drops of rain and just before the skies unleashed a torrent of water.

Chapter Thirteen

As the rain poured, Jake found himself quickly distracted with the myriad of trinkets and items in the Barefoot General Store. It didn't help that he kept being distracted by his and Rachel's talk at Alligator Adventure. It had been a long time coming, and truth be told, it had been a long time coming in being apparent to him. He realized he began to understand what Rachel had said earlier, about feeling something but not being able to coalesce that feeling into words. It had taken him years to recognize the insecurity he felt and to be able to work up the courage to tell her about it.

Jake's dad had been a wonderful man, a great husband and father, but one of his few faults had been a low emotional quotient. He seldom expressed feelings, either verbally or actively. Jake had never seen his dad cry. Whereas Jake made jokes when his emotions bubbled to the surface, Jerry Taylor had walled them off behind a stubble-clad iron jaw.

To some degree, he was a product of his generation, raised by a father who had fought the Nazis and Nips in the 1940s, who had himself lived through the Great Depression. Raised on and inheriting a self-sustaining farm, Jake's dad had likely been too busy trying to survive and put food on the table for his three sons to mess around with emotions. And Jake knew his dad had loved him—never doubted it—even though he could only recall a few times when he'd actually heard it in so many words.

By comparison, he and his brothers were emotionally healthy. Rachel had confirmed it on several occasions. Some of that was due to Jerry and Jennifer's passing. That jarring tragedy had loosened up all three Taylor men. Having daughters had finished Jason, who now cried at the drop of a hat. Jake wasn't there yet—didn't really want to be—but he could see a change in his way of dealing with emotions. Rachel, no doubt, had played a role in that too. Now, to keep her from expecting this to be a regular sort of deal.

The rain lasted for thirty minutes, and Jake felt like Noah when he stepped out of the store to check the sky. The clouds were already parting.

With a little over three hours to spare, he and Rachel took their time, starting by crossing the lake via one of three footbridges and browsing at the iconic Ron Jon's Surf Shop. They moved on and found a South Carolina-themed board game for Rachel's sister's kids and boxes of saltwater taffy and fudge for various people back home, plus a sack of taffy for themselves. After purchasing homemade ice cream from a place reminiscent of a Ma & Pa's, they sat down on a now dry bench and people watched by the lake.

"So let's get something out of the way," Rachel said, spooning her ice cream.

"Okay," Jake said. His was of the cone variety, and he licked a pre-drip.

"We've never officially said it, I think because in our case it doesn't need to be said, but no matter what, divorce is absolutely never on the table."

"Is this your equivalent of asking Mom and Dad for a tattoo so they'll let you go to a party?"

"It's not that. It's just a starting point for a conversation."

"Okay, agreed."

"We realized from the beginning that love alone wouldn't keep us together. It had to be love with commitment, even when we didn't feel like it, combined with prayer and reliance on God."

"Right."

Rachel spooned more ice cream. "So since we both agree that we're stuck with each other and have resolved to at least maintain a functioning relationship, let's set the bar a little higher."

"We'd almost have to."

"What I'm trying to say is, I don't think either of us is content to let our marriage devolve to little more than a legal contract, hanging on because we refuse to let it dissolve out of principle but having no benefit or value."

"Wow, when you aim high, you aim high."

"You know what I mean, Jake? I don't want to settle for a crummy marriage or even an okay marriage. I want a good one."

He nodded.

"But I'm not going to strive for something if you're not with me."

"Agreed. No settling. Lots of striving. Sounds fun."

She raised her eyebrows at him but also smiled.

He licked.

"That means we're going to have to hold each other accountable. Call each other out if we think we're settling."

"Are you setting me up so you can point out a case of settling?" he asked.

"No. I just want to make sure we're on the same page, commitment-wise."

"The C-word."

"You've never been scared of commitment."

"No, not really. And I'm with you. If we're committed to being honest and straightforward, that means pointing out what needs to be pointed out."

"And it can't just be us pointing out issues and problems."

"You think that's what we've been doing?"

"It seems like it quite a bit."

"It's a starting point," he said.

"It is. But it can't be all there is, or we haven't accomplished anything. We need to follow up, push each other, push ourselves. If this is going to work, if we're going to rekindle things and be any different six weeks or two years from now, we've got to hold each other to a higher standard."

"Even when it hurts?"

"Even so."

"I ask, because I'm not the one who gets hurt feelings very often."

Rachel looked down. "I know. I need a thicker skin sometimes."

"You're a woman."

She raised her eyebrow again.

"What? Woman are often more emotional, more fragile. It's science."

"And men are often indelicate and cold and need to be more gentle."

"Science?"

She nodded and raised another spoonful to her mouth.

"You're a woman, and I'm a man. Really making breakthroughs here."

"Jake, sometimes . . ."

He stuck the rest of his ice cream cone in his mouth, filling it almost to the point where he couldn't chew. But he got it down, while Rachel rolled her eyes.

When she was finished eating, they crossed back to the north side of the lake, spending another hour ducking in and out of various shops. They bought a few more knickknacks and gifts and, in Rachel's case, considered a lot more. That included two shirts and a sundress, all of which she liked and all of which she passed on for the time being. Shortly before six, they returned to the Barefoot General Store, where it had all started.

"Now what?" she asked.

"We still have over an hour."

"I think I want to go back and get that necklace for Lisa," she said, referring to an only semi-tacky seashell necklace she'd seen at a store at the far end of the promenade, shortly after crossing back over the lake. "And then the tigers are supposed to be out at six."

"How about I meet you there? I want to get something for Jimmy at Dixie Outfitters."

"We didn't even stop there."

"I know."

"So how do you know you want to get something for him there?"

"It's his kind of store."

She shrugged.

"I'll catch up with you in a few."

"Okay."

She strolled down the promenade and Jake ducked into Dixie Outfitters. He wasn't sure he'd find anything for Jimmy or not, but Rachel had looked at jewelry for her sister for fifteen minutes on the first visit, and he wasn't in the mood for any more.

Jake browsed for five minutes and spent another two debating between a "Dont Tread on Me" T-shirt that mimicked the popular Gadsden flag showing a coiled snake on a yellow background, and a red hoodie with a "Southern cross" on the back and a small Confederate flag on the front. As it had for many people, the Confederate flag had become a symbol to his brother of standing up to political correctness and government overreach. Recognizing that it was also offensive and controversial to many people—and that Jimmy's wife wouldn't like it—Jake opted for the "Dont Tread on Me" shirt.

He had just paid for it and was examining a row of coffee mugs when Rachel popped into the store. He frowned, wondering what she was doing there, and raised his hand to signal her.

He dropped it when he saw a flash of black beneath her neck. Rachel's dress was Kelly green, not black. Trying to be discreet, Jake studied the woman. She was maybe a little thinner and bonier than Rachel, too much so. Her skin was a shade darker, despite Rachel's recent time in the sun, and her eyes were wide circles compared to Rachel's almonds. Under the auspices of checking out some more T-shirts, Jake got a little closer. Her hair was black, on further inspection, with a few brownish highlights, and choppier and shorter than Rachel's. Still, at first glance—and even second—she bore a striking resemblance to his wife.

Jake exited the store and headed toward the T.I.G.E.R.S. Preservation Station. The free attraction allowed visitors to get up close to full-size tigers. For a fee, they could even have their picture taken with a tiger cub.

Spotting Rachel's dress through the crowd, Jake pressed toward the glass cage. She stood with one palm against the glass, eying a white and black tiger as it slowly stalked around through the foliage. Two other tigers lay at the back of the cage, their massive bellies slowly heaving in and out.

"Incredible," Rachel breathed when she saw Jake beside her.

"Want to know something funny?"

"What's that?" she asked warily.

"I could have sworn you just walked into Dixie Outfitters."

Rachel frowned.

"I saw a woman and had to do a double- and triple-take to realize it wasn't you."

Her frown intensified. "You know, the same thing happened to me the other day, coming back from the beach. A man got into the elevator, and I was halfway toward asking you what you were doing getting on at the third floor when I realized it wasn't you."

"Huh. They say everybody has a doppelganger."

"I guess."

"Did you get the necklace?"

"No," Rachel said sheepishly. "I got this far and got distracted."

"Well, you'd better get moving."

"I want to see the cubs first."

"You didn't let me finish. While I get in line to have your picture taken with one."

Rachel looked at him with something akin to shock on her face.

"Call it an anniversary gift."

"I thought this trip was the gift."

He shrugged. "So this is the cherry on top."

The look intensified.

"Miss the mark again?" he asked.

"No. No, you nailed it head on."

He smirked. "Go on. I'll get in line."

She gave his arm a quick squeeze and darted off toward the store in question. Jake smiled at her departure and then looked for the back of the line for having pictures taken with tiger cubs. It was hard to discern where the line ended and the mass of people trying to get to the glass or just trying to get by the mob began.

Jake had just made the determination when a man appeared at his right side. He had Jake by a few inches and maybe twenty pounds, and at first glance, Jake deduced the guy knew how to handle himself. Even so, he wasn't in the least bit threatening. He wore blue pants and a light gray shirt, tucked in, buttoned all the way except for around the neck. A striped tie that matched both the shirt and pants hung loosely around his neck. He looked like Jake after a long day's work.

"Excuse me, sir, can I have a moment of your time?" he asked with a Southern drawl that was more cultured than casual. He flashed a somewhat crooked, yellowed smile that Jake found trustworthy. He'd been about to blow the guy off, thinking he was hawking something or wanting to conduct a survey. Instead, he nodded, figuring he could spare a minute the way Rachel shopped.

They stepped out of the flow of traffic and beside a palm tree. A dozen feet away, a kiosk sold remote control helicopters and similar gadgets. The salesman was flirting with a couple of young women and paid Jake and the newcomer no attention.

"Are you Jake Taylor?" the man asked.

Jake's hackles went up suddenly. "How do you know who I am?"

The man reached for his pocket, and Jake flinched for just a second until the man held up a wallet. It contained a badge. "I'm FBI Special Agent Eric Butler, and I'd like to ask you a few questions."

Chapter Fourteen

Rachel was torn between two necklaces. One featured polished seashells, the sort of thing that could look tacky or refined. She leaned toward the latter but wasn't sure her sister would agree. The other was a small glass dolphin that was beautiful but a touch kitschy. After going back and forth, holding both of them against her skin and checking in the mirror, she decided on the seashell necklace. If Lisa didn't like it, Rachel would keep it for herself.

She paid and headed for the exit, pondering how heavy tiger cubs were, if their paws were manicured, and if kissing was allowed. She smiled. Not if she wanted to kiss Jake tonight.

"Excuse me, ma'am," a voice called from her right as she exited the store. She turned to see a woman get off a bench beside a grove of bushes and flowers. She was shorter than Rachel by several inches, with pale blue eyes and long, somewhat messy blond hair half pinned behind her head. She wore low heels, gray slacks, and a white scoop-neck blouse under a three-quarter-sleeve blazer.

Rachel stopped. "Yes?"

"I'm sorry to interrupt you," the woman said, pulling back one flap of her blazer. "I'm Special Agent Laura Holmes, FBI. I'd like to ask you a few questions."

Rachel focused on the gold badge clipped to the woman's waistline until she let the blazer drape back over it. "FBI?" Rachel asked.

"That's right."

"What's this about?"

"I can answer that when we meet up with your husband. He should be with my partner now."

"Jake?" Rachel asked. She turned away from the woman and started toward the T.I.G.E.R.S. station.

"Ma'am," the woman called after her.

Rachel strode quickly, searching for Jake's blue and white striped shirt. She spotted him under a palm tree, talking to a black man in business attire. She quickened her pace.

"Hey, Hon," he said, opening his arms to her.

Not until she felt his arm around her and had similarly embraced him did she turn to see the female FBI agent approaching.

"Jake, this woman says she's with the FBI and wants to talk to me."

"I know," he said. "This is Agent Butler."

"Ma'am, I'm sorry if we frightened you," he said, offering a hand. After a moment's hesitation, she shook it. "Special Agent Eric Butler," he said. "The titles are a bit intimidating at times, so call me Eric. This my partner, Agent Holmes," he said to Jake.

"Laura," she said, almost resignedly, as they shook hands.

"What's this all about?" Jake asked.

"This is a rather public place, and what we have to talk about is of a somewhat sensitive nature," Butler said, smiling. "Can we buy you folks dinner—place of your choosing—and we'll explain it all there?"

"We're actually meeting someone for dinner at the top of the hour," Jake said.

"We know," Holmes said. "That's what we want to talk to you about."

Rachel and Jake exchanged glances.

"Can you give us a little more than that?" Jake asked. "You have to admit, this is pretty peculiar."

Butler looked around before continuing the tag-team. "Suffice to say, your dinner companions tonight are not who they say they are."

"You know who we're meeting for dinner?" Rachel asked.

"Yes, ma'am, we do."

"And who are they?" Jake asked.

"If you ask them, in a moment of honesty, international acquisitions specialists," Butler said.

"If you ask us," Holmes interjected, "thieves."

Rachel looked at her husband, his face contemplative.

"Okay," he said. "Captain Squid's a mile or two back, a big pirate's hat over the entrance."

"I know it," Butler said.

"Meet us there at seven."

"Thank you, Mr. Taylor," he said with a nod. "We'll make the reservation under your name."

Jake nodded.

"A word of advice, don't make any contact with Jamison or Frost."

"Who?"

"Sorry, we shouldn't have assumed they used those names. Their real names are Liam Jamison and Gabrielle Frost."

Jake nodded. "That's them. We just didn't know last names."

"Okay. We'll see you shortly," Butler said, then guided Holmes toward the parking lot.

Rachel turned toward Jake. "What is going on?"

"I don't know, Babe. I don't know."

"Do you think this is tied to the break-in?" Rachel asked when they were back in the car. "Or to whatever you found in your pocket?"

"I don't know. A lot of coincidences if not."

She rubbed her forehead.

"You have your phone?" Jake asked.

"In my purse."

"See if you can get online."

"Okay," she said, already digging through the small purse she'd brought with her. "What am I looking for?"

"FBI field offices in South Carolina."

"Why?"

"Just being cautious."

She searched while Jake navigated his way out of the parking lot. Traffic on Kings Highway hadn't diminished, and he sat waiting for the light to turn.

"Only one is in Columbia," she said.

"You have a number?"

"Yeah."

"Call it."

"What?"

"Call the number."

"Okay, but I'm not talking."

He held out his hand, and a moment later, she plopped the phone into his palm. He glanced down to make sure it was facing the right way, then put it to his ear as he accelerated and turned onto the highway. After two rings, an automated attendant answered, and he listened to several options before tapping the correct button on the screen. He did the same for a submenu, then the phone rang again. This time, an actual person picked up.

"FBI Columbia Field Office, this is Agent Lawrence."

"Agent Lawrence, my name is Jake Taylor. I was just approached by two persons claiming to be FBI agents, and I'd like to verify their identities."

"Certainly. What were their names?"

"Eric Butler and . . ."

"Laura Holmes," Rachel whispered.

He repeated her name to Agent Lawrence. "They each had badges and IDs, but I don't know how easily such things can be forged. Can you describe them to me?"

"Sure. Special Agent Butler is African-American, six-foot-one, two hundred pounds, brown eyes, short hair faded out at the temples. He has a small mole on his right jaw, a misshapen nose, and coffee-stained teeth."

That fit to a T.

"Special Agent Holmes is Caucasian, five-five, a hundred and twenty pounds. She has long blond hair, blue eyes, and a small mouth. She is known for her brevity."

Two for two.

"That sounds like them. Can you confirm what it is they want to talk to us about?"

"I'm afraid I'm not privy to that information, Mr. Taylor. I can have you transferred to their supervisor?"

"That's not necessary," Jake said after a moment. "Thank you, Agent Lawrence."

"My pleasure, sir."

They exchanged the usual pleasantries, and Jake lowered the phone. "They're legit. Else class-A imposters."

"That's not exactly reassuring," Rachel said, taking back her phone. "The FBI. I can't believe it."

"Believe it, Babe," Jake said as he signaled for a turn. "Wait 'til I tell Jason and Jimmy."

The parking lot at Captain Squid's was packed, but Jake found a spot around back.

"What do fibbies drive?" he asked as they got out.

"Please don't call them fibbies to their face," Rachel said.

"I won't." He checked his watch: 6:57. He figured Liam and Gabrielle would give them ten minutes before trying to call.

From the outside, the restaurant looked like an old bait-and-tackle shop that had been renovated by a miniature golf course designer—right up to the giant, smiling squid wearing a pirate hat affixed to the roof over the front entrance. Inside, it wasn't much better, with fake fish and sea creatures on the walls, nets and paddles and a canoe hanging from the ceiling, and servers in cartoonish pirate garb. But Jake had seen advertisements all around town, bragging up the Calabash seafood and large portions.

A hostess—also dressed like a pirate—led them to a booth in the back corner. Agents Butler and Holmes were already there, ice waters in front of them. Butler got out of the booth and stood as Rachel slid into the opposite side, followed by Jake.

"Thank you both very much for meeting us," Butler said. "I know this is highly unusual."

"That it is," Jake agreed.

"I just got a text from an Agent Lawrence at the field office in Columbia, said you wanted to verify our identities?"

"Can't be too careful these days."

"I appreciate that, and your diligence, Mr. Taylor."

"Jake."

"And Rachel."

Butler nodded. "Is there anything else we can do to alleviate your concerns?" he asked, looking at both of them.

"No," Jake said. "But to be honest, we'd really like to know why we're here."

"Certainly. If it's okay with you, we'll order—our treat, get whatever you're in the mood for—and then once that's all out of the way, we'll be free to talk."

Jake nodded for what felt like the tenth time as a waitress brought menus and two more glasses of water. Awkwardness fell over the table as the group scanned them. Nobody was in a picky mood, and within just a few minutes, they had all decided on meals and ordered.

"If I could ask one more thing of you," Butler said, "and I know this might seem odd, but could you please turn off your cell phones and place them on the table? We don't want to risk anyone possibly listening in."

"Is that a real concern?" Rachel asked.

"Considering who we're dealing with, it is."

With a shrug, Jake complied, and Rachel followed suit.

"Thank you," Butler said. "Laura, you want to start?"

She reached into a valise beside her and pulled out a manila file folder. Jake watched with surprise as she opened it, thinking all this was done electronically now. Then again, it was hard to bug a manila folder.

Holmes brushed her water glass to the side and quickly mopped up the condensation with a napkin. Then she spread two eight-by-ten snapshots on the table. "Liam Jamison and Gabrielle Frost, more aliases than are worth mentioning. They are rather high-end thieves—fine jewelry, rare artwork, anything unusual or of extreme value. They're suspected of half a dozen high-value thefts from New York to Paris to Amsterdam to Hong Kong. They are the best in the world at what they do."

Jake studied the photographs as she talked. They looked just like they would in the movies, shots of each of them in unsuspecting moments. Liam was getting out of a luxury car on a busy city street. Gabrielle was looking over her shoulder, but not at the camera, in front of what appeared to be a fountain. Her hair was a little shorter, his a touch darker, and they both appeared a few years younger. But it was undeniably the couple Jake and Rachel were scheduled to be dining with at that very moment.

"How come they've never been arrested?" Rachel asked.

Holmes flitted her eyes at her. "Because they're the best at what they do."

"They've actually been arrested several times," Butler chimed in, "most recently five years ago in Johannesburg."

"They have a very good, very expensive lawyer, and they're—"

"The best at what they do."

Holmes eyed Rachel as if angry at being interrupted, but nodded nonetheless.

"We had no idea," Rachel said. "We just met them at the beach and—"

"Don't worry," Butler said. "You're not in any trouble."

"Then what do you want with us?" Jake asked.

"Three weeks ago," Holmes continued, "word began to leak about a black market auction. Interpol picked up chatter coming out of Frankfurt, and several South American governments intercepted similar communiques from inside their countries. Naval Intelligence hacked an e-mail between a crooked ensign and his handler. They busted him for smuggling tobacco products into the U.S. aboard a Navy frigate and got him to turn on his handler, who in turn ratted out his boss, a man named Mitchum. This man Mitchum is a known antiquities trafficker, and when grilled by NCIS, the FBI, and Interpol, revealed intel that matched with what Interpol and Brazilian and Chilean intelligence agencies had picked up. Then, two weeks ago, we decrypted several messages on the dark web related to an auction, specifying details that, again, were in line with the other intel we'd gleaned."

Rachel had her hands on her forehead, elbows on the table. She looked up. "I'm sorry, black market auctions, Chilean intelligence, the dark web? What does any of this have to do with us?"

"I'm getting there," Holmes said. "The intel all suggested this auction was going to take place two nights from now, and our decryption experts believe it will take place here in Myrtle Beach or one of the surrounding communities. Interpol agrees."

"Myrtle Beach?" Jake asked. "Don't these things usually take place at poker tournaments in Macau or warehouses by the docks in Istanbul or something?"

Butler grinned. "They take place wherever is convenient, for a number of reasons."

Holmes sighed. Jake took it she didn't like interruptions of any kind.

"As I mentioned, Jamison and Frost are wanted around the world, including here in the U.S. We expect them to show at the auction, but more importantly, we also expect a man known as *La Fantôme* to be there."

"The Phantom," Jake said.

"Technically 'the Ghost' in French. He is one of the biggest black market art collectors in the world."

"The biggest," Butler said.

"And nobody knows who he is, where he is, or much of anything about him. But we suspect he is involved, if not as the buyer, then as the seller."

"Why are all these thieves involved in an auction?" Jake asked.

"Keep in mind it's a black market auction," Butler said, "not a Christie's or Sotheby's auction. It's essentially robbery to the highest bidder."

"What's being auctioned off?" Rachel asked.

"We don't know," Holmes said, looking down. "We just know that many of the key players we've been after for a long time are going to be here, or at least be involved, in our jurisdiction."

"This is all very interesting," Jake said, "and I hope you catch these people. But what does that have to do with us?"

Holmes looked at Butler, who nodded. She retrieved a second manila folder, a duplicate of the first. She set it on the table and opened it. "Have you ever seen one of these?" she asked.

Jake looked down at another eight-by-ten photo, his eyes widening. It was a close-up shot of a small object on what appeared to be a wooden table or counter. The object was rectangular with two rounded corners, white except for silver trim at the square end. Size was hard to determine, but judging by the grain on the table, Jake placed it at half an inch by three-quarters, and maybe one-eighth-inch thick.

It was an exact replica of the mysterious object he had discovered in his jacket pocket Sunday night.

Chapter Fifteen

Rachel felt as if she was going to throw up. The charming couple she and Jake had been prepared to have dinner with were actually international thieves in town for a black market auction that had the interest of the FBI, Interpol, foreign governments, and someone called *La Fantôme*. And now she was looking at a picture, supplied by the FBI, of the very device Jake had found in his pocket. How? Why? And what had happened to their romantic getaway?

Jake glanced her way before nodding. "What is that?"

"It's called a paddle," Butler said.

"A paddle?"

"P-A-D-L. Purchase And Delivery Liaison. They're all the rage in these black market auction circles. Stolen art, weapons, you name it."

"But what is it?"

"It's an electronic device that can be plugged into a computer or other device with a USB or HDMI port," Holmes said. "The PADL contains identification, perhaps an encrypted password, and, often times, the owner's bid, payment information, and instructions. When the PADL gets uploaded to a device—say, a laptop—it transmits all that data to the seller, who can then transmit return data—verification of receipt, declaration of victory, delivery instructions, etcetera—back to the bidder. And it's all strictly anonymous."

"So someone like *La Fantôme* could bid on an auction in Myrtle Beach and still be a continent away," Butler said.

"But there was nothing on the device," Rachel said. "Jake's a network engineer."

"You have one?" Holmes asked.

Rachel swallowed.

"I found it in my pocket Sunday night after we got into our condo," Jake said. "But Rachel's right, there was nothing on it."

"The software is incredibly well hidden and disguised," Butler said. "The only way it's even activated is when introduced to a system that has the required proprietary software to set up or read a PADL."

"I took the device to the cops," Jake said. "They had no idea what they were looking at."

"No surprise," Holmes said. "This is above their pay grade."

"We weren't even aware of PADLs until late last year," Butler said. "And by this time next year, they'll probably be passé. But for the time being, we have an opening. And that's where you come in."

The sick feeling returned to Rachel's stomach. It didn't help that the waiter chose that moment to deliver a salad for which she suddenly had no appetite. Holmes pushed hers to the side, Butler crumbled oyster crackers into his soup, and Jake sat thinking, having asked for double fries with his seafood platter in lieu of a soup or salad.

"We come in?" Jake asked.

"How did you get a hold of the PADL?" Holmes asked.

"I told you, it was in my pocket when we got to our condo."

"Before or after the break-in?"

Rachel gasped slightly but caught herself. Of course, the FBI would know about the break-in if they had investigated her and Jake. And obviously they knew enough to know about their dinner plans with Liam and Gabrielle. The question was, how much else did they know?

"After," Jake said, briefly explaining the events of their arrival Sunday night. As he spoke, Butler consumed his soup almost ritualistically, stirring, spooning, pausing to blow, and slurping each bite. Meanwhile, neither woman touched her salad.

"And you have no idea how it got there?" Holmes asked.

"Don't you think we'd tell you if we did?" Rachel said.

Butler held up a hand. "Sorry, Rachel. We didn't mean to imply anything. I realize you're overwhelmed and this doesn't make sense. Unfortunately, we're in the same boat to a degree."

"PADLs are incredibly hard to come by," Holmes said. "Only select persons have them."

"Like *La Fantôme*?" Jake asked.

Holmes nodded.

Rachel slipped her hand down under the table and over to Jake's.

"Did you encounter anyone suspicious in your travels?" Holmes asked. "In the airport, on the plane? Anyone who could have slipped you the PADL?"

"Why would someone have slipped us the PADL?" Rachel asked.

"Working theory, they mistook you for someone else."

"I still don't understand. Who would they think we were?"

"A proxy," Butler answered. "The greatest feature of the PADL is the anonymity it provides. Anyone could show up at an auction with a PADL and submit a bid, without the seller knowing who they were or who they represented—since in many cases only numbered accounts and PINs are used. It would enable someone, like *La Fantôme*, to conduct his business while remaining insulated."

"We ran standard FBI background checks on both of you," Holmes said. "You're clean, so we don't suspect you of being complicit. That's why we think this was a mistake. Someone passed you the PADL accidentally."

"Jake . . ."

"I know."

"What?" Holmes asked. "Jake what? What's 'Jake'?"

"A few minutes before you showed up at the mall, I spotted a woman who was a pretty good ringer for Rachel. A couple of days ago in our condo, she spotted my double. We thought it just a weird coincidence, until now."

Under the table, Rachel squeezed his hand harder. He squeezed back.

"Describe them. Anything you can remember."

Jake first, then Rachel, described the woman and man they had spotted. She felt bad that her description was based largely off Jake, but that's whom the man had looked like. Holmes took notes, sighing when they were finished.

"What do we do now?" Jake asked. "I assume you want the PADL?"

"Actually, no," Butler said. "The FBI got its hands on one two months ago outside a strip club in Miami. Our experts and the best NSA, Homeland, and DOD had to offer all analyzed it and were unable to come up with anything. No hint of any software. However it's hidden is something beyond what we've ever seen—we being the collective U.S. government."

"That's comforting," Jake muttered.

"We only know what the device is thanks to an informant working in Zurich and the confession of a black market seller apprehended outside Shanghai."

"So what then?" Rachel asked, a pit forming in her stomach. She had a funny feeling she knew what the answer would be.

"It's very possible that whoever passed you the PADL by mistake doesn't know he's made a mistake," Holmes said. "That gives us an advantage."

"How so?" Jake asked.

"The PADL likely contains all required information to submit a bid at the auction—buyer ID, bank info, and bid amount. It doesn't matter whose hands it's in as long as it makes it to the auction."

"You want us to go?" Jake asked. "Undercover."

"It may be our only chance to catch *La Fantôme*."

"It's certainly our best chance," Butler said, moving his soup bowl aside. "This guy is what his name says—a ghost. If we can get a foot in the door at the auction, we can possibly gain intel we've never had before."

"How? This isn't his PADL, is it?"

"Could be," Holmes said.

"Even so, you yourselves said it, he could be half a continent away, and you're at square one when it comes to interpreting the software on the device because you can't even find it."

"All true," Butler said. "But if the PADL is his, we're confident he'll have the high bid, based on everything we know about him. When the bid wins, assuming this auction follows the standard protocol, the owner of the—I should say, the possessor of—the PADL will be notified, and delivery arrangements will be made. It's possible that's the end of the line for the proxy, but we expect *La Fantôme* would have hired them to arrange to pick up and deliver to him, somehow, whatever it is he's buying." Butler tapped the table with his finger. "And that's where we move in."

"On whom?" Rachel asked. "We're the proxy. That is what you're asking, isn't it?"

Butler nodded. "Yes, Rachel, it is. We'll move in on the seller, the one person who has access to all the bids and bid information. That info will hopefully lead us to *La Fantôme*. Not to mention, this gives us an excellent chance at recovering whatever is being auctioned, which is almost certainly hot."

"What if it's not *La Fantôme's* PADL?" Jake asked.

"If it has the high bid, it still gets us the seller," Holmes said.

"And if not?"

"Then we 'swoop' in and announce we've recovered a PADL from two unsuspecting tourists, thus clearing you of wrongdoing in the eyes of its owner, and we ship it to our boys in the lab and hope they can find something on it they haven't previously."

"And you have no idea what this item up for auction is?" Jake asked.

"The message off the dark web that we decrypted contained the phrase 'arch,' we think," Holmes said. "That could make it the Archibald Diamonds, lost artwork depicting the Archangel Michael, any number of priceless parchments, something historic related to an archduke, or numerous items we haven't even thought of."

"So no," Rachel said, a little snarky, but not unwarrantedly so, given the circumstances.

"No."

"We realize this is a big ask," Butler said. "And we never would, except you have the PADL and we, so to speak, have you."

"If we say no?" Jake asked.

"We can't compel private citizens to be a part of an FBI investigation," Butler said. "I don't know about Laura here, but I'm not above begging." He smiled for the first time in a long time. "If that doesn't work, then we'll take the PADL and do what we can. But you two obviously fit a profile, so it makes you the best candidates."

"Why did someone break into our condo?" Rachel asked.

"I'm sorry?"

"Well, you said whoever gave us the PADL by mistake doesn't know we're the wrong people. So who broke into our condo?"

"We said 'we think,'" Holmes said.

"And why would our doubles, the likely supposed proxy, be following us?" Jake asked.

"Do you know they were?"

"I suppose they *could* just happen to be staying at the same condo and be shopping at the same time and place as us."

"These are all working theories," Butler said. "Another possibility is that the PADL's owner—say *La Fantôme* for the sake of discussion—hired

113

someone to pass the PADL to the proxy, and he's the one who screwed up and gave it to you by mistake. Somebody like that might be hesitant to report their mistake to their boss, meaning as far as *La Fantôme* and the auction are concerned, the PADL is in the right hands."

"But won't that put us in danger?" Rachel asked.

"Conceivably, yes. But the break-in was three days ago. Whoever this is found you within hours of your arrival to Myrtle Beach, so he or she could certainly have found you again by now. The fact that no further attempt has been made to recover the PADL tells us they either believe you don't have it or have opted for an alternate strategy to attain the item up for auction."

Rachel looked at Jake, searching for wisdom behind his eyes. All she saw was uncertainty. And healthy fear.

Their entrées arrived, and Rachel tried to summon an appetite. She tried to think of questions to ask, but knowing only what she saw on movies or spy-themed episodes of *NCIS* or *24*, she and Jake were in the dark. Where either of them did have questions, Butler and Holmes willingly answered all they could and went over things two or three times with patience—at least on Butler's part.

Jake, still, had an appetite, and halfway through his plate of four kinds of fried seafood asked, "Can we think about it? Sleep on it?"

Butler looked at his partner. "I think that's fair."

"I realize it's scary," Holmes said, looking between Rachel and Jake but mostly at Rachel, "but we wouldn't be asking you to do this if we didn't think you could pull it off or if we thought it placed you in any real danger."

Rachel forced a smile in response. She appreciated Holmes' kinder, more compassionate tone, but couldn't help notice the qualifier "real" before the word danger.

Only Jake finished his meal. Rachel did little more than pick at her food, and the two FBI agents were too busy talking to clean their plates. They all took food to go, and when Butler had settled the check, he offered his hand to both of the Taylors.

"Thank you very much for taking the time to meet with us and for considering this. If you have any more questions that can help with your decision, please give us a call," he said with a nod at dual business cards Holmes had provided.

"We'll be in touch tomorrow morning," Jake promised.

Butler nodded and stood. Rachel and Jake slid to do likewise, but Holmes stopped them as she leaned across the table. "Do not have any contact with Jamison or Frost. Not until we speak tomorrow. If they left you a message or call again, ignore them."

The Taylors nodded.

They said goodbyes again in the parking lot, and Rachel and Jake walked to the car. More clouds had moved in, and for all intents and purposes, darkness had fallen. They sat in the Mustang for several minutes, neither of them speaking.

"What are we going to do, Jake?" Rachel asked finally.

He stared blankly ahead at the trees beyond the parking lot. "I don't know."

"Jake, Honey, are you sleeping?"

He rolled over, his eyes half open. He blinked them a few times. "I'm not now. Rach?" She wasn't in bed beside him, and he sat up. His eyes took a moment to adjust to the darkness of the bedroom before spotting Rachel in an armchair in the corner. The drapes were pulled back a few inches so she could look out the window, which she did with her chin resting on top of her knee.

Jake sat up all the way. "Babe, what's the matter?"

"I'm just watching the lightning. Thunder woke me up."

Admittedly not great at reading Rachel's signals, Jake was smart enough—even in the fog of an interrupted REM cycle—to know Rachel wasn't pensively looking out the window because of an overnight thunderstorm. He glanced quickly at the red numbers on the clock by the bed. It was 2:12, or roughly three hours after they'd finally gone to sleep after regurgitating everything they'd heard from Butler and Holmes at dinner and weighing every pro and con of helping them. It hadn't taken a cryptanalyst to pick up on Rachel's concern, and it had been hard to conceal his own.

They had laid every option on the table: Playing along exactly as the FBI agents asked. Going to the local police, explaining things, and getting a "second opinion." Simply saying "no" and giving the PADL to Butler and Holmes. Booking an early morning flight home, or to Key West, or to Jamaica. Neither of them was big on running away from problems, nor weaseling out of a tough spot. It was part DNA, part Midwestern values—you faced a challenge head on, persevered, and beat it.

But Midwestern challenges rarely involved the black market, covert "acquisitions specialists," and characters named *La Fantôme*.

They had also researched some of the potential items Holmes had mentioned as possibilities to be auctioned: the Archibald Diamonds, paintings of the Archangel Michael, and valuables known to have been possessed by Archduke Ferdinand. Aside from a Wikipedia-level crash course on high-end art and antiquities, they'd come away with nothing to aid in their decision. So, finally, after much pacing and pondering, they'd decided to do what they'd told the FBI agents they would do—sleep on it.

Jake had meant for a full night. He brushed aside the covers and walked over to his wife. He eased her out of the chair, took her place, and then settled her onto his lap. He locked his arms around her waist and kissed her cheek. "I'm not going to let anything happen to you."

She laid her head back on his shoulder. "That's very sweet, but you and I both know you can't guarantee that promise."

"There's one way I can," he said, whispering for a reason he couldn't figure. "We can say no."

"I don't think we can, Jake."

"I know it's important to you to do the honorable thing, Babe, and I agree. But we're in over our heads here."

"I'm not talking about that. I know what Agents Butler and Holmes said, but I can't help but believe that ever since somebody slipped that PADL into your pocket, we're in this until the end. If we run away, aren't we always going to be looking over our shoulder for *La Fantôme*?"

"Holmes said they'd cover for us if we did."

"And I'm sure an international art thief named 'The Ghost' would believe the FBI. And even if he did, he might still come after us for ruining his play at the Archibald Diamonds or some historic parchment or whatever it is by involving the feds in the first place."

Lightning flashed vividly out the window, and, for the first time, Jake heard rain drumming against the building. He'd thought Rachel was looking at distant lightning out over the ocean again, not effects of a present storm. At any rate, he smiled.

"What?" Rachel asked

"What 'what'?"

"You're smiling."

He looked down at the top of her head, wondering how she knew.

"I can hear it," she said.

"I was just thinking about how in the movies, lightning always flashes when somebody says something dramatic like how a guy named 'The Ghost' is going to hunt them down and haunt them."

She slapped his stomach and sat up. "I'm serious, Jake."

"I know you are. And I share the same fears."

Even in the darkness, her eyes studied his. "I think the only way forward is to work with them and finish this."

He nodded. "I think you're right."

"And that is what worries me," she said, laying her head back on his shoulder. "That's why I'm sitting up watching lightning at two a.m."

He dropped a kiss onto her hair and rested his cheek on her head. "Well, you can say this at least: we're out of the rut."

Chapter Sixteen

The pit in Rachel's stomach from the night before had returned, and it had nothing to do with the rapidly shrinking ground beneath her and Jake. This was not her first time in a helicopter, although it was a long way removed from the aerial tour of New York City that had been her thirteenth birthday present from her grandparents. It was also a long way removed from that festive atmosphere.

Special Agent Holmes had called while Rachel and Jake were eating breakfast. She'd apologized for the intrusion and asked them to meet her and Agent Butler at Helicopter Adventures at ten, saying she would explain when they arrived.

"You don't suppose Jamison and Frost are the real FBI agents and these two are phonies, and the plan is to abscond with us to some secret lair, do you?" Rachel had asked Jake.

He'd winked in return. "Only a little."

Despite his dislike of planes, Jake had no qualms about a helicopter ride, so they agreed. After finishing breakfast on the balcony while enjoying the return of sunshine and low humidity, they headed out from their condo. Liam and Gabrielle—or rather Jamison and Frost, as they were known in the "intelligence community"—had called twice the night before and once that morning, and as she and Jake cruised down Ocean Boulevard with the top down in the Mustang, Rachel wished their problems would disappear with the breeze. How nice it would be to enjoy Myrtle Beach without worrying about running into art thieves, mysterious doubles, or federal agents.

Helicopter Adventures, which advertised its $20 helicopter tours in Rachel's guidebook, online, on billboards, and behind planes that flew up and down the coast, was only a few miles from their condo. It consisted of a small, blacktopped parking lot, two buildings—an office and a hangar or small warehouse—two big red- and white-striped tent canopies, and five concrete helicopter pads. Three of them were occupied with Robinson R-44 helicopters—a detail Rachel knew because she'd browsed the Helicopter Adventures website briefly after breakfast. She'd also discovered that the $20 advertisement was a bit misleading. The company did offer rides for that price, but they only lasted a few minutes, basically just circling the immediate area. To really tour the Grand Strand, you had to purchase a higher-level package, with prices running well over $100.

Special Agent Butler was waiting for them just beyond the parking lot. He wore khaki pants and a royal blue polo shirt and looked like an associate at Best Buy.

"Good morning, Jake and Rachel," he said, flashing a yellow but friendly smile. Rachel didn't mind him. He was at least congenial, for a G-man. Holmes, on the other hand, had a chip on her shoulder, it seemed. Plus she had that "messy blonde" look down to a T. Rachel knew some guys found it appealing, but she couldn't understand why. Maybe the carefully tousled look now and again, but Holmes looked, well, as if she'd just stepped out of a helicopter. Remembering some of her more stressful, hair-won't-cooperate days, Rachel sighed and made sure her ponytail was tight as Butler led them toward the nearest chopper.

"Agent Butler, can you tell us what this is about?" Jake asked.

"Once you're airborne, we'll explain everything."

"What, are helicopters the new run-the-water-in-the-bathroom spy trick, a Maxwell Smart cone of silence?"

Butler looked right at Jake. "That's not all that inaccurate."

That's when Rachel's stomach started to tighten.

Butler passed them off to Holmes, who had emerged from one of the tents. She could have been wearing the same slacks as yesterday, but with a bright green top, an odd contrast to her pale blue eyes. Her hair, it appeared, had been wadded up and stapled to the back of her head, and Rachel concluded the previous day had not been an aberration.

Holmes offered cursory handshakes, then guided Rachel and Jake to the back seat of the chopper, identifying headsets and seatbelts. She slid the door shut behind them, then got in front, on the left side. Beside her, a tall, well-built man dressed in a white polo shirt and dark trousers finished checking various gauges and switches, then turned around to face Rachel and Jake.

"Can you both hear me?" he asked into a headset like theirs.

They nodded.

He offered a hand. "I'm Special Agent-in-Charge Simon Vaughn."

Rachel shook his hand, studying him briefly. She placed him in his mid-forties, with brown hair just starting to gray around the temples. His face was tanned and weathered, but friendly. He had mere slits for eyes, she could tell because Vaughn's gold-rimmed aviator sunglasses were clipped over the buttons of his shirt instead of covering his eyes.

"Mr. and Mrs. Taylor, pleased to meet you," he said after introductions and handshakes. "I don't stand on pretense, so no need for any 'Special Agent Vaughn' stuff. Call me Simon, and thanks much for coming out here today."

"You're welcome," Jake replied.

"Just give me a few minutes, and we'll be airborne, and then we can talk freely."

Rachel hadn't been sure if conversation at ground level could somehow be intercepted or if Vaughn had merely meant less of his focus would be required on flying once they were in the air, but it had indeed been just a few minutes. Holmes had checked—a little late—if either of them got airsick and explained that Butler would be waiting "as a lookout" on the ground, "just in case."

Combined with the weight of what she and Jake were undertaking, all the spy craft was almost too much for Rachel, and she tried to take her mind off her turbulent nerves by focusing on the scene out the window. The chopper was facing southwest, and out her window, Rachel saw the Intracoastal Waterway, golf course communities, and miles of South Carolina low country. Turning to look past Jake, she spotted the Broadway at the Beach shopping center, a venue similar to Barefoot Landing. Beyond it, rows of hotels and condos lined the cerulean waters of the Atlantic.

The view had a calming effect, as did Jake when he grabbed her hand. Perhaps spotting the gesture out the corner of his eye, Vaughn turned back to them. "Don't let Agent Holmes scare you," he said in his baritone voice. "We don't anticipate any trouble. But when you're dealing with someone like *La Fantôme*, you want to keep all your bases covered."

Rachel again watched the scenery as they leveled off and turned north. Smooth as you please, Vaughn eased the cyclic forward, and the helicopter followed. Beneath them, the Intracoastal Waterway was a ribbon of blue, gradually tapering the land between it and the ocean as it ran northeast.

"You're getting the Grand Adventure," Vaughn said. "We'll follow the ICW practically to the North Carolina border, then swing back along the beach. Be about twenty-five minutes total."

"Excuse the bluntness, Simon," Jake said, "but can you tell us what this is all about?"

"Mr. Taylor, if you'll—"

"Jake."

Vaughn nodded. "All right, Jake, if you'll excuse the bluntness right back, I'm here to hold your and your wife's hands. I'm sure you folks probably have a lot of questions and can't even begin to figure out which one to ask first. I don't mean that to talk down to you, but in my twenty years with the Bureau, I've worked with a lot of 'civilians,' and I've come to expect it. So fire away."

Before Jake could think of a question, Rachel spoke. "You're Agent Butler and Holmes' boss?"

"Yes, ma'am."

"If you don't mind me asking, is there a reason you've come now instead of initially?"

"Of course I don't mind you asking," he said, and Jake noticed for the first time a very faint Southern drawl, not nearly as pronounced as Butler's. And perhaps a touch more refined. "It's like I said, we thought you'd have some questions."

"I'm sorry, but isn't hand-holding usually a job for rookie field agents, not a special agent-in-charge."

"Often times, Rachel, yes. But in this case, Agents Butler and Holmes reported that you had some . . . misgivings—perfectly natural, under the circumstances—so I decided to slip down to the coast and see if I could provide any reassurances."

Jake looked at his wife as she sat back. "How did you know to contact us?" he asked. "How did you know we were meeting with this Jamison and Frost, when, and where? It seems pretty coincidental that your agents just happened to intercept us thirty minutes before we met them."

"A number of things played into that," Vaughn said. "For starters, Agent Holmes said she briefed you on the various intel we have about the upcoming auction."

"She did."

"That, of course, drew our attention in the first place. When Jamison and Frost arrived at Myrtle Beach International, their faces popped in our database, among others. While they're both suspected of a variety of illegalities, there isn't any actionable evidence, so they can travel freely under their actual names. But not without being noticed."

Jake scanned the view out his window as Vaughn talked. It was mostly forest and marsh. He glanced past Rachel and saw sparkling ocean in the distance.

"Once we were aware of their arrival, we studied airport surveillance to see who else may have arrived with them or interacted with them."

"We didn't," Rachel said.

"No. They flew in from New York, arriving about the same time, however. And from as far as we can tell, you had no interaction with them."

"No," Jake said.

"We did pull images of everyone at the airport at the time, which put the two of you in a 'database' of sorts."

"Is that legal?" Jake asked.

"Yes, sir, it is."

"Hmm."

"Should have voted for Rand Paul," Holmes muttered.

"You certainly didn't monitor everyone in the airport at the same time as them," Rachel said.

"No, but then your condo was broken into. That drew our attention."

"We went back to the airport security footage and spotted this," Holmes said. She turned in her seat and handed a small tablet to Jake. "Just tap the screen."

He did, holding it so that Rachel could see as well. A black screen faded in to show a greenish-gray security feed. It took him only a moment to recognize the Boardwalk Café inside the terminal of the airport. It showed him ordering coffee and tea for him and Rachel, then fiddling with the zipper on his jacket as the cashier filled the order. Another figure appeared in the shot. He was short, wiry, had unkempt, light-colored hair. He brushed Jake's elbow, said something to him, and then spoke to the cashier. Seconds later, he disappeared.

"Do you remember him?" Holmes asked, watching Jake as he watched the video.

"Yeah, he bumped into me as he was asking about the restrooms or something."

"Did he speak to you?"

"I think he said 'Excuse me.'"

"You think?"

"It was 'Excuse me' or 'Pardon me' or something of that nature. That's it."

"Who is he?" Rachel asked.

"We don't know," Holmes answered.

"We *think* he's a man by the name of Spencer Flynn," Vaughn said. "But he never let his face be fully photographed by a security camera. Always looking down or away or shielding himself behind another person. The little bit we can see of him matches the description, however."

"Who's Spencer Flynn?" Rachel asked.

"A stooge," Holmes replied.

"The technical term is henchman," Vaughn said. "He's an independent contractor, one we think has ties to *La Fantôme*."

"You think?"

"When it comes to *La Fantôme*, nothing is for certain. But we're reasonably confident, based on a variety of intelligence reports, that he's working for him."

"Okay, so what?" Rachel asked. "An . . . independent contractor with ties to *La Fantôme* bumped into Jake while asking where the restrooms were, and that drew you to us?"

"Jake, you said you found the PADL device in your pocket," Holmes said. "By any chance your right jacket pocket?"

"Yeah," Jake said. "You don't think . . ."

"There's no other reason for Mr. Flynn to be at the airport," Vaughn said. "He didn't pass through security, didn't come or go on a plane. From what we can tell from security footage, he neither arrived nor left with another passenger."

"But how?" Rachel asked. "He barely brushed his elbow."

"An expert pickpocket could do it," Vaughn said.

"Let me guess, Flynn's a pickpocket," Jake said.

"Among many other things."

"We slowed the footage down frame by frame," Holmes said. "We can't confirm he passed it on to you then, but we certainly can't deny it. In hindsight, that appears to be what happened."

"Okay, but you didn't know we had the PADL until last night. What made you think so?"

Holmes continued. "We expected that if *La Fantôme* was indeed going to bid at the auction, he'd use a proxy, and that means he'd somehow have to get the PADL to them."

"Couldn't he have just mailed it?" Rachel asked.

"Given the technological complexity, black market value for a PADL is just under a million dollars. It's not the type of thing you want to ship through the mail. Plus, the proxy would then have to bring it through airport security, which could alert TSA. A person-to-person passage would be safer."

"Assuming they passed it to the right person," Jake said.

"Right."

"When we saw what we thought was an exchange," Vaughn said, "we ran you both through a comprehensive FBI background check. The break-in already suggested there'd been some sort of mishap, but we wanted to be sure. You both passed with flying colors, and that's when we decided to contact you."

"That took three days?"

"No. Agent Holmes was about to approach you when she spotted you having drinks with Jamison and Frost. That raised our suspicions again, but you came through the vetting perfectly. We began to suspect they were scoping out the competition or hatching some sort of a plan."

"How could they have known who we were?" Rachel asked.

"Our guess is the same way we did. Jamison is known to be a techie—can hack anything, including airport security footage and federal databases."

"Any idea what they wanted with us?" Rachel asked.

"Only guesses. They didn't seem malevolent, so probably to use you as an alternate play for whatever is being auctioned."

"This is so bizarre."

"Agreed, Rachel. Anyhow, to finally answer your question, we had you and them surveilled most of yesterday, and Agent Butler actually heard you use their names and mention a dinner meeting while you were shopping at Barefoot Landing. That's when I authorized them to move in."

They had drifted inland, over the Intracoastal Waterway, and Vaughn used the gap in conversation to make a slow bank to the right, tipping the chopper as he did. Jake looked down and out Rachel's window at a shallow marsh and river outflow.

"Little River," Vaughn said. "Everything to the left is North Carolina."

"How far are we from the airfield?" Jake asked.

"About twenty miles. I'm going to drop down a little lower, give you a better view of the beach. No reason we can't mix business and pleasure."

Vaughn brought the craft around until it was lined up with the beach, then dropped to within a hundred feet of the ocean's surface. Jake felt like he was riding with T.C., skimming the waves on their way to Maui or Molokai.

"One thing I still don't get," Rachel said.

"If it's just one, you're doing better than me," Vaughn said, still flying effortlessly while carrying on a conversation. "Fire away."

"If this is such a high-stakes deal with big-league players, how could Flynn have accidentally passed a million-dollar piece of equipment to the wrong people?"

"That's a good question. Best guess is he only had a rough description to work off of. Proxies or middlemen can't advertise in the newspaper or on Craigslist, and they certainly don't want their actual IDs known. Flynn could have been told that two people matching your descriptions would arrive on such-and-such a flight from Chicago, maybe even be wearing a red jacket or perform some mannerism your husband unknowingly mimicked, and he made the exchange."

"Any idea who the real proxies are?" Rachel asked.

"No, unfortunately not."

"We took the descriptions you gave us last night and tried to match them with people on your flight. We came up with several possible hits, but nobody who's raised a flag."

"We were delayed," Jake said. "If our flight to Chicago had been on time, we would have been here in the afternoon, and none of this would have happened."

"The Lord works in mysterious ways," Vaughn said.

"The Lord?" Rachel asked.

"Well, He's not the only one."

"One other question," Jake said.

"Shoot."

"Why haven't you read the cops in on any of this? They had no idea what I had when I showed them the PADL, and have no leads to the break-in. Shouldn't you be working jointly with them?"

"We're keeping the chain of need-to-know as small as possible," Vaughn answered. "Obviously, since we're in their jurisdiction, we've made them aware we're conducting an op. But the fewer people who know the details, the better. Until the need-to-know changes, we felt it's best that they not be involved."

"Anything else we can clear up for you?" Vaughn asked.

"What specifically will we need to do?" Jake asked.

"The auction is Friday night. We'll need you to go, submit the PADL, and let us know of any response back from the sellers. Based on what that word is, we'll go from there."

"That simple?" Rachel asked.

"It actually is. We can go over a few more details, but it's little more than attending the auction and handing the PADL to someone who will plug it into a computer and return it to you."

"PADL," Jake said. "Purchase And *Delivery* Liaison. Agent Holmes said last night that the device is used to communicate back to the buyer about the delivery arrangements."

"Often times, yes."

"How will we know what that communication is? We don't have the software and, from what we were told last night, neither does the FBI."

"If that were the case," Vaughn said, "we think *La Fantôme* would have made provision for his proxy to be able to interpret the message. As it is, they'd need to return the PADL to him before he could determine if he'd won or lost and what arrangements were to be made for delivery. We don't know for sure, but we assume that will be communicated another way, likely to you as the proxy directly."

Jake nodded. He looked at Rachel. Agent Vaughn—like Agents Butler and Holmes the night before—had answers for everything. But Jake still felt uneasy, and Rachel's jade eyes conveyed the same sentiment. But the slight upturn at the corner of her pursed lips told Jake she hadn't changed her mind. And neither had he.

"Okay," he said.

"Okay?" Vaughn asked.

"We'll do it. We'll go undercover and help you take down *La Fantôme*."

Chapter Seventeen

A sliver of moonlight, instead of distant lightning, lit the sky over the ocean as Rachel and Jake walked slowly at the water's edge. Despite the darkness, the air was still warm—almost hot—with a minimal breeze. It was the definition of balmy, and their hand-in-hand stroll was the perfect ending to a relaxing afternoon and evening spent poolside and dining at the Cypress Room.

If only Rachel could relax. She hadn't been able to stop thinking about their conversation in the helicopter with Special Agents Vaughn and Holmes. After she and Jake had told Vaughn that they were "in," he had flown them back to the Helicopter Adventures base by way of the coastline, including a few minutes hovering over some dolphins playing in the surf. He'd given them some final instructions before touching down, which he had only done after radioing Agent Butler, who'd given the all clear. Rachel and Jake had disembarked from the helicopter and returned to their car like any other tourists, having been told that Butler and Holmes would be in touch.

They had called back later that afternoon and scheduled lunch with the Taylors on Friday. They would brief them on all the auction details and provide them with any last-minute instructions then. It all seemed so . . . routine, so easy. Yet Rachel couldn't stop thinking about how she and Jake were in way over their heads and of all the things that could go wrong. Jake had been quieter than usual, and she speculated his mind was occupied similarly.

They had debated getting away for the afternoon, running to Brookgreen Gardens, Hopsewee Plantation, or one of several museums, but had decided to veg instead. That ran the risk of encountering Jamison and Frost, so they'd stayed at their own condo until dinner. Now, walking north on the beach—away from Jamison and Frost's hotel, if they had told the truth about where they were staying—Rachel hoped they were safe.

"What do you think it is?" she asked at length, tired of her own thoughts.

Jake looked down at her. "What what is?"

"The item being auctioned."

Aside from some crabbers way up ahead and a pair of women jogging south, they were alone on the beach. The constant swish of waves made conversation unlikely to travel anyhow.

"I don't know," he answered at length. "Diamonds are the most exotic, but in the movies, diamonds are always what terrorists use to finance their operations or how bad guys pay for stuff. Nobody ever buys the diamonds; they buy with them."

"They have to get them sometime."

"I suppose."

"And the Archibald Diamonds are more like the Hope Diamond or the Great Star of Africa, not a bunch of tiny little gems a warlord dumps out of a velvet pouch."

"What about you?" he asked.

"Some lost Michelangelo painting of Michael fighting the devil or something—a priceless work of art."

They walked a while longer, the cool water lapping at Rachel's ankles providing a refreshing contrast to the warm night air.

"You know what'd be kind of fun?" Jake said.

"Mmm?"

"Just keep walking up the beach and slip into some out of the way motel and lay low from everybody for a while. Forget this whole FBI business."

"Don't tempt me, Jake."

"I admire you, you know."

She turned her head toward him. "For what?"

"Having the courage to do this. I know it scares you. It scares me too. But that's one of the things I've always loved about you—you're not some tough, old, battle-scarred broad who isn't afraid of anything, but you're also not a weakling who just clings behind her man like Olive Oyl."

"Jake, your compliments are the strangest things ever."

"At least it's a compliment."

She dipped her head in concession.

"You know what I mean though?"

"I think so," she said. She raised her eyes to find his. "And that's one of the things I've always loved about you too."

"My odd compliments?"

"No," she said, swatting his arm. She quickly took his hand again. "You don't let fear stop you. You press on and do what has to be done."

"I'm the son of a farmer."

"And you roll up your sleeves and do it yourself," she said, hoping her subtlety wasn't being lost on him. Growing up amongst the wealthy and privileged, Rachel had observed plenty of men who farmed out all the dirty work, the difficult, hands-on stuff. There were certainly "rich" guys who did their own hard work, but the majority of the men who ran in her parents' circles were the former. Even as a girl, Rachel had been drawn to men who valued a hard day's work, who could fix problems themselves. Men like Jake. It was one of the reasons she would never—despite the fact that he did have simpler tastes than she had long been accustomed to—lose interest in him. But how to tell him that without coming right out and telling him that?

"I'm the son of a farmer," he repeated to her latest compliment.

"It's more than that, Jake."

"You mean my 'tireless good character'?" he asked, turning his head.

Rachel slowly smiled. "You remember my vows?"

"Bits and pieces."

She drew herself closer as they trudged through the damp sand.

"You want to turn back?" he asked after a few more steps.

"No. Do you?"

"No, you just slowed. You slow whenever you're trying to hint that it's time to turn for home or when you want to head a different direction in the mall."

She smiled again and stretched up to peck his cheek. "I also slow when I'm enjoying lingering in the moment."

"I see."

"And it's so nice out here," she said, turning her head to let a wisp of hair blow off her forehead. "All that waits for us back at the condo is going to bed—"

"Guess that answers my next question."

She barely hesitated despite rolling her eyes at him. "—which leads to waking up, which brings preparation for tomorrow night, which actually brings tomorrow night. Not to go all Olive Oyl on you," she added.

He responded by releasing her hand and pulling her toward him, his arm around her waist. She reciprocated, and they strolled onward. Rachel tried to enjoy the moment, but couldn't stop thinking about all that was in store the next day. Maybe Jake was right—maybe they should hide out in some lonely seaside motel and let the oncoming hurricane blow over.

Jake and Rachel left the condo early Friday morning. They stopped for breakfast at a value-friendly family restaurant named John's before heading to Coastal Grand Mall out by the airport. Jake left Rachel browsing for formal dresses at a Belk and quickly got fitted for a tuxedo at Jos. A. Bank. It would be ready by three, which was plenty early. He returned and sorted through the racks to find Rachel with two dresses over her arm.

"You're just in time," she said. "There's one more I want to try on."

Jake tried very hard not to sigh. He'd been dress shopping with Rachel before, and he'd yet to see her try on an evening gown that looked anything short of stunning. But whenever he said as much, she put her hands on her hips and huffed, as if he was just trying to get out of work. So he was forced to find fault with certain dresses—without in any way insulting Rachel's appearance and while making sense with his critique—and approve others, all without taking up an entire morning. It was the case with most clothes, but dresses were the worst. Fortunately, he and Rachel didn't run in circles that required her to shop for formalwear all that often.

He trailed behind her as she wound through racks of dresses and ultimately selected a third, which she carried over her shoulder to the fitting rooms. Jake had a seat while Rachel entered the dressing room to try on the first dress. He watched her bare feet and ankles under the door as she slipped the dress on, then realized a sales associate was giving him an eye as if he was some sort of creep. So he studied his cell phone until Rachel emerged.

"Well," she said, hands out.

The dress was purple with a modest halter top. Tapered at the waist, it flared slightly as it hung to her ankles. It wasn't fancy, had no frills, but had a simple yet exquisite look. Jake liked it but knew he'd have to see all three anyhow. So he emulated an Olympic judge and gave the first "competitor" a medium score.

"I like it," he said. "And there's ample room for, say, a big diamond necklace."

"Right, I'll just wear it out of there." She held up her hair behind her head, turning and looking down at her posterior. "Does it work with my eyes?"

"I think so."

She wasn't convinced, pursing her lips as she looked in the mirror. "What about the back?" she asked over her shoulder.

"How so?"

"Too much, too little?"

"Just right?"

She sighed and ducked back into the dressing room. Jake looked back to his phone. No new messages from Jamison and Frost. Per Special Agent-in-Charge Vaughn, he had called them the previous afternoon and apologized, saying he and Rachel had both come down with a terrible stomach virus or food poisoning and had been sick all night. Liam had bought it, or at least faked buying it convincingly. Now, not to run into either of them again. Vaughn had said he didn't think, based on what had transpired so far, that Jamison and Frost would pose a danger to the Taylors, but Jake would prefer to avoid them nonetheless.

The next dress was navy blue, a one-shoulder number that was a little less form fitting.

"Why is it always the right shoulder?" Jake asked as Rachel posed for him.

"What?"

"The one-shoulder dresses always have the right shoulder covered."

"I take that as a no."

"I'm not big on its asymmetrical nature," Jake said.

Rachel retreated to the dressing room.

The last dress was black, with both "sleeves" off the shoulder. Like the first, it nicely accentuated Rachel's figure and left plenty of room for jewelry.

The dress tapered at the knee, then flared, looking almost like a mermaid's fin. Jake said as much.

"Didn't you want to go see that pirate show with mermaids?" she asked.

"They weren't really the selling point."

"So another no?"

"I'd go with the first one, the purple one."

Rachel's hand went to her hips. "It wasn't purple. It was sangria."

"What color's sangria?"

"It's a burnt red."

"Like I said, I like it."

"It wasn't very fancy."

"You don't need a fancy dress."

She lowered her chin.

"I'm serious, Babe. It looked great on you, and besides, we do want to keep a low profile."

"So which point are you making?"

"It really was good, Rach. I like the look of it, like the lines."

"It's not a Porsche."

"And it does work with your eyes. Besides, I'll be wearing black, so we'd be black and black."

"We are going to be spies," she said. The sales associate was gone, and they were alone.

"Yes, but not obvious about it."

"You're not just saying this to shut me up?"

"I really like the purple one."

"Okay. I'll get 'the purple one.'"

Jake sighed with relief as she turned.

"We just have to get shoes," Rachel said as she ducked back into the dressing room. Jake dropped his head into his hands.

Chapter Eighteen

As a gift for her senior prom, Rachel's mom had bought her a $499 Alyce Paris dress. She had looked magnificent and had turned more than a few heads, all without feeling the least bit of guilt at the extravagant price tag. Now, half her life later, dropping just over half that on a dress and a pair of heels felt like a mortal sin. And while she liked the look of the sangria-colored halter-top dress, it wasn't on the level of her prom dress. Nor was she sold by Jake's endorsement.

But that was in the rearview mirror for now, as was Myrtle Beach. With Jake at the wheel (Rachel had to start throwing her weight around to get more time in the driver's seat of the Mustang) they were headed south on Business 17, through more sprawl and outskirts than she thought possible. How many waterparks, strip malls, themed eateries, and stores selling beach apparel could one community support? Not to mention campgrounds, grocery stores, and offbeat souvenir shops.

They were running late, and incessant stoplights didn't help. Finally, just before he missed it, Jake spotted the sign signaling the turnoff for Murrells Inlet. They left the sprawl behind and took a narrow, two-lane road into the heart of a saltmarsh. Suddenly, Rachel felt millions of miles from Myrtle Beach and its commercialization.

They didn't drive far, just half a mile or so, before spotting the Dead Dog Saloon on their left. Jake missed the turn but took the next, which led to a gravel parking lot adjacent to the restaurant—a parking lot that also serviced the Crazy Sisters Marina ahead of them. They got out and were immediately hit with the salty smell of the marsh and the squawk of seagulls flitting through the air. A sign beside access to a wooden boardwalk welcomed them to the Murrells Inlet MarshWalk.

The inlet itself comprised several square miles of swampland and feeders around a creek that emptied into the Atlantic about a mile south. The MarshWalk built alongside the marsh was home to restaurants, boat docks, and vistas of the marsh. Rachel knew from her travel book that the area was much livelier and festive come evening. Now, as she and Jake strolled along the boardwalk past several docked Jet Skis and jet boats, along with plenty of brackish water, it felt oddly vacant, like a house the morning after a big party.

Known as the "Seafood Capital of the World," Murrells Inlet featured an array of dining options, from casual to upscale. The first in line along the MarshWalk was the Dead Dog Saloon, and Rachel had no idea why Agents Butler and Holmes had selected it over any others. Jake told the hostess they were meeting someone, and she led them out onto the deck, overlooking the marsh.

"Hi!" Holmes called cheerily when she saw Jake and Rachel. She wore a peach and white striped shirt, white capris, and flip-flops. Only her chaotic hair was the same. Butler wore a polo shirt and board shorts, flip-flops as well, and greeted them with just as many teeth.

"Act like we're old friends," Holmes said as she gave Rachel a quick squeeze. "In case someone's watching."

Rachel received a quick air kiss from Butler before the quartet sat down.

"Sorry, I know this is odd," Holmes said, her voice back to the usual grumpy tone.

"Who would be watching here?" Rachel said, sweeping her eyes over the marsh. It was a mixture of torpid backwater and seagrass extending for half a mile. The exception was a low row of tree-covered earth in the distance that was home to eight or ten goats. That, and a pier extending out from the marina several hundred yards. It was connected to the boardwalk, and neither was terribly populated, and none of the occasional passersby paid the group at the table the least bit of attention. Nor did the handful of other outdoor patrons at the Dead Dog.

"You never know," Butler said as he scooted in his chair. "But we can't be too careful."

A waiter brought drinks and menus. As they looked them over, Holmes asked, "How is preparation coming?"

"I bought a dress and shoes this morning," Rachel said. "And Jake has to pick up his tux this afternoon."

"Save receipts. The Bureau will reimburse you."

"What about mileage?" Jake asked.

"Of course."

"Don't be a cheapskate, Jake," Rachel said as he smiled to show he'd been joking.

"Have Jamison or Frost made any further contact?" Holmes asked. "A few more minutes," she added as the waiter approached them.

"No," Jake answered. "Not since I left Lia—Jamison a voicemail yesterday."

"Good."

"Have you spotted anything else unusual?" Butler asked.

"Should we have?"

"Nope. Just making sure."

"What about our 'doubles'?" Rachel asked. "Are they a threat to us?"

Butler shook his head. "They appear to be observing you, but that's all. The fact that they haven't made any sort of a move would suggest they won't."

"Not until after the auction," Holmes said.

Rachel dropped her chin into her palm. "That's comforting."

"Everyone seems to be taking a step back," Butler said. "Likely waiting to see how the auction plays out. If there's a 'move'—so to speak—to be made, it will be at the exchange. But we'll be there to make sure nothing happens to you, and we're getting ahead of ourselves."

They took a few minutes to peruse menus and order. They made awkward small talk until drinks and appetizer plates of fried green tomatoes and buffalo shrimp—ordered by Butler and Holmes—arrived. Clearly, the FBI was sparing no expense on its agents or to wine and dine its undercover operatives.

"So about the auction," Holmes said after depositing one of the shrimp into her mouth. "It's taking place at a residence called Coral Manor, which just sounds contrived to me. It's located on North Ocean Boulevard, practically at the city limits of Myrtle Beach. We flew over it yesterday, in fact."

Butler took over. "It's owned by a man named Crenshaw Banks—he from a long line of Charleston money—and his wife Priscilla, who has family ties back to the Ottoman Empire. They also have homes in Hawaii, the Scottish countryside, and the south of France. They're incredibly philanthropic, with their charity of choice being third-world literacy and education. Tonight's auction is a yearly deal on behalf of such charities, this time to raise money for a girl's school in Cameroon."

"How very Oprah," Jake said.

"The Bankses mean well," Butler said. "In fact, they do well."

"But," Holmes said, picking up the pause after downing another shrimp, "there are also rumors—and they are just that, but they're what we call credible rumors—that Priscilla Banks has some connections to the underworld. In particular, to a man named Jonah Blackaby, an international arms and commodities dealer who is thought—again credibly—to have past connections to *La Fantôme*."

"What kind of connections?" Rachel asked.

"Mostly money trails suspected to be a part of a major art deal years ago. Again, nothing provable. But where there's smoke . . ."

"All this to say," Butler said, "when we picked up the intelligence clueing us in to the auction and to it taking place here, tonight, the Banks's mansion made perfect sense as a locale."

Rachel leaned forward. "The other night you mentioned various governments picking up chatter and something about a Navy ensign and decrypting this and that. I don't mean to be rude, but can you condense all of this into the bare facts? What do we know about this auction tonight?"

"Fair enough," Butler said. "I apologize for getting too technical." He set his appetizer plate aside and leaned on the table. "The auction is taking place this evening at Coral Manor under the guise of a charity auction benefiting the Cameroonian school."

"Guise?" Jake asked. "So it's not a real charity auction?"

"No, that's real. I used the wrong term. The auction we're interested in will be conducted alongside the actual auction."

"How does that work?" Rachel asked.

"We're not entirely sure," Holmes said. "Since the charity auction is legit, there will be a lot of people there, the majority of whom have no knowledge of anything underhanded and who just want to help girls in Cameroon learn to read and write. Or buy expensive artwork. Or who want to look prestigious and win the approval of their peers."

"But along with them will be a handful, we're guessing five to seven bidders, who want whatever it is that's being auctioned off secretly."

Holmes took over for Butler again. "Now, there's a good chance this item will be out with the others, or it might be in a private room. Either way, the bidders will want to see it and authenticate it."

"Which can also be done remotely, where the object is off-site, and a satellite feed is set up so that the bidders can see the object, without it having to be on location. And it could be that the bidders have received confirmation previously."

"Since we don't know what's being auctioned, we can't say one way or the other."

Rachel felt like her head was spinning, in no small part due to the back-and-forth from the two FBI agents. Why couldn't the Bureau have saved some tax dollars and just sent one of them?

"So how do we make the bid?" Jake asked.

"That part's a little tricky," Butler said.

"Just that part?" Rachel asked.

He smiled back at her. "We think the pass phrase to get access to the item and to make a bid is either 'Charlotte' or 'Rose.'"

"Mitchum, the man the Navy ensign led us to," Holmes said, "used the word Charlotte twice. He said it was code for something, but he didn't know what. We also decrypted it from the dark web chatter we picked up, along with several references to a rose or roses. Charlotte could be the name of the seller, could refer to the Charlotte Parchments, or could be the code word you use to identify yourselves as bidders. Similarly, rose could be a codename for some object—maybe jewels—could be a person. We're not sure."

"So what do we do?" Jake asked.

"Play it by ear."

"Speaking of that, are we going to have comms or earwigs or something so you can listen in and talk to us?"

"No," Butler said. "Unlike in the movies, people can actually spot an earpiece in your ear more often than you'd think. Especially if they're looking for them, and we suspect they might be."

The group's lunches were delivered, causing a break in conversation. Shopping made Rachel hungry, so despite the unease returning to her stomach, she had no trouble polishing off her turkey avocado sandwich while Butler and

Holmes went over more details of the auction, how Rachel and Jake should handle themselves, and—most importantly, Holmes stressed—when and how to get in touch with the FBI afterward.

With ample reassurances and plenty of smiles—from Butler—Rachel and Jake were as ready as they could be. After lunch, at the suggestion of the agents, the two of them took a walk out to the end of the pier. It was odd, feeling so isolated and far away from everything but nature. And yet, half a mile across the saltmarsh were rows of beachside homes and condos.

"How you feeling?" Jake asked as they leaned on the pier railing.

"It's too surreal to feel much of anything," Rachel answered.

Jake put his arm around her. "When this vacation is over, we should go on vacation."

She smiled at him. "You're enjoying this, aren't you? James Bond meets Danny Ocean meets Bruce Wayne?"

"Only a little," he said with a grin. "And only," he said with an added squeeze, "because Bond always gets the girl in the end."

She patted him on the stomach and turned away. "We'll see about that."

Chapter Nineteen

One of Jake's favorite episodes of TV was an episode of *Everybody Loves Raymond* where "Ray," spurred on by his father, threatened his wife, "Deborah," that he would leave for an important event without her if she weren't ready at the appointed time. She agreed to the deal, and when she wasn't ready on time, he made good on his threat and left without her. Unbeknownst to him at the time, she was late because a last-second touch-up resulted in her curling iron getting stuck in her hair. Jake couldn't even remember how they "made up" at the end of the episode, or if they had. His takeaway image from the episode was of Patricia Heaton walking around with a curling iron hanging from her hair.

Over the years, Jake had grown accustomed to waiting for Rachel, as had all husbands and boyfriends and fathers, according to stereotype. He usually didn't mind, for several reasons. Most significantly, the wait was usually worth it. And Rachel was conscientious and never too terribly tardy. Plus she was usually the one who had set the schedule or deadline they were falling behind anyhow, which didn't matter much to him.

Tonight, however, was different. Tonight, he empathized with Ray. The auction at Coral Manor "began" at five, with drinks and hors d'oeuvres being served at five-thirty. Butler and Holmes hadn't advised a particular time to arrive but suggested it not trend toward late. So Jake checked his watch intermittently while pacing the confines of their condo living room. He'd been in his tux for forty-five minutes, his hair as close to good as it was going to get that night.

After leaving Murrells Inlet, he and Rachel had bummed some of the backroads of South Carolina, in part to kill time, in part to see the countryside, and in part because Jake had wanted to spot a tail if they had one. Rachel had told him he was buying into the feds' paranoia. He'd countered that if the feds were paranoid, it was probably called for. Then she'd asked if he could spot a tail anyhow.

They'd circled back to Coastal Grand Mall, where Jake had picked up his altered tux. It fit him perfectly without being constrictive. Just in case they had to make a break for it or something.

"You're not wearing that, are you?" Rachel asked as she emerged from the bedroom and caught Jake looking at his cuff watch. It didn't go terribly well with a tuxedo, admittedly, but it was the only watch he had.

Jake shrugged it under his sleeve and said as much. Then he studied her. Rachel was downright resplendent in her new dress, which she'd complemented with a teardrop diamond pendant he'd given her for their fifth anniversary and matching teardrop earrings, both in gold settings. That had been another of the rare occasions when he'd picked out the proper gift, and he always smiled when she wore them.

"I told you that dress was great," he said, and couldn't help but notice a slight flattening of Rachel's smile. "Then again," he said, "maybe it's not the dress."

"Nice save."

"Seriously, you look great, Rach."

She smiled, for real, and rubbed her palm over his cheek. "You're getting scruffy."

"I'm playing an international man of leisure. The scruffy look is in."

"Are you ready?" she asked.

He held out an elbow in response. Rachel grabbed her clutch purse—which she'd thought of as they had been leaving the mall the second time, triggering a twenty-minute return venture—and they headed for the door.

"I'd let you drive," Jake said as they entered the parking garage. He pulled the key fob from his pocket and, pointing it at the Mustang, gave the unlock button a double-tap. "But Bond never lets the Bond girls drive."

"Bond also shaves."

The weather had held, with the afternoon build-up of clouds now thinning. The air was warm but not overly humid, and a refreshing breeze blew in off the Atlantic. Jake and Rachel followed Ocean Boulevard north, out of what Rachel termed "Myrtle Beach proper" and through blocks of private houses. Then the road jogged, paralleling the coast with only a few, one-room houses between it and the beach. They were accessible by private walks. On the left, another string of high-rise condos and apartments towered against the sky.

"I want you to take the lead tonight, Jake," Rachel said. She was reclined slightly in her seat, looking totally comfortable and at ease. Jake had felt awkward since putting on the penguin suit. He always did when dressing up. Rachel, on the other hand, never seemed out of her comfort zone.

"You mean as Double-0 Proxy?"

"I mean in general. You should be more assertive. You know what you're talking about, you're never out of the loop, and you're good at making decisions and thinking on your feet. It's the analytical nature I always complain about proving its worth."

He nodded, checked the road, then looked back at her. "Are we still talking about tonight?"

"Yes, but more than that too. I know I'm anything but a wallflower, the 'epitome of girl power' according to your brother."

"Which one?"

"Jimmy. But you're the head of our family, Jake. I trust you to lead. I trust you to respect my thoughts and feelings. I know you'd never trample over me. So don't be afraid to take charge. If you get out of line, I'll go all 'girl power' and call you on it."

"Jimmy said that?"

She nodded.

He shrugged, then nodded as well. "Okay."

Rachel smiled.

"Is this something new?" he asked.

"No. I've been leaving hints . . ."

"That I've missed."

She shrugged. "With what's going on now, it seemed like a good time to bring it up."

He looked at her again. "I'm glad you did."

Another smile.

"And I think I should probably lead by driving everywhere we go."

"The captain's not always the quarterback."

"He is on this team."

She sighed. "I've created a monster."

"Seriously, though, I've been thinking. We should keep a low profile, tonight. We're clearly in over our heads, and we have no idea who knows who we are and who knows who we aren't. The less attention, the better."

"I agree. But it's going to be hard with you looking so dapper in that tux," she said, reaching over to stroke the back of his head.

"Unshaven as I am."

She tapped his head lightly, then withdrew her hand.

Ocean Boulevard had cut back inland and now snaked through a posh, tree-lined neighborhood. Several roads or private drives cut through the trees, but massive two- and three-story homes blocked the view of the ocean.

"There," Rachel said, pointing to a small plaque built into a wrought-iron fence. It was a peachy salmon color—coral, to be precise—with flowing white cursive letters that announced the property as Coral Manor. Another sign, canted slightly to the north, likely bore the same message to travelers from that direction. Between the two signs, the fence formed an eight-foot-high arched gate spanning a cobblestone driveway. The gate was open, and Jake signaled for a turn.

The driveway ran straight for a hundred feet, lined on either side by a solid hedgerow and, beyond it, palm trees so picture-perfect they almost appeared fake. Dozens of cars, most of them sleek, fancy sports cars or shiny luxury models, also lined the drive. Jake drove slowly until the driveway ended in a cul-de-sac, in the middle of which was a tiered fountain atop which a bronze statue depicted a trio of leaping dolphins. It was a magnificent sculpture that momentarily took Jake's attention away from the house. But not for long.

The square house was three stories tall, covered in pink-shaded white stucco that was broken in places by reddish brick, giving it a charming vintage appearance. A dozen stairs led up to the front porch, which was flanked by faux-marble (or maybe real marble) columns that supported a portico covering the dual front doors and the huge, curved-top window above them. On either side of the columns, bays contained massive windows on the first floor and balconies on the second and third stories. The pyramid-hip roof was covered in clay tile shingles to accompany the stucco and brick. Matching shingles also topped a wall that ran north and south from the house, giving more privacy to the "backyard" and beach, as well as presumably a carport or lower-level garage entrance beyond a gate in the south wall.

As if the house wasn't magnificent enough, flowers of every color filled beds around the front steps and circling the corners, and more palm trees—scattered haphazardly—cast the perfectly clipped grass in a mixture of yellow sunlight and indigo shade. Something of a lawn-care freak himself, Jake was in awe. This sod resembled the field at the Rose Bowl or an Augusta National fairway. Immaculate was an understatement.

"We are so out of our league," he said to Rachel as he parked the car in front of the steps. Before he could reach for his door, a valet had it open for him. Another did the same for Rachel, even lending her a hand. Jake got out and tipped the guy a five-dollar bill, which seemed chintzy given the atmosphere, but was still the limit for a Midwestern boy. He circled the car and extended his arm to Rachel, as he had in their condo some twenty minutes earlier.

"Shall we, my dear?"

Her neck was still craned up at the stairs in front of them.

"Out of our league," she said quietly. "We're not even playing the same game."

🌴 🌴 🌴

Arm-in-arm with Jake, Rachel climbed the front steps of Coral Manor, where a man in a tuxedo with tails held the door for them.

"Good evening, Madam and Sir," he said.

"Good evening," Rachel said. They entered a wide, grand hall that ran the length of the building and was open to balconies on the second and third floors. Curving staircases on either side of the hall—one from front to back and one from back to front—led to second-floor catwalks that spanned the hall, essentially cutting it into thirds. Three large chandeliers hung between them, the one in the middle unlike any Rachel had ever seen.

Her heels clicked on the marble floor, a warm coral- and blue-flecked blend that complemented the walls and nautical décor. Rachel had grown up surrounded by money, vacationed in the Hamptons, and attended high-end parties. Still, this was impressive. Everything from the intricate molding and trim to the ornate spindles on the staircases to the exquisite artwork (and that just in the main hall) exuded wealth that was so abundant and ordinary the owners likely didn't realize they were flaunting it. And they weren't, not in any overt way. But the scale of things, the grandeur, did so without any effort.

At the far end of the hall, paned-glass doors opened to a patio or deck, and Rachel could see the ocean sparkling in the evening sunlight. Almost as magnificently as the chandelier in the center of the hall, which again drew her eyes. It was a combination of soft white bulbs and mirrors that gave it the appearance of something almost magical.

"Three hundred and forty-three."

Rachel lowered her eyes to see an old man standing in front of her. No, not old. Although he was likely in his sixties or early seventies judging by his silver, thinning hair and somewhat weathered skin, his posture and the energy with which he smiled and extended his hand was that of someone much younger.

"Crenshaw Banks the third," he said, taking Rachel's hand as she offered it to him. He cupped strong, soft hands around her fingers and lifted them to his lips. "Welcome to Coral Manor. I couldn't help notice you admiring the chandelier. If you're like most guests, you're wondering either how many bulbs or how much it cost, am I right?"

Rachel couldn't help but blush a little as she nodded.

"I hope they're long-lasting bulbs," Jake said as he shook Banks' hand. Rachel hoped his smart-aleck remark hadn't offended their host, but he showed no signs that it had.

"Of course. Crenshaw Banks."

"Jake Taylor," Jake said. They'd debated using aliases, but the FBI agents had said there was no need since the proxies whose place they were taking were unknown. And it was possible Banks or the black market auctioneer would be employing some form of facial-recognition software to identify his guests, and the last thing Rachel or Jake wanted was to be caught in a lie. So they were sticking with their real IDs.

"My wife, Rachel."

"It is a pleasure to meet you both," Banks said. His voice was smooth and refined, carrying a tinge of inflection so subtle it couldn't really be called an accent. Besides, it only enhanced his crisp, perfect diction. "Please, enjoy something to eat or drink as you make your way through the house. There are items up for bid on each of the first two floors, and you can register and get your bidder number in here," he said, extending a hand toward the gallery.

"Thank you," Jake said, and he stepped aside so Banks could meet additional guests.

"That just coincidence?" Rachel asked. "We meet him thirty seconds after we arrive?"

"Guessing so."

"You didn't mention Charlotte or Rose."

"Call it a hunch, but I don't think he's in on this whole black market deal."

"A hunch?"

"Questioning my leadership already?"

"Just your gut."

"Speaking of, let's say we find something to eat and do some mingling."

"Lead the way."

They spent the next thirty minutes in tandem, finding fancy and delicious appetizers for Jake and exploring Coral Manor. Half of the downstairs was consumed by a dining room, kitchen, and breakfast nook—the latter two of which were off limits to guests—and a solarium on the southeast corner. It was open to the second floor, allowing maximum sunlight to enter through enormous windows. Its spacious floor made room for half a dozen unusual sculptures and two or three times that many smaller three-dimensional works of art. The other half of the lower level was cordoned off into a gallery, a sitting room, and a living room. The only difference between the latter two rooms seemed to be a fireplace in the sitting room and variations in décor. The rooms contained sports memorabilia, event or experience tickets and vouchers, jewelry and other accessories, and a variety of celebrity items—everything from dinner with someone famous to autographed mementos—whereas the gallery exhibited more traditional pieces of artwork, namely paintings.

The second floor housed the library, the items on display a wide assortment of old books and rare bottles of wine, and three bedrooms immaculately decorated. Everything not bolted down, along with designer clothes, shoes, and VIP shopping experiences, was up for auction. In front of every item was a placard with a description, the owner in most cases, and often a starting bid. There was also a register with a place for names and bid amounts. As opposed to the more common English "open outcry" auctions where a fast-talking auctioneer called out bids, this was a silent auction. Bids would accumulate until the end of the evening, at which time the high bidder in the register would win the item. Even had Rachel and Jake been interested in bidding on anything, short of taking out a second mortgage on their home back in Omaha, they would have had no shot.

After half an hour of browsing, and having spotted no items tabbed "Black Market Goodies" or seeing signs directing underworld characters to do some back-office bidding, Rachel and Jake exited to the patio. It, like the interior, was getting crowded with men and women of all ages in tuxedos and evening gowns, many of them holding champagne flutes or small appetizer plates.

Rachel and Jake wandered to a corner of the patio and leaned on a concrete railing. The breeze was stronger at the beach, and Rachel tucked loose strands of hair behind her ear as she marveled at the color in the bubbling clouds out over the ocean. Just steps off the patio, a row of dunes maybe five feet high separated the house from the beach and mostly buried a wooden fence. Tufts of grass poked up here and there, but otherwise, the sand was warm and inviting.

"Do you think that's a real fence with a purpose," Jake asked, "or just there to look rustic?"

"Is that really what's on your mind right now?"

"No, I'm trying to figure out where to drop a pass phrase."

"Maybe I should go around introducing myself as Charlotte Rose," she said with a country twang.

"Isn't that a clothing store for young women?"

"That's Charlotte Russe."

"Hmm. You sure?"

"Mm-hmm."

Jake shrugged. "Well, from what I can tell, except for the kitchen downstairs and the billiard room on the second floor, we've been everywhere."

"Except for the powder rooms."

"Right."

"Billiard room? Seems like the place for this sort of thing."

"Else . . ." His eyes drifted upward.

"What?"

"Third story," he said, eying twin balconies facing the ocean. "Master bedroom, probably, but quiet and out of the public eye."

"You want to go kick in doors?"

"No."

She nodded. "Well, you think about our next move, captain. I'm going to go use one of those powder rooms."

"Look for secret messages left on the mirror or something."

"That only works where there's a shower to steam them up."

He shrugged, and Rachel shook her head as she left him and weaved through the crowd. The nearest powder room was at the end of a short alcove just before the base of the stairs leading up to the second level, and Rachel quickly checked her makeup and hair. Both were holding up fine. She didn't feel an urgent need to use the bathroom, but figured it was best to now instead of later—once she and Jake were in the spy business up to their armpits.

No man could ever properly empathize with a woman in a full-length evening gown having to use a toilet. As Rachel washed her hands, she smirked at the thought of Jake always pacing, waiting for her as if she was just piddling around. Having helped her into and out of gowns before, he should get it, but of course, he continued on in the typical male ignorance.

On second thought, Rachel added a touch-up of lipstick, a mauve she'd brought with her that matched the sangria dress almost perfectly. Content, she smiled at her reflection in the mirror and exited the powder room. She stepped out from the alcove and surveyed the hall to see if Jake had come back in.

"Feeling better, I trust."

Startling slightly, Rachel turned to her right, knowing who had spoken to her by the accent before she saw the face.

Gabrielle Frost.

Chapter Twenty

Jake had to admit, the scenery was fantastic. As much as he hated waiting for Rachel to get all dolled up, he loved seeing her in fancy gowns and loved the romantic mood it usually put her in. He also liked that she didn't wear such outfits to Wal-Mart, meaning she was usually accompanied by a lot of other gorgeous women similarly attired.

Tonight was no different. Jake was not a creep; he didn't stand around lusting after other women. Nor was he a cad, leering or even admiring other women while with his wife. But it was like an old friend of his had once said, God made a lot of beautiful things, including women. And it was sure more enjoyable to be surrounded by good-looking women than, well, all Iowans—Rachel exempted. To that end—and that end only—he certainly enjoyed the scenery.

And the appetizers, minuscule and unfilling as they were. The few hors d'oeuvres he'd consumed—at such a venue, they were probably called amuse-bouches—likely cost more than a prime rib dinner at Brother Sebastian's. He spent a few moments wondering if there were better ways to provide education for Cameroonian schoolgirls, then went to find something more to eat.

Rachel approached him from the side, out of the solarium, as he entered the main hall. Then he realized it wasn't Rachel. This woman wore a black halter-top dress, tight at the waist, with a slit almost to it. Her hair was darker, piled up in some fancy updo, and her eyes were a few shades greener. And her nose, if he was being straightforward, was just a touch more perfect. It was the woman he'd spotted at Dixie Outfitters at Barefoot Landing.

Her eyes raked over Jake as she approached. "You're not here alone, are you?" she asked with what could only be described as a brief smirk.

"No, my wife's here too, somewhere."

"Yes, well, so is my husband," she said, tipping up her champagne flute. "But he is obsessed with art, leaving me to play his mistress."

"His loss," Jake said, hoping it came across as a gentleman's compliment and not a cheesy pickup line.

"You're very kind. You don't mind if I stand here until your wife or my husband returns, do you? It will save us from having to explain we're not single and hopefully ward off any more 'What do you think of such-and-such a piece?' or 'Have you seen the bids on this or that?' questions." Her voice, void of any inflection or even emotion, was flat and quick, perhaps a result of boredom. "Unless you go for that sort of thing?"

"No, I'm quite happy not to talk about art and auction prices."

"A kindred soul at last," the woman said, tipping back her flute again.

Jake's mind was racing, not so much because Rachel might come back and find him hanging out with a beautiful woman, but because he was pretty sure that woman was the person who should have received the PADL, not he and Rachel. The same PADL that was in his pocket now. Did she know or suspect that? Was she some master thief/pickpocket who could point out a piece of art on the wall and have the PADL in her possession by the time he got his eyes back around? He was suddenly overcome with the compulsion to check his pocket and make sure it was still there. But that would only clue her in to its location. So he tried to play it cool.

"Where you from?" the woman asked.

"Omaha. Yourself?"

"Chicago. What do you do there?"

"I'm a network engineer."

"Sounds boring."

"It is." He extended his hand and rubbed his fingers against his thumb. "But it puts money on the table."

"Enough money to buy all this . . . stuff here?"

Jake, not sure if she was playing a part or not, decided to meet her halfway. He smirked. "Not all."

The woman returned the smirk and took another drink.

Jake decided to pry a little, see what she said. It couldn't hurt to ask a few questions. "How about yourself? What do you do in Chicago?"

"I'm a corporate headhunter. Never boring, and . . ." She made the same thumb-and-fingers gesture.

"Your husband?

"Day trader. Your wife?"

"Photojournalist," Jake said, embellishing a little. Rachel worked for a small photography service, doing mostly weddings, senior pictures, and family photo shoots.

"Why Omaha?"

"Good beef," Jake said with another smirk. He wasn't sure if they were flirting or dancing like boxers in the ring, but he found himself oddly—either way—enjoying the repartee.

"I'd make a snarky comment, but the only thing going for Chicago is cold and wind. That and racist cops killing black thugs, depending on your point of view."

Now she was throwing politics at him? Was this one of those unsuspecting interviews or something? Like that one reality show where Richard Branson had posed as a cab driver to see which of the "contestants" would disqualify himself or herself before the game even started?

"You grow up there?" he asked.

"All over. Military brat. You?"

"Born in Chicago, actually."

"You don't say."

"Moved when I was six."

"Cubs or Sox?"

"Bears. More of a football guy."

"Too bad." Another drink.

Jake checked his watch. Rachel had been in the powder room for quite a while.

"Nice watch," the woman said.

"Yeah, well," he said, retreating it into his sleeve.

"No, I mean it. Might clash with a tux, but at least it's you. Everyone looks the same in those things. I like a little flair. Sets you apart from all the stuffed shirts."

Jake nodded.

"Can I see it?"

He slowly raised his arm.

"My husband wears some generic department store thing. I've been looking to get him something new, and this is his style. Not that he'd ever wear it with a tux."

The woman's fingers touched Jake's skin, not an unpleasant sensation. He was reasonably sure she could not, while touching his left wrist, pick his right pants pocket, no matter how good she was.

Rachel quickly composed herself, hoping her expression didn't give anything away.

Gabrielle Frost stood tall and confident in a striking royal blue gown. She wore her hair down, letting it flow in layers onto her bare shoulders. The diamond-crusted heart necklace around her neck made Rachel's look like a cereal box prize, as did bracelets on each wrist. Gabrielle looked like a cover model for *Vogue*.

"Yes," Rachel said, avoiding stammering. "Yes, much, thanks," she said, keeping to the cover story that she and Jake had been sick. "I'm so sorry about dinner."

Gabrielle waved it off as if it meant nothing, and her smile, which Rachel had found snakelike at first, was laidback and amicable. "So what brings you here?"

That was a good question, and one Rachel hadn't expected to answer. "It was Jake's idea," she said, stalling, hoping to spot him in the crowd. "His brother spent time as a missionary in Nigeria," she continued, amazed at where the lie came from. "So it's a cause near and dear to his heart."

"He's here then?"

"Somewhere. Liam?" she felt compelled to ask.

"Coming this way," Gabrielle said, looking up as he approached with a drink in each hand. Talk about James Bond. His tuxedo cut perfectly, his hair immaculate in its untidiness, and his jaw and chin clean-shaven, Liam lacked only the gun in his pocket or he was a perfect imitation of the infamous spy. Rachel took a moment to remind herself that he was a high-end thief. And quite possibly had a gun in his pocket.

"Good evening, Rachel," Liam said. "I hope you and Jake have recovered."

He said it with a beaming smile as he handed Gabrielle her drink. She too grinned, yet Rachel couldn't get rid of the feeling it was the smile of a predator closing in on its prey. The way they flanked her and managed to back her against the wall didn't help matters.

"We have, thanks."

"Is Jake around?"

"I don't see him at the moment," Rachel said, begging with her eyes for him to appear.

"In that case, maybe we could just speak with you," Liam said.

"About what?"

"It might be better in private," he said, nodding toward the front door.

Rachel narrowed her eyes. "Why? What's going on?"

"Trust us," Gabrielle said, her dark brown eyes now slits.

"I'd really rather find Jake first," Rachel said.

"Perhaps I was a little vague," Liam said. He gently but firmly placed his hand on Rachel's elbow and began to turn her. "Please come with us."

Rachel looked for Jake, for anyone she could use as an excuse to get away. She could always resort to a self-defense class she had taken in college, if she could remember the techniques and if they worked in real life and not just against a BOB dummy. But she preferred not to attempt anything so drastic, not yet anyway. So she let herself be escorted by Liam, giving him the impression that she was fully compliant.

As they neared the front door, she began to think he was taking her outside. She was about to change her mind regarding putting up a fight when he instead steered her into the dining room. A long, brilliantly polished table was surrounded by more than a dozen chairs. The table's surface caught almost as much of the evening sunlight as did the silver and crystal plates and bowls arrayed on top of it, containing numerous ostentatious appetizers and treats. Condensation on carafes of water and pitchers of tea and lemonade glistened in the sun's golden rays, and Rachel had to squint until Liam stopped in a small alcove created by a huge bay window and further secluded by large potted ferns on either side of the window. They were on the opposite side of the table from a temporary bar, where a server was ready to mix drinks for guests. Several other couples and singles were filling plates of hors d'oeuvres, refilling their drinks, or chatting in the corner, so Rachel breathed easy knowing she wasn't alone with Liam and Gabrielle. Even so, they crowded her back into the window, intimidating her with their posture.

"We know you and Jake weren't really ill," Liam said in a quiet but stern voice.

"What do you me—"

"We know," he said, "so don't bother playing innocent with us. Clearly, someone got to you. We want to know who."

Rachel may not have had Jake's analytic brain, but she wasn't completely inept when it came to putting together mental puzzles. She noted that Liam hadn't bothered to identify himself and Gabrielle, nor had he made any pretense about them not being just Liam and Gabby on holiday. Instead, he got right down to the point, wanting to know which other "players" were involved.

Rachel decided to stall, for lack of any better answer. "No one," she said.

"Who is it, exactly, they told you we were?" Gabrielle asked.

"I'm sorry, but—"

"Foreign government agents, thieves, spies?" She said the last word as if it was the most ridiculous thing ever conceived.

"Until five minutes ago, I thought you were two nice people we met at the beach."

"Oh, we're quite nice," Liam said. "Reasonable too, really. Which is why all we need to know is who you talked to. Who told you to avoid us?"

Rachel exhaled slowly. Again. She let her countenance fall, the way she did when she knew Jake had won an argument. "He didn't say," she said. "Only that you weren't who you said you were," she added quickly. "He said you were dangerous and we should have nothing to do with you. Jake dreamt up the food poisoning thing himself," she added with a shake of her head, trying anything to deflect.

"So a stranger approached you and told you not to trust us?" Liam asked.

"That's right."

"Without identifying himself?"

"We asked him several times, but he wouldn't say anything."

"And you believed him?"

"We didn't know what to believe. But given what he said, we thought it best not to take any chances."

"What did he say?"

"That you were . . . I'm trying to remember the exact phrase—private operatives."

"Did he tell you why we were masquerading as if on holiday in Myrtle Beach?" Liam asked.

"Something about the dark web and the black market," Rachel said.

Liam and Gabrielle looked at each other.

"Believe me or not," Rachel said, "it's the truth. Now, do you mind telling me what this is all about? Who are you people?"

They exchanged looks again. "What did this man look like?" Gabrielle asked.

Rachel proceeded to describe the man Vaughn and Holmes had identified as Spencer Flynn. If Liam and Gabrielle were working in league with him somehow, they'd know it was a lie right away. But if not, if they were another party after the auction item as the FBI claimed, maybe Rachel could set them on a wild goose chase.

Liam and Gabrielle looked at each other yet again when she was finished.

"Why are you here?" Liam asked.

"Better question, I think, given the accusations, is why are you?"

"We're asking the questions here."

"And I'm done answering them. I don't know who you are, but I've had enough of this."

Rachel moved to walk between them, and they slid together to block her. She anticipated their potential response and was ready. Walking more toward Gabrielle than Liam, she pulled her right arm into her body, as if recoiling from their pincer movement. Then she rammed her elbow into Gabrielle's midsection, aiming for an imaginary circle halfway between the neck and groin, just under the ribcage.

Rachel heard an "oof" from Gabrielle and saw her body convulse forward, chin down as she reacted to the shot to her solar plexus. Immediately, Rachel swung her other arm upward, aiming her ulna for Liam's neck. As she had expected, he had inched closer to respond to the attack on Gabrielle, his posture slackening in surprise at Rachel's attack. It left him vulnerable to a quick swing of the arm. Although it lacked the force of her body weight behind it, her arm connected with his Adam's apple, stopping him in his tracks.

Rachel quickly looked around the room. Two men stood chatting with the bartender as if they were old buddies. An older couple was standing by the drinks on the table, and a young couple was just turning Rachel's way from the other end of the table, where they were analyzing the hors d'oeuvres.

"Help, I think they're choking," Rachel said, the first thing that came to her mind. "I'm going to try to find a doctor!"

Without waiting for a response, she took off as fast as her heels and dress would allow, to her right since the couple from the table blocked her way to the left. She skirted the old couple and made a beeline for the door to the kitchen.

"Ma'am, you can't—" the bartender started.

Rachel ignored him, casting a quick glance back to see Gabrielle leaning against the wall, bent over, hands on her stomach and Liam on one knee, fiddling with his collar or tie. Then she pushed through the kitchen door with no intention of slowing down.

Chapter Twenty-One

The kitchen was like any other kitchen, only huge. And occupied by half a dozen cooks and servers. They cast a wary look at Rachel, who thought about keeping up the "somebody's choking" charade before deciding against it. They made no move to stop her as she rushed through and into a vacant breakfast nook. It opened via a pair of pocket doors to the solarium, and Rachel's emergence drew several more looks. She did her best to act as if she belonged, taking a deep breath and striding toward the main hall and, hopefully, Jake.

What were they to do? Talk about things that could go wrong. She was reasonably certain Liam and Gabrielle wouldn't try something in a crowd, but then again, they had just sort of tried something, hadn't they? What were they doing at the auction? How much did they know and how much didn't they? And how were she and Jake to make a bid on some unknown object with a couple of private operatives or acquisitions specialists or whatever they were lurking about?

Rachel entered the main hall and stopped. Standing just inside the door were Jake and a woman who at first appeared to be Rachel's reflection. It only took Rachel a fraction of a second to realize she was looking at her double, almost certainly the woman Jake had spotted shortly before Butler and Holmes had made contact the other night. What was *she* doing here? And why did Jake seem to be chatting her up, smiling, and . . . showing off his watch?

The circumstances didn't matter a whole lot. Rachel stood tall and marched toward them. She announced her presence with an ever so soft clearing of the throat.

"Oh, there you are," Jake said, looking away from his watch. He had been showing the woman something on the dial, one of its many useless features that had excited him so much when he'd bought it. He'd practically been like a little kid the whole ride home.

"This is my wife, Rachel," Jake said, turning to the other woman. "Rach, this is . . ."

"Tory," the woman said, finally dropping Jake's wrist. "It's nice to meet you."

"You too," Rachel said, absent any conviction. She was not the jealous type, but practical handholding went a little far, especially with a woman—unless there had been a genetic glitch—they suspected of being connected to *La Fantôme*.

"We were just keeping each other company until our spouses returned," Jake said, doing a good job keeping the desperation out of his voice.

Rachel nodded, her eyes mostly on Tory.

"Trying to avoid boring art conversations," he continued.

"Tory, would you mind if I had a word with my husband?"

"Not at all," she answered as if she hadn't a care in the world. She drained the remaining liquid in her champagne flute without making eye contact with Rachel.

Loosely grabbing Jake's arm, Rachel led him toward the patio. "Showing off your neato watch?" she asked as they stepped outside.

"She was interested in it. Said her husb—"

"Didn't you notice she looked just like me?"

"Not half as beautif—"

"Save it, Taylor. What's going on?"

They walked to the far corner of the patio from where they had been not long ago.

"She approached me," Jake said. "Started talking. Didn't stop."

"I didn't see a lot of talking going on."

"Are you jealous, Babe?"

"I'm confused," Rachel said, keeping her voice low as two men approached the north railing. She and Jake turned toward the ocean. "I thought we had accidentally taken the place of these 'doubles' of ours, but here they show up at the auction and she's flirting with you."

"She wasn't flirting."

"'Oh, this watch is so cool. Can I press one of these buttons?'"

"Well, that's not even close to how she sounds."

"And I just got the third degree from Liam and Gabrielle or Jamison and Frost or whatever we're calling them today."

"What? They're here?"

"Yeah."

"Where? You said the third degree?"

"Asking all sorts of questions about who warned us about them and who we thought they were."

"What'd you tell them?"

"I'm fine, by the way. And I told them the quickest pack of lies I could think of."

Jake exhaled. "Where are they now?"

"Last I checked, gasping for breath in the dining room."

"Gasping for breath?"

"They wanted to ask me more questions. I wanted to leave."

Jake looked at her, shaking his head as a way of asking for more info.

"I elbowed her in the solar plexus and punched him in the neck."

Jake frowned, almost stone-faced. "Wait, you what?"

"I flashed back to my old self-defense class. I anticipated their movements and got lucky, but I don't know how long they'll be down or how they'll respond."

"And you're all right?"

"I'm fine. Don't worry, I'm tougher than I look."

Jake ran his eyes up and down her.

"What?" she asked.

"A woman who can beat up two international thieves while being dressed like this . . ."

Rachel put up a hand. "Jake, please, none of your weird fantasies right now." She sighed. "What are we going to do?"

"What we came to do. Find the private auction, make our bid, and get out. And unless nature calls, we stick together."

"Okay."

159

"I'll be the leader, you can be the muscle."

Rachel finally permitted herself to smile. "Someone has to be."

"Ouch, right in the male ego."

Jake led the way inside and into the living room on the northeast side of the house. With a tray ceiling and floor-to-ceiling windows looking out at the grounds, the room appeared even larger than it was. Adding to that sentiment was the adjoined sitting room, the focal point of which was a large fireplace on the south wall. Both rooms were crowded with potential bidders examining the collection of items. Jake figured these two rooms and the gallery on the far side of the sitting room were the best places to find "bigwigs," the type of people who might know where the secret auction was being held. His plan was to hang around several of the pricier items, hoping to use them as conversation starters. But he didn't generate much conversation, and when he felt a tug on his arm, he turned to see Rachel nodding subtly over her shoulder. Jamison had entered from the far side of the room.

"This way," Jake said, guiding her into the gallery. A glance back at Jamison showed him moving their way, although not giving away that he'd spotted them. Jake led Rachel toward the gallery's other outlet, back into the main hall at the front of the house. "You know," he said, "cat-and-mouse wouldn't be so hard if you didn't cut such a striking figure in that dress."

"Don't bother trying to distract me, Jake. It's no use."

"Distract you? Just trying to get out of the doghouse for earlier."

"That's no use either."

They passed through a small anteroom to the gallery and into the main hall, where they nearly bumped into a gentleman in a tuxedo with long coattails. Positioned as he was in front of a small coatroom, Jake took him to be something of a concierge. He was dressed to match the man who had held the door for them on their arrival, with one small exception. Pinned to the lapel of his tuxedo was a red rose.

Jake looked at Rachel as they approached the man. "Good evening," he said with a trace of Southern gentility.

"Good evening," Jake returned.

"Enjoying the auction?"

"We are."

The man nodded and smiled. He was maybe sixty, mostly bald, with a grandfatherly glint to his eyes. Even so, Jake had a feeling he was the man to see and wondered how they had missed him on the way in. He blamed it on the multitude of people in the entry hall and on their being so enamored with the house.

"Where are you folks from?" the man with the rose asked.

Jake glanced at Rachel before answering. "Charlotte."

"Ah, Charlotte, the Queen City. Beautiful place," the man said with a broad smile.

Jake hoped there was no further piece of the code he needed to know.

"Well, I hope you enjoy your visit to Coral Manor. I suggest you take a stroll around the grounds while you're here. Particularly the pool house. A wonderful piece of architecture."

"We'll do that," Jake said, placing a hand on Rachel's back. He guided her through the hall and toward the patio.

"Was that what I thought it was?"

"I'm pretty sure it was."

"How'd he know . . . ?"

"Maybe we just had that look. Or maybe he asks all the guests."

She patted his arm. "Your very first coded spy exchange."

"Ba-da-ba-dum," he said, imitating the James Bond theme.

There were two exits off the patio, one in the southeast corner and one in the northeast. "You know what'd be fun," Jake said as they slipped through the crowd to the northeast exit.

"What's that?"

"Before we leave, placing a quarter-million-dollar bid on something."

"Under the name Liam Jamison or Gabrielle Frost," Rachel finished as they took several steps down to the lawn.

"Exactly."

The grass was like carpet, and Jake and Rachel wandered around a trio of palm trees. A head-high hedgerow ran between the stucco wall extending from the front of the house and the dunes between the lawn and the beach. Halfway between the wall and the dunes, an arched wooden trellis provided a path through the hedges.

"Pool house?" Rachel asked.

"That or an alternate world with talking beavers."

Rachel rolled her eyes as she led the way through the trellis. It led to a miniature version of the property—a square building in the midst of a perfect lawn, surrounded by haphazard palm trees, and flanked by dunes on one side and a stucco wall on two others. The far wall was covered by vines and ferns and other manner of foliage. But the focal point was clearly the two-story house constructed in the same fashion as the main house. A smaller staircase led up a couple feet to the "front" door, which faced south, toward the hedgerow, and a patio and pool spanned the distance between the house's eastern wall and the dunes. Back in Omaha, this would be an upscale, medium-family home. Here it was the pool house.

"Front door?" Jake asked.

Rachel shrugged, and they crossed the lawn, noticing no signs of other people or any indication that anyone was inside. Two windows on either side of the door and five more on the second floor were all dark or had blinds drawn.

"I guess we knock," he said as they climbed the steps, and he rapped on the wood door.

Thirty seconds passed, and Jake was about to knock again when they heard a click, and the door swung open. A man in a dark suit—not a tux—stood like a sentinel between them and the inside. His short-cropped hair, muscles straining against the arms of his suit jacket, and ramrod posture all spoke to his being private security. So did his mouth, a mere slit, when he said, "I'm sorry, the pool house is off limits to visitors."

"A guy with a rose on his lapel suggested we check it out," Jake said.

The man's features softened a fraction. "Are you visiting from out of state?"

Jake hoped there wasn't a second password required at this "level."

"Yeah, from Charlotte."

The man nodded, looked beyond them, then stepped to the side. "Please, come in."

As a gentleman, Jake usually let Rachel go first, but he made an exception and stepped in front of her into a high-ceilinged but single-level hallway. It ran for a dozen feet before widening and opening to a living room. The floor was the same coral- and blue-flecked marble as the main house, and the décor was also similar.

The man closed the door behind Rachel, then led them past a closed door on the left and an entrance to the kitchen on the right. They stopped at the base of a staircase leading left. Directly ahead of them and down a couple of stairs, was a large living room featuring several seating areas around a fireplace and a huge flat screen TV. To the right, the hall turned and led to sliding glass doors opening to the patio and pool. The hall was bound on the left by a half wall and on the right by a granite countertop fronted by four barstools and backed by the kitchen. The man nodded at the counter, on which rested a large ceramic bowl.

"Please place your cell phones or any other communications devices in the bowl," he said.

Jake dug his phone from his pocket, wondering if the PADL counted as a communication device. He decided it didn't. He and Rachel each placed phones in the bowl, along with one other. The man nodded and then extended a hand back into the hallway. "If you'll walk this way, please."

He guided them to the first door they had passed and stepped in front of them to open it. "Please wait in here and make yourselves comfortable. It should be just a few minutes."

Jake nodded, and Rachel mumbled a thank you as they stepped into a den made to resemble a captain's quarters aboard a ship, right down to the desk that appeared to have been salvaged from an old schooner built into the right wall.

"I don't like this," Jake said after the man closed the door behind them.

"It certainly is very cloak-and-dagger."

"Be ready to run."

"Run? Run where?" She looked down. "In heels and this dress?"

He shrugged.

Rachel wandered to a window and parted the Venetian blinds with her fingers.

"See anything?"

"Four heavies with guns coming this way."

"Cute," he said, and she turned to smirk at him. Jake exhaled. "There was another phone in the bowl."

"I saw that."

"Another bidder? Is this just the waiting room?"

"My guess."

He nodded. "I still don't like it."

Rachel walked to him, smoothing out an imperfection—real or otherwise—in his sleeve. "Have you had much to eat?"

Jake looked her in the eye. "You trying to distract me now?"

"Maybe in a manner of speaking, but I'm asking for real."

He shrugged. "I've nibbled."

"I should have eaten before we left," she said, crossing her arms over her stomach and feeling it with one palm.

"I'm sure there's more back in the main house. And I doubt Liam and Gabby are still lurking by the crab cakes."

"It's not that. I just feel like more than hors d'oeuvres. I'm thinking about a big, juicy cheeseburger."

Despite the circumstances, Jake couldn't help but smile. "You are the woman I fell in love with."

"When we get out of here, wanna go grab a burger? *If* we get out of here," she added with a wink.

Before Jake could answer, the doorknob turned, and the man took a step into the room. "Please come with me," he said, and motioned for them to follow. He led them back to the base of the stairs, where he said, "If you'll bear with me, I do need to wand you." He reached into his suit jacket and withdrew a small wand metal detector, similar to what TSA agents used at the airport. He instructed them to extend their arms and proceeded to wave it meticulously around their arms, legs, and torsos. Content, he nodded and returned it to his pocket. "Please head upstairs and then bear left. I will be waiting here when you're finished."

Trying to conceal a frown, Jake nodded and reached a hand for Rachel, allowing her to go first. They climbed a wide set of stairs that reversed itself halfway up, leading them to a hallway above the first floor hall. Following the man's instructions, they turned left and found themselves at a pair of French doors with curtains on the opposite side. Jake was about to reach out and knock on the glass when the doors both swung inward.

A woman greeted them with the thinnest, flattest possible smile. She too wore a suit, only without a tie, her dark hair pulled back into a tight bun at the base of her skull. She stepped back so they could enter a bedroom that spanned the north half of the second floor. Complete with a fireplace, four-poster bed, a private seating area, an attached bathroom no doubt containing every possible amenity, and doors leading to a private balcony, it was more opulent than Jake and Rachel's condo. Whereas beach-themed knickknacks could come across as kitschy, here—like everywhere at Coral Manor—they were refined and luxurious.

Sitting on a folding chair in front of a temporary table was a man smaller and less intimidating than the one downstairs. Two laptop computers were open on the table in front of him. He looked up to Jake and Rachel, who both followed the woman's eyes to him. No one spoke, but the man stood and extended a hand.

Wordlessly, Jake reached into his pocket and withdrew the PADL. He held it up between his thumb and forefinger for a second, then let it fall into the man's palm.

"It will be just a few minutes," the man said.

"Please sit down if you'd like," the woman said, gesturing at a fainting couch under a window.

"We're good, thanks," Jake said.

The man plugged the PADL into one of the computers and immediately began typing as if he was a TV secret agent desperately trying to hack a runaway missile or something. Jake looked down at Rachel, seeing the same look of confusion, disbelief, and amusement on her face as he felt inside him. He reached his arm around her waist as the man stopped typing and sat back. He waited less than thirty seconds for a soft, techie chime to sound. Then he removed the PADL and stood.

"Here you are," he said extending it to Jake.

"That's it?"

"That's it."

The woman reached into her jacket pocket and withdrew a small manila envelope. "This contains a burner phone. You will be notified, if applicable, via text message," she said.

Jake nodded. He wondered if a real proxy for *La Fantôme* would know the appropriate way to end such an exchange. Instead, he simply said, "Thanks."

She opened the French doors for them, and they took their cue to head back downstairs, where the first man was waiting for them. He gestured toward the bowl on the counter and said they could retrieve their phones. They were the only two in the bowl, and Jake pocketed his and handed Rachel's to her.

"This way please," the man said, walking ahead of them to the sliding glass doors. He pulled them open, nodded at Jake and Rachel as they passed, and slid them closed behind them as soon as Rachel's heel crossed the threshold.

"Well, dear, you think we won?" Jake asked. He stuffed the manila envelope into his jacket pocket, feeling very Bond-villain like as he did so.

"Honestly, I hope not." She looped her arm around his. "I want to get back to vacation."

The patio stretched for a dozen feet before dropping down a few steps to a terrace that bordered a square, turquoise pool on three sides. On the fourth, it was framed by a brick wall and then the dunes, which still caught a few rays of sunlight, in contrast to the patio that was completely in the shade. Off in the distance, the clouds over the Atlantic were every color imaginable, tumbling over each other like dolphins showing off. Taking a deep breath, Jake could almost feel the tension of the last few days slipping off his shoulders. Yes, getting back to vacation sounded like a good idea.

He squeezed Rachel's hand and nodded toward the main house. "What do you say we blow this party and go have our own party?"

"If by 'our own party,' you mean supper, I'm game."

"Party pooper."

Without looking back, they strolled across the lawn. Jake let Rachel go through the trellis first. He followed closely, as she had trailed her arm behind her to hang onto his fingers. A distant police siren carried on the wind, then faded, replaced by the lapping of waves and shrieking of gulls. It was the same old sound, but it never grew tiresome. In Nebraska, all there was to hear was the whistling of the wind or the absolute silence of hot, summer nights. (Hearing growing corn popping was a legend, as far as Jake was concerned.)

They were almost back to the main house patio when Jake heard the sirens again. He stopped, giving ever so slight a tug on Rachel's fingers.

"What is it?" she asked, turning to face him.

"Hear that?"

"Sirens, so?"

"Getting closer."

She shook her head. "You don't think . . ."

"I don't know. I've just got sort of a bad feeling again."

The sirens were piercing now. Multiple tones, drawing yet closer. Guests on the patio had noticed too. Jake looked at the palm trees in the side yard, their trunks in the shadow but the fronds still high enough in the air to catch the golden tint of the setting sun. And the reflection of red and blue strobing lights as police cars rolled up the driveway of Coral Manor.

Chapter Twenty-Two

The eastern sky had turned a hazy amber color, the clouds quickly fading to shades of purple and gray. The calm Atlantic beneath them was a midnight blue, laced with lines of white as waves rolled gently onshore. The dunes in the shade of the house were a shapeless taupe, the wisps of seagrass losing their distinction in the shadow. Although Rachel's eyes took in the panorama, it didn't register with her. Instead, she observed the rarely seen uneasiness on the face of her husband, uneasiness that hadn't been there during any of the conversations with the FBI agents, when she'd explained running into Jamison and Frost, or even when he expressed anxiety before the very odd "bidding process" just a few minutes ago. His look told her something was off, even though she didn't know what it could be.

"Rach, do one of those collar-fixing, tie-straightening, lapel-patting things women do."

"What?"

"More importantly, just stand here," he said, taking a half step to the left.

"What's going on?" she asked, reaching up to smooth his lapel, which didn't need any smoothing.

He didn't answer, his eyes roving over her shoulders while he as deftly as possible removed the manila envelope from his jacket pocket. He held it at waist level and retrieved the PADL from his pants pocket. He inserted it into the envelope.

"What are you doing, Honey?" Rachel asked, tracing his cheek with her hand.

"Trying not to spend the night in the slammer," he said, folding the manila envelope over on itself. He looked pensively around again. Then he took her hand. "Come on."

Instead of leading her up onto the patio, they walked between it and the dunes on a narrow strip of grass. Rachel heard car doors slamming. Guests on the patio had taken on confused expressions, muttering to themselves. Several headed inside.

Movement to Rachel's left caught her eye, and she turned to look at Jake. He had his free hand in his pocket, casual as you please.

"Where's the envelope?" she asked.

"What envelope?"

Rachel stopped.

He pulled her on. "We have nothing on us. We're just two guests at an auction, here mostly to see the items since they're probably out of our price range. Stick to the truth but leave out anything about the FBI."

"Lie to the cops?"

"Omit. Remember what Vaughn said about them not being in on this? Let's keep it that way, for now."

"Jake—"

"And this is the important part. If they happen to arrest us or take us in for questioning, say nothing without a lawyer and without talking to me. Nothing."

"Jake, you're scaring me."

"Just a precaution. But remember, we've done nothing wrong, so we have nothing to worry about."

"Tell that to my amygdala."

"I always thought it was a-myg-DA-la."

"Jake."

"Just lightening the mood," he said, turning her onto the patio at its southeast corner. "Smile, act natural."

"Where is the phone?"

"Better you don't know."

The patio was clearing, and Rachel and Jake followed the guests inside. Several uniformed officers had already entered the front door and drawn the attention of Crenshaw Banks III.

"What is the meaning of this?" he boomed.

"Are you Crenshaw Banks?" one of the officers asked.

"I am. And you are interrupting a charity auction benefitting Camer—"

"Mr. Banks, we received a credible tip that there is a black market auction of stolen goods taking place at this facility this evening."

"A what? That's absurd!"

Rachel scanned the crowd, looking for the man with the rose on his lapel, or for Jamison or Frost or her double, the lady fascinated with Jake's watch. She saw none of them. She did see that everyone in the hall was standing and watching the scene just inside the front door.

"We'd like to look around, if that's okay," the officer said.

"It most certainly is not."

"This event is open to the public, is it not?"

"It is, but this is also private property, and I have the right to ask anyone to leave, which I am doing now."

The officer tilted his radio attached to his shoulder to his ear. Rachel couldn't hear the gibberish that came through it. "Sir, we just were granted a warrant to search the premises and question your guests. It will be here within minutes."

Banks was furious but relented.

Rachel expected a stampede of people trying to leave, but everybody remained frozen in place. The officer began instructing his fellow police officers to cordon off the area. He then uttered the words, "Make sure nobody leaves," and a murmur went up from the crowd. Rachel found Jake's hand and squeezed, and he returned the gesture.

"We might as well get comfortable," he said.

Rachel tried to relax. She realized maybe this would be the end of their problems. The cops would break up the auction, capture the item—whatever it was—and arrest those responsible. The FBI wouldn't be happy, but it would be the end . . .

"Jake," she said, suddenly uncertain.

"Mmm?"

"What if we were on camera in the pool house?"

"We weren't."

"How do you know?"

"Because with all the precautions they took, they'd never let it happen. Or rather, they'd never let the footage fall into the hands of the cops."

"If they did . . ."

He shrugged. "We tell the truth. Vaughn will back us up if it comes to that."

"Are you sure?"

He shrugged again. "Pretty."

"Or what if I'm on video attacking Jamison and Frost? Surely Banks has security cameras out today."

"We'll play it by ear," Jake said. "And I'll be right beside you."

The officers had fanned out, having received reinforcements, and were circulating among the guests.

"Looks like they're looking for someone," Jake said.

Rachel watched as they spoke for a few seconds to various people before moving on. One of the officers made brief eye contact with her, then turned to the officer next to him.

"Jake . . ."

The officers casually walked their way.

"Stay cool," Jake said in his best ventriloquist voice. It wasn't very good.

"Ma'am, sir," the lead officer said. He had short black hair and a kind— albeit forcedly so—face. "Sorry for the intrusion, but we'd like to ask you a few questions."

"Sure," Jake said.

"May we talk where there's a little more privacy?"

Rachel's heart sped up. None of the other guests had been singled out in such a way. The officers knew something. Had they been tipped off, perhaps by Jamison and Frost?

"Sure," Jake said again. "The patio was pretty empty a few minutes ago."

"That will be fine."

The officer gestured for them to lead the way, and Jake placed a hand on Rachel's back, guiding her toward the door. She stepped out onto the patio, noting how the balmy evening air felt cool on her suddenly hot skin. She hoped her anxiety didn't show.

She walked to the side railing and turned around, Jake beside her. "What can we help you with, Officers?" he asked.

"You may have heard a few minutes ago," the same officer said, "we received a tip that this auction was actually a cover for a black market auction here on the premises."

Jake frowned. "What's that mean?"

"Likely stolen or contraband merchandise being auctioned illegally."

"What can we do to help?"

Rachel had to hand it to Jake. He was good. She tried not to let the pensiveness play on her face, but she wasn't a great liar. Or fibber. Even deceiver. She hadn't even been able to pull off a surprise birthday party for Jake when they were dating.

"We were actually told to look for persons matching your descriptions," the officer said. "They fit you to a T."

"And what is it we allegedly did?" Jake asked.

"Conspired to buy or sell contraband items."

"Officer, I'm a network engineer from Omaha and my wife is a photographer. We know nothing about any of this. I know that's not exactly a rock-solid alibi, but I think I may be able to shed some light on things."

"Go ahead," the officer said with a "this should be good" sort of smile.

"About an hour ago, I had a conversation with a woman who was the spitting image of my wife. She had darker hair and a black dress, but they could have been sisters. She also mentioned that I bore a resemblance to her husband. Is it possible, through some weird coincidence, we've been mistaken for them?"

The officers glanced at each other. "It's possible," the first one said.

"My wife was also accosted by another couple who seemed to think she had taken something that belonged to them. They actually got a little physical with her, and she had to rely on moves she learned in an old self-defense class to get away from them."

"This took place here, at the auction?"

"Yes, sir."

"In the dining room," Rachel said, glad her voice didn't break.

"We thought it was just a strange case of mistaken identity at the time, but I wonder if it's not tied to whatever it is that's going on here."

"It's possible," the officer repeated. He nodded with conviction as he spoke. "We'll look into it. But to be thorough, we do need to ask some more questions."

"Of course," Jake said.

"To start with, do both of you have some ID?"

"Sure," Jake said, producing his wallet. Rachel dug into her purse for her driver's license. The second officer checked them and handed them back while the first asked a series of routine questions. What brings you to Myrtle Beach? How long are you here for? Why are you at the auction? Have you seen anything suspicious? Jake answered most of them, with Rachel pitching in a few times so it wouldn't look like he was a spokesman for the two of them, which might suggest he was covering for her.

Then the officers asked about the altercation with Jamison and Frost, and Rachel hoped shifting eyes and a slight hesitation in her speech didn't come across as lying. In actuality, she told as much truth as possible, while keeping with Jake's original story about Jamison and Frost thinking she had taken something of theirs. If the officers suspected duplicity, they didn't show it. Instead, they asked her for a description of them.

"And you have no idea who they are?" they asked when she was finished.

"No," Rachel said, realizing that wasn't really a lie. At this point, she doubted everyone's identity—Jamison and Frost, her and Jake's doubles, the FBI agents, even the cops themselves.

The first officer, who had been taking notes as they spoke, dotted his notebook with some force, then flipped it shut. "Mr. and Mrs. Taylor, thank you very much for your cooperation. I think that's all for now. It's possible we may have more questions later, and we're asking everyone to remain on the premises for the time being, but we have nothing further at the moment."

"Thank you, Officers," Jake said. "I hope you find whoever's responsible."

With brief nods, the two officers retreated, and Rachel heaved a sigh of relief and leaned back against the patio railing. Jake put his arm around her shoulder and pulled her into him. "You did great," he whispered.

"Jake, you remember that line from *The Rainmaker*, about how a murderer makes twenty-five mistakes and is lucky if he can remember five?" She looked up at him. "I can think of at least five."

"We didn't murder anybody."

"No, but they can catch us in our lies in so many ways . . ."

"If they do, we fall back on what Vaughn told us. FBI trumps local police. At least, they always do on TV."

She wrapped her arms around him and squeezed. "You were really quick on your feet."

"I just channeled my inner spy."

"Throwing suspicion on our doubles, who probably are complicit, and dragging Jamison and Frost into it—genius."

"I don't know about that. Very clever, maybe, but genius?"

"Wishing them luck catching 'whoever's responsible' might have been a bit much, though."

"That part was true."

Rachel let go and sighed. "So now what?"

"Now we hang loose and hope no beach-combing crabbers spot a manila envelope in the dunes."

Chapter Twenty-Three

"Jake, this is crazy."

"You have a better idea?"

"No."

"Well?"

"That doesn't validate yours."

"We need to get that envelope back," Jake said, coasting to a stop, the tires of the Mustang crunching on gravel. "And the sooner, the better."

They'd been detained at the party for over an hour while the police questioned guests and searched the premises. A detective—not Detective Robinson—arrived and asked them a few follow-up questions. He seemed content with their answers, and if they had been identified as the Jake and Rachel Taylor who'd experienced a break-in their first night in Myrtle Beach, it wasn't brought up. And if the cops hadn't figured it out, neither Jake nor Rachel was going to connect it for them.

When they were allowed to leave just before eight-thirty, they knew nothing about the nature of the investigation and didn't hang around to find out. Instead, Jake drove only a few houses south before turning into a stub of paved driveway that gave way to gravel. He drove through some encroaching shrubs and trees and parked behind a half-finished garage. It was a few steps farther along than the house, a two-story box that was framed but little more.

He parked between a tool trailer and a towable cement mixer, and he and Rachel got out.

Darkness had fallen during their sequestration and short drive, for which Rachel was at least grateful. She picked her way carefully in heels on gravel, following Jake around the side of the house. "There's a path here," he called, slowing to wait for her.

"I cannot believe we are doing this in a tux and gown."

"I told you, time's a priority."

"I know, I know. Here, hold me."

"Anytime, Babe," he said with a dumb wink she could just see by moonlight. She leaned on his shoulder while unfastening her three-inch heels. After more than three hours, it felt good to set her feet free. Holding her heels with one hand and lifting her gown so as not to drag it through the sand with the other, Rachel nodded for Jake to lead the way.

"How are we supposed to spot an envelope in all this?" Rachel asked as they passed through a gap in the dunes.

"With the flashlight app on my phone," Jake said.

"There are still guests at the auction. Won't they see it?"

"They'll think it's crabbers."

"Is this even a public beach?"

"Yeah," Jake said confidently. "I'm sure it is."

Rachel sighed and followed him north, counting the properties until the familiar three-story outline of Coral Manor towered over the dunes. With the lights on in all the rooms, not to mention soft floodlights aimed at the sides of the house as part of the décor, it stood out. It also, Jake argued, minimized the likelihood of anyone spotting their light as they searched. And the dunes, from the beach, were at least five or six feet high, so Jake and Rachel's heads would be the only part of them—if any—visible to someone on the estate grounds.

"Okay, we're about in line with the patio," Jake said. He withdrew his phone and switched open his flashlight app. "I think it went pretty much straight east."

"How far? Over the dunes?"

"Cleared the top, at least."

"And do you mean magnetic east or straight to the ocean?"

Jake stopped. "Magnetic east?"

"Like magnetic north as opposed to true north. Like east on the compass."

"Straight toward the ocean," Jake said, pointing. He looked down at his watch, pausing.

"What's the matter?"

"My compass isn't working."

"You have a compass on your watch?"

He nodded.

"Well if you know which direction it went, what difference does it make?"

"It doesn't, I guess."

"So somewhere around here?" she asked.

"Yeah, about."

Rachel dropped her heels and used both hands to hold up her dress. "What?" she asked, noticing Jake was staring at her.

"You're just cute, you know, in that dress, barefoot on the beach."

"Really? Do you just sit around dreaming up these 'looks' for me? Barefoot in a dress on the beach? Evening gown ninja? Feisty farm girl in boots?"

He shrugged.

"Can we just find this envelope and get out of here?"

He nodded. "Feisty farm girl in boots. I could—"

"Jake."

He smiled, and they resumed searching. It took five minutes before he spotted the envelope nestled at the bottom of the dune. He quickly opened it as Rachel approached. "Phone and PADL," he said.

"A real Moses in the reeds moment. Let's go," Rachel said, looking around. So far, it appeared they had avoided detection.

They made it halfway back to the car before Rachel remembered her heels, and it took another ten minutes to retrace their steps and find them. Another five were spent using Jake's heretofore unused—he promised—handkerchief to brush all the grains of sand from between her toes. While she did that, leaning on him again, he powered on the cell phone given him in the pool house.

"Nothing," he reported. "We didn't miss anything."

"Bullet dodged then."

"It would appear so."

"Good," she said, reaching to fasten her second sandal. "Then let's get out of here. I'm starved."

Rachel looked beautiful.

It wasn't just her relaxed posture, elbows extended as they rested on the table, or her striking dress, or the way the her hair hung around and over her shoulders—although those things all helped.

It was her . . . aura. She was carefree and comfortable, albeit out of place. So was he, decked in formalwear at the throwback diner several blocks south and west of their condo. It had been Rachel's idea, and her rumbling stomach's, to eat without stopping to change. Never mind they clashed with the '50s décor, particularly her dress with the sky blue vinyl booth they sat in. Nor, after noshing on potato croquetas with saffron aioli, mini zucchini and goat cheese tartlets, and gravid lax, were cheeseburgers and fries an appropriate main course. But hunger and taste buds dictated.

Rachel's demeanor was also tied to having survived the evening. She had noticeably relaxed after they returned to the Mustang, left the construction site, and made several miles' progress south on Ocean Boulevard. Coral Manor, the auction, international thieves-turned-assailants, doppelgangers, and police inquiries were in the rearview mirror. They had pulled it off, and she wasn't the only one breathing easier. Then again, that might have been because Jake had finally loosened his bowtie.

"When do we have to call Butler and Holmes?" Rachel asked.

"When we get back."

"Won't that be kind of late?"

Jake shrugged. "They can deal."

"And sweat in the meantime."

"Serves them right for not reading in the cops. Would have saved us a pile of trouble."

"They're probably mad that the cops almost blew their op." She grinned as she lifted her cheeseburger. "Besides, you managed just fine."

Jake grinned, admiring a woman who could eat a sloppy cheeseburger in a pageant-worthy gown, and do so with aplomb.

"We did fine," he corrected after taking a drink.

"You did all the work."

"Except for fighting off Jamison and Frost, filling in details with the cops, keeping me calm."

"How did I do that, exactly?"

"By looking so great in that dress."

She tipped her head to the side.

"Seriously, Rach, you were spectacular."

"Just following your lead."

He grinned again. "We sound like those cartoon squirrels. 'After you.' 'No, I insist, after you.' 'How very kind of you.' 'Indubitably.'"

Rachel wrinkled her nose. "Weren't they chipmunks?"

"Whatever."

She gave a somewhat sultry smile as she reached for a fry. She plopped it into her mouth, dangling her hand in front of her chin afterward. "So I noticed something tonight."

"What's that?"

"We work pretty well together."

"You want me to quit my job and become your lighting and backdrop guy?"

"No," she said with a slight eye roll-turned-smirk. "I also thought we did a good job communicating. Very straightforward."

"You're hinting at something . . ."

"Maybe you have a point at being more direct with each other. At least in certain situations."

"Like our next covert sting operation?"

She kicked him under the table.

"Ow."

"Maybe I do need to be a little more overt at giving you signals and hints, not be so worried about having to come right out and tell you something. And you don't have to be afraid to ask me what I mean or what's going on. Like you said, be direct with each other."

"Certainly worth a try."

"Good." She hefted her burger again.

"What was the name of Hammett's husband and wife team?"

"Nick and Nora Charles."

"Weren't they from Omaha?"

She frowned. "I don't think so."

"Hmm. But they were spies, right?"

"Detectives, I think."

"Maybe they'll write a book about us someday."

"And call it what, *The Accidental Detectives*?"

"I read those as a kid. No fooling."

She shook her head at him.

Having taken a brief break to chat, he re-attacked his burger, loaded with bacon, cheese, barbecue sauce, and onion strings.

"We should get out and do something active tomorrow," Rachel said. "Burn some calories."

"If you didn't order the fattest thing on the menu . . ."

"I was hungry," she said, sliding her chocolate milkshake over and taking an exaggerated slurp through the straw.

"Hit the golf course again?"

"I was thinking more in line with a nature walk, maybe a flower garden."

"We've yet to hike the Boardwalk, shop, find kitschy souvenirs."

"And soft pretzels and chili dogs and loaded nachos? I know how you think. Accuse me for what I eat."

He shrugged.

"Tomorrow's Saturday. I'd rather save that for a weekday when it isn't so crowded."

"Sure," he said.

They ate for a while, reminiscing about the evening, citing observations, admitting fears, and guessing at explanations.

Finished with her burger, Rachel took her milkshake in hand. She slouched a little in the booth and rested her head on top of the backrest. Then she extended her legs, propping her feet beside Jake on the booth. She took a slurp. "You know, in an odd way, tonight was sort of fun."

"Fun?" Jake asked. He wiped his left hand on his napkin, then dropped it under the table. He felt inside Rachel's gown and leisurely rubbed her calves.

"Yeah. Don't get me wrong, it was nerve-racking and stressful too. But dressing up with you, hobnobbing with high-society folks, exploring the grounds of a beachside mansion at dusk."

"Are you being a romantic or just messing with me?"

Having closed her eyes, Rachel opened just one of them. "Little of each."

He patted her calf, then withdrew his hand to clean up his fries.

"Makes me think," she said, opening both eyes again.

His head down to sip from his pop, he raised his eyes. "About?"

"We should do this more often."

Jake swallowed as he sat up. "To be clear, you mean gorge ourselves on greasy food or hobnob with 'high-society' folks?"

"I mean go on dates."

"We do go on dates."

"We go out to eat once a week and to the occasional movie. There's no variety."

"I can see when the next auction in Omaha is, or try to get in touch with the local black market. Else Nate's our website guy at work—maybe he can get me on a dark web chatroom."

Rachel ignored his wisecrack. "We should do more things together, get out, experience life."

"Like what?"

She reached for a stray fry, munching it from one end to the other. "I don't know. Anything. Dress up and go to some formal art gala or the opera."

"Oh, could we?"

"Or go golfing. Or disc golfing. Take a day trip somewhere. Take a class. Whatever. We'll hit some, and we'll miss some, but we'll have experiences."

"Not sure experiences is all we're after. I mean, POWs have an experience."

"Don't be extreme or anything," Rachel said, withdrawing her feet and sitting up. "Look at tonight. That wasn't fun by any definition, and yet, it was oddly . . ."

"Fun," he said.

"Right. So we go golfing and I lose all our balls and bounce a tee shot off your knee. It'd be fun. Or we go to the opera and hate it, but then spend a few hours ripping on it from a corner table at a hole-in-the-wall pizza place. The point is, we try something."

"You wear a dress like that, you've got a deal."

She sighed.

"I'm kidding. I'm with you, Sweetie."

"And we should talk. Even if it's just about nonsense. We sit at dinner and go through the formalities and banalities of life, and that's about it. We never talk about real stuff, about our marriage. Even this—my ponderings and your cartoon references is—"

"Fun," he said again.

"Good for us, I think. At least it's something different."

Jake had a final fry and nodded. "Yeah, I agree."

She smiled thinly.

"You about read—"

From inside Jake's jacket pocket, a brief chime sounded. His eyes widened, and he looked at Rachel.

"Them?" she asked.

He reached into his pocket as the phone sounded again, still in its envelope. He withdrew it and tapped the screen to see the new message.

"'*Congrats. You're the winner,*'" he read.

"You're kidding."

"Nope."

"That's it?"

"There's a second message." He scrolled to it. "'*2nd Ave Pier 6:30 pm tomorrow. Further instructions to follow.*'"

Rachel smiled without enthusiasm. "I guess we're going to the Boardwalk tomorrow after all."

Chapter Twenty-Four

One of Rachel's rules on vacation was no eating at chain restaurants. Sure, the occasional Whopper or McChicken was acceptable in a pinch, but by and large, she wanted to experience local cuisine, not something she could find on West Dodge Street. Yet here she and Jake were sharing the same side of a booth at a Denny's in southern Myrtle Beach. It had been Butler and Holmes' idea, figuring it was about the least likely spot for anyone to follow or observe them.

Jake had called them when he and Rachel had returned to their condo the night before, briefing Butler and Holmes on events at the auction, including interactions with Jamison and Frost and the arrival of the police. Once they'd learned of the two text messages, the FBI agents had set up a breakfast meeting for the morning. Now, as the foursome waited for their breakfast to be cooked and served, Holmes asked, "Any further word?"

"Nothing," Jake said. He had already shown them the phone, which Butler had looked at for several minutes. They recorded the sending number but were sure it was a "burner" and thus untraceable.

"There's a good chance the 'further instructions' won't come until six-thirty, or close to it," Holmes said. "They don't want to tip you off."

"So what do we do?" Jake asked.

"If you're up for it, make the exchange," Butler said. "We'll be there as well, undercover, and as soon as you take possession of the object, you can give it to us."

"Why don't you just take the phone and take it from here?" Rachel asked.

"Because they might be expecting you. It's possible the people who took your bid last night won't be involved in the exchange, but they might be. And even if not, they might have passed on your descriptions or even a secretly snapped photo."

"Then how do we make the exchange? What if they follow us?"

"They won't," Holmes said dismissively. She was dressed like an agent again, her hair in a messy ponytail. She seemed, if possible, less friendly than their previous meetings. "They'll want to verify you're the people who submitted the bid, but once they pass the item to you, it's no longer their concern."

"Our plan is to have you take a taxi or Uber to the pier tonight," Butler said. "Laura will be there already, and I'll be waiting to pick you up in another 'Uber.' All you have to do is proceed with the exchange and get in the car. I'll drive you back to your hotel, and Laura and I will conduct a full debriefing. Then you'll be done."

"Until *La Fantôme* comes after us for not giving him his purchase."

"You'll be the least of his worries," Holmes said. "I'll be tracking the person making the exchange so I can take them into custody. We'll have the object and the phone as evidence, plus your testimony. Once word gets out that we've intercepted the transaction, *La Fantôme* will be on the run. He'll certainly have no motive to come for you because we'll have whatever it is he wants."

"What about revenge?" Rachel asked.

"Not his style."

"It initiates risk," Butler said. "And it doesn't pay. *La Fantôme* is all about return on investment."

"Speaking of," Jake said, "how does the money in all this work out?"

"We don't know," Butler answered. "Could have been a wire account number on the PADL, could have been an arrangement made ahead of time that we aren't aware of. Either way, there's been no mention of the proxy making payment, so I wouldn't worry about it."

Rachel noted a lot of "don't worry about it" type responses from the FBI, and they were having the reverse effect.

Their server arrived with plates of pancakes, omelets, chicken and waffles, and biscuits covered with sausage gravy. And more coffee for Jake and Agent Butler. When she was gone, Jake cut into his biscuits. "Any word on MBPD's investigation last night?"

"Not that we're aware of," Butler said as he buttered his toast. "But we're not working with them, per se."

"I ask because they complicated things for us. We were in a real pickle," he said, explaining how they had dealt with the police's arrival by tossing the phone and PADL over the dunes. Butler seemed to approve, whereas Holmes nearly choked on her pancakes.

"We figured Jamison and Frost might be there," she said after swallowing.

"Thanks for the heads up," Rachel said.

"But we didn't think they'd accost you in any way," Holmes finished with a glare.

"As for your double, that was quick thinking," Butler said. "We didn't think they'd be there at all, given they didn't have a PADL."

"And speaking of, we may have a line on them after all," Holmes said. She retrieved her phone and tapped and swiped the screen a few times. She handed it to Jake, and Rachel leaned over to look.

"Is this her?" Rachel asked.

"Yeah, I think so. Only her hair was dark."

Rachel looked at Holmes. "Who is she?"

"Her name is Victoria Masters. She's a private contractor, which basically means criminal-for-hire. Largely espionage work, thefts, smuggling. She didn't pop when we originally ran everyone on your flight through our database because of the blond hair. Swipe to the next photo."

Jake did so. The image now showed what looked like another security photograph from an unfamiliar location, maybe a city street or train station. Rachel noted the timestamp of the previous February.

"This was taken earlier this year in Prague."

"Same woman?" he asked.

"We think. It hasn't been confirmed, largely because the hair doesn't match, and facial recognition hasn't been able to get a clean enough image to match enough data points, but several intelligence organizations speculate it is." She looked from Jake to Rachel.

"Yeah, that looks like her," Jake said. "Her hair's still darker now, and the nose is a bit more . . ."

"Chiseled," Rachel added.

"We think she may have had it altered. Now this," Holmes said, reaching to swipe the phone, "is a composite of the two faces—best we can do without a higher quality image—and with darker hair."

"Oh my goodness," Rachel said. "That could be me."

Holmes nodded as Jake added his agreement. "That's her. That's the woman. And she said her name was Tory, so that fits."

Rachel reached for her orange juice. "What about the guy I saw?"

Holmes took the phone back and called up several more photographs. "We're assuming he's Dane Paul, an Australian-born hitter who has worked with Masters on several previous engagements. Every photo of him in the system shows him with long, blond hair, so he again didn't match the profile. And airport security never got a clean shot of his face for facial rec. But here he is . . ."

Rachel studied the two photos side by side on the screen. They showed a man who resembled the one she had seen Monday, but it was hard to be sure five days later. She'd only seen him briefly, and whenever she pictured him, she also pictured Jake.

"And here is a computer rendering with shorter, darker hair."

Rachel gasped. "That's him. Oh, wow."

"Now when you say 'hitter' . . . ?" Jake asked.

"A number of things," Butler answered. "Thefts and retrievals, personal attacks, assassinations."

"Oh, awesome," Rachel muttered.

"Like we said yesterday, they haven't made any move to harm you. Our guess is they'll try to take the object once you take possession of it. But we'll be there. And now that we know who we're looking for, we're several steps ahead of them, seeing as how they don't know we're onto them."

"Why would they change their appearance to match ours?" Jake asked.

"Coincidence," Butler said. "There would be no reason."

"They're wanted," Holmes tag-teamed again, "if not by governments in various locations, then by people they've worked for, marks, or competitors. A new haircut or style, even the odd nose job, isn't that unusual."

"And you don't think these two are a danger to us?" Jake asked.

Butler shook his head. "I won't tell you that there's no danger to you and Rachel, Jake. There is. These two are unsavory characters, and this is a high-stakes game. But, they've done nothing since arriving here to indicate they actually mean you any harm. Even if they or *La Fantôme* were to show up at your condo, all you have to do is come clean. They'll leave you alone then."

"But it won't come to that, honestly," Holmes said. "The heat will be on them soon enough."

"There is danger," Butler said, "but we think it is a low probability of danger. We wouldn't ask you to go through with this, even as much as is on the line, if we didn't have every confidence that we'd be able to keep you safe."

Rachel wished she shared the FBI agents' confidence. She looked at Jake, who seemed to be satisfied, and decided to trust his lead. They finished their breakfast, discussing details and contingencies. Jake promised to call as soon as he received any further details via text, or if there were any developments of any sort. Butler and Holmes agreed to do the same.

"You still want to get out and do something today?" Jake asked as they split at the back of the Mustang.

It was a breezy but clear morning, and Rachel had to brush hair out of her face before answering. "Why, what'd you have in mind?"

"We've been saving a little money eating on the FBI's dime. How about a relaxing afternoon at a spa?"

"A Calabash dinner and breakfast at Denny's don't equate to much in the way of spa treatments."

"There was also lunch yesterday," he said with a shrug.

"And what are you going to do, get a mani-pedi with me?"

"I'll play nine."

She leveled her eyes at him. Sensing no ulterior motives, she said, "You have got a deal."

Chapter Twenty-Five

The sun was sinking in the western sky, but it was still plenty warm as Jake and Rachel waited for their Uber out front of their condo. It was a quarter after six, which would give them plenty of time to reach the southern end of "Myrtle Beach proper," the 2nd Avenue Pier. The seller had texted at precisely six o'clock, as Jake had been lacing up his shoes. The message had been short and simple, telling them to walk out to the end of the pier. Jake had called Butler, who had confirmed that he and Holmes would be in place.

The morning breeze had brought heavy early afternoon storms that had cut short Jake's round of golf. They had not impinged on Rachel's spa treatments. The Taylors had returned to the condo around two-thirty, as the rain was finishing, and watched a movie on DVD to kill time. That had been followed by a brief walk on the beach in the post-rain heat and humidity to expel nervous energy, and a snack supper with plans to celebrate the end of this ordeal by going out for something more substantial later.

"Just a few more hours," Jake said, squeezing Rachel's hand. She wore a pink tank top and dark denim shorts, along with her ASICS. Jake's blue shirt was matched with gray shorts and athletic shoes as well. They were as nondescript of outfits as they could think of, and matched the colors—pink and blue—they'd promised the FBI agents they would be wearing.

"Tomorrow, let's get out of town," she said.

"Okay."

"Go to Charleston or somewhere, make a day trip of it. Just get away from this all."

"Okay."

"When we get back, it'll be like a new vacation."

"Make sure you wear something with no pockets."

She smiled as a car pulled to the curb. "You Jake and Rachel?" a young female driver asked, rolling down the window.

"We are," Jake said, opening the back door for Rachel. He slid in after her. He confirmed their destination and sat back. The driver had a heavy foot, both on the gas and brake pedals, and they reached the pier several minutes early. Better than late, Jake reasoned.

The 2nd Avenue Pier extended over nine hundred feet into the Atlantic from a towering base that housed a gift shop, a restaurant, and an open-air bar on the top floor. It was set back a few hundred feet from the street to make way for a parking lot that Jake scanned as they started walking. It was half-full of cars, none of them a Hyundai Accent containing an FBI agent posing as an Uber driver. But it was early.

Jake checked the cell phone—nothing—as he and Rachel neared the pier. Coming from the parking lot, it looked like a beach house on stilts. Aside from a few port windows and glass doors on two different levels, the east side of the building was made up mostly of beige slats that, on closer inspection, formed the second-level railing and partial enclosure for the stairs leading to the second and third levels. Or, technically, the first and second levels since the "first level" was the beach.

"Stairs or elevator?" Jake asked.

"Stairs," Rachel said. They climbed one story and entered the air-conditioned gift shop. It sold T-shirts, various snack foods, and knickknacks— like all the other gift shops in the world. To their right, a glass wall separated them from the mostly full Pier House Restaurant. The smells lingered to the gift shop and made Jake's mouth water.

They paid a dollar each for admission to the pier and stepped back into the warmth. Red umbrellas, most of them unfurled, topped picnic tables lining the center of the pier. Crude benches and stands for fishing poles flanked them alongside the railings. The pier was busy with fishermen, people enjoying cold drinks sold at a small stand immediately on Jake and Rachel's left, and sightseers gazing at the SkyWheel and hotels and condos north along the Strip or watching parasailers out over the ocean.

Jake and Rachel walked slowly, him checking the phone several times. Even late in the day and with the ocean breeze, it was hot, and Jake used the shade of an umbrella to cool down as well as to see the phone's screen better.

"Anything?" Rachel asked.

"No."

"Maybe they'll find—"

The phone chimed. They crowded together to view the incoming message.

Far end of pier. Gray shirt, red had. Lean on railing to my left.

"Think he means red hat?" Jake asked.

"Even black market art dealers are susceptible to typos," she said.

He grinned.

"You going to call Holmes?"

"No. They might have eyes on us."

"I haven't seen her," Rachel said, sweeping her eyes up and down the pier.

"I'm sure she's here," Jake said. "In disguise."

"I suppose. Hid that rat's nest of hair somehow."

"Let's go."

They continued farther onto the pier, observing straggler sunbathers on the beach on either side. More high-rises lined the beach to the south, whereas the buildings to the north—at least for several blocks—were a little more modest. Ahead of them, the pier widened at its end, with a wood canopy in the middle and fishing posts at either end. Late in the day, most were occupied by people with reddish-brown, weathered skin. Shirts and shoes were optional, which made spotting a man in a dark gray shirt and red hat that much easier. He stood with several fishing poles to his left, propped between a wood stand and the pier railing. His elbows rested on the railing with his head turned out to sea, oblivious—so it would seem—to his surroundings.

Jake gave Rachel's hand a squeeze and, walking on her right, approached the man. He imitated his stance on the railing, leaving four feet—and the fishing poles—between them.

"Evening," the man said with a quick turn of his head. Then he looked back out to sea.

"Evening," Jake said. It was not the man from the night before at the pool house. It was not a man he had ever seen.

The man continued looking at the ocean. Jake assumed it was all part of the cover, and put his arm around Rachel.

"You fish?" the man asked again after a minute or two of silence.

Jake hesitated, wondering if there was some sort of coded response he should give. If so, he had no idea what it would be. He opted for the truth. "Now and again, yeah."

"Mind these poles for me, will ya? I gotta take a leak."

"Okay, sure," Jake said, doing his best to commit the man's features to memory, in case he was asked later. They were pretty ordinary. Dark eyes, slightly crooked nose. A few days' worth of beard, same color as the brown hair peeking out from under the hat—an Anheuser-Busch cap. The shirt bore the logo of a local bait shop.

"I suspect you'll get a bite on the pole nearest you in about five minutes," he said quietly as he turned. Without another word, he began walking down the pier.

Jake followed him with his eyes for a moment, then looked at Rachel. Her eyes flashed with questions her mouth didn't ask. At first. Then, after looking from Jake to the man walking down the pier to the pole, back to the man, and to Jake again, she said, "You don't suppose . . ."

"That or in the bucket of bait over here."

"Jake, if we have to gut a fish to get at this 'prize.'"

"You've gutted fish before."

"I've also thrown up eleven times in a day from the flu. It doesn't mean I'm willing to do it again. Sort of like your 'experiences' comment last night."

"Point taken. One minute down?"

"You've got the fancy watch."

He concluded it had been one minute as he checked his watch, figuring he might as well start keeping time, in case five minutes meant five minutes and not in a little while. Then he leaned on the railing again, trying to play it cool. Rachel stood beside him, facing him, so she could easily look back at the pier without seeming to be looking for anyone in particular.

"See anything?"

"I see a lot," she answered.

"See the man in gray?"

"Far end of the pier."

"Think he's leaving?"

"Looks that way."

"Any chance he's just a fisherman who has to pee, and we somehow got the wrong guy?"

"The way this week has gone, there's a chance of anything."

"See Holmes?"

"Nope," she said after scanning the pier and the beach. "Nor do I see a gray Accent in the parking lot, but I can't see much of it from here."

"If Butler doesn't show, we take whatever this is, pawn it, and get an appetizer with every meal from now on."

"Woo, living large."

"Two and a half minutes."

They spent them in silence until Jake began to count down the final thirty seconds, five at a time. At ten, Rachel said this wasn't an atomic clock, and since he'd been winging it the first minute, he could probably just go ahead and haul in their catch. With a sheepish smile, he lifted the pole and began reeling in the line, feeling a little tension in it.

"See anything?" he asked as Rachel peeked over the railing.

"Um . . . yeah. A black bag."

"Like a garbage bag?"

"Smaller."

He kept reeling until the bag was level with the pier deck. It was the size of a small gift bag but made of the same material as a garbage bag. Jake reeled in the remainder of the line and set the pole down, reaching out to unhook the bag, which had been tied to the end of the line with more string.

"Do we open it?" Rachel asked.

"This is just the waterproof container," Jake said. He spent a moment attempting to untie the string, then tore open the bag. Half a dozen ball bearings tumbled out, bouncing off the pier deck and into the water.

"Smooth."

He cast her a quick glance before peeling back the torn bag to reveal a small pouch about six inches in length and maybe two around. It was pliable as if filled with putty. Jake met Rachel's eyes again, then dropped the object into his shorts side pocket, snapping the button on the pocket flap to make sure the pouch didn't slip out. Then he looked around. No sign of the man in gray or of anyone paying them any attention. A teenage boy used a stainless steel sink mounted to the pier railing to rinse off his catch, a couple of young lovers stared back toward the evening sun, and a few fishermen watched their bobbers and lures in the water.

"Okay," Jake said. "Let's get out of here."

With the pouch jostling in his pocket and brushing against his leg with each stride, he and Rachel headed back toward the building at the end of the pier. A few clouds speckled the sky, including one that momentarily blocked the low-hanging sun. It was a beautiful evening, and Jake was eager to be rid of the pouch and the responsibility it bore and enjoy the next week in Myrtle Beach with his wife.

They reentered the gift shop and quickly made their way through the people milling inside. As they reached the double glass doors leading back outside, Jake's eyes were already looking for Butler's car. He spotted the gray Hyundai Accent the agent had promised to be driving idling at the near end of the parking lot, and turned toward the enclosed stairway, one step ahead of Rachel.

Then she screamed.

Rachel was used to Jake opening doors for her and gently placing his hand on the small of her back to guide her through automatic doors. It was something he'd done since their first date and had never quit, one of those little chivalrous, outdated but still nice gestures. The only exception was when he sensed danger or uncertainty of some sort, so it made sense when he exited the gift shop in front of her.

She was about to ask if he saw Butler's car when a whiff of cigarette smoke infiltrated her nose. Almost instinctively, she turned toward the smell to identify its origin and spotted a woman dressed in a pink halter top and white shorts. Her hair was pinned behind her head, leaving an open view of her face. It was Tory, Rachel's double, the woman Butler and Holmes had identified as Victoria Masters.

Rachel tried to call Jake's name, but it came out as more of a scream. He stopped suddenly and turned her way. At the same time, Rachel saw movement from the stairwell. It was a man, charging at them out of the darkness. Rachel began to turn back toward Tory, prepared to face a more equal match and leave the man for Jake.

But before she could, Jake's arm pressed her back into the doorway. In the same motion, he grabbed the plastic smoker's receptacle beside the door. Taking hold of its thin, upstanding top, he hefted it into the air. He moved fluidly, like a trained action hero in a choreographed scene, holding the top with both hands and swinging the stubby base in a wide arc toward the charging man—likely Dane Paul. A routine pop-fly hitter in his few years of beer league softball, Jake didn't swing off his back foot this time. He stepped forward, putting some weight behind a perfectly timed swing. The base of the receptacle crunched into the surprised man's face.

He staggered back with the force of the blow and into the wall. A plastic container full of cigarette butts wasn't exactly a ball-and-chain flail, but on impact, the base had cracked, releasing the butts like candy from a piñata. The man closed his eyes, but not in time to keep the ashes from penetrating them. He slid down the wall and immediately slapped his hands to his face.

It all happened in a few seconds. As the man slumped to the floor, Rachel turned and lashed out at Masters with her right foot in a simple push kick. It was far from textbook, but it grazed Masters as she charged forward, deflecting her slightly, taking away her momentum, and leaving her vulnerable.

Rachel was off balance, but Jake had turned his attention her way, and he swung the receptacle back. It was little more than a plastic stub, and Masters ducked it and plowed her shoulder toward Jake, driving him back into the wall. Rachel abandoned all fighting tactics she'd learned in self-defense class or observed over the years. She reached for the back of Masters' head, digging her fingers into the clump of hair pinned behind it. She pulled back with a grunt, at the same time raising her knee and driving it into the small of Masters' back as she dragged her away from Jake.

Masters gasped in pain as Jake pushed off from the wall. He charged under Masters' legs and flipped her up, heels-over-head and over a ducking Rachel. Masters tumbled upside down into the railing, her knees cracking against the wood just before her head thudded to the deck.

The immediate threat neutralized, Rachel's first impulse was to rush back inside, for help. But Jake took her hand and, without asking if she was all right, pulled her to the staircase. She glanced over her shoulder and saw

Masters crumpled in a ball—dead, unconscious, or just in pain. To Rachel's left, the man was on hands and knees. Technically, elbows and knees, his hands still over his eyes, prohibiting her from identifying him. But it had to be Paul, Masters' known associate. Cigarette butts and ashes were spread around him, almost concealing the blade of a knife he had dropped.

Jake let go of Rachel's hands at the top of the steps and took them two at a time. She followed one at a time but just as quickly and hit the ground running after him toward Butler's car. Rachel chanced one look back up at the deck. Masters was crawling like a boxer trying to get his bearings during a mandatory eight count.

Reaching the rear door of the car first, Jake opened it for Rachel, who practically dove in. Jake followed right on her tail. He pulled himself forward using the rear of the passenger seat. "Let's go. Mast—"

Rachel turned to see why he had stopped mid-sentence.

"Butler?" Jake asked, leaning farther forward to peek into the front seat. He shook the FBI agent's shoulder and called his name again.

Instead of responding, Agent Butler slumped over, falling across the center console and into the passenger seat.

It was then that Rachel saw the gaping knife wound in his neck and the fresh blood staining his shirt.

Chapter Twenty-Six

Rachel was not a screamer, but for the second time in as many minutes, she did just that. Jake couldn't blame her. Hunting with his brothers and his dad back in the day, he'd seen his share of blood and guts, but this was different. He didn't have time, however, to be sick about it.

"Out," he said, pointing at Rachel's door. "Get out."

To her credit, she responded quickly, throwing open the door and exiting the car.

"Jake, they . . . they killed him."

"Yeah." He looked around the parking lot for signs of anyone watching them. Or for Holmes.

"Paul had a . . . a kn-knife. That was them, wasn't it? Paul and Masters?"

"I think so." He reached into his pocket and pulled out his phone, swiveling his head from side to side again. "You see Holmes?"

"Holmes?" She turned her head. "No."

Jake looked up toward the entrance to the gift shop and restaurants, where Masters had staggered to her feet, hunched over the railing, still dazed. Paul was out of sight. If their fight had attracted the attention of anyone inside, they weren't rushing to help. Nobody in the parking lot or on the Boardwalk seemed to have noticed either.

"Come on," Jake said, taking Rachel's arm with his free hand. "Let's go."

"Where?"

"Away from here. Are you okay?"

"Yeah."

"Forget what you saw, Rach. For now, forget it."

She nodded.

"I'm going to call Holm—"

A black BMW turned into the parking lot, and for some reason, his eyes were drawn to it.

"Jake?"

He looked down and finished dialing, then watched the BMW, at the same time pulling Rachel with him, toward the front of Butler's car. "This way," he said.

Jake shot another glance up toward Masters as Holmes' phone rang.

The BMW drew closer and swung into a parking space about fifty or sixty feet away as the phone rang for the second time.

He stopped, waiting as the doors of the BMW opened.

A third ring.

"This is FBI Special Agent Holmes. I can't take your call ri—"

A dark-haired female emerged from the passenger side of the BMW. Gabrielle Frost. Jake disconnected the call and dropped his phone into his pocket as Liam Jamison's head peeked over the roof.

"Rach, come on!" he shouted, pulling her with him. He flung a quick glance at the deck outside the gift shop. Masters was out of sight.

Letting go of Rachel's hand, Jake led her across an empty lawn, past some stubby palms and a wood-chipped flowerbed. The Boardwalk—here technically a concrete promenade—curved gently so that they intersected it almost on a straight line, in the process looping around a woman on rollerblades.

Jake had gone running with Rachel a number of times, and if anything, she outpaced him. But that was technically jogging, not a full sprint. Jake wasn't sure how fast she was in a dead heat, nor how long he could run full speed. Jason Bourne had said he could do half a mile at altitude, but maybe he'd just been trying to impress that gypsy chick—and Jake was no Jason Bourne. At any rate, he checked over his shoulder every few seconds to make sure Rachel was with him—she was—and to check on pursuers. He saw Frost, but not Jamison, Paul, or Masters.

They had been dressed like him and Rachel. He'd worn a blue shirt. She'd worn a pink top. Coincidence? Or did they somehow know? And if so, why had it mattered?

The promenade continued to meander north. Dunes covered by tufts of seagrass and interspersed with more stubby palms lined the promenade to the right, as far as the eye could see. A slat-wood fence topped the dunes, barring access to the beach except by way of intermittent wood footbridges. On the left, grassy open spaces separated the promenade from low, boxlike hotels and condos. More palms and landscaped flowerbeds created an aesthetic flow to the promenade, which was lined with benches and unlit—as of yet—lampposts.

Jake took it all in as they ran. He was also conscious of the pouch in his pocket, the pouch containing an unknown item that had caused all this mayhem. Butler was dead because of it. Holmes wasn't answering her phone. Paul and Masters—a "hitter" and a "criminal-for-hire"—had followed Jake and Rachel to the exchange and attacked them. Jake thought about dropping the pouch along the path and being done with it all.

Rachel's heavy breathing a pace behind matched his own, and their mad sprint probably drew some odd looks from people on chaise lounges and lawn chairs in front of a condo a hundred or so feet to their left.

Up ahead, the promenade widened under a series of triangular blue and yellow tarps stretched between white poles. Benches and garbage cans were placed at corners of the intersection between the promenade and a path leading to 3rd Avenue on the left and a wide bridge to the beach on the right. Jake looked back, saw Frost maybe twenty-five yards behind, and decided to push on. In the instant he swept his eyes across Rachel's face, he saw flushed cheeks but the same determination in her eyes as was in him.

A group of twelve to fifteen teenagers reached the intersection from the beach just before Jake and Rachel. They were decked in swimwear, shorts, T-shirts, odd caps, and towels. They were laughing and flirting and talking over one another, a few of them walking backward. A few more looked over their shoulders to talk to others. All of them seemed oblivious to anyone else.

Glancing again to see that Rachel was with him, Jake ducked around the first few teens, cutting like a skier around a slalom pole. He heard a couple shouts from the group and shot a quick look back to see that they had largely blocked the path. It would slow Frost momentarily, and he focused his attention on pushing his body to gain every ounce of speed.

Rachel knew that under normal circumstances she could "run" all the way back to their condo, twenty-some-odd blocks north. But having just taken possession of a black market auction prize, fought two thugs, and seen a dead FBI agent, her adrenaline was pumping and throwing her system out of whack. She also wasn't a sprinter and didn't know how long she could hold their current pace.

As long as Jake could, she resolved, training her eyes between his shoulder blades and concentrating on putting one foot in front of the other. Jake kept glancing back, and she tried to send the message with her eyes that she was with him. Then again, maybe he was checking for pursuers. She'd learned running track in high school never to look back, as it only slowed you down.

They passed a few other "runners" going half their pace. Then, suddenly, Jake slowed.

He came almost to a stop and turned onto a footbridge to the beach. Rachel saw nothing ahead to cause him to take the detour but trusted he knew what he was doing.

The bridge was up a few steps, and maybe twenty feet long. It did not take them directly to the beach, but rather to a rutted sand path that bisected the seagrass as it ran parallel to the promenade. A much thinner path continued from the footbridge across it to the beach. Rachel followed Jake onto the beach, glancing right once, looking for signs of pursuit. She saw none. Maybe they'd lost them.

When he reached the beach, Jake slowed and took her hand. They half walked, half jogged north. The sun still bathed the sand in warm light, and more than a handful of people were soaking up its last rays on the shore and in the ocean.

"Take off your shirt," Jake said, looking back over his shoulder a few times.

"What?"

"We need to blend in," he said. Having dropped her hand, he was finagling out of his shirt.

Rachel reached for the hem of her tank top. Before leaving the condo, Jake had advised her to wear her swimsuit under her clothes, just in case the exchange went sideways and they had to bail off the end of the pier. He'd been mostly joking, but serious enough that Rachel had donned her black bikini top in place of a bra. Now, as she pulled her tank top over her head, she was glad for Jake's precaution.

"Here," he said, taking her shirt. He balled it up and wedged it into his shorts pocket. "Undo your hair too," he said, looking back again. They continued to walk north, cutting over to the broadest section of beach, in front of a few sunbathers and umbrellas near the "top" of the beach. Rachel quickened her pace, feeling odd about her outfit of a bikini, jean shorts, and running shoes—and about wearing said shoes on the beach. But this wasn't the time to be embarrassed by her apparel. So she plodded through the sand, at the same time pulling out the band binding her hair into a ponytail.

Jake reached for her hand and slowed to a casual walk. "We'll try to blend in, act natural."

Rachel nodded, her heart pounding, her breath coming in gasps.

"Frost wasn't far behind us," Jake said, looking over his shoulder again.

"Did she see us cut over?"

"She got lost in those kids. I don't think so."

"Jamison? Paul and Masters?"

"I think he ducked back into the car, probably to cut us off. It's why I got off the path."

She nodded and chanced a look back herself.

"Masters was gone last I looked," Jake said. "Probably in the stairwell."

"Chasing us."

"Yeah."

Rachel used a few steps to catch her breath. They were even with another footbridge, this one leading to 4th Avenue. She saw no signs of anyone chasing them.

"How does this end, Jake?"

"I don't know. We find a safe spot to hide out for a while and think. One step at a time."

Rachel nodded her assent and looked back again. The dunes and seagrass created enough of a wall that someone on the promenade would have trouble spotting—much less identifying—people on the beach. But if Frost had seen them jog over . . .

A four-wheeler zipped south on the rutted path between the beach and the promenade. Rachel grabbed Jake's arm.

"What is it?"

"Did you see that four-wheeler?"

"Yeah. It went north a minute ago."

She looked back. "I think . . . I think it was Flynn."

"The guy who passed me the PADL?"

"Yeah. Jake, he's turning toward the beach."

Jake whipped his head back, then around. "Into the water."

"What?"

"We'll be harder to spot in the water," he said, pulling her toward where the waves were rolling onshore.

Rachel briefly debated taking off her shoes, but figured leaving them on the beach would be a giveaway if Flynn or Frost spotted them. She didn't have time to decide because Jake was already plowing into the waves. There were eight or ten other people in the water in the general vicinity, wading only to their knees, boogie boarding, or riding the waves at their breaking point. Rachel and Jake plunged forward until their torsos were submerged so that, to someone on shore, they looked no different than anyone else in the water.

"They're looking for blue and pink shirts," Jake said. "Not your hot bod and my ripped abs."

Rachel managed to grin at his effort at humor, at the same time looking back to see the four-wheeler trolling north, now on the actual beach. The driver wore a black T-shirt and gray pants. Even with dark sunglasses blocking his eyes, Rachel was sure he was the man from the security footage Vaughn and Holmes had shown them.

Jake nodded confirmation as she looked at him. Then he wrapped his arms around her and kissed her.

"Jake, what are—"

"It will look a little weird just standing here facing away from the beach. So we'll be the amorous couple kissing in the waves."

"I'm really not in the mood right now."

"Just pretend then," he said, sliding his arms over her back.

Rachel bounced with an incoming wave, then reached up and kissed Jake for his bravery. She leaned her head against his chest, using him as a barrier against another wave. Then she raised her head.

"Jake!"

"What is it?"

"He stopped," she said, looking at the four-wheeler. It had parked, facing south now, and the driver had dismounted.

Jake pulled her into another kiss, which she withdrew from, cutting her eyes back toward land. Flynn stood with hands on hips, surveying the people in the water. Rachel's inclination was to turn away or dive under the water, but she feared that would draw his attention. She felt Jake's eyes focused on her, but couldn't keep from turning hers back toward Flynn.

As she did, she saw him raise his sunglasses up on his head as if he'd locked in. He suddenly charged into the water, and Rachel gripped Jake tighter. Flynn was clearly coming directly at them.

Jake stood straight, turned to face Flynn, subtly slipping his body in front of Rachel's. But he didn't fully block her view. Peering around his shoulder, she saw Flynn reach for his waist and unholster a pistol.

Chapter Twenty-Seven

Jake knew as Flynn reached for his waist that he was going for a gun. Instead of moving farther in front of Rachel, Jake took a half step to the right. As Flynn removed an elongated pistol from its holster, Jake shoved Rachel as hard as he could to his and her left, hoping she would fall beneath the waves and out of sight. Then he dove backward, away from Flynn, who had entered the water almost to his knees.

Just before submerging, Jake heard a thwip-thwip as two bullets shot through a silencer. He felt no pain and assumed they missed.

A wave had crested just as Jake dove into the water, and he found himself underwater and thus out of sight of Flynn. He wanted to stay there, move as far from his original spot as possible before coming up for air. But he wasn't sure Rachel had made it all the way under and feared Flynn might hone in on her. So he rode the next wave and popped to the surface as it crested.

Flynn had taken several steps farther into the water, toward where Jake saw Rachel's arm poking above the surface. Somewhere in the distance, he heard a scream, likely another swimmer or person on the beach who had seen what happened. He hoped they called the cops. But he didn't have time to think about it because Flynn was taking aim toward where Rachel was floundering and had just stuck her head above the surface.

"Hey!" Jake yelled, and Flynn swiveled his aim.

Jake again dove underwater, this time at a forty-five-degree angle toward Flynn and toward shore. Hoping—praying!—that Rachel ducked down again, he swam with the incoming waves. He hoped the froth and foam would keep him hidden until he reached Flynn. But his lungs gave out, and he had to come up for air.

He was in thigh-deep water, some twenty feet almost directly to Flynn's left. Flynn had moved to his right and a little farther into the water, toward Rachel. Now, he swung his gun back toward Jake. A wave rocked him and threw off his aim, and his bullets sailed harmlessly into the shallow water.

Not seeing Rachel, Jake submerged again, stroking in a roundabout way toward Flynn. The roiling of waves crashing against the beach made it hard to see as he half swam, half crawled on the seabed. He spotted a gray form, took a chance, and drove his shoulder into what he hoped was Flynn's leg. He felt initial resistance before it gave way. Jake surged up out of the water, lifting the leg with him. He broke the surface and felt Flynn's weight on his shoulder and back. He rotated his upper body, trying to drive what momentum he had left into the heart of Flynn's body mass. But they were both off balance, out of control, and soon plunged back beneath the waves in a jumble of arms and legs.

Their fall coincided with a wave. Uprooted, they were both carried with it toward shore. Jake scrambled to his feet as soon as possible and turned to look for Flynn and Rachel. He saw a blur coming his way and ducked just as Flynn's arm crashed down on his head. He no longer held the gun but seemed poised to murder Jake with his fists.

The blow only grazed Jake, but it still knocked him backward. Off balance, he fell beneath the surface again. He tried to get up but found a weight pressing him down, then hands around his neck.

Jake jerked and wiggled, trying to get free. But Flynn's hands were like a vise, choking the life out of him. He flailed his arms, trying to swing a punch, but underwater, he could get no force behind the blows.

Through the shallow water, Jake saw another blur, this one of tan and black. He felt the hands release, and the pressure on his neck was gone. He sat up, hacking and spluttering and drawing in air. Rachel had come flying out of nowhere and plowed into Flynn, knocking him back into shallower water. She rolled to her side beside him, instinctively reaching for her shoulder.

Still gasping for breath, Jake realized Flynn would get up sooner than Rachel. He willed himself to his feet and charged, tackling Flynn into the mucky sand created by a receding wave and pressing his face into it. An elbow reared back and missed its mark, but Flynn managed to wriggle enough to generate the body leverage to roll Jake to the side. A second elbow missed, but Flynn's forearm connected with Jake's face and knocked him onto his back just as a wave sloshed over them.

Rachel attacked a second time, something between a roar and a growl escaping her mouth as she plowed all of her one hundred forty-five pounds into Flynn, leading with her shoulder and aiming for his head. She missed, connecting instead with his shoulder, and bellowed a second cry of pain as they both tumbled backward.

Again Jake got to his feet, slogging through knee-deep water. Rachel's blow had rocked Flynn as well, and Jake straddled him as he got on hands and knees. Looping his right arm under Flynn's neck, he pulled back, locking Flynn's head into the crook of his elbow, then clamping his right hand on his left arm. It was a basic sleeper hold his brother had shown him after four years in the Army. Shown him by demonstration, so Jake knew it worked.

He fell backward, using his momentum to carry Flynn with him. They landed with a thud in the soft sand and silt, thrashing as a wave washed over them. Flynn had more experience than Jake and used his left hand to reach for Jake's face and eyes while driving his right elbow into Jake's stomach.

Jake pinched his eyes shut as tightly as possible and willed his abdominal muscles to hold. He felt his grip slipping and risked opening his eyes to what was happening. He was just in time to see Rachel, her shoulder noticeably lagging, try to wrap her arms around Flynn's shod feet, which were kicking at Jake's kneecaps. Flynn fought her off with a kick to the side of the head that sent her flying.

Fueled by visceral rage, Jake squeezed Flynn's neck with everything he had, willing his bare arms to be a garroting wire. Flynn continued to struggle, but Jake's hold was strong. Rachel returned, this time coming around from the side. With Flynn's hands occupied attacking Jake, they weren't prepared for Rachel, who dropped all her weight down toward Flynn's groin, using her knee as a point of contact.

Flynn's head jerked up in reaction, and a groan tried to come out of his mouth. It didn't make it, and his upward motion only increased the tightness of

Jake's grip on his neck. With a growl of his own, he pulled him back, his muscles throbbing as he felt Flynn's body go limp in his arms.

He released him and rolled to the side. Flynn lay half in the water, half out, at least until the next wave came. Jake didn't give him a chance to recover. Despite being out of breath, with his stomach aching and his muscles burning, he lifted Flynn by his shirt and drilled him in the cheek. He swung again, and again, savage fury coming out at the man who had injured his wife.

"Jake!"

He reared back to swing again.

"Jake!" Rachel called, looping her arm in his before he could punch. "Let him go. Let him go, he's out."

Jake's breaths came in huge heaves as the adrenaline and rage washed out of him. He released his grip on Flynn's shirt and dropped the unconscious, bleeding man. He looked around. Their entire fight had lasted maybe two minutes, but that was time for the others in the water and most everyone on the beach to gather. Shocked, scared, unsure of whose side to take, they did little more than watch.

His wits quickly coming back to him, Jake decided to use them to his advantage.

"Somebody, call the cops!" he said. "This guy just tried to kill me and my wife. He was shouting '*Allahu Akbar.*'"

He didn't care if there were those in the crowd who could verify that wasn't the case. He just wanted to get most of them excited. And it worked. He took Rachel's hand and pulled her up onto dry ground. At the same time as his eyes roved the beach for signs of their other pursuers, his hand felt his pocket. The pouch was still there, even though the pocket had come unsnapped.

"Come on," he said, pulling Rachel's hand. She had a small cut high on her cheek, washed clean by the saltwater but starting to ooze a trickle of blood again. His arms and abdominal muscles ached like he'd spent an hour in the gym toning them. But it didn't matter.

Several voices in the crowd asked questions. Jake only heard bits and pieces.

"—for the cops?"

"Who was that—"

"Are you hurt?"

"—terrorist?"

"—your names?"

Jake didn't spot Frost—she'd been wearing a white shirt and dark shorts—in the crowd, but he knew it would only be a matter of time before she and the others were drawn there. He and Rachel had to get away. Maybe inside one of the condos, or to the street where they could find a taxi . . .

"Jake, are you okay?" Rachel asked as they stepped higher up onto the beach.

"Yeah, fine. Are you?"

"You're bleeding."

"Where?" He looked around.

"Your side."

He turned his eyes down and saw a small gash at the bottom of his ribcage. Had one of Flynn's bullets winged him? Maybe something underwater during their tussle? Either way, it wasn't too deep, and he hadn't felt it until she mentioned it.

"It's fine. Your shoulder?"

"I'll live."

"That's the idea, anyhow." He looked up and down the beach. A blur of pink caught his eye. Then blue. Masters and Paul, just joining the crowd, which had started to disperse and spread out.

"Come on," he said, grabbing for Rachel's hand again. He missed, but she joined him as they dashed up the beach, headed for a path between the dunes. He spotted green to his right and turned his head. The four-wheeler.

He diverted course and pounded through the sand for it. "Hop on!" he called over his shoulder to Rachel. He straddled the seat, turned the key, and pushed the starter button. Paul and Masters had to have seen them, but he didn't waste a look in their direction.

He felt the engine grumble to life as Rachel wrapped her arms around him. He twisted the grip on the handlebar, and the four-wheeler took off with a jolt. Rachel screamed in his ear, and he picked up a blur of movement to his side. Blue. Paul, running alongside them. Jake coaxed a little more speed out of the four-wheeler, swerving into the dunes as he did. Seagrass whipped against his legs, and they bounced over a rut that threatened to throw them both. They held on, and Jake quickly outdistanced Paul on foot.

Just ahead, a tan box that stored public umbrellas and beach chairs marked the path to the promenade. Jake slowed and hollered for Rachel to hang on. He leaned into the turn, Rachel's arms squeezing his already sore midsection. He grimaced through it and made another immediate turn, back north onto the sandy path between the beach and promenade.

Paul had seen the maneuver and darted across the dunes. He came up short. Masters took a better angle, and Jake heard Rachel in his ear again. Masters was lining up a shot, it appeared to make a flying tackle and take them off the four-wheeler. It was a daring move, and Jake countered with one of his own.

Knowing Rachel held tightly to him, he veered into the dunes, directly at Masters. Instead of being able to size up a leap, she had to dive out of his way, sprawling into the tall grass.

Twice more, Jake and Rachel were nearly bounced off the seat, but they held on as he swerved back to the path. Waiting for a gunshot that never came, he straightened out and accelerated again. Chancing a look back, he saw both Paul and Masters headed for the street. Giving up? More likely going to their car, planning to catch up to them farther ahead.

The path was designed for emergency and maintenance vehicles, and Jake prayed for one to show up. Instead, as they zipped past the 5th Avenue access point, all he saw were stunned onlookers on the promenade and beach. Even in Myrtle Beach, it couldn't be often that two drenched, shirtless people plowed full speed along the beach on a four-wheeler.

Halfway between 5th and 6th Avenues, Jake had to bring the four-wheeler almost to a stop as a trio of graying women trekked back from the beach across his path. They regarded him and Rachel with bemusement before continuing to a footbridge to the promenade. As soon as they were out of the way, Jake cranked the throttle, and they shot forward again.

With nothing to concentrate on but driving the four-wheeler, Jake's other senses were open. He smelled the coppery scent of blood in his nose, likely a result of Flynn's blows to the face. Rachel hadn't mentioned it was bleeding, and it didn't hurt, so he doubted it was broken. He felt her grip on him, her body pressed tightly to his to absorb shock. He also felt wet socks and sneakers, and the pouch resting on his thigh, like a glowing orb from a Spielberg production that had come to life in his pocket.

Rachel said something indistinguishable in his ear, then one arm loosened and she pointed toward the beach. Jamison and Frost, facing south, had stopped and watched them zip by. As Rachel locked her arms around him again, he glanced over his shoulder. The two thieves turned and started running.

Jake and Rachel passed the path to the beach at the end of 6th Avenue and raced onward. He tried to remember from looking at a satellite photo of the northern end of the Boardwalk and Promenade what become of this path. Did it continue all the way to the 14th Avenue Pier? Should he cut over to the beach? Cut to the street?

His choice was made for him just past a footbridge leading to the promenade. Up ahead, at 7th Avenue, a silver Nissan had utilized vehicular access to the beach to cross the dunes. It turned onto the path and took aim for Jake and Rachel.

Chapter Twenty-Eight

"Jake!" Rachel screamed.

"I see it."

He stopped. The Nissan didn't, barreling down the path in a cloud of dust.

"Get off," Jake said.

"Jake!" she yelled, fearing he intended to do something heroic and leave her behind.

"Get off!"

She loosened her grip and slid off the four-wheeler. Jake, meanwhile, straightened the handlebars. Then he twisted the throttle, at the same time leaping from the four-wheeler. It shot forward toward the oncoming car as he tumbled into the seagrass.

Rachel watched as the four-wheeler and the Nissan continued on a collision course. Jake had timed things perfectly, waiting until the Nissan was close enough that it couldn't stop in time. Realizing what was happening, the driver slammed on his brakes. But the four-wheeler had enough momentum and was jolted around little enough that it plowed into the grill of the car with a crunch. Rachel saw airbags deploy, just before Jake appeared at her side and took her arm.

They beat a quick retreat twenty-five paces back to the footbridge that crossed over to the promenade. Rachel looked back and saw Jamison and Frost pounding down the dirt path, maybe a hundred feet from the footbridge. She tried to utter their names to warn Jake, but she was out of breath.

Once on the promenade, Jake turned back north. Rachel pushed her body to the limit to match his stride, but the fight in the water had sucked her energy, and the short ride on the four-wheeler hadn't been sufficient for it to replenish. Not to mention she was running in wet socks and shoes.

As they passed the crashed four-wheeler and Nissan, Rachel looked over and saw both Paul and Masters struggling to extricate themselves from the airbags. They must not have guns, Rachel concluded. Else they'd have used them. That was something, at least. But they did have—or had had at one point—a knife. And a knife fight terrified Rachel more than anything. It was so close and . . . violent. Even on TV, she could watch shootouts with no qualms. But knife fights caused her to tense up and dig her feet into the arms of the couch or Jake's legs.

They had caught the breaks so far and did again as they approached 7th Avenue. A pickup truck with a trailer was backing up toward the beach, Jet Skis on the trailer and empty kayak racks in the bed of the pickup. Jake and Rachel darted past it while the driver adjusted the wheels of the pickup. He then continued backing, blocking the promenade. A cloud of fire, so to speak.

The promenade continued to curve through seagrass, palms, and woodchip-lined flowerbeds. From their left, the sound of live oldies music wafted from the Hammerhead Grill, where outdoor patio tables were full of customers soaking up good food, cheap beer, the music, and the atmosphere. Few even glanced at the bare-chested man and bikini-clad woman running full speed along the promenade.

An old man with a dog did, hollering a "Watch it!" as they weaved past him. The dog added a bark.

"Jake . . . I'm dyin'," Rachel managed.

He slowed, his breaths coming in huge gulps as well. Just beyond the restaurant was a small strip mall with a deck overlooking the promenade and the beach. Shortly ahead of them, the promenade gave way to a plank-lined boardwalk. The next street, 8th Avenue, also marked the beginning of a block-long open, undeveloped area.

"In here," Jake panted, and he turned onto a path leading up to the deck. Rachel's eyes swept over the signs above the glass doorways: an internet café, a frozen yogurt shop, a beachwear store, and a pizzeria. Jake honed in on the beachwear store, and Rachel followed with a look back. She didn't spot any of their pursuers. Or rather, didn't see Masters' pink shirt, Paul's blue shirt, Frost's white shirt, or Jamison's navy shirt. She didn't have time to detect much more than that before they were inside.

Loud pop music blasted from overhead speakers, and air conditioning quickly cooled Rachel's exposed skin. It had mostly dried, but her top and shorts were still wet. Her hair hung in clumps, a tangled, knotted mess, no doubt, and she tucked it behind her ears in an attempt at civility.

The shop was dark, and her eyes widened to take it in. An abundance of clothes—mostly T-shirts, mostly with crass puns and slogans—lined the walls to the ceiling. Racks offered sale items and deals, everything from more T-shirts to swimwear to dresses to flip-flops.

"Hey, guys, no shirts, no service."

Rachel turned to see a young man, his beard a scruffy, fuzzy mess, his blond dreadlocks knotted in a bun behind his head. He had several piercings on his face, and his head bobbed to the music—LL Cool J, Rachel was pretty sure—even as he spoke.

"Really?" Jake asked. "On the beach?"

The guy shrugged.

"Tell you what," Jake said. "Let the dress code slide, we'll give you fifty bucks for two T-shirts."

"They're only nine ninety—"

"The rest is a tip, for you accommodating us."

The guy looked at them. "You guys fall off a boat or something?"

"Something like that," Jake said as he reached for his wallet. Fortunately, it had not fallen out during the fight in the surf. His and Rachel's shirts, apparently, had.

The guy shifted his eyes from Jake to Rachel, who hoped the small cut she felt on her cheek wasn't bleeding noticeably.

Jake extended three soggy bills to the man. "Make it sixty."

"They're wet."

"They'll dry and be just as good."

The guy hesitated. The seconds felt like minutes. It took all of Rachel's nerves not to look over her shoulder to see if anyone had followed them into the store.

LL Cool J gave way to Nicki Minaj.

"Okay, sure. Why not, right?"

Jake dipped his head in agreement as he slapped the three bills on the counter. "Thanks." He grabbed two shirts off the rack and tossed one to Rachel. She smiled at the man before following Jake toward the door, which opened to the sidewalk beside Ocean Boulevard.

Sun blinded her for a moment, hanging just above the building across the street. It was a scooter rental store, which caught her attention.

"Quick, put that on," Jake said.

She slipped into her T-shirt, pulling her wet hair out the back. The shirt was a deep berry color—almost sangria, her brain noted—with the logo from the South Carolina state flag—a crescent moon over a palm tree—stamped on the front. It was actually kind of nice. Jake's was black and depicted Bob Marley smoking a bong while wearing a red, green, and yellow rastacap.

Rachel was about to mention the scooter rental when Jake nudged her elbow. There was a brief break in traffic, and they jaywalked across the four lanes of Ocean Boulevard. Jake didn't hesitate, turning north, past store display windows full of beach towels, boogie boards, and a sign advertising free hermit crabs. The store was on the corner of 8th and Ocean, with its main doors angled to face the corner. Briefly surveilling the street, Jake turned the corner and ducked inside.

"Hey, folks, where you from?" a black man behind a small counter asked. The counter and the wall behind him were plastered with brochures. Rachel and Jake had encountered such booths a few times already, with hawkers promising them huge discounts—if not outright free deals—on everything from restaurants to shows if they would sacrifice a few hours to come to a presentation.

Jake ignored him and turned down the second aisle, past a cage containing painted hermit crabs. Rachel followed, looking over racks of women's clothing for signs of pursuers. The windows were mostly blocked by merchandise and advertising, and it was a fool's errand.

"What's the plan?" she asked as Jake continued to the back of the store.

"I'm hoping they didn't see us enter the beach store," Jake said. "They definitely don't know we've switched clothes."

"So we hide in plain sight?"

"Yeah. Give them time to pursue us further north."

"Can we call the police? Or Holmes again?"

"She didn't pick up when I tried before," Jake said, tugging on a sleeve of a shirt on a rack. "Our phones are probably waterlogged anyhow. Pretend we're shopping."

Rachel swallowed and tried to act natural. She picked through a few shirts on racks, her body on autopilot. She had so many questions and knew Jake didn't have answers. She asked anyhow.

"What happened, Jake? Masters and Paul were waiting to ambush us."

"I know. Either the FBI has a leak, or they've been tracking us some . . . how." He looked down at his watch. "Of course."

"What?"

"Masters. She didn't like my watch."

"What?"

"I knew something was off about her talking to me. I just couldn't figure out what."

"You think she bugged it somehow?"

"Probably." He took it off. "That's why the compass didn't work too. Their bug probably threw off the magnet."

"We need to move then. They can hone in on us."

"Only if their bug is waterproof." Shielding his hands from the checkout counter with his body, he fastened his watch around the end of a display rack. I'm going to go check the door."

"Aren't we leaving?"

"I don't want to expose ourselves unless we're sure they're tracking us. I'll look. You drift toward the west door, just in case. Act like you're browsing."

Rachel nodded.

"They have no idea that we aren't."

Not easily excitable herself, Rachel wasn't sure how Jake was keeping so calm. Then again, he was always easygoing. She'd just never witnessed him in a situation like this to know if that was really *always* true.

Rachel ambled through aisles containing all sorts of knickknacks and souvenirs: ceramic lighthouses, wooden pirate ships, bamboo chimes, water globes, polished-glass ashtrays and animal figurines, jewelry boxes, gel candles, and a host of toys and stuffed animals. She feigned interest, keeping her eyes on Jake, who was doing a pretty good job of "examining" boogie boards by the east windows. Rachel looked at shot glasses and coffee mugs emblazoned with Myrtle Beach slogans and artwork, seashells and starfish and sand dollars, ornaments, refrigerator magnets, and other tacky keepsakes. She felt the eyes of the storekeeper on her and tried to convince herself it was because her hair and shorts were wet and not because she was acting suspiciously.

Jake was coming her way, his face calm, his eyes sending no furtive message. Rachel drifted toward some T-shirts hanging on the wall, again feigning interest. Instead of just acting natural, she tried to concoct escape plans. Should they buy more T-shirts so they were prepared to change their appearance again? Should they use a phone to call the cops or a taxi or the National Guard? She asked herself, what would Sydney Bristow do? Her sister had tried to hook her on *Alias* back in the day, but it hadn't worked. It was all too far-fetched for Rachel. But just the thought of it now brought a smile to her face.

Jake met her at the back of the store. "All clear," he said.

"Now what?"

"We hang a little while longer. Then, assuming they've gone on, we double back."

"To where? How does this end, Jake?"

"We get a scooter, take it south to a dive motel, hide out for the night."

"They'll find us. Security cameras, desk clerks who talk."

He put his hand on her shoulders. "Calm down, Babe. We'll be okay. We just—"

"Jake?"

He leaned around her and peeked out the north windows of the store. Then he tugged her sleeve.

"Jake, what is it?"

He pulled her toward the door through which they had entered a few minutes ago.

She opened her mouth to question again, but then closed it when she saw the door in the northwest corner of the store open. Gabrielle Frost stepped through it, her eyes widening almost instantly as she recognized the Taylors.

Rachel felt her hand out for Jake's shoulder as she turned her head. Once again, they took off running.

Chapter Twenty-Nine

Jake and Rachel burst out of the store, past a surprised Jamison, and into the street. Fortunately, traffic on Ocean Boulevard was hung up at a red light, and they only had to navigate vehicles waiting to turn off 8th Avenue from the west and one hybrid exiting the parking lot that was east on 8th. Jake forced a south-turning car to slam on the brakes and had to sidestep the rear end of the westbound hybrid. Other than that, he and Rachel—who had stayed right with him—bound up onto the eastside sidewalk amid honking horns and startled gasps from onlookers. They ignored them and started sprinting.

Jake's lungs burned, but he forced himself on. He was the trailblazer, picking his way through crowds and around palm trees planted in the sidewalk. There was nothing but open grass to their right, or across the street to their left, meaning they had nowhere to hide. So he ran as fast as his aching muscles and organs would allow, and as fast as Rachel could keep up behind him. She never lost a step.

He thought about darting across the grass toward the Boardwalk a hundred feet away. But for all the hassle the pedestrians on the sidewalk caused, they balanced it out by hiding the Taylors from pursuers.

At the end of the lot, three sand volleyball courts were layed out side by side. Two of them were occupied, and it occurred to Jake to use them for cover. But if he and Rachel had lost Jamison and Frost, the last thing he wanted was surprised cries and shouts to attract their attention.

So he focused on the intersection of 9th and Ocean. The towering yellow and faux-brick wall of Ripley's Believe It or Not Odditorium dominated the northwest corner. The northeast was home to Peaches Corner, a café Jake remembered from browsing Rachel's guidebook. Beside it, along the north side of the pedestrian-only 9th Avenue, were a series of shops and restaurants. And continuing north on Ocean, the eateries and stores lined both sides of the street for several blocks.

Jake slowed at the corner, considering options, looking behind them. The light at 8th had turned shortly after they crossed the street, as evidenced by moving traffic, and Jake suspected they'd created some distance between themselves and Jamison and Frost. He certainly didn't see them.

"Babe," Rachel said, tugging his sleeve. He turned and followed her nod across the corner. Paul and Masters, recognizable more than anything by their now familiar shirts, stood under the overhang of Ripley's, beside a giant, granite ball floating on a thin sheen of water. They were elevated several feet above the sidewalk and were scanning in all directions for the Taylors.

"Here," Jake said, using a sudden pack of people headed north as cover. They crossed 9th and turned east, toward the ocean. "They don't know what we're wearing," he said as much to himself as Rachel.

"Back to the Boardwalk?" she asked.

"No, in here," Jake said. Halfway down the block, they veered toward a building with a logwood façade. Large white letters in Playbill font identified it as The Bowery. Famous for being the home of super group Alabama in the 1970s—and in current times for its fun, festive, Southern atmosphere featuring plenty of live music—The Bowery brought the 1940s honky-tonk back to life.

Jake and Rachel paused inside to let their eyes adjust to the darkness. Even before The Bounty Hunters—the house band—took the stage, the joint was hopping with country western music. Women in boots and short skirts or tank tops and shorts, and guys in cowboy hats and bolo ties or board shorts and flip-flops worked the dance floor, crowded tables, or lined the bar. Confederate flags, Alabama posters and memorabilia, beer signs, and random roadhouse knickknacks covered the walls.

A waitress in a black T-shirt told them to find their own seat, and they proceeded deeper into the bar.

"Looking for a table facing the door, I assume?" Rachel said.

"Actually, not thinking of staying."

"What?"

"If anyone saw us duck in here, I want them to spend some time looking."

"Where are we going?"

"Out the back."

He led the way deeper into the bar and spotted an LED exit sign above a door in the corner beyond some red-felt billiard tables. They had to duck around a pair of games to get to the door, but a moment later, they stepped out into an alley cast in shadow. That was in contrast to the sun-drenched brick wall of the building on the other side of the alley.

Jake looked back at Rachel as the door closed behind her. A delivery truck blocked the alley toward the street, so he turned right. They briskly walked past a dumpster and found themselves facing a second. Beyond it, a wood fence screened the alley from the Boardwalk.

A garbage bag flew over the far end of the second dumpster, and Jake held up a hand. He fast-walked beside the dumpster and turned the corner to see a door swinging shut. He quickly lunged forward and grabbed the handle just before it closed. He waited fifteen seconds, reading the label on the door—Oceanfront Bar & Grill—before leaning back. "Rach!" he hissed.

She peeked around the corner of the dumpster, and he motioned for her to join him.

"What are we doing?" she asked.

"I think the technical term is the pizza parlor trick," Jake said. He pulled open the door, and he and Rachel sneaked inside, entering the main dining room through a back hallway. No one seemed to notice them or think anything was out of place, so Jake led the way to a vacant table, and he and Rachel sat down on wood barstools. The bar, most of the other tables inside, and the numerous tables outside on the deck were full. Huge garage-door-size windows were open, providing views of 9th Avenue and the field beyond it to the south and the Boardwalk and ocean to the east.

Jake exhaled.

"So what, we eat now?"

"We wait again. We can see two directions and exit two directions."

"Whatever you say. It's been working so far."

Jake exhaled again, letting his eyes drift up to a lattice-board ceiling and a spinning fan. What had been working was mostly dumb luck and keeping one step ahead of pursuit. Neither could be expected to continue indefinitely.

A blond waitress approached the table. "Didn't see you folks come in," she said, placing menus in front of them. "What can I get you to drink?"

"Couple of waters for now," Jake said.

"Coming up."

He leaned forward. "Your cell happen to be dry?"

Rachel reached for it. "It's gone. Must have fallen out in the ocean."

"Or the four-wheeler or anywhere." Jake set his phone on the table. "Soaked." He pried it open and removed the battery and SIM card. He'd heard that was the way to make it untraceable. He didn't know if that was true or not, or if anyone after them had means to track it, but he wasn't taking chances.

He placed all the components in his pocket. "I saw a payphone in the hall. I'm going to try Holmes again."

"You remember her number?"

"I think so." He slid off his stool. "You see anything, stay cool. If they see you, run to me, and we'll go out the way we came in."

"Okay."

"You're doing great, Rach."

He patted her arm as he walked back to the hallway. It had been years since he'd used a payphone, and he had to read the instructions on it before dialing. His only coin was a quarter, and he deposited it and tapped in Holmes' cell number.

It rang three times before her voicemail greeting told him to leave a message.

"Agent Holmes, it's Jake Taylor. Something went wrong. Paul and Masters ambushed us and Butler . . . I'm sorry, but he's dead," he said, holding the phone close to his mouth and speaking quietly, even though he was alone in the hallway. "Paul, Masters, Frost, Jamison, and Flynn are after us, our cells are toast, and we're . . . We'll check in when we can."

He hung up, having passed on giving her their location. At this point, he didn't dare trust anyone. And he had a sinking feeling that even if Holmes was on the level—which she probably was—she had been incapacitated same as her partner.

He returned to the table where Rachel reported seeing nothing. Two glasses of ice water sat beside their menus, and Jake gulped half of his before reporting.

"You want to call Vaughn?" Rachel asked.

"Out of change."

"You could get some at the bar if you have money."

"I don't remember his number anyhow."

"What about the cops?"

"I don't know, Rach. I've been thinking. The FBI hasn't read them in on any of this. Last night, they suspected us of being part of a black market auction. Now with Butler dead . . ."

"What, you think they'd suspect us?"

"Maybe."

"Vaughn will vouch for us."

"Maybe. Unless he suspects we double-crossed him."

"Why would he?"

"I don't know."

"We can't just avoid the FBI forever. And we'll need their help."

"I know. I just want to wait until I can think." He took another big drink of water. "Same plan as before: we find a place to lay low for a while, sort things out, think."

"Here?"

"Still thinking back south. We just have to give Jamison and Frost time to work their way past us."

"What about Paul and Masters? How long do we give them? What if they double back at the same time?"

"I don't know, Babe. It's all a crapshoot."

"Great."

He put his arm on her wrist.

"You folks ready?" the waitress asked.

"Uh, no, we need a few more minutes," Jake said.

"No problem. Take your time."

She drifted away, and Jake opened his wallet. "I've got . . . thirty-seven dollars on me. You hungry?"

"No. Just thirsty," she answered, reaching for her glass.

"Me too." He stuffed the wallet back into his pocket. His shorts had mostly dried. His underwear was another matter, as were his socks. Least of his worries for the time being.

"We can put her off one more time," he said, nodding at the waitress who was talking with patrons at the bar. "Gives us about five minutes, which should time out okay. By now, Jamison and Frost should have made their way this far and will keep working north. Paul and Masters . . . Who knows. We'll go south on the Boardwalk or maybe the beach anyway."

"What do you think happened to Flynn?"

"Hopefully his brain hemorrhaged."

"Jake."

"He shot at us, kicked you in the head. These aren't nice people, Rach, and I don't much care what happens to them."

She took another drink. He scanned the Boardwalk and panned his eyes over 9th Avenue. He spotted blue and nudged Rachel.

"What?"

"Sorry, false alarm."

She sighed.

He was just breathing easier when he saw a blue shirt on the street again. This time there was no doubt it belonged to Dane Paul.

Chapter Thirty

Without looking her way, Jake touched Rachel's arm. "Very slowly, very naturally, get up and walk out onto the Boardwalk," he said, keeping his eyes trained between patrons standing and talking at the corner of the bar and a table on the other side of the restaurant. Rachel followed his gaze, spotting Paul and Masters outside, beyond the barrier separating the outdoor tables from the foot traffic on 9th Avenue.

She eased off the stool and turned for the wide opening leading to the exterior Boardwalk seating area. Jake followed her as they sharply turned the corner and started walking north. Rachel looked back twice, expecting their waitress to holler after them and draw attention. She didn't, and as soon as she and Jake were clear of Oceanfront's outdoor seating, they started jogging, knowing that if Paul and Masters didn't spot them inside, they were likely to wander to the Boardwalk next.

After a few dozen paces, Jake had them slow back to a walk, not wanting to attract attention. The Boardwalk was wide, close to twenty feet, all of it in shadow now. Every so often, staircases led down to the beach or buildouts provided seating and viewing areas. Curved iron lampposts cast a warm glow on the Boardwalk, accompanied by the bright neon and LED lights from businesses on the left. The Boardwalk was crowded, which worked in their favor as they tried to blend in.

They had reached the backside of the Gay Dolphin Gift Cove when the crowd thinned. Looking ahead, Rachel spotted the beautiful but scary form of Gabrielle Frost backlit by the magenta and blue glow of the SkyWheel. She was looking side to side as she meandered down the Boardwalk, checking every face for theirs.

Rachel squeezed Jake's arm.

"I see her," he said, stopping and causing a couple behind them to nearly bump into them. "In there," Jake said, pointing at the entrance to the Gay Dolphin. A dozen windows faced the Boardwalk, each full of curios and keepsakes. The door was at the far left, shielded partially from the north by a V-shaped sign that reached from the Boardwalk deck up some fifteen feet into the air. Rachel hoped it would enable her and Jake to enter the shop unnoticed, and it probably would have had she not been looking back at Frost. In so doing, she bumped into a woman who was reaching for the door at the same time.

"Watch what you're doing," the woman snapped.

Rachel mumbled an apology while turning back, just in time to see Frost's eyes lock onto the source of the cry.

"Go," Jake said, following close on Rachel's heels. She nearly ran over the woman a second time as she entered the store.

The inside was just like the windows, with shelves lined with every trinket or souvenir imaginable. Hanging strings of starfish and seashells, display cases of jewelry, models of ships and lighthouses, ceramic dishware and ornaments, and a wide assortment of wall hangings were just a few of the items that seemed to crowd Rachel as soon as she stepped inside.

"Stairs," Jake said, pointing. She stepped around the same woman again, fortunate that looks could not indeed kill. They climbed to the next level, where woodcarvings of pirate-era schooners, mermaids, parrots, sailboats, and dolphins lined shelves. Sharks' teeth, alligator heads, and thousands if not millions of seashells filled bins. Waist- and chest-high lighthouses and painted wooden pirates stood in the corners beside stacked treasure chests. More decorations hung from the ceiling. Despite being chased, Rachel couldn't help letting her eyes survey it all.

"Rach," Jake said, taking her arm, "find your way through the store and exit onto Ocean."

"What, just me?"

"I'll try to hold her off in here."

"What? How? No, Jake—"

"She won't try anything in here."

"Then we should both stay."

"No." He reached into his pocket and pulled out his wallet, then a soggy twenty-dollar bill that he placed in her hand. "Cross the street and find a way to change your appearance. New shirt, hat, something. Then head south."

"Jake."

"Babe, there's no time to argue. They're looking for two of us, so individually, we'll be better able to blend in."

"Where—"

"There's a Nathan's on 8th, just behind the Bargain Beachwear store. Wait for me there."

"Nathan's by Bargain Beachwear. Jake, can't we—"

He leaned in and kissed her forehead. "I love you, Rach. Now go!"

She didn't like leaving him, but she wasn't going to stop trusting him now. "I love you too," she said as she crumpled the bill into her pocket. Then she turned to leave.

Jake said a silent prayer for Rachel's safety as she headed toward the street. He turned around and peeked over bins of seashells at Frost as she entered the store. It would only take her a few seconds to determine that Jake and Rachel weren't in the rear part of the store. Then she would go either up or down. He lingered, waiting to see if Jamison was with her and which direction she chose. When she started toward the stairs leading up, he headed for a staircase leading down.

He took his time, wanting Frost to spot him and pursue him instead of thinking he and Rachel had hurried through the store, doing so herself, and spotting Rachel. He halted at the top of the stairs until he saw Frost's head appear from the staircase leading to the ground level. He then dashed down the stairs, hoping his quick movement would catch her attention.

Jake paused at the landing halfway down a reversing staircase, watching to see if his ploy had worked. When he saw tanned legs and black shorts coming his way, he deduced it had and took the second flight of stairs down to the basement. He was surrounded by bargain T-shirts, turquoise and jade jewelry, ladies' hats, placards and signs to hang on the wall, and a nearly life-sized black and gold Pharaoh.

Jake drifted from the stairs, looking for alternate exits from this lowest level and keeping an eye on other customers. He also looked for something under seventeen dollars that he could use as a weapon. He wasn't real keen on physically assaulting Gabrielle Frost, and not just because she was a good-looking woman. He felt the same way about Jamison. They'd talked—as friends. They'd had drinks together, planned to dine together. And while they were clearly chasing him and Rachel, they had yet to attack them. Even counting their "interrogation" of Rachel the night before, the most they had done was physically usher her to another room and crowd her. Jake wouldn't hesitate to use violence if it became necessary to defend Rachel or himself, but he wasn't seeking to mete it out on either Frost or Jamison.

Paul, on the other hand, and Masters had escalated things. He'd had a knife. Jake had seen the malice in Masters' eyes. Jake and Rachel had been lucky the first time, and he wasn't counting on finding a conveniently located smoker's receptacle—or it working as a weapon if he did—a second time.

Frost descended the stairs, and Jake ducked into an aisle.

This was nuts. Maybe he could reason with her, explain things to her.

Right, because she was easy on the eyes she couldn't possibly be a ruthless criminal who would stop at nothing to get what she wanted.

Jake crept along the ends of several aisles. He spotted Frost advancing slowly, looking down each one, the way he did when he lost Rachel at Hy-Vee.

Frost stopped.

So did Jake.

They looked at each other, her brown eyes honing in.

She was between Jake and the stairs, between him and access to the front of the store. All he had were restrooms behind him. He waited, playing a game of chicken, buying Rachel time.

"Excuse me, ma'am."

Jake saw a heavyset woman waddling toward Frost from the aisle to her left. He'd spotted her before, browsing the XL T-shirts. None of them would fit. She had to weigh three hundred pounds, her legs so fat they rubbed together at the knee as she walked. Jake knew she would fill the entire aisle and immediately darted to his right.

Frost took off down the aisle after him. He took the second aisle to his left, running now, sure the security cameras would catch him, and an employee would be dispatched to tell him to knock it off.

At the end of the aisle, across the intersecting aisle, was a three-foot-tall painted carving of a mermaid, her tail wrapped around a pier pylon. Jake grabbed it and slid it back into the middle of the aisle he had just vacated, at the same time that Frost turned down it. Seeing her path blocked, she turned around to take the next aisle. She reversed direction a little too fast and lost her footing on the tile floor. She fell backward into a shelf, causing an assortment of trinkets to wobble and fall.

Jake didn't wait to see the carnage. He headed for the steps and quickly climbed back to the level where he'd parted with Rachel. He followed in her footsteps, to another level full of T-shirts and a life-sized shark hanging from the ceiling. He looked back and didn't see Frost yet, so he slowed. He was gaining confidence and wanted to buy Rachel more time.

When he saw Frost climb the stairs again, he ducked behind a rack of discounted T-shirts. Frost looked around, then spotted him. She said something, but Jake couldn't hear over Ed Sheeran playing on the store's speakers. He turned and nearly ran over a teenage boy who'd started to browse from the same rack.

"Sorry," Jake said. Frost was quickly closing the gap, and Jake brushed past the kid. He took a half flight of stairs to the ground level and turned left, away from the front cashier's counter. He ducked into an aisle containing blown glass sculptures and glass figurines.

And literally ran into Liam Jamison.

Chapter Thirty-One

Rachel hurried through the Gay Dolphin Gift Cove, her eyes taking in all its treasures and treats while also looking for her and Jake's pursuers. The way things were going, she almost expected Jamison to appear in the Ocean Boulevard entrance as she tried to exit.

He did not.

The sun had set behind the buildings, leaving the street in shadow. Already, the lights of shops and eateries and dozens of cars on Ocean lit the dusky night. It reminded Rachel of Las Vegas. She and Jake had visited a few years ago, for some work conference he'd had to attend. She mostly disliked the place, but couldn't help but feel an aura as night fell on the Las Vegas Strip. Now, in Myrtle Beach, she got a similar feeling as the Strip of Ocean Boulevard was transformed.

Rachel remembered Jake's words: "Cross the street and find a way to change your appearance. New shirt, hat, something." She still didn't like the plan. She was more than capable of thinking on her own and didn't *need* Jake to survive. But he sure helped. How many times had he spotted something she hadn't or vice versa? They were better together. Two were always better than one.

More than anything, she just didn't like being away from him, didn't like not knowing what might happen. She may not be able to stop something bad if she were with him, but the illusion that she could made it hard to go on alone. But she knew it was what he wanted, and what he expected. She couldn't turn back now.

Just a few steps north, a brick crosswalk bisected the road, and Rachel, along with several others, used it to cross to the west side of the street. Several cars stopped to allow the pedestrians the right of way, one of them an all-black, new model Dodge Challenger that revved its engine just as Rachel passed in front of it.

She jumped and heard the driver laugh through his open window. She wasn't sure if he'd revved it at her, in anger at having to wait, or just because. And she didn't care. She hurried across the street and turned south.

Before she had taken more than a few steps, a loud, blood-curdling scream sounded from her right. Rachel jumped again, emitting a quiet scream herself. She turned and saw two teenage girls laughing and covering their mouths. A third stood back, hands on her heart, while a fourth pointed at a cardboard box in front of the entrance to Ripley's Haunted Adventure. "Free kittens" was written on the box, and Rachel realized it was a scream box, designed to lure people toward it and trigger a sensor that would emit the scream when they peeked inside.

Her heart going back to normal, Rachel resumed walking beside the ghoulish Ripley's building, made to look like an old steel mill or a factory of some sort. Rachel didn't get why people would willingly try to scare themselves. Whatever thrill it produced, wasn't it mitigated by intending to produce it in the first place?

Twice, Rachel looked back at the towering glass front of the Gay Dolphin, then down to the front door from which she had exited. She hoped to see Jake coming, or even Frost, meaning she had missed him inside. When Rachel turned her head back the second time, she saw Paul and Masters coming toward her, several storefronts away.

She tried to hide behind a palm tree, hoping they hadn't spotted her. But their quickened pace indicated they had. Panic swelled in Rachel's chest. She looked left, but traffic was continually moving south on Ocean. She flitted her head back toward Paul and Masters. They were running now. She turned right, her only option an open doorway. She didn't even know which building she was entering until she came to a small ticket counter. The signs identified it as Ripley's Mirror Maze.

Rachel hesitated. It was that or go back onto the street, north, trying to outrun two criminal operatives who would be right on her heels.

She dug the crumpled twenty-dollar bill from her pocket and practically threw it on the counter. A girl, maybe teenage, maybe early twenties, and clearly bored, processed it and returned twelve dollars in change. Rachel snatched the trio of bills and pushed through the turnstile toward the maze entrance.

Jamison appeared as shocked as Jake as they collided into each other. For an instant, they stared at each other. Jamison reacted first, reaching for Jake. He responded by turning around and making a beeline for the wrought-iron staircase inside the glass tower at the front of the building.

The staircase circled around a feature of multiple dolphins spitting water into a coin pool at the lower level. Jake opted to go down and heard Jamison's footsteps on the iron stairs behind him. He made a quick left and then a quick right, getting into the "heart" of the store as quickly as possible.

He turned another corner, nearly knocking drinking glasses off a shelf.

"No running!" someone shouted. Jake hoped the same person would be prepared for Jamison and would scold him more severely. Say, with a forearm to the neck.

Jake passed Pharaoh again, and a sarcophagus. He turned once more and ducked behind a shelf containing a variety of dolls. He squatted low, identifying several possible escape routes. Stairs led up both to his right and left. At this point, he was getting confused about how many levels there were and which staircases led where. Maybe after an hour of running for his and his wife's life, he was just losing it.

His wife. Had he been wrong to send Rachel away? She was smart and savvy and could survive on her own. But it wasn't just on her. Even with Jamison and Frost tied up cat-and-mousing around the Gay Dolphin with him, Paul and Masters were out there somewhere. And what if something happened to him, if he couldn't meet up with her? She had no phone, little money, nobody to trust.

Jake briefly closed his eyes, praying that Rachel was safe. The analytical engineer in him liked to offer detailed, specific prayers, laying out everything on his heart and mind. But he knew that God knew all that before he voiced it, and he didn't have time anyhow. He opened his eyes and peeked through the dolls. He saw Jamison turn the other way. At the same time, Frost came down the stairs to his left. She slowly made her way toward him, and he realized he had to move.

Flicking his eyes toward Jamison, Jake crept to his right, around several display cases. As he looked for Jamison's position again, his foot caught the edge of a rack holding rows of baby sharks preserved in bottles, tipping it and them over. He saw Frost's legs come around a shelf and, paying no attention to the potential mess he had made, he stood and ran again.

Rachel was lost immediately. Amidst flashing—strobing, really—pinkish red and purplish blue lights, she was looking at what appeared to be rows and rows of hexagonal columns, spaced out equally and connected by arches. They created what appeared to be square sections between four columns but were in reality triangles, as evidenced by glowing and pulsating lights stretching from column to column on the otherwise dark floor.

From her vantage point, it looked as if Rachel could walk straight to the far end of the room. If she turned her head right or left, the same apparition was there, and she knew it was just that. From reading a brief paragraph in her guidebook while in the Chicago airport, Rachel knew the maze provided multiple ways out, and the challenge for "maze-runners" was to find the best and quickest route. Ostensibly, not while being chased by psychopaths, but this was Ripley's.

Rachel was not concerned with appearances. She could only imagine being there with Jake, him trying to make it through the maze "clean," without any mistakes. She just wanted to put as much distance between her and Paul and Masters as possible. And quickly. To that end, she felt her way with both hands, looking like a zombie as she staggered forward, left, then right.

The music sounded like a Halloween haunted house mixed with *The Phantom of the Opera* intermingled with screams and wails. The lights slowly turned from blue to red, then flicked on and off in an effort to give maze-runners a seizure. Then they went off entirely. When they came back on, Rachel was looking at three of her reflections, all facing different ways.

She sighed in frustration, knowing she'd hardly moved from the entrance. She touched a mirror as the lights blinked off again. They came on at the same time as a ghoulish growl sounded, and Rachel found herself face to face with an ogre in a trench coat. She jumped back and screamed, her heart threatening to pound out of her chest until she realized it was just a holographic image.

"That way," she heard a hissed voice declare. The next moment, she saw a feminine hand reaching for her. Rachel jumped back and crashed into a mirror. The hand groped at nothing, being not a real hand but a reflection an indeterminate number of quadrants and angles away. Rachel moved to her left, encountered another mirror, and reversed her course.

She had luck, making a couple turns before reaching a dead end. She turned around and found herself face to face with a scowling yet smirking Dane Paul.

Chapter Thirty-Two

Jake darted up the steps to ground level and thought about exiting to the street. But that would just continue the chase, and he would either lead Jamison and Frost to Rachel or have to run away from her himself. So he opted to go up, using the curving staircase around the dolphin sculpture and fountain to climb to the second story.

It was stocked with large model boats, surfboards, and paintings. There wasn't much place to hide, so Jake continued climbing, winding around the staircase. It circled the inside of the glass tower for several more stories, but a gate blocked customers from going to the top. Knowing he was trapped, Jake looked down once and, not seeing Jamison or Frost, clambered over the gate. He continued climbing, aware that he was likely on security footage and thus about to get in trouble. It was a risk worth taking.

He made another loop around the tower and flattened himself on the catwalk between sections of staircase. Prostrating himself, he raised one eye over the side and peeked down toward the floor of the store.

Another minute passed before Jamison and Frost met up at the front of the store, almost directly below him. Their movement suggested they were making a systematic, slow advance so as not to allow him to double back again. They paused for a moment at the base of the staircase, and he feared they would talk to someone who had seen him climb up. They didn't, but Jamison began to ascend the staircase anyhow.

Jake continued to peer carefully over the edge of the catwalk as Jamison climbed to the second level. He searched it quickly, while down below, Frost milled around the front of the store.

His search of the second level completed, Jamison stood at the landing and looked up. Jake jerked his head away from the edge and flattened himself against the metal. He had no choice but to wait and hope. If Jamison climbed higher, Jake's only choice would be to keep climbing. He'd seen an external staircase beside the tower when driving by the other day. Maybe he could get down and to the roof and then . . .

He heard footfalls on the staircase and chanced a look. Jamison was going back down. Careful not to be spotted by Frost as she looked up at Jamison, Jake continued to watch. They conferred quietly for a moment, then pushed toward the exit. Jake shifted on the catwalk and reoriented his head to look through the glass at the street. He'd given Rachel ten minutes at least, maybe closer to fifteen. He hoped that was enough.

Jamison and Frost spent a moment looking around. Then Jamison crossed to the west side of Ocean Boulevard, and they both continued north. Internally pumping his fist, Jake watched them until they were out of sight. Then, before his already pressed luck ran out, he climbed down the staircase.

🌴　　　　🌴　　　　🌴

Rachel thought it was just a reflection again until Paul lunged at her. She dove down and to the right at the same time as the lights went black again and a death scream echoed through the maze. Paul's arm glanced off her shoulder. He reached back, grabbed her arm, and threatened to pull her back into a grappling match with him. She kicked and swung with her free arm, nearly breaking her ulna—or so it felt—when it crashed down on his. Somehow, the flailing in the dark worked, and she was free.

As the lights blipped back on and changed colors, she darted back the way she and Paul had come, twisting left and then right through an opening. She realized she wasn't going to be able to cleverly pick her way through the maze, differentiating actual paths from reflections. At least not with Paul and Masters after her. Hoping there were multiple paths through it, she settled on a plan of making only left turns. She also rolled the left sleeve of her T-shirt up to the shoulder. With all the multiple mirrors, it was easy to lose her sense of right and left when she spotted her reflection.

Holding to her pattern, she continued at a painstaking pace. Twice she encountered Masters' reflection, once apparently right beside her and another time way off in the distance that proved to be much closer. But, by that time, Rachel was more adept at finding her way through the maze than Masters and eluded her.

The lights strobed again, the music switched beats, and Rachel saw light ahead. It vanished with a left turn, so she retraced her steps, abandoned her strategy, and stepped through a curtain and into a dimly lit exit room. A door on the right announced street access, and Rachel wasted no time pushing through it.

She was not on the street but a thin, tunnel-like alley. The whoosh of traffic and the murmur of pedestrians told her the street was on her left. She thought for a moment about going right, toward a parking lot and off the beaten path. Remembering Jake's instructions and knowing that Frost, Paul, and Masters all had seen her in the berry-colored shirt she currently wore, Rachel headed for the street.

Even at dusk, the lights were momentarily blinding after the mirror maze. Squinting, Rachel panned the street in case she happened to spy Jake, or Frost or Jamison. Seeing no one familiar, she turned south and walked fast.

The first store on the right sold shirts and other beachwear, but Rachel wanted to put a little distance between herself and Paul and Masters, so she kept going. The next building was a grill and deli, and then another beachwear store. The lone entrance was crowded with people, and instead of pushing through them, Rachel continued on, hoping Paul and Masters were still stuck in the maze.

As her eyes searched for another store, her ears honed in on the beat of the street. Every store blasted music onto the sidewalk, mostly pop or hip-hop, but some oldies, reggae, and country too. Most of the cars added to it, contributing rap or modern rock. Salesman hawked their shop's particular wares or various show and restaurant deals. Cars idled, honked, accelerated. To Rachel, it became one steady background cacophony.

She passed a couple smaller stores before seeing a bright Kings sign towering over the sidewalk. The marquee advertised airbrushed tees, sharktooth necklaces, and an abundance of cheap clothes. With a look back over her shoulder—she didn't spot either Paul or Masters—Rachel ducked inside.

Toby Keith boomed through speakers, deafening compared to the sounds of the street or even the maze racket. Kings offered hundreds if not thousands of shirt designs, in addition to swimwear, the typical souvenirs, and beach accessories. In a hurry, Rachel browsed for a cheap shirt. She stayed away from pink or shades of red and found a green that matched her eyes. The logo said "Myrtle Beach" and "South Carolina" above and below a printed palm tree. The price tag was $3.99.

On the way to the checkout counter, she stopped at a rack selling hats. She found a black trucker's cap with "Myrtle Beach" scrawled on the front in cursive. It cost $6.99, and Rachel snagged it off the hook and took it and the T-shirt to the checkout counter.

She was second in line and waited nervously.

"I can help you over here," a woman said, and Rachel moved to a second register. She placed three crumpled bills on the counter and got fourteen cents in change.

"No bag," she said as she stepped away from the counter. Instead of exiting the store, she ducked behind a display case and quickly peeled off her shirt.

"Whoa!" a male customer said.

"Hey, what are you doing?" the checkout woman asked.

Rachel ignored them both and put on her new shirt. Clenching the bill of the hat in her teeth, she gathered her hair with both hands and pulled it into a ponytail, which she bound with a band around her wrist from earlier. She held the ponytail with one hand and put the cap on with the other, feeding the pony through it. She took just a moment to settle the cap on her head, then grabbed her old shirt and peeked around the display. The coast was clear, so she exited to the sidewalk.

Rachel retraced her steps to a garbage can just a few paces north. She deposited the berry shirt with a hint of regret, having liked the color and the logo. She spun around and felt someone grab her arm.

She knew it wasn't Paul or Masters. She'd been looking for them. She thought it was a random person bumping into her, but the grip tightened. Jerking her head around, she found herself looking at the bruised face of Spencer Flynn.

Chapter Thirty-Three

Flynn's grip was like fire on Rachel's arm. His voice was a razor, albeit with a bit of garble. "You scream or yell, I break it off," he said, and Rachel didn't doubt he could and would.

He took her south, headed for the intersection of Ocean and 9th. Rachel's eyes frantically scanned the crowds for a police officer, Jake, or a do-gooder who would recognize her distress. Her eyes widened hopefully as a few passersby cast dubious looks at them, but Flynn continued to force her south.

"Where are we going?" Rachel asked.

"Somewhere private."

As they approached the intersection, Rachel knew she had to do something. If Flynn got her away from the crowds, he could do whatever he wanted to her to get her to talk. And he'd already proven, he wasn't much into talk, but into actions. Like shooting at people.

She was shocked at how strong he was, considering he wasn't much bigger than her—in height or, it appeared, weight. His iron grip was unbreakable though, and with her shoulder already sore from a previous fight with him, she knew it wouldn't take much for him to make her scream in pain. She thought about appealing for mercy but knew it would do no good.

Lord, please help me out of this! I'm scared.

The light had changed, stopping traffic on Ocean Boulevard, and a throng of people crossed from under the light by Peaches Corner. They forced Flynn, as he turned Rachel west, to climb a couple of the steps leading up to Ripley's. In doing so, he lost leverage on Rachel's arm.

Feeling a loosening of his grip, she resisted the urge to pull away. Instead, she drove her weight into Flynn, knocking him off balance. His grip slipped, and Rachel threw her body weight forward, breaking his grip completely. She made a quick U-turn, using the crowd of people as a shield.

A car turning right onto 9th blared its horn, nearly clipping her as she strayed onto the curb. She instinctively turned left and took off running north on the sidewalk along Ocean Boulevard. She thought about calling for help but didn't want to attract any more attention to herself, knowing Paul and Masters couldn't be far off.

With her peripheral vision, she saw Flynn was back on his feet and chasing her. Doubting she could outrun him for any long period of time, Rachel looked for a way to put distance between herself and Flynn. She mentally ran through the stores and shops on her side of the street. Aside from the mirror maze again, there was no good place to hide. Plus Paul and Masters had to be coming her way.

As the light turned, southbound traffic began to accelerate. Rachel took advantage of the initially slow progress and darted between a pickup flying huge American and Confederate flags from the corners of its bed and, of all things, a red Mustang. She paused for a revving motorcycle in the second southbound lane, feeling the whoosh of a car right behind her. Its horn sounded a quick blast that faded as it accelerated through the intersection.

Behind her, Rachel heard a shout—maybe Flynn, maybe someone wondering why she was playing chicken on Ocean Boulevard. She ignored it and continued across the street in the motorcycle's wake, cutting in front of a slow-starting southbound SUV and at the same time glancing right.

Northbound traffic had already crossed 9th Avenue. Rachel knew if she hesitated, Flynn would catch her for sure. Besides, she was already in the middle of the street; turning back was no safer than continuing. So she sprinted across both lanes, hearing a squeal of brakes as she did. She looked at a skidding Corvette and not at her next step, and her foot came down on the side of the curb. Pain shooting up her leg, she tumbled forward, rolling onto the sidewalk.

At the same time, she heard a screech and a crunch. Then several gasps and screams, followed by a thud and more screams.

Rachel rolled over, reaching for her ankle, looking back toward the street. The Corvette had squealed to a stop where she had just been. A black shoe lay by its front tire. Spencer Flynn, his legs bent at an obtuse angle, lay just beyond its back bumper and just in front of a pickup that had also slammed on its brakes and, in so doing, been rear-ended by another muscle car.

Rachel used a palm tree trunk to pull herself to her feet. She was distantly aware of more screams, of questions directed at her about what happened and if she was all right. Her eyes were drawn to Flynn's body, immobile, blood gushing from several cuts and gashes on his head. She was sickened and relieved at the same time.

"Whoa, lady, are you okay?" a male voice asked.

Rachel turned to see a guy in his twenties, long colorful tank top, a faded Mohawk.

"Yeah, I'm fine," she said, unsure yet if it was true.

"Somebody should call 9-1-1," another voice said, and Mohawk turned to look at the guy.

Rachel hobbled north, ignoring more questions directed her way. Pain shot through her ankle with every step, but she was able to grimace through it and quickly get away from the accident.

She looked around. Neon lights above her blinked the words "FUN PLAZA." The alley that connected to The Bowery and Oceanfront Bar & Grill was just to the south, and beyond that, Peaches Corner and 9th Avenue. Rachel knew she was supposed to go south, but didn't know if her ankle would carry her all the way to Nathan's. And, after dodging Paul and Masters, being captured by Flynn, and seeing him splattered on the street, she just wanted to find Jake. She wanted to hold him and be held back. She wanted to be back in their living room in Omaha, snuggled in front of a boring movie with a bowl of popcorn.

"Cowboy up, Chel," she mumbled under her breath, using the nickname her high school track coach—and no one else—had used. He'd been an enigma among high school girls' coaches in that he'd been an old-school, tell-it-like-it-is coach who wasn't afraid to dish out tough love. "Chel" had been what he'd called Rachel when she needed to toughen up or dig deep. She'd hated it—and him—but found herself using the nickname when she needed to power through the end of a tough run or finish a long, stressful day.

Buoyed by her renewed resolve, Rachel turned around to continue south. As she did, her eyes swept over the street. She couldn't believe them. Traffic had come to a stop because of the accident, and a blue-clad man and a pink-clad woman were using the break to cross over to her side of the street.

Paul and Masters.

Again.

After descending the spiral staircase inside the glass tower of the Gay Dolphin Gift Cove, Jake quickly made his way back through the store again, wary of store employees who had tabbed him as the troublemaker who'd been playing hide-and-seek for the last quarter hour. He also feared Jamison or Frost would return to the store when they didn't spot him on the street, so he didn't waste time.

Exiting onto the Boardwalk, Jake paused a moment to catch his breath and take stock of things. By now, Rachel should be to Nathan's, unless she'd run into trouble. Jamison and Frost had gone north, so worst-case scenario, even if they had turned back, he was ahead of them and was separated from them by the buildings between Ocean and the Boardwalk. He had no idea where Paul and Masters were—last he'd seen them they'd been approaching Oceanfront Bar & Grill from the south, and had probably made their way north in the last fifteen minutes. That meant he should be in the clear, barring the dumb luck of running into them. The way things had been going, however, dumb luck was distinctly possible, and Jake considered cutting over to the beach where he was less likely to run into anyone.

He dismissed that notion for two reasons. One, running or even walking on sand was harder than the wooden boardwalk, and he didn't need any more stress on his leg muscles. Two, if Rachel got into some kind of trouble, he had a chance of being in seeing or hearing distance if he stayed on the Boardwalk. Not so from the beach.

With that resolved, Jake started south. He was sustained by the hope that this might all be over soon, that he would be reunited with Rachel and be free from their pursuers. That hope fell quickly when he remembered the grotesque image of Agent Butler's slit neck, of the unconscious Spencer Flynn lying in the waves amidst a crowd of onlookers, and of the auction prize he and Rachel still had to deal with one way or the other.

Already tired, Jake opted to walk instead of jog. He passed a shop selling gyros, an arcade, another shop offering Italian ices, and another T-shirt and souvenir store. The sky above him wasn't yet black, but on the east side of the buildings, it was as good as nighttime. The crowds of people, if anything, had increased on the Boardwalk. They were a two-edged sword, making it easier for Jake to blend in, but also enabling his pursuers to approach him unseen.

Paintings of tipped over Coca-Cola bottles spanned either side of a neon sign reading "FUN PLAZA" on a blue building on his right. The smell of burgers and hot dogs wafted from an attached eatery, followed by the clanging and rattling and beeping of arcade games. The noise drew his eyes, and they spotted a woman in a pale green shirt and a black baseball cap, running and limping toward him.

Jake's eyes widened as he recognized Rachel.

"Rach, are you okay?" he asked, his eyes going down to her ankle as she seized his arm. "What hap—"

"Paul and Masters! They're right behind me."

Although he wanted to go south and although Jamison and Frost were likely north, Jake knew that aside from a couple of restaurants, there was nothing south but open ground. He and Rachel, especially with her limping, would be sitting ducks. That meant going north, which in turn meant a renewal of the cat-and-mouse game, this time with different cats. Somehow, he had to find a way to end it.

First, he needed to tend to his wife. He looped his arm under her and they "ran" north. After a dozen yards, it became apparent that Rachel wasn't going to be able to outrun anyone. Jake looked over his shoulder and didn't see Paul and Masters yet.

"Quick, in here."

"What?" Rachel asked as he guided her toward another gift shop.

"Hide in here. I'll distract them."

"Jake, no!"

"You can't run. I'm going to get help."

She started to protest, but Jake gently ushered her toward the door. As soon as she entered the shop, he turned and continued north, praying for her safety and his own wisdom. With Rachel hobbled, he had to find a way to change the status quo. Having avoided the authorities thus far because of the complexity of explaining everything and the potential of him and Rachel getting into trouble, Jake realized it was now his only option. His and Rachel's immediate safety took precedence over anything else.

Jake looked back and saw both Paul and Masters emerge from the arcade. He lingered, hoping they'd spot him and give chase. Since they had been following Rachel, he wasn't sure if they would suddenly make a play to catch him, but it was worth a try to lead them away from her. He hoped he could then lose them in the crowds at Plyler Park, just beyond the Gay Dolphin and on this side of the Sky Wheel. Then he could find a police officer and bring him to Rachel. All while avoiding Jamison and Frost, who were still out there somewhere.

He looked back again and saw Paul pointing his way. Jake picked up his pace, dodging a group on Segways and a couple walking hand-in-hand with a toddler between them.

Iron patio furniture encroached on the Boardwalk in front of the gyro shop, forming a bottleneck of foot traffic. Slowed, Jake looked back. He caught a glimpse of Paul's blue shirt, closing fast. Jake turned around and pressed through the crowd. He nearly tripped over a woman's stroller—incurring a shout from her as a result—and peeked over his shoulder to see Paul gaining still.

The Boardwalk cleared momentarily, and Jake summoned all his energy to sprint, his shoes thudding on the wood surface. He didn't look back, and didn't need to—he could hear Paul's footsteps behind him.

Up ahead, the Boardwalk narrowed again to make room for outdoor restaurant seating, this time for Moe Moon's. A group of people, arms full of shopping bags and to-go food containers, stood in the Boardwalk, blocking his route. Another beachwear shop didn't appear to go all the way through to Ocean Boulevard, and an alley just beyond it was blocked by a closed gate. So Jake twisted through a trio of college-aged guys loitering by a buildout, then abruptly turned and jumped down a short stairway to the sand.

It was maybe forty feet to the beach. Spying a few people still there, Jake headed for it, hoping to use them as screens or obtain some sort of help from them. He never made it.

Five feet from reaching the open sand of the beach, Jake felt a weight drop across the back of his legs. His forward momentum stopped, and he plunged face-first into the sand.

The gift shop was just like all the others, selling many of the same T-shirts, sweatshirts, and beach shorts; the same shot glasses, coffee mugs, and water bottles; and the same assortment of knickknacks, trinkets, and décor. Rachel made her way to the back of the store as quickly as possible and removed her hat, tossing it into a bin of cheap bargains where it could ostensibly belong.

Hiding behind a tiered T-shirt display table, Rachel took the weight off her injured ankle. Only two other customers were in the store at the moment, and Rachel felt conspicuous. The clerk, a good-looking young guy, had been eyeing her since she entered, and kept furtively—or so she thought—glancing her way. She decided she'd better pretend to be shopping or browsing, while at the same time watching the window for Paul and Masters.

Lord, keep Jake safe. Give him wisdom. Get us out of this!

Rachel fiddled with a shirt in front of her. When she lifted her eyes, she saw Paul and Masters walking by. She instinctively ducked down, wincing as she put weight on her ankle. It was a useless move anyhow, as the windows of the store were so plastered with items that it would be almost impossible for Paul or Masters to identify her.

Jake had maybe a minute head start. Probably less. More like forty-five seconds. Max.

And what was he going to do? He'd said get help. From who? Cops? From where? Besides, these people had already killed Agent Butler—or had that been Flynn? What if they killed the cops too? How would she and Jake ever get out—

Pink flashed in the doorway as Masters entered the store. Having just stood up, Rachel tried to step behind a display case but was late. Masters spotted her and stalked toward her. Rachel backed up, looking for an escape avenue. There were fitting rooms and restrooms, but those were all dead ends, as was a wall full of T-shirt designs and a counter of cheap jewelry behind her.

She tried to drift toward the front of the store, hoping to circle toward the door. But Masters was onto her, edging that way, moving to cut Rachel off while closing in. Neither of the other customers was in the same half of the store, and the man tending the counter was suddenly busy on a phone call.

Her heart pounding, Rachel tried not to panic. She looked for something she could use as a weapon. Clothes, stuffed animals, shirts were of no use. Memories of brief kickboxing lessons and taekwondo classes—both weight-loss measures—and of her college self-defense course flashed through her head. A bout of nausea flashed through her intestines.

Masters drew closer. Her hair, once pinned tightly behind her head, was now something of a mess, wisps hanging everywhere. A bruise on her forehead was a blend of purple and yellow. And blood had clotted from a gash just above her knee.

But it was her eyes that stood out. They were green and vivid, and laser-focused on Rachel.

On the verge of terror, Rachel looked right and left. She realized there was no escape. She only had one choice.

Fight.

Chapter Thirty-Four

Before Jake could roll over, Paul was on top of him, pushing his head into the sand, attempting to suffocate him. Jake flailed backward with his arms, wriggling and squirming, and managed to topple Paul off him. He turned over and started to get up, but before he could, a shoe lashed out and connected with his jaw, knocking him back. That quickly, Paul jumped on him and began swinging.

Jake's buddy had once invited him over to watch MMA on pay-per-view. Nearly naked guys attempting to beat each other to a pulp for sport—it wasn't his thing. But he'd learned terms like "ground and pound," which applied to what Paul was doing to him now, and "tapping out." That was how a fighter who couldn't take it anymore signaled to the referee that he quit. With Paul on top of him and swinging away, Jake needed a referee. But the hubbub on the Boardwalk and the stragglers on the beach might as well have been a mile away.

In the distance, Jake thought he heard a woman scream or shriek. He didn't have time to process it because Paul kept swinging, and Jake had all he could do to divert some of the punches. He tried raising a knee toward Paul's groin, hoping to roll the "hitter" off him so he could make a break for it. But Paul was too strong, and retaliated with an uppercut that had Jake seeing stars.

Jake was slightly more fond of boxing, the "sweet science." In boxing, a fighter didn't tap out. The referee sensed that he was no longer capable of defending himself and stepped in to end the fight, resulting in a TKO—a technical knockout. But Jake still had no such referee at his disposal.

Instead, having knocked Jake semi unconscious, Paul knelt on his chest and pawed him, rifling through his shorts and otherwise frisking him.

"Where are they?" Paul practically spat.

Jake blinked several times, trying to revive himself. He hacked on blood from a split lip. "Where . . . where are who?"

"Where?"

Jake said nothing.

"The girl," Paul said, rising to his knees. Having rolled Jake onto his side, he now flipped him onto his chest, his face thumping into the sand. Paul pushed it deeper into the sand as he got to his feet. "Trust me, she'll give them up."

Rachel inched backward toward the jewelry counter, hoping to convince Masters that she was passive and scared. The latter part wasn't hard, because she was terrified.

Rachel had never been in a "fight" fight. She had gotten into a kindergarten wrestling match with Charlie Carson because he'd taken her crayons. She'd slapped her sister once, three days before Rachel's wedding. Lisa had deserved it. And one New Year's Eve, a particularly chaotic trip to Super Saver had gotten a little tenuous when Rachel just beat another woman to the last of the deli's potato salad.

This was different. Masters' eyes made that clear as she felt her way around a T-shirt display table.

"Give me the—"

Packing her fist, Rachel sucker-punched Masters in the nose. Even though it almost immediately drew a trickle of blood, it wasn't an extremely effective blow long-term. It was a tone-setter, Rachel hoped.

She didn't wait to find out, instead making a mad dash away from Masters. That meant going deeper into the store, and she frantically looked for something to assist her. Seeing nothing obvious, Rachel was about to turn and take her chances in a fight, when a thought hit her. She and Jake had been ducking in and out of back entrances to all sorts of shops and restaurants. Maybe this gift shop had a back entrance to an alley leading to Ocean Boulevard or even back to the Boardwalk. Rachel loathed the idea of getting into another chase, especially with her bad ankle. But it beat getting into a fight with someone like Masters.

Flitting a look over her shoulder, Rachel saw Masters on her heel. Her eyes also raked over the other customers and the clerk, none of whom had moved to intervene. She began flailing at items on shelves, swiping them off behind her or trying to find something she could throw at Masters. She spied bottles of spray-on sunscreen, and her hand knocked over a pair of them before she could wrap her fingers around one.

Clenching it tightly, Rachel ducked around a T-shirt rack. As she fumbled with the tamper-evident band, she turned around. Masters was rounding the rack, blood still dripping from her nose. Her eyes practically smoldered. Quelling the fear that made her fingers borderline useless, Rachel finally ripped the band free. She turned the cap and sprayed the sunscreen in Masters' face.

Masters ducked to the side and threw up a hand to block it, at the same time stopping her advance. Even so, and before she could reflexively close her eyes, some of the spray penetrated them. Emitting a gasp-like cry, she spun farther away, immediately reaching her hands for her eyes. Rachel sprayed a little more for effect, then turned toward the hallway leading to the restrooms.

She looked back once, seeing the clerk edge around the checkout counter and between the two customers. They both stood slack-jawed. Rachel's eyes turned to Masters, who was digging the heel of her wrists into her eyes, trying to expel the sunscreen. Rachel emptied the can onto the tile floor, hoping it might slow down Masters. For good measure, she heaved the empty can at her and turned to run.

There were three doors in the hall, two next to each other across from the entrance to the hall, and a third down the hall to the left. It was marked "Employees Only," whereas the other two were identified as the men's and women's restrooms. There was no exit.

Rachel thought about ducking into the bathroom and locking the door behind her, assuming it even locked. But then what would she do? She had no phone. Wait for the clerk to get help? Hope Masters didn't convince him she was the good guy?

Rachel looked back out into the store and saw Masters coming her way, blocking escape. Her only option was to run to the Employees Only door, hoping it opened and contained something she could use to defend herself. She yanked on the knob, but nothing happened. She tried twisting it, and the knob turned. The door opened just as a dull thud sounded behind her.

Rachel spun around and saw Masters sliding on her backside into the hallway. The sunscreen on the floor must have done the trick. The fall had not knocked Masters unconscious, however, and she quickly scrambled to her feet. Rachel entered the closet, desperately fumbling around in the semi-darkness for a makeshift weapon. She found a wet mop in the traditional yellow bucket and yanked it out. She tried to swing it around to extend the mop, but the confines of the closet kept her from doing so. She pulled the handle back, managed to turn it, and shoved the mop forward just as Masters charged into the closet.

The mop hit her in the chin, slid down into the neck and chest, and stopped her cold. Rachel pulled it back and thrust it again, knocking Masters back into the door. She came again, this time lower, ducking under the mop. She charged into Rachel's midsection and drove her back. They crashed into a shelving unit, and all manner of items fell onto and around them.

Rachel could hardly see and resorted to flailing her elbows and trying to punch someone she couldn't make out. She felt several blows to her midsection, then a hand pushed against the side of her face. She slid out from under it and fell to the side, losing her balance and falling into the wall. She had dropped the mop and reached for whatever her hands could find, in this case a plastic bottle of something. She swung it in the general direction of Masters' head, as hard as she could, emitting a guttural yell in the process.

She felt the bottle break, or maybe the screw-in sprayer and handle came off. Then she felt liquid on her hand and arm and heard Masters scream. Rachel had no idea what chemical she had just luckily splashed in Masters' face, and didn't care. She turned for the door. Seeing the mop leaning against it, she grabbed it and stabbed toward Masters. She felt some resistance and heard the sound of Masters being knocked into the shelves again.

Rachel stepped back and slammed the door. Almost without thinking, she lifted the mop and snapped it down on her raised knee, like a baseball player who had just struck out might his bat. The mop handle splintered and broke just above where it attached to the mop. Rachel discarded the handle and wedged the stub under the door, a near perfect fit. She kicked the mop twice with her shoe, wedging it as tightly as possible. It wouldn't hold forever, and Masters could likely find something to jab it out with. But any amount of time she was slowed was a win.

Rachel turned and exited the hallway, nearly colliding with the clerk and then nearly falling on the sunscreen.

"What is going on?" he asked, wide-eyed.

Rachel ignored the mess and headed for the exit. "Call the cops," she said over her shoulder. "She's a wanted criminal."

The clerk's mouth widened to match his eyes. "Who . . . are you?"

"I'm working undercover with the FBI," Rachel said, surprising herself with her lucidity.

"What's your na—"

She pushed through a pair of young guys, whose faces registered a combination of shock and amusement, and out into the evening air. The breeze on her skin drew her attention to a cut on her arm. It wasn't anything major. She'd also split her lip somewhere along the line but, considering, was okay.

Jake had told her to wait for help, but she was sick of waiting and being a sitting duck. She didn't want to answer questions, and she didn't want to risk Masters escaping from the closet and starting another round. Limping, she turned north, wary of running into Paul and hoping Jake was having better success.

Chapter Thirty-Five

Jake slowly rolled over and spat out a combination of saliva, blood, and sand. His head pulsated like a jackhammer. He was aware of the buzz of voices in the periphery of his cognizance, but couldn't tell if it was related to him and Paul or not. He pushed to his hands and knees, and a wave of dizziness washed over him. He wanted to crumble back to the ground. But even more vivid than the pain from Paul's furious punches was the memory of his parting words.

"The girl. . . . Trust me, she'll give them up."

Jake got to one knee, then stood. He wobbled, nearly fell, but kept his balance. He sucked in a lungful of salt air, both painful and curative at the same time.

Paul was fifty feet ahead of him, staying on the beach as he walked south. Maybe to avoid the limelight after the fight. Maybe because he had a better view of everyone on the Boardwalk from a distance. Or maybe because he knew that Masters had Rachel in her custody and he was going to meet her somewhere.

Jake looked around. If anybody had observed the fight—the beating— they hadn't come to his aid but had gone back about their business. No one on the Boardwalk seemed to notice he was there, and the few people on the beach had moved on. Jake was on his own.

Summoning strength he didn't know existed, he took off running. He knew engaging Paul in another fight wasn't likely to end well, but he didn't know what else to do. He'd come after Jake alone, meaning Masters had lagged behind, likely to search stores. She'd find Rachel for sure.

His footfalls muffled by the sand, Jake sprinted toward Paul, planning to drive into his back. If he could catch him unaware, he could drop him into the sand and deliver a knockout blow to the back of the head. If only.

Paul turned just as Jake approached. He wasn't in time to defend himself, but instead of Jake nailing him in the small of the back, his blow was absorbed by Paul's arm. As they fell, Jake slid toward Paul's chest, knocking him back into the sand.

They tumbled and rolled and came up with Jake on top. Spitting in fury, he threw a mammoth punch that he felt should have broken Paul's face. Instead, he merely turned his head with the blow, deflected another, and rolled Jake to the side.

Their positions now reversed, Paul had the upper hand and picked up where he had left off, pummeling Jake. He managed to get his hands in the way of a few blows and landed a punch to Paul's chin that knocked him back momentarily.

Jake tried to get up, but before he could make it, a punch rocked him sideways into the seagrass. He felt his body being picked up, then a knee slammed into his midsection, and he crumpled like burning paper.

Next thing he knew he was rolled onto his back, and Paul resumed punching his face again, with Jake too weak to offer any defense.

Rachel heard several calls from behind her.

"Hey, lady, wait a second!"

"Who is that?"

"What's going on?"

She ignored them and pushed herself forward, her ankle throbbing, pain pulsing in her side, and her entire body shaking with adrenaline and fear. Her eyes roved left and right, looking for Jake, for Paul, for a uniform and badge. She must have looked a sight, limping, with a cut on her arm and one on her cheek, a bleeding lip, and her hair hanging in the last little clump of a ponytail. She saw the looks of passersby, confused, a little worried, avoiding her.

She ignored them too and kept going, the lights and neon store signs and hum of conversation and beats of background music all a blur around her. She felt like she was in slow motion.

God, help.

Her world was spinning. It felt like hours that she and Jake had been on the run, seeing a murdered FBI agent, dodging a man with a gun, running and hiding and running some more, escaping Flynn, the crash, now her fight with Masters. How long could they go on?

Out the side of her eye, Rachel saw flashes of movement on the beach. She looked, saw black and blue, and somehow knew it was Jake and Paul. She saw Paul slam his knee into Jake's stomach, saw his body crumble.

"Jake," she little more than breathed.

She had stopped at the railing of the Boardwalk and saw Paul flip Jake over and begin to wail on him.

"Excuse me, ma'am, are you okay?"

Rachel ignored the voice and, without thinking, swung over the railing. She landed in pain, her ankle rolling slightly again. She ignored the burn and ran through the seagrass. She hurdled the slat fence halfway across the dunes, sending more pain shooting through her ankle as she pushed off it. She landed on her good foot and kept going.

Remembering something from her self-defense class, she sized up Paul's neck. A few steps away, she hollered, little more than an out-of-breath growl. He turned from Jake to look at her.

Rachel charged, her forearm in front of her. She envisioned it as the hood ornament of a one hundred forty-five-pound truck barreling down on the soft tissue of Paul's windpipe. He raised a hand at the last second, but it was too late.

Rachel plowed through Paul, colliding at full speed. The two of them toppled over into the sand in a tangle of arms. Her momentum carried her farther as she rolled through the sand, onto her bad shoulder, her head thudding into packed sand for good measure.

It took Rachel a few seconds to gather her bearings, and she sat up and turned back toward Jake and Paul. She began to crawl toward Paul, who was on his knees and one hand, his other reaching for his throat. He was gasping, the wheezing, gurgling sound of a man unable to get his breath. Rachel gulped, knowing she had to strike while he was still down. Her self-defense class had taught her—drilled into her, really—that, as grisly as it seemed, when it came to life-and-death situations, kill or be killed was real. When dealing with sociopaths, any other mentality was a death sentence. That had been a shock to her system at the time, and she'd brushed it off as hyperbole. Now, Rachel knew it to be the truth, and she knew Paul was a sociopath. So was Masters, judging by the look in her eyes just before their fight.

Before Rachel could act, Jake came flying in like a drunk in a bar fight. She wasn't sure what his intention was, but his upright midsection crashed into Paul's shoulder, neck, and head, knocking him back into the sand. Unable to brace himself, Paul landed hard, his head taking the brunt of the blow.

Jake rolled to his feet, then dropped to his knees beside an immobile Paul.

"Jake," Rachel said, crawling toward him.

Jake rolled Paul over, pushing his face into the loose sand.

"Jake, what are you doing?" Rachel asked, getting to her feet.

With both hands, he pushed Paul's neck into the ground. There was no resistance.

"Jake!" Rachel nearly shouted, wrapping both arms around her husband. She pulled him back, off and away from Paul, and they both fell back into the sand and seagrass.

Jake immediately moved to get up, half crawling toward Paul. Rachel grabbed him, clinging to his arm. "Jake, no. Jacob!" she said, turning his head. Her hand came back with blood.

Her eyes met Jake's. They were wide and distant. One was swollen. Then her eyes flitted toward the Boardwalk, failing to spy any police officers.

Jake staggered to his feet, and so did Rachel. She continued to pull his arm. "Come on, Baby. We need to get you help."

"I'm fine," he said. He too looked to the Boardwalk, where a few people had gathered and were gesturing toward them. Most just kept walking. His eyes cut to Paul, who hadn't moved. "We gotta get out of here."

"Jake, wh—"

He now took her arm, turning her north. "We gotta go."

Arm-in-arm, helping each other walk, they staggered away from Paul's body. Rachel looked back over her shoulder. Paul still wasn't moving, and she feared the worst.

Chapter Thirty-Six

The beach was empty. Jake and Rachel staggered on, he in something of a daze. His vision was blurred, and he was only distantly aware of the ocean to his right, the noise and lights from the Boardwalk and Plyler Park to his left, and Rachel's questions right beside him. One thing that was crystal clear in his mind was the need to keep moving. Somebody on the Boardwalk had to have seen what happened and where he and Rachel had gone, and it wouldn't be long until someone came after them.

Had he killed Paul? It had been in self-defense, sort of, to make sure Paul was unable to hurt him and Rachel again. Or maybe it had been vengeance or had crossed the line halfway along. Either way, after leaving Flynn half-dead in the waves, after being in the car with a dead FBI agent, with his and Rachel's running through crowds and bobbing and weaving in and out of various establishments, and now with his fight with Paul, they had to have attracted attention. And it was attention he didn't want at the moment. Somehow, he had a sinking feeling the facts wouldn't be clear enough or properly disclosed so as to stack in their favor.

Pain began to crystallize in his consciousness. His stomach felt as if he had the flu. His head felt as if it was in a vise and on fire at the same time, worse than any sinus headache he'd ever experienced. Particularly painful was his left eye, and he realized it might account for his blurred vision.

Screams and shouts distracted him and drew his head to the left. They emanated from crowds at Plyler Park and around the SkyWheel. Music from LandShark Bar & Grill temporarily drowned them out, accompanied by the murmur of conversations from its outdoor deck.

Jake turned around and saw a crowd had gathered five hundred feet behind them, but no one seemed to be coming after them. Somewhere, a siren sounded, but Jake didn't know if it was related to his fight with Paul or some other mayhem in Myrtle Beach.

Walking while looking over his shoulder caused him to stumble, and he would have fallen if Rachel hadn't caught him. He realized they were walking less in tandem, but more with her bearing his weight. She asked some sort of question but sounded like the teacher on a *Peanuts* special. He swung his arm off her shoulders, determined to walk on his own strength.

"Jake."

"We've gotta keep moving," he said, concentrating on putting one foot in front of the other and staying upright. Rachel was content to hold onto his hand, looking back several times.

"Jake, there's an ambulance."

He stopped and turned, seeing the flashing red and white lights as the ambulance slowly turned onto the beach from an access point just behind them. It headed south. After quickly scanning the beach for anyone coming their way, Jake took Rachel's arm again. "Come on."

Up ahead, the dark form of the 14th Avenue Pier loomed against the night sky. Less formidable than the 2nd Avenue Pier, and jutting a much shorter distance into the ocean, it was still an impressive structure boasting a restaurant and gift shop at its base. The entire edifice was constructed on a series of cross-braced pylons, and accessible by a similarly supported bridge from the Boardwalk.

Jake's steps faltered twice, and Rachel tugged on his hand. She led him toward the pier, and he lacked the energy to resist. They ducked under a cross brace and into the darkness. Rachel helped Jake to a large support pillar, and he let it bear his weight.

Rachel stood in front of him, her hands gently probing his face. "Oh my, Jake," she said, her voice on the edge of breaking.

He took her wrists and lowered her hands. "I'm fine, Babe."

"You're not fine. Your face is a mess."

"You used to say I was handsome," he said with a painful smile.

"Jake."

"I'm feeling better," he said, inhaling the salt air.

"We don't lie to each other, Jacob William Taylor."

"It's not a lie," he said. "And we need to keep moving."

"No. Here, sit down."

"Rach."

"Jake," she said. It was too dark to tell, but he knew her eyes were vivid. "Sit down."

"We need to keep—They're going to come for us."

"No one is coming. Now sit down."

He allowed his legs to give way and slid down to his rear with her help.

"Wait here."

She turned and picked her way through the braces and pylons and into the darkness. Jake concentrated on breathing deeply, trying to clear his head. No one had followed them, likely all too focused on Paul. They would have no idea who he was or who the couple who had left him in his current condition was. But somebody had to have seen them go north. Word would spread eventually and, when the confusion died down, someone would seek them out. Looking like a punching bag, Jake wouldn't be hard to spot. They had to keep moving, but his legs felt like jelly.

Rachel returned, her shirt in her hands. As she knelt down in front of him, Jake tried to stand, but she stopped him.

"We have to move," he said to her. "Somebody will find us."

"Wasn't that your idea a few minutes ago?"

"Not like . . ."

"This is going to sting a little," she said, and just before she touched the shirt to his face, he realized it was wet, soaked in saltwater.

"Wha—Ow."

"I'm cleaning you up."

"Rach, it's fine."

"Jake, if you tell me you're fine one more time . . ."

"What are you—Ouch—going to wear?"

"It's the beach. Half the women here are in swimsuits."

"None as hot as you."

"Shut up," she said with a thin smile.

She shifted to one side, straddling his leg. The movement brought her face out of the shadows and into the faint ambient glow cast by the city lights, most notably the blue and purple of the SkyWheel. Her hair was a mess, half of it hanging in a tuft held by a hairband a few inches from the end. The rest was a jumble of wisps and loose ends in her face and sticking in various directions. That much was cute. But in addition to the cut on her cheek from before, she now had a split lip and another gash on her arm.

Suddenly indifferent to any of his wounds, Jake sat up a little straighter. He took Rachel's hands and lowered them. "Honey . . ."

She pursed her lips.

"Are you . . . Does it hurt?"

"No. Not as much as my ankle."

"What happened to it?"

"Tripped on the curb when . . ."

"When?"

"Flynn."

"What about him?"

"He found me. As I was coming out of a store. I got away, ran into the street, and . . . a car hit him."

"A car?"

"I think he's dead, Jake."

He sat back against the pylon. She resumed dabbing his face.

"Masters?" he asked. "Did she find you? Is that what happened to your lip?"

Rachel nodded, running her shirt through her hands to get a clean section.

"What happened?" Jake asked.

"She came into the store, cornered me." She dabbed his face. "I punched her in the nose, then attacked her with a mop and locked her in a closet."

"That's my girl."

"How much trouble are we in?"

"I don't know," he said, rolling his head. He met her eyes and slipped his hand under her ear, cradling her neck. He wished he could say something to make her injuries go away, but he knew it didn't work that way. "I'm so, so sorry, Babe."

"No. This isn't your fault."

"If I pressured you into going along with this—"

"You didn't."

She leaned forward and kissed him, a quick peck on the lips.

"I love you so much," he said.

"I love you too, Jake. A ton."

She kissed him again, slower and softer, then backed away. "Ouch."

"What?"

"My lip."

"Right. I'm going to kill that woman."

"After she gets through me."

Jake laughed. "I've never loved you more than I do right now."

Rachel shook her head at him. Then she lowered the shirt, dropped to a hip, and slid into his chest, resting her head against his shoulder. He wrapped both arms around her.

"Brad and Angelina have nothing on us," he said.

"What?" She lifted her head. "Who?"

"Brad Pitt and Angelina Jolie."

"They're divorced, Jake."

"I mean in that movie."

She frowned.

"*Mr. and Mrs. Smith.*"

She laid her head back down. "Definitely concussed."

He held her even tighter.

Rachel wanted nothing more than to lie in Jake's arms for the rest of the night. But preferably not in the sand under the 14th Avenue Pier. And maybe after a long, hot bath. And some food.

And a legal pardon.

After several minutes, Jake said again, "We should get going."

Knowing he was right, Rachel sighed and sat up. Then she helped him to his feet. "Are you sure you're okay to keep walking?"

"Aside from one knee to the stomach that was too low to break any ribs, all his punches were to my head."

"That's kind of why I'm worried."

"Quiz me if you want."

"Maybe later."

"Then let's get going," he said. "Your ankle is okay?"

"If I made it this far, not to mention fighting with Masters, then I'll be fine."

"Okay."

Jake looked south, to where the lights of an ambulance still flashed, joined now by the red and blue of the Myrtle Beach Police. Rachel followed his gaze until he turned her away. He peeked out at the beach before taking her hand and leading her north. Maybe they had gotten away completely unnoticed. It had been dark, and maybe all anybody saw was commotion. Maybe when they found Paul's body, they had no idea what had happened to him or any inclination to be on the lookout for anyone else. Or maybe nobody had seen where she and Jake had gone, or the police had decided against combing the beach for them. Whatever the case, they appeared to have gotten away clean.

The Boardwalk ended just north of the pier, and, with it, so did the crowds. There were still stragglers on the beach, but with the only light coming from a thin curl of moon behind them and scant lights from hotels and condos on their left, nobody could tell they were beaten and bleeding. Rachel's limp was minimal, and Jake's slow pace looked natural for a couple walking hand-in-hand.

"What's my middle name?" Rachel asked.

"Huh?"

"Testing your brain. My middle name?"

"Elizabeth."

"Birth date?"

"January 4."

"Year?"

"Nineteen eighty-three.

"Anniversary?"

"June ninth. Twenty-oh-eight."

They took a few steps.

"Satisfied?"

"For now."

Another few steps.

"So now what?" she asked.

"Assuming Frost or Jamison don't pop out of the sand like those guys in *The Four Feathers*?"

"Assuming that. Walk back to the condo?"

"No."

"We're halfway there."

"No. We need to . . ."

"Jake?"

"Your shirt."

"What about it?" she asked, holding it in her free hand.

"We need to get a cab."

Rachel frowned, less satisfied with Jake's mental status than thirty seconds ago.

"It'd be a little more natural if you were dressed," he said.

"Well, I can put it on, but the bloodstains might be a little off-putting."

"It is the beach, like you said. Just flirt with him."

"Do we have money for a cab? I used all you gave me."

"I've got some. But we need that . . ."

"Jake?"

"Credit card, but I hate to use that. They can track it."

"They who? Where exactly are we taking the cab?"

"Not far. I just don't want anyone knowing where we are until I can sort things out."

They walked the equivalent of a few blocks, then used a tree-lined walkway to get back to Ocean Boulevard. It was narrower there, just two lanes, with far less traffic. They sat on a concrete bench a few feet from the sidewalk. The muted glow of a street lamp revealed that Rachel's third shirt of the evening was indeed smudged with reddish brown streaks and smears. Jake's face, however, was looking a little better, albeit bruised and swollen. Her being in a bikini top wouldn't be the biggest hindrance to getting a cab.

Jake rested for a moment, his eyes always moving. They settled on the entrance to a mission-style building just south of them, a Mexican restaurant judging by the smell. "I'm going to see if there's a phone," he said.

"Here, I have a dime. Does that still get you anywhere?"

"I can ask for change. Wait here."

"Okay."

Rachel watched traffic, thinking every car looked suspicious until it passed. After the way their evening had gone, she half expected Frost to grab her from behind or Jamison to appear in the middle of the street from behind a passing car. Else for several SWAT vehicles to suddenly screech to a stop in front of her. Was this how spies lived all the time?

Jake was back in two minutes and announced that a cab would be arriving in about ten minutes. They waited on the same bench, her head on his shoulder. Jake wasn't a stud, but his shoulders were broad and strong. Rachel always felt safe whenever she leaned on him or against him, the same as she had around her father as a little girl. Tonight, however, Jake's shoulders were sagged and slumped. She'd never seen him so worn out—physically or mentally—not even after ten- or twelve-hour days of hard, manual labor.

And yet, he had a plan, was always thinking about their next step, always focused on keeping her safe. And yet, he was the one concerned about a small cut on her lip when he'd been beaten to a pulp. And yet, he was the one who cradled her in his arm and assured her she would be fine. Not "we'll be fine," but "you'll be fine." A small distinction, maybe. A discomforting one, in a sense. But also one that warmed every inch of her soul, because she knew Jake would do anything—including give his life—to keep her safe.

And yet, he was the one to help her up when the lights of a cab approached from the south and pulled to the curb. The driver, if he noticed Jake's face or thought Rachel's apparel odd, said nothing. He just took Jake's credit card and asked their destination.

"Bargain Beachwear," Jake said. "Corner of 8th and Ocean."

"You got it."

Rachel turned a quizzical eye to Jake, but his face gave nothing away.

It took just three minutes to drive seven blocks south. Rachel searched the businesses out her window. Ripley's Haunted Adventure and Mirror Maze. Beach Bums. Kings. She turned to see where Flynn had been hit, the scene now clear and traffic moving again.

"Bargain on your right, boss?" the driver said.

"No, 8th and Ocean."

"No problem. Just checking."

They stopped at the light at 9th, where Rachel had broken free from Flynn's grasp in front of Ripley's Believe It or Not. She stared at the spot, the people walking by, oblivious to what had happened there not long ago. She half expected his face to suddenly press against the window like a zombie. He didn't, and as the light turned, the cab continued south.

"Can you park on the side here and wait?" Jake asked when they arrived at 8th Avenue. "We'll only be a minute."

"Meter keeps ticking, but sure."

Frowning at her husband but following his visual cues to keep silent, Rachel got out of the cab. She followed Jake across the street, and they entered the store from which they had made a mad dash to escape Jamison and Frost a little more than an hour ago. The same guy was still hawking freebies and deals from his counter by the entrance. He frowned at Jake but said nothing about Rachel's lack of shirt or their injuries. The clerk at the checkout counter to the right cast them a glance too, but also said nothing.

Jake made a beeline to one of the middle aisles. Still bewildered, Rachel followed. "What are we doing here?" she asked.

"Just wait," Jake said, stopping in front of several dozen ceramic sharks. He reached toward the back and began lifting and gently shaking various figurines. After three or four, he selected one and stood upright. "Okay."

"Okay what?"

He said nothing as he walked to the counter. Rachel followed a pace behind and waited nervously while Jake paid for the ceramic shark. The clerk, a kid with bedhead, gave them each a onceover. "Rough night?"

"You have no idea," Jake said.

"You want a bag?"

"Please."

The kid bagged the shark and handed it to Jake, who nodded at Rachel. "Let's go."

They returned to the cab, and Jake set the bag on the bench seat between them. "Sea Captain's House," he said, referring to a family seafood restaurant on the beach, a few blocks north of their condo.

"Pretty sure there's a dress code," the driver answered, nodding at Rachel.

"We'll be all right," Jake said, holding up the bag.

"You got it, boss."

When they had pulled away from the curb and made a U-turn, and the driver's focus was on Ocean Boulevard traffic, Rachel looked at Jake. She waited until he acknowledged her, then gave a "What gives?" shake of the head to him.

Deftly, he reached down for the bag. He slid out the shark and tipped it over, revealing a two-inch diameter hole in the bottom. He reached into the hole with his thumb and forefinger and pulled. Then he tipped the shark back upright and removed his thumb and finger.

The pouch they'd fished out of the ocean from the 2nd Avenue Pier some two hours prior tumbled into Rachel's lap.

Chapter Thirty-Seven

Rachel hobbled out of the bathroom to the aroma of . . . chicken tenders and French fries?

After the cab had dropped them off in front of Sea Captain's House, she and Jake had waited for it to drive off before skirting a small waterpark beside the restaurant to make their way back to the beach. They had walked several blocks' worth of beach south to their condo, conscientious that Jamison and Frost were staying—or so they had claimed—a few buildings down from them. Aside from a pair of crabbers with their flashlights and two other couples out strolling, they had encountered no one.

They'd entered the condo off the beach and taken the elevator to the nineteenth floor, saying nothing, as had been the case while on the beach. When they had entered their room via key code and had locked and bolted the door behind them, they had both collapsed onto the couch.

"Wow, you really look terrible," Rachel had said, breaking the silence. In the light, Jake's face looked like something out of a, well, Ripley's attraction.

"Yeah, well, your hair is—"

"Never more attractive?"

"I was going to say nest-like, but we'll go with that."

Rachel swung her bad ankle onto the coffee table. "Okay, fess up."

"When we got to Bargain Beachwear, I was afraid we wouldn't be able to outrun everybody forever. After I checked the window, while you were checking the far entrance, I hid the pouch in the shark. I figured if somebody did catch up to us and we didn't have it, they'd assume we'd lost it in the water with Flynn or something."

Rachel shook her head. "Why didn't you tell me?"

"Wasn't a great chance."

She stared at him.

"Plausible deniability," he said. "Now you fess up. After we split at the Gay Dolphin, how'd Flynn find you?"

"We can exchange war stories later," Rachel said. "Right now, I need a hot bath and a hot meal."

"Don't you want to see what we risked our lives for?" Jake asked, holding up the pouch.

"Not half as much I want that bath."

"Fine. We'll have a grand reveal. I wouldn't mind a shower myself."

She leaned forward. "Are we safe here?"

"Nobody knows what room we're in."

"Jake, they've known everything every step of the way. Jamison and Frost knew when and where to 'bump' into us, Paul and Masters bugged and tracked your watch, the FBI found us at a giant outdoor mall . . ."

"Good points. We ditched the watch, so Paul—if he's out of traction—and Masters can't track us anymore. No idea on Jamison and Frost, and the FBI is the FBI. But none of them ever came to our room. They found us at the beach, the elevator, at restaurants . . . And even if they did, they'd have to break down our door. We're as safe here as anywhere."

"Then I am going to take a hot bath."

"I'll shower and order something from the bistro for us to eat. What are you in the mood for?"

"Something hot and hearty."

Jake had apparently concluded chicken strips fit the bill, considering the Styrofoam containers on the coffee table. While Rachel had soaked for nearly forty-five minutes, letting the jets of the whirlpool tub massage sore muscles, he'd used the bathroom's separate shower, his winces and grimaces audible over the sound of the water. After proudly showing Rachel his wounds— they'd concluded one of Flynn's bullets had grazed his midsection—he'd taken to finding food. Rachel had soaked a while longer, amazed at how much every part of her body ached. Given all they'd been through, it made sense.

Tempted to drift off to sleep, she had forced herself to get out when Jake had peeked his head back into the bathroom to announce that he was back with dinner. Rachel had quickly toweled dry and dressed in cotton pants and a comfy T-shirt. She'd spent a few minutes cleaning the cuts on her face and arms and her split lip—none were as bad as she'd thought—before wrapping a cold compress around her ankle with an elastic bandage. Both had been part of the first-aid kit she'd packed for the trip, despite Jake's mocking.

"You order off the kiddie menu?" she asked.

"It was hot, quick, and easy," Jake answered. He sat sideways on the couch in shorts and a T-shirt, one leg extended along the back cushions, one bent and hanging over the edge. He patted the spot on the sofa between his spread legs.

Rachel plucked a chicken tender from one of the containers and plopped down in his "lap," tucking one foot under her and extending the other, wrapped with the compress, beside his.

"You're the only woman I know who can look sexy in sweats and an ACE bandage," he said.

She tore off the tip of the tender with her teeth, chewed, and swallowed. Then she pecked his lips. "And you're the only guy who would be thinking about that at a time like this."

He raised his eyebrows.

"Okay, so you're not." She took another bite, then fed him one. "So," she said and swallowed, "where's the pouch?"

Jake reached into the crevice between his leg and the side of the sofa and lifted the pouch.

"You didn't peek, did you?" she asked. She sat up and swung around to face him.

"Nope. I'm a man of honor."

"Well, let's do it," Rachel said before taking another bite. Her eyes were drawn to the pouch as she chewed.

It was black, velvety in appearance, and lacking any particular shape. Jake worked a knotted drawstring at one end for several seconds before handing it to Rachel. She wedged the rest of the tender into her mouth and, not seeing any napkins, wiped her hands on Jake's shirt.

"Nice."

She shrugged as her fingers dexterously undid the knot. She put the end of her index finger into the opening to pry it wider. Then, with a glance at Jake, she tipped the pouch upside down over his cupped hands.

After a moment's hesitation, a necklace studded with marble-sized diamonds tumbled out and slid into Jake's palms.

Jake lay back against a couple of pillows and the arm of the couch. Rachel lay between his legs and against his chest, his arms around her waist. The cold compress on her ankle had long since warmed to the point that it no longer chilled his calf, nor did it provide her any medical benefit. Neither of them had the energy or the incentive to do anything about it, however.

In fact, neither of them had moved in quite a while. The TV, turned on to watch the late local news, was now black. The balcony doors, open wide when Jake wandered out to think, were still cracked, the sheer curtains floating softly with the breeze that carried the sound of the waves up nineteen stories to their room. It was the only sound, aside from the very faint hum of the lamp in the corner that gave the room its lone light. Most of the fries and all the chicken tenders—save for the third that had fallen out of Rachel's gaping mouth and onto the floor—had been consumed.

And the diamond necklace that was the source of so much contention, hassle, and death rested on an extra pillow in the middle of the coffee table. Jake couldn't take his eyes off it. Even with the meager light, it sparkled like the treasure at the end of a fairy tale. Every time he looked, the diamonds seemed even bigger, more magnificent. He was anything but a jeweler or an expert on facets and karats—he'd needed major help just picking out Rachel's engagement ring—but he could tell these stones were flawless.

Rachel had stared at them for several minutes, disregarding the chicken tender that had fallen out of her mouth. Then she'd said his name over and over: "Jake . . ." She had been unable to get out much more, until finally taking the diamonds from him and fingering them. There were seven, with the one in the middle the largest—the size of a quarter—and each outside of it marginally smaller. Even those on the outside were huge. She'd said his name a few more times.

Finally, she'd looked up at him and constructed a sentence. "What do we do?"

"I hear Monte Carlo is nice this time of year."

They'd started by eating and Googling. They'd confirmed, as best they could, that they were holding the Archibald Diamonds, a set of brilliant cut stones whose history went back centuries. Originally the property of Catherine Maria, daughter of the Duke of Savoy in seventeenth-century Austria, they had been passed down to heirs, given away as usury, paid as ransom, stolen and recovered multiple times, and lost for decades at least thrice. The origin of the stones—provenance, Rachel had said was the appropriate term—was unknown, as was the current owner or location, according to their online research.

The Archibald Diamonds were valued at somewhere between forty and fifty million dollars. Conservatively. Rachel had said for that price, they should have been able to afford better than chicken tenders. Jake had declared that a few scrapes and a twisted ankle were well worth it.

Then they'd actually debated what to do next. The local news had mentioned a murder investigation outside the 2nd Avenue Pier in Myrtle Beach, as well as a pedestrian being hit by a car on Ocean Boulevard. It hadn't given names, listed Flynn's condition, referenced Rachel's fight with Masters or Jake and Paul's battle on the beach (nor Masters' and Paul's whereabouts and conditions), or mentioned any of the other chaos that had taken place along the Myrtle Beach Boardwalk and Promenade that evening. There had been no speculation as to whether the murder and the crash were connected, and no further information—such as suspected tourists from Nebraska being identified by name and photograph—had been provided.

After a brief debate, Jake and Rachel had concluded the best path forward was to contact the FBI—in particular, Special Agent Vaughn. Although both of them were lacking in the trust department, they'd agreed they had no reason—other than everything going wrong for the last few hours—to doubt Vaughn or the FBI. And if he backed them, which they had every reason to believe he would, any remaining legal trouble they might potentially find themselves in should be mitigable.

Using the condo's phone since their cells were shot, Jake had called Vaughn and left a message. He had tried Holmes again, getting the same voicemail as before. He'd called Vaughn a second time—still no answer—and he and Rachel had been toying with the idea of calling Detective Robinson when Vaughn had returned Jake's call.

"Taylor, where are you?"

"Safe," Jake had answered.

"You have them?"

"We do. Are you . . . Do you know about Butler?"

"He's dead, I know," Vaughn said. "Holmes too."

"Holmes too?" Jake asked, cutting his eyes to Rachel. She sat beside him, nibbling a French fry. She stopped chewing and listened.

"Found strangled under the 2nd Avenue Pier."

"I'm sorry."

"Me too. I'm pulling info from MBPD, but I'm out of the loop. Can you update me?"

Jake did, giving him a brief recap of their night. Vaughn swore several times throughout, and again at the end. "You and Rachel, you're okay?"

"A few scrapes and bruises, but yeah."

"I am on my way. I'm in Columbia, but I can be at the coast in a couple of hours. Stay safe, and I'll call you when I arrive. I'd wait until morning, but this has clearly escalated beyond what we anticipated."

"Should we call the police?"

"If you're safe, I'd recommend not until I get there and can liaise with them. After all that's happened tonight, it'd be easier."

"Okay," Jake said. "I'll wait for your call."

That had been a little after eleven. He and Rachel had cleaned up dinner and snuggled on the couch, where they'd lain together for quite a while. At first, the excitement of the day had ebbed out of them in conversation. They'd recounted their shared adventures, answered questions about their experiences apart, and speculated on everything from how Jamison and Frost had known to show up at the 2nd Avenue Pier to how Vaughn would smooth things over with the authorities.

Gradually, they spoke less and less. Twice Jake thought Rachel had fallen asleep until her near-whisper asked another question. Once or twice, he felt himself on the verge of sleep. But a memory of his fights with Flynn and Paul or the horrifying thought of his wife having to fight Masters and evade Flynn kept him from sleeping.

He gave her a gentle squeeze before whispering in her ear, just a few inches from his lips. "I've been thinking."

"Hmm?"

"That gown you wore the other night, to the auction."

"That was just last night."

"Was it?"

Her head nodded beneath his chin.

"Huh. Anyhow, I was thinking it would look pretty good with that string of diamonds around your neck."

She slapped his leg.

"I, of course, meant you would look good in the dress and the diamonds."

"Jake, a shapeless mannequin would look good in that dress and those diamonds."

"Yes, but it'd lack your convivial personality."

She slapped him again, and he smiled.

"I've been thinking," she said after a few minutes.

"About how good I'd look, diamonds or not?"

"You know how you don't appreciate something until it's gone?"

"Like that Counting Crows song?" he asked.

"It's actually a Joni Mitchell song. And I was thinking more like breathing when you have a cold or cheering for a football team that used to win conference titles."

He jabbed her lightly in the stomach, causing her body to wriggle. He tickled her waist, and she giggled with a moan and grabbed his arms. "Ow . . . I'm too sore for tickling."

"Then you shouldn't sass my Huskers."

"Says the guy who constantly mocks women from Iowa."

"You were saying?"

"I was saying I've realized, with all that we've been through this week and especially tonight, just exactly how much you mean to me." She rotated her head so her eyes could look up at his. "I mean, I've always known it, and little things enhance it. But tonight, when we were separated, or when I saw him—" She gulped. "When I saw him beating you . . ." She laid her head on his chest.

"The same way I felt when I heard about you getting in a fight with Masters."

"And when I think of everything you went through to try to protect me. I always knew you would Jake, in theory, but to have it happen not just in theory . . ." She slowly, painfully it appeared, turned over. "I love you so much. I know those are just words, so I'd add a bunch of so's, but they're still just words. They don't accurately represent how much I care about you—and I realized that anew tonight."

Jake smiled thinly as she kissed him.

"What?" she asked.

"You know how when you say you love me, I kind of have to say I love you back?"

She lifted her head a little to give him a cockeyed look.

"I do, like when someone says 'Merry Christmas' or 'Happy New Year' you can't just nod at them."

"Okay?"

"The point is, the fact that I have to say it sort of cheapens it when I do mean it."

"*When* you mean it?"

"You know what I mean."

"Wanna keep digging?"

He wrapped his arms around her waist and pulled her into him. "I'm trying to tell you, Rach, that I feel the exact same way. When I see how you fight through exhaustion and pain and stay with me every step of the way, how you dive into the fray to save me from getting pounded to soup, or when you agree to help the FBI out of responsibility or put your trust in me over and over and tell me that you'll follow my lead, I realize what an absolutely incredible wife I have and how much you truly mean to me."

As he spoke, he saw her eyes melting, the jade warming into a pool of Caribbean water.

"And I want you to know I'm not just saying that because you said it. It's the sincere truth."

"I know it is," she said, her words being swallowed up by a return kiss that would have likely lasted much longer had they not both been so exhausted and sore.

He gave her a quick pat on the butt. "It'll be a while before Vaughn calls. We should try to get some sleep. Or at least lay someplace more comfortable."

She sighed, her head on his chest, if anything snuggling into him a little further. "In a minute."

One arm around her waist, he gently stroked her hair. Her breath was warm on his neck, and he reconsidered if any place could be more comfortable.

The next thing he knew, Special Agent Vaughn's call woke them up.

Chapter Thirty-Eight

Rachel shook awake as a boom echoed through the condo. Her heart thudded in her chest for a moment until she realized it was thunder. She lifted her head, wincing immediately, and looked down at the couch pillow that, along with her hand, had been her cushion. How long had she been out?

Vaughn's call had come just before two a.m. He'd asked Rachel and Jake to come meet him at Peggy's, an all-night diner a few blocks north and west of their condo. Jake had said he'd be there at two-thirty.

While he'd gone to the bathroom and changed into jeans with pockets, Rachel had removed the body-temperature compress, then changed herself, swapping lounge clothes for a nicer shirt and a pair of jeans. She'd been zipping them up when Jake exited the bathroom. He had frowned.

"What are you doing?"

"I wasn't going to meet an FBI agent in sweats, no matter how sexy you find me."

"I'm going alone, Rach."

"What?"

"Just a precaution."

"I thought we trusted Vaughn."

"I do. But I don't trust anybody a hundred percent right now. And I don't want to risk something happening to you," he said, walking into the living room.

Rachel flicked off the bedroom light and followed him. "You think I'll be safer here by myself?"

"This is the safest place there is, Babe. Look, we don't know who's out there yet or what they know about us and where we are. But we do know they're brazen and determined. I don't want to take a chance that they're lying in wait in the parking garage or something and shoot us so they can lift the diamonds off us."

"So what, they just shoot you?"

He shrugged.

Rachel dropped onto the couch with a sigh. "You're not planning to take the diamonds yourself and run off to some exotic locale full of beautiful women, are you?"

"Nope," he said, picking the pouch off the coffee table. He tossed it into her lap. "I'm leaving them here."

"Here?"

"Not real keen on walking around with fifty million worth of diamonds in my pocket, now that I know what they are. Anyhow, I'll meet with Agent Vaughn, make sure everything's okay, and set up a time to hand them over to him."

"And why not now?"

"Call it a gut instinct. I don't know if I'm paranoid or subconsciously aware of something. I just want to see how the chips have fallen before I give them up."

She bit her lip.

"Rach, you've trusted me this far. One step more?"

She nodded. "Of course."

Jake leaned down and kissed her on the forehead. "I'll be back soon."

Rachel reached for his hand and pulled him down to give him a more proper kiss, on the lips. "Be careful, Jake."

"I will. Try to get some sleep. This is almost over."

"You keep saying that . . ."

She had watched him leave, then laid down on the couch, knowing going to bed wasn't worth it—there'd be no way she'd sleep. Truth be told, she had still been a little mad that Jake left her behind. At the same time, she'd realized he was actually doing what she wanted him to do—looking out for her, not taking her for granted. He was putting her needs ahead of her wants, which was an act of true love. Of all the times for him to start being perfect.

It had been thundering in the distance then, she remembered now as she came to, wondering how much she'd actually slept and how long it had really been. Just a few minutes, maybe? The thunder still sounded distant.

Rachel sat up halfway, hearing another rumble. Only it didn't sound like thunder. More like . . . a drawer closing.

Her heart began to race, and she looked around the dark condo. Jake must have turned off the lights when he left. Why couldn't she remember that?

The rumble sounded again, more of a clack-clack. Rollers of a drawer closing, or was that her imagination? She looked around, trying to convince herself she was hearing things, that her sleepy brain was playing tricks with her.

Then she heard it again and knew it wasn't something conjured up by her sleep-deprived mind, nor was it thunder. A muted, very white light—as might be cast by an LED penlight—shown through the open bedroom door.

Somebody was in the condo.

Muted thunder sounded in the distance as Jake crossed Ocean Boulevard and walked to the parking garage where he'd left the Mustang. He wasn't leaving Rachel without qualms, and his "precautions" struck him as a little over the top. Maybe he'd watched too many spy thrillers and had gotten too caught up and influenced by the events of the last thirty-some-odd hours. But he wasn't taking any chances. If anything, Special Agent Vaughn—having lost two agents that night—would appreciate his discretion.

Jake was not into praying his way out of every bind. As his dad had told him when he was a kid, you can't practice like a scrub and pray to play like a star. Even when he wasn't in a pickle because of his own negligence or carelessness, Jake knew God wasn't a magic problem-solver to be used like Jim Rockford used that blond chick every time he got arrested. But he also knew the Almighty was a refuge in trouble and did tell His children to come to Him like an "Abba" or "Daddy." So as Jake guided the car through the parking garage, he prayed for his and Rachel's safety and for wisdom. And for whatever else he might need.

Peggy's looked like little more than an Airstream trailer parked between loblolly pine trees. It was set back from the road to make room for one row of parking stalls accessed via the road. Two of them were filled, one by a black, governmenty SUV, and Jake eased the Mustang into a spot between the two vehicles

From somewhere in the distance, lightning flashed, followed a few seconds later by a clap of thunder. Gusts of wind shook the trees, and the apostrophe in the neon green "Peggy's" sign on the roof flicked off as if affected by the storm.

The front door was in the middle, with a short set of stairs on the far side and a ramp on the near. Jake bounded up the ramp and opened the door. He was immediately hit by the greasy smell of frying bacon and the strains of country music—Martina McBride if he wasn't mistaken. A counter stretched the length of the diner, dotted with eight or ten padded barstools. A trio of tables lined the blinded windows both left and right. Special Agent Vaughn and another man sat on opposite sides of a booth in the right corner. The only other patron was a guy nursing a beer at the left end of the counter, a plate with uneaten burger fixings beside him.

Jake nodded at Vaughn as he approached the table. Both men were dressed in the casual agent style: khakis, jackets over polo shirts, no smiles. Half-empty coffee mugs flanked a carafe between them, and two more mugs were turned upside down next to it.

"Your wife not with you?" Vaughn asked.

"No, sleeping."

"Yeah, well, I'm sorry about the hour, but given the circumstances . . ." He gestured at the booth next to the other man. "Have a seat."

Jake did and shook the hand offered to him.

"Probationary Agent Darren West," Vaughn said. "D, this is Jake Taylor."

"Pleasure," West said.

"Same here."

"Jake, I'm sorry for all you and your wife had to go through," Vaughn said. He scrunched his face. "Are you all right? You said you got into a fight with Paul, but it looks more like you went through a meat grinder."

"One and the same. I'm all right."

"Rachel?"

"A little shaken, but she's okay too."

"Jake, believe me, if I'd anticipated this sort of a situation developing, I would have never asked the two of you to go through with it."

Jake nodded. "What's done is done. I'm sorry about your agents."

"Thank you."

"If I may, what went wrong?"

"We think Paul and Masters got wind of the exchange, possibly even your plans with Laura and Eric. We think they were the ones who . . . took them out." He reached for the carafe and topped off his cup. "Thirsty?"

"No."

"You're welcome to order if you'd like."

"No, I'm good. Thanks. Is there any word on Paul or Masters?"

"Paul was taken to Grand Strand Medical Center," Vaughn said. "He had a ruptured trachea, a mild concussion, and some other lesser injuries."

Jake nodded.

"MBPD was called to the gift shop, but by the time they got there, Masters was gone. We've got a BOLO out for her."

Jake suddenly felt a pit in his stomach, knowing Rachel was alone and Masters was still out there. If something happened to her . . .

"As for Spencer Flynn, he was pronounced dead on arrival at Grand Strand. Severe head trauma, not to mention his legs pretty much being cut in half."

Whatever appetite Jake might have had was gone. He took a deep breath. "Are Rachel and I . . . Are we in trouble?"

"Not once I talk to MBPD." Vaughn took a sip of coffee. A gulp, more like. "I should clarify that. I don't know if you are or not, but I know you won't be once I talk to them. Darren here's been on the horn with contacts at MBPD and the state police most of the way down from the capital. From what you've told me and from what he's gleaned from reports of various witnesses, you and Rachel acted in self-defense. And you were working for us. You'll be fine," he added as he lifted the mug to take another drink.

"Besides," West said, "MBPD is still way behind the curve right now. They're still trying to figure out if the rash of activity along the Boardwalk tonight is connected."

Vaughn nodded. "If they do link it up to you, and they probably will, in all honesty, we'll have your back."

Jake exhaled again.

"So, I'm not much of one to beat around the bush, Jake. You said on the phone you had them?"

"That's right."

"Do you know what we're dealing with?"

"We believe they're the Archibald Diamonds."

Vaughn's nod confirmed it.

"Agent Holmes mentioned them as a possibility for what was being auctioned, so when we saw the diamonds, we looked them up online. Neither of us is a gemologist or anything, but they seem to be a match."

Vaughn glanced at the guy on the stool at the other end of the diner, then behind the counter. "You bring them with you?"

"No. I was hesitant to transport something that valuable in the middle of the night, especially given all that we've been through tonight."

Vaughn nodded, looked to West, nodded some more. "That makes sense." He clapped his hands on the table. "Let's go to your condo and pick them up."

"They're not there either," Jake said. He wasn't sure why, but he had a nagging feeling that something was amiss.

"Where are they?"

"Somewhere safe."

Vaughn extended his tongue, clamping his teeth on it. He retraced his tongue and pursed his lips while glancing at West. "Jake, are you shaking me down?"

"No, sir. But something's off here, and I just figured out what it is."

Vaughn shook his head, a puzzled expression on his face.

"You're right, on the phone, I did tell you we had the diamonds. But only after you asked if we had 'them.'"

Vaughn repeated the head shake. "So?"

"Thing is, nobody—not you, not Holmes, not Butler—knew what was being auctioned. I didn't think much of it at the time—it didn't really register. But then when I got here tonight, you said 'them' again. So what I'm wondering, Special Agent Vaughn, is how you knew to use a plural term for the diamonds when the FBI supposedly didn't know what we had."

Vaughn pursed his lips again. He made the subtlest of nods at West, and before Jake knew it, a cold object was pressed into his side.

"That is what you think it is," Vaughn said. He leaned onto the table. "Now, because I'm something of a patient man, I'm going to ask you again. And because I'm not a violent man and because there's been enough bloodshed already tonight, I'm going to offer you an easy way out of this. But rest assured, I'm also not one to mess around, so you'd better not play with me."

He stared at Jake for several seconds, letting his threat sink in.

"Now, where are the diamonds?"

Chapter Thirty-Nine

Jake swallowed hard. He wanted to kick himself for not catching Vaughn's slip of the tongue earlier. He wanted to kick himself, while he was at it, for showing his hand and revealing what he knew. Most of all, he wanted to kick himself for ever coming to Myrtle Beach in the first place. He should have just bought Rachel some flowers and chocolates and let her pick the movie to watch.

But that was all in the past, and the present was very vivid. Vaughn stared at him with intense brown eyes. Probationary Agent West, if that was his title or name, had a look of hardened steel. Despite Vaughn's recent statement about patience and pacifism, Jake had no doubt that these men would kill to get what they wanted, especially if it was fifty million in diamonds.

For all he knew, they had killed already. He didn't know if they were corrupt FBI agents or imposters. Had they been telling the truth about Paul and Masters' identities, about them being Holmes and Butler's likely killers? Maybe Vaughn had killed them himself. Maybe they were legit agents who'd served their purpose, or maybe they were corrupt agents no longer necessary in his evil plan. Or maybe they weren't agents at all. Holmes might not even be dead.

Jake knew nothing for sure, except that he had to stall.

"I'll get the diamonds for you," he said. "I'll bring them to you."

"No," Vaughn said, "you'll take me to them."

Jake wanted to kick himself again for leaving the diamonds with Rachel. The last thing he wanted to do was take Vaughn to her. Maybe he could propose a deal. Maybe he could get Rachel to bring the diamonds to them. Either way, she would be in danger, and for that, Jake couldn't forgive himself. But he might mitigate the danger by having her come to a public place rather than take Vaughn and West to their condo, where there would be no witnesses."

He tried to stall. "I can't do that."

"Why not?"

"Because I don't know where they are."

"You're lying."

"No, I'm playing my insurance card. See, I was suspicious," he said, fabricating as he went, "and didn't want to bring the diamonds to you until I could alleviate my suspicions. I also didn't want a scenario where you forced me at gunpoint to take you back to our condo to the diamonds and to Rachel. So I told her to go somewhere with them, without me knowing where, just in case. So you see, I can't take you to them."

Vaughn grinned. "You might think you're clever, Taylor, but it won't matter. Call your lovely wife, tell her to bring the diamonds, or she'll be going back to Nebraska a widow."

"Considering the trouble I've gotten her in, that may not be your best leverage."

West pushed the gun a little farther into Jake's side.

He pretended to mull for a moment, but he'd gotten exactly what he wanted—or at least as much as he could hope for under the circumstances. So he nodded.

"Call her," Vaughn said.

"My phone got busted during our escapade this evening," Jake said. "Borrow yours?"

Vaughn planted his tongue in his cheek for a moment. Then he reached down to his waist and brought out a new-model iPhone. He slid it across to Jake. "On speaker."

Jake swallowed and dialed the condo's room number, which he fortunately remembered.

Trill, silence. Trill, silence. Trill, silence.

Vaughn reached over and tapped the screen to end the call after seven rings. "Are you playing me, Taylor?"

Jake shook his head, suddenly dry of spit. Where was Rachel? Asleep? In the bathroom? Had something happened to her?

Vaughn nodded and redialed. After six or seven more rings, he ended the call. "You know what I think, Jake? I think you're lying to me."

"I'm not."

"Then why isn't your wife answering her phone?"

Rachel sat up and eased to the edge of the couch, wary of making a sound. She couldn't believe it. How had somebody broken into their condo? The same way they had before. They'd left the balcony door open, she realized as the curtain fluttered again. Had someone rappelled from the roof? Had they picked the lock on the front door? Had they accosted Jake and tortured the key code out of him?

Maybe it was Jake. Maybe he'd come back and was looking for something. What though? And why in the dark? So as not to wake her?

The light flashed across the floor, then shown at a different angle.

Another clack-clack, this one enveloped by a distant peal of thunder.

Rachel stood, a dull shudder going up from her ankle. She debated making a break for the door. But to go where? With or without the diamonds? She couldn't leave them, but she couldn't go on the run with them and no car, no purse, no money.

She crept toward the bedroom door, barefoot on carpet, but with her heart beating so loudly she feared it was audible to whoever was in the room. Rachel scanned for something she could use as a weapon. She thought about picking up a coffee table book from a bookcase by the wall, then selected a glass sculpture from the top of the bookcase. The sculpture was an odd piece, resembling a mermaid with ocean waves for a tailfin. Rachel and Jake had commented about it all week, and she'd even examined it and found it quite heavy.

Moving slowly so as not to make any noise, Rachel picked up the sculpture, her fingers curled around the mermaid's torso. She held it up by her head, edging toward the bedroom door. She peeked around the corner, and her heart jumped out of her chest.

A figure was hunched over by the end table beside the bed, a flashlight in its mouth as it looked through the drawers.

Rachel watched for a few seconds, and the glow cast by the flashlight's beam revealed strands of long hair. A woman? Frost? Masters?

Knowing it wasn't Jake, Rachel crept forward. She wouldn't make any noise on the carpet, but her bones could creak or the figure might "sense" Rachel was there. She took one slow stride after another, forcing herself to take her time. The intruder slid a drawer shut and started to turn, and Rachel planted her left foot and swung. She brought the sculpture down on the intruder's left temple, knocking her into the side of the bed.

The sculpture shattered into a dozen fragments as Rachel delivered the blow. She jumped back as the intruder fell on the floor, toward Rachel's feet, the flashlight tumbling to the ground and going out. Rachel felt the wall behind her and edged away from the broken pieces of glass, suppressing the urge to scream.

The intruder lay unmoving on the floor. Rachel crossed the room and felt for the light switch. She blinked twice as light flooded the room, revealing Gabrielle Frost, dressed head to toe in black, a rivulet of blood streaming down her head.

She stirred, and this time Rachel did yell. She jumped back into the wall.

What should she do? Suffocate Frost with a pillow? Stomp on her neck? Run?

For whatever reason, she swiped for her purse, nearly knocking it off the dresser.

Shoes!

She was barefoot, and opted for flip-flops, which she'd left . . . by the front door, for going down to the beach.

Frost rolled over, reaching for her head. Rachel darted through the doorway into the living room. Jake had thrown the diamonds—back in their pouch—to her before leaving, and she'd lain down on the couch with them beside her.

She banged her shin on the coffee table, pain shooting up her leg. She lifted a pillow off the couch and grabbed the pouch.

A moan came from the bedroom. Rachel darted to the door, jabbing her left foot at a flip-flop. It took her two tries to wedge it between her toes. The other flip-flop was upside down, and she rolled it over and stabbed her foot at it.

She missed.

A creak from the bedroom. Rachel's heart nearly exploded.

She poked her foot at the flip-flop's strap twice more, then reached down with her hand and grabbed it. She spun around, jerked open the door, and darted into the hallway.

Rachel ran toward the elevator, her purse in one hand, her flip-flop and fifty million in diamonds in her other. Her ankle and shin protesting, she relived her old track and field days.

She pressed the down button on the elevator and looked back, hopping on one foot, trying to put on her other flip-flop. She considered taking the stairs but remembered her ankle and shin.

The elevator hummed and the cables ground and creaked. Rachel growled as the strap refused to slide into place between her toes. She looked back toward the room again, just as Frost staggered into the hallway.

Chapter Forty

The elevator dinged and the doors opened. Frantically now, Rachel hopped-slash-tripped inside and mashed the close button with her right hand. The pouch of diamonds slipped from it, tumbling toward the gap between the elevator and the floor. The pouch landed straddling the gap, and Rachel reached down to pick it up, falling to her knees in the process. Her hand bobbled, nearly knocking the pouch sideways and into the crevice.

Instead, she snatched it, then rolled backward into the elevator as the door whooshed shut. Rachel flailed at the L button for the lobby, and nearly cried with relief when she felt the elevator descending.

She pulled herself up, wondering if Frost could somehow take the stairs down to intercept the elevator. Could she catch a second, faster elevator? What if someone else called for Rachel's elevator? Not likely at this hour, but not impossible.

She watched the numbers tick down, leaning back and finally getting her flip-flop on. She hung her purse over her right shoulder and across her neck, unzipped it, and put the pouch inside. She zipped it shut again as the elevator passed the seventh floor.

What did she do when she got to the lobby? Run? Call 9-1-1? What if Jamison was waiting for her? Or a reincarnated Flynn, the way things were going?

The elevator slowed, wobbled once, and stopped. The doors opened, revealing a vacant lobby.

Rachel didn't hesitate. She rushed for the exit, passing through the double set of automatic doors.

Thunder growled overhead as Rachel stepped out into the night air, a hot breeze whipping her face. She had to figure Frost would be on her soon, and she needed to find a place to hide. She looked left and right, then darted across the street. Headlights from the north bore down on her as she passed through a small, foliaged island between northbound and southbound lanes. She just reached the curb before a pickup truck rolled over the crosswalk. Its horn blared, and a bearded passenger yelled something at Rachel in passing.

She ignored it and turned south. Thunder cracked again, this time with a distant lightning flash.

Rachel reached the south end of the parking garage and immediately turned onto the sidewalk of a westbound street. Palm trees lined the right side of the street, beside the parking garage. A three-story apartment or condo complex was on the south side, its parking lot to its west. Rachel hurried, giant droplets of rain splotching down on her.

Through all that had happened that day—seeing Butler's slit neck, running, being grabbed by Flynn, having to fight Masters, seeing her husband being assaulted—Rachel had experienced near-crippling fear. It was nothing compared to what she felt now, walking the dark streets alone, unsure where to go, being chased. She tried to pray, tried to think, and did neither very well.

She cut across the street, looking back. She didn't spot Frost yet.

An alley cut behind the apartment complex and several commercial buildings south of it. Rachel turned into the alley, angling south and west in the general direction of Peggy's. Without a phone, with the odds of finding a taxi at this hour between slim and none, Rachel figured maybe she could walk the less than a mile to where Jake was meeting with Agent Vaughn. Unless her ankle gave out. Adrenaline had masked the pain initially, but now it was throbbing with every step.

The raindrops had increased, now falling in a steady rhythm. Lightning flashed frequently, and the thunder was almost constant.

Rachel looked back again as she reached the next street south. Not seeing anyone, she turned west again, walking in the street since there was no sidewalk. Small cottages sat on tiny lots on either side of the street, with burned—if any—grass, cracked asphalt or gravel driveways, and little or no vegetation. Except for the obligatory palm trees. It was as if she'd switched counties in a block. Jake had repeated Peggy's address aloud when talking with Vaughn, but now Rachel wondered if she would end up lost, trudging through rundown neighborhoods until dawn.

She looked back, saw nothing, and looked up ahead. She spotted what looked like a major road—Kings Highway, probably—several blocks west, and willed herself to carry on. She was beat, worn not just from a long day but also from the events of it. She reminded herself that she was a distance runner. A mile was nothing, even in flip-flops and with a turned ankle. She thought again of her old track coach, the one who called her Chel. He'd had a slogan, "Find another gear or finish in the rear." Remembering it, Rachel quickened her pace.

Then the heavens opened, and the rain began to pour.

Jake could feel himself sweating. He tried to think at warp speed so it wouldn't be obvious that he was stalling. So far, Vaughn didn't know he was lying, and he tried to maintain that illusion as he searched for an explanation as to why Rachel hadn't answered the phone.

"I don't know. Maybe she's driving."

"I think you're full of crap," Vaughn said. "I think your wife's asleep in bed at your condo with the diamonds tucked under her pillow."

Jake shrugged.

"So here's what I suggest. Either I can send Darren here over there to rouse her and see what he finds, or we can all go."

Jake swallowed again. They were calling his bluff. What could he do, but stall some more? So he shrugged again.

Vaughn did as well. "D, go check the Taylors' condo. If Mrs. Taylor is there, take care of her."

West nodded.

"No," Jake said. "No, I'll take you. We'll all go."

"Smart man," Vaughn said. He leaned forward. "Just so we're clear," he said quietly, "the Archibald Diamonds are worth almost fifty million, and my cut is ten percent. I don't know about you, Jake, but there isn't much I wouldn't do for five million dollars. And I'm already in this up to my elbows, so if you get any bright ideas like shouting for help to that drunk at the barstool or somebody behind the counter, or maybe to the janitor at your condo, it's not going to save your life. It's going to cost them theirs. Are we clear?"

Jake nodded.

"We're going to find your wife, Jake. If you cooperate, we'll treat her well. If not, well, then her blood's on your hands. Got it?"

He nodded again.

"Good."

Vaughn flipped a five-dollar bill on the table and nodded at West. The trio rose and exited the diner. Vaughn told Jake to get in the middle of the SUV, a GMC Yukon. He got behind the wheel, while West got in beside Jake and kept the gun trained on him.

"Are you really FBI?" Jake asked as Vaughn backed out of the stall.

"Twenty years." Rain was starting to fall, and he switched on the wipers. They were noiseless as they squeegeed the windshield.

"Why?"

Vaughn met Jake's eyes in the mirror. "Why what? Sell out?"

Jake nodded.

"Five million not enough of a reason?"

"For some people. You seem like a clean-cut guy, unless it's all an act. Wouldn't have pegged you for it."

"Not that it's any of your business," Vaughn said as he swung the Yukon in a left turn, "but I've got a pair of exes who took half of everything and then half of that, a daughter I've supported for twenty years but never see, I've been watching buddies and colleagues drift toward retirement with no prospects, and the opportunity came along to make a couple million. And nobody gets hurt if they play ball. It was an easy choice."

"Were Butler and Holmes in on that choice?"

"I didn't kill Eric and Laura. Paul and Masters did that." He looked at Jake again through the mirror. "Just because I'm doing a 'bad' thing, doesn't mean I'm all black inside. And I was telling you the truth before. You and your wife play ball, you walk away from this. You don't . . ."

Jake turned to West. "And what's your cut? Ten percent of his ten?"

West smirked. "Won't work, pal, so save it."

They parked in a public lot a block from the Taylors' condo and hurried to it, the raindrops now coming down steadily. They were all soaked by the time they reached the condo lobby, but there was no one there to see them. They rode the elevator to the nineteenth floor in silence, Jake's heart thumping. Could he trust Vaughn not to harm Rachel, especially once he found out Jake had been lying? Would he kill them both and make it look like Paul and Masters or Jamison and Frost had done it? Or would he set them up to be the patsies, making them look like jewel thieves and killers?

The doors opened, and they advanced down the hall. Jake spotted a reddish brown mark on the wall to his right. Blood. His heart rivaled the thunder.

Jake's fingers shook as he punched in the code. He swung open the door, entering first and flipping on the light.

Rachel had vacated the couch, and he didn't see the diamond pouch on it, on the coffee table, or nearby on the floor. He did see drops of blood on the carpet and followed them into the bedroom. Shards of glass surrounded the bed, and a small patch of red stained the carpet by the near nightstand. A flashlight he didn't recognize lay beside it.

Vaughn stood behind him, looking at the scene.

"She's not here," West reported.

Vaughn turned to Jake, who tried to keep a calm face as he processed what he was seeing. Blood. Rachel's? The shards of glass, from what looked like the hideous mermaid/wave sculpture. Had there been a fight? Rachel and who?

More importantly, where was Rachel now?

Rachel was drenched by the time she reached Peggy's, several of its neon green lights flickering. The Mustang was parked to the left side of the small lot, the only vehicle there. Wiping the rain from her forehead, Rachel mounted the steps to the diner's front door as a crack of thunder seemed to shake the very air.

The diner was empty. No one at the counter in front of her. No one in any of the booths. No one working?

"Hello?" Rachel called. She wiped her face again, the water dripping off her clothes and body and puddling on the linoleum floor.

"Be there in a minute!" a male voice hollered from somewhere. It was more like two until a heavyset guy with a scraggly red beard appeared from through a white door with a port window in it. The door swung back and forth on its hinges behind him, which wasn't easy since there was plenty of him behind him too. He had to weigh three hundred pounds, most of it covered in a greasy, stained black apron.

"Whaddya want?" he asked. He reached up to punch off a stereo playing very loud Dierks Bentley.

"I'm looking for my husband," Rachel said. "He was meeting someone here."

"Ain't nobody here," the guy said.

"His car's outside," Rachel said, and briefly described Jake.

"Ain't seen 'im. Course, I've been in back emptyin' grease traps for half an hour."

"Is there anybody else working here?"

"Sally just went home. She might'a served 'em."

Rachel's shoulders fell.

"You want somethin' to eat?"

"No, thanks."

The guy nodded and pushed back through the door. Rachel turned around. "Jake, where are you?" she muttered. Had Vaughn taken him somewhere else in his vehicle? Had Jake been kidnapped before Vaughn arrived? Was Vaughn really a black market art thief masquerading as an FBI agent?

Rachel exited the diner and stood atop the small stoop, under the awning and protected from the rain that drummed against the awning and dripped off it all around her. Now what, she asked herself. Did she wait here or go back to the condo? She couldn't go back, not if there were any chance Frost was still there. She could try calling Vaughn, but didn't have his cell number, and wasn't sure if anyone was answering the FBI's phones in Columbia at this hour to patch her through to him.

She was still debating when a dark sedan slowed and turned into the parking lot, its headlights sweeping across her as it parked. Almost immediately, the door opened, and a man got out. The headlights were still shining in Rachel's general direction and shielded her from identifying him until he was almost to the steps.

Rachel recoiled and backed against the diner door. It was Liam Jamison.

Chapter Forty-One

Jake's eye stayed focused on the small pool of blood beside the bed. Thinking of the drips on the carpet and the smear in the hallway, he tried to put together events. Something had happened to Rachel. Someone had broken into their condo—or been let in by Rachel, which he doubted. There had been a struggle, somebody had been hit with a statue, then exited the condo. But who? Whose blood was it? Rachel's? The other person's? And where were they now?

"Place is clean," West reported. He'd made quick work of searching the condo, presumably for the diamonds. Vaughn had remained with Jake, saying nothing.

"You have any idea what happened?" he now asked.

"No."

"D?"

West looked around. "A struggle . . . Somebody got hit, probably over the head. They left, not real fast, probably woozy, seeing as how the blood was smeared on the wall outside."

Jake wanted to throw up. For all his jokes about Rachel being a ninja in an evening gown, kicking butt and taking names, the thought of her being seriously wounded was almost more than he could take.

"You really don't know where she is, do you?" Vaughn asked Jake.

"No, I don't."

"But you were lying to me before. She was here."

Jake saw no point denying it. He nodded.

"Tell me what happened."

"Simon, we should go," West said.

"In a minute."

"I left Rachel here, with the diamonds, as a failsafe. I was stalling before. I was afraid you'd kill her."

"I'm not going to kill her unless you or she force my hand. You cooperate, you'll both be fine. You have my word, whether you trust it or not."

Jake nodded. It turned to a shake of his head. "I don't know how to cooperate. I'm in the dark."

Vaughn pursed his lips as he nodded.

"We really should go," West said. "Somebody could notice the blood, the comings and goings. Taylor might go to the police."

"You're right. We'll check into a motel and figure out what to do next." Vaughn turned to Jake. "You know your wife. What would she do with the diamonds, assuming she still has them?"

Jake hesitated, in part because he was wondering what had happened to Rachel if she didn't still have the diamonds, and in part because he feared that if he told Vaughn the truth—that she'd go to the cops—he'd react poorly.

"Tell me the truth, Jake. It's your best play."

"She'd try to get in touch with you. That failing, she'd go to the police."

"We need to walk and talk," West said.

Vaughn nodded, and West led the way out of the condo. Jake looked for any signs in the hallway that would tell him whose blood he was looking at or what had happened to Rachel.

"D, get on the horn and see if anybody at MBPD has any updated info," Vaughn instructed.

West nodded as he jabbed the elevator's down button.

"Be vague."

"Of course."

The doors opened, and they got in. As the elevator began to descend, Jake felt sick, leaving behind the condo and any potential link to Rachel.

Rachel felt for the door handle, retreating farther into the doorway. She was hesitant to enter the diner, where she'd be cornered and where she had no ally except that heavyset, bearded man behind the counter.

Jamison held out a hand as he took the first step. "Mrs. Taylor . . ."

She edged toward the ramp, thinking of making a run for it. She doubted she could get very far in flip-flops, and she had nowhere to go if she did.

"I just want to talk to you," Jamison said. She backed away, taking one step down the ramp. Rain splattered down her face, and she blinked it away. When her eyes opened, Jamison was to the top of the steps.

She turned and ran, bolting for the Mustang. At the same time, she fished into her purse for her car key. Sloshing through a puddle in the cracked, uneven parking lot, Rachel heard Jamison behind her. She rounded the front of the car, hand still in her purse. She tripped over the concrete parking block and fell, banging her elbow, bad shoulder, and head into the asphalt. One-flip-flop came off, and the other slid crooked.

Panting, she glanced up at Jamison, who had reached the bottom of the ramp and was coming around the front of the Mustang. Fumbling around in her purse, she reached up with her other hand for the door of the car, hoping it was unlocked. If she could get in, she could lock herself in and find her key—

Jamison grabbed her, and she screamed. It did no good. No one was around to hear it.

"Mrs. Taylor, I'm not going to hurt you," he said, holding her arms as she tried to push back. He then stepped back, his hands up. "I just need to talk to you."

Rachel panted, looking for truth in his dark blue eyes.

Still holding a hand up, he reached his other into his back pocket. Rachel recoiled against the door of the Mustang as he brought out a small wallet. He flipped it open, displaying what looked like credentials of some sort.

"I'm with Interpol. Gabby and I are the 'good guys,' Rachel."

"Interpol?" she breathed.

"That's right. Based out of Lyon, France. We've been tracking a man codenamed *La Fantôme*, French for 'The Ghost.' We're trying to capture him and the Archibald Diamonds."

"*La Fantôme*?" Rachel asked. Her brain was racing, trying to put the pieces together, trying to make sense of all the information she'd been given. "The FBI said you were thieves."

"The FBI is compromised, we believe by someone working with *La Fantôme*."

"What?"

"I can explain it all, but would you mind if we went inside? I feel like I'm back home in Knightsbridge."

He smiled, and it seemed sincere to Rachel. She reasoned that if he had wanted to hurt her, he could have. He certainly wouldn't be suggesting they go inside where there would be potential witnesses. So she nodded.

For the second time, Rachel entered the diner and dripped all over the floor. Jamison invited her to sit down while he approached the counter. When he got the attention of the diner's sole worker, he ordered two coffees and brought them to the table, setting one in front of Rachel as he slid into the other side of the booth. She didn't drink coffee but figured she could make an exception.

"I'm sure you have a lot of questions," Jamison said, "and I'm willing to answer them all. But let me start by saying we think your husband may be in trouble."

If the overnight desk clerk at the dodgy two-story motel thought anything odd about three men checking into a room at three in the morning, he didn't vocalize it. He provided Vaughn with a key—an actual key—on a ring and gave him directions to the second-level room. The motel was shaped like a U, with all the rooms facing the inside of the U, overlooking a dingy green pool. Across the street, a high-rise blocked the view of the ocean, but it didn't stop the motel from advertising "ocean views from every room" on its marquee. Well, technically, "ocean veiws."

Jake, Vaughn, and West climbed the covered exterior staircase and entered the room. West had made several calls during the short ride south from the Taylors' condo, and he placed and received a few more shortly after they checked into the room. After the last, a call that had come to him with no perceptible ring or warning, he reported that MBPD had no further developments. Meaning Rachel had not contacted them.

Vaughn then stepped out onto the terrace to make a short call. Jake turned to West, who had sprawled out on one bed, eyes closed, yet totally aware, Jake was sure. "You actually a probie?" he asked.

"No."

"An agent at all?"

West opened his eyes and rotated his head toward Jake. "No."

"You realize he's going to kill you when this is over, right?"

West smiled as he closed his eyes again. Jake gave up, turning his attention to Rachel. Where was she? Was she okay? What had she done with the diamonds? And how could he reach her?

If she hadn't gone to the police, then she had probably tried to get to him at Peggy's. But she had no car, meaning she would have had to walk in the rain or try to find a late-night taxi. Or maybe she too was holed up in some dive motel, trying to figure out how to reach him. Jake tried to remember the condo bedroom, picturing the dresser. Had Rachel's purse been there? He couldn't recall. Without it, she'd have no way to book a room. So maybe she was hiding out in a lobby or another all-night café. Maybe she was wandering the streets.

Or maybe she wasn't free to do anything. Maybe she was in someone's custody. Or maybe . . . Jake couldn't bring himself to think she was dead. Hadn't she just been in his arms an hour ago? Hadn't they laid together on the couch talking about how much they meant to each other? And now, could they be torn apart?

Vaughn returned. He held up his phone. "This your wife's cell?" he asked Jake.

He only glanced at the number displayed on the phone. "No."

"Then who were you calling before?"

"The condo. Her phone is waterlogged, just like mine."

"She still have it with her?"

"No."

Vaughn ran his tongue over his upper lip as he sat down. "Okay, so your wife is on the run. Let's assume the best, that she's okay. She doesn't go to the cops. What does she do?"

"I don't know."

"Think, Jake."

He shrugged. "I told you, she'd come for me and you."

"The diner," Vaughn and West said at the same time. "Their car's still there," Vaughn added.

"I'll check it out," West said.

"Don't hurt her," Jake said.

"That's on her," Vaughn said. "If she cooperates, she'll be fine."

He nodded at West, who slipped out the door.

⚓   ⚓   ⚓

"Jake's in trouble?" Rachel asked. "He was meeting with a Special Agent Vaughn."

Jamison nodded. "We're not certain, but we think he may be *La Fantôme's* inside man with the FBI."

"Inside why?"

"In case his first plan to get the diamonds failed, which it apparently did."

"And you've known this all along?"

"We've been putting together pieces, but yes."

"You and Frost? She's Interpol too?"

"She is."

"I . . . She broke into my room. I hit—"

"I know. She and I just spoke."

"Is she—?"

"She's fine. She's much tougher than she looks."

"I didn't . . . Why? Why did she break in?"

"The truth is, Rachel, we have been a little unsure about you and your husband from the beginning. We were in the airport, arriving from New York, when your flight from Chicago landed. We saw Spencer Flynn make a drop to your husband. Interpol has linked Flynn to an associate of *La Fantôme*, and we thought you were agents working on his behalf, perhaps even unwittingly. So we set up surveillance. Gabby put a tracker on your car," he said, nodding out the window, "and we arranged to 'run into' you and Jake, hoping to strike up a friendship and keep an eye on you."

Rachel nodded and sipped the coffee. It tasted like electricity.

"When you blew off dinner with us, we thought you were onto us. That's why we approached you at the auction. The way you responded there convinced us you weren't just a network engineer and photographer, and that you were conspiring with someone. We upped our surveillance, hoping you would lead us back to *La Fantôme*."

"Why didn't you tell me then who you were?"

Jamison swallowed a drink. "Not trusting you, we didn't want to reveal our identity."

"The FBI said you were thieves. Was that all part of Vaughn's lie?"

"Not entirely. Doing undercover work, we do take on several personas now and again, including rather high-end thieves. Their intel could have been legit, so to speak."

Rachel nodded, wishing she could make sense of this all.

"Anyhow, we hacked into the condo's security cameras, enabling us to see when you left the condo. We saw you headed down this evening—that is, last evening—and figured you were going to your car, which we could tail. When you got into an Uber, we had to hack their database, which enabled us to trace you to the 2nd Avenue Pier. We assumed you were going to receive the diamonds, and we planned to intercept you and get you to tell us what we needed to know about *La Fantôme*."

Rachel's brain continued to spin, one step behind it seemed, trying to fit what Jamison was saying with her perception of reality—a perception largely formed by the words of various FBI agents.

"When you eluded us, we determined our best play was to continue surveillance and see if you led us to *La Fantôme*. We assumed you were in for the night until the tracker in the car activated. We split up. I followed the car, in case you were going to meet *La Fantôme*, and Gabby broke into your room in case you'd left the diamonds behind. We didn't take the time to check the security footage to see only Jake had left. If we had, we might have planned things differently."

Rachel nodded. "So you knew all along what was being auctioned?"

"We did."

"How did the FBI not?"

"Because they're relatively new to the game when it comes to pursuing *La Fantôme* and the Archibald Diamonds. Or because they were kept in the dark. Special Agent Vaughn likely was aware it was the diamonds, but he kept it from his subordinates because the reason he knew wasn't because of FBI intelligence but because of his connections to *La Fantôme*."

"So what now?" Rachel asked, cradling the mug for warmth. The diner had the A/C cranked and, being soaking wet, she was starting to shiver steadily.

"That depends."

"On?"

"Where the diamonds are."

Rachel swallowed. Everything about Jamison—his eyes, his smile, his words—was persuasive. And what he said rang true, at least theoretically. But she was hesitant to trust him fully. If he was telling the truth, she and Jake had been duped by the FBI. Couldn't she just as easily be being duped now by Jamison? He could have flashed her a fishing license before. Even if she scrutinized his credentials, she wouldn't know a legitimate Interpol badge from even a rudimentary forgery. Nor would she be sure, if she called some Interpol office to verify the duo, that she was actually talking to Interpol and not Frost with a disguised voice on a patched-in line, just like in the movies. So she chose to play her cards very carefully.

"J-Jake has th-them," she said, stuttering from the cold. "He was t-taking them to V-V-Vaughn. We th-thought he-he w-was tr-trustwo-worthy."

"He has the badge to back it up," Jamison said. He took a drink. "I don't mean to alarm you, but with what we know about Vaughn, it's imperative we find your husband, and soon."

Chapter Forty-Two

"F-find them," Rachel stammered. "I thought you w-w-were f-following them."

"I was. I tracked your car here. A few minutes after I arrived, Jake exited the diner with Vaughn and another man. They all got into a black SUV. I tailed them until it was clear they were headed back to your condo. Since Gabby was already there, I had her take up surveillance. And since she reported you had fled on foot, we concluded you were coming here, so I doubled back."

"So if she's at the c-condo, she can confirm th-they're th-th-there?"

"Maybe. Let me call her."

Rachel sat back and held herself in her arms, trying to stop her shivering, unable to quit worrying about Jake. If Vaughn was bad, and if Jake didn't have the diamonds as Vaughn expected, what would he do to him? And what could Rachel do to help him?

Jamison lowered the phone from his ear. "She says the SUV just left."

"L-left? Left for wh-where?"

Jamison asked the question into his phone, then reported. "Turned south on Ocean is all she knows."

"Was Jake . . . Was he inside?"

"I'm sorry, I don't know," he said after a moment. He continued to talk to Frost, and Rachel tried to ignore his half of the conversation. She needed to think.

No, she needed Jake. She wasn't a spy, wasn't prepared to figure this sort of stuff out. Neither was he, for that matter, but he'd been doing it pretty well so far.

"What changed your mind?" she asked Jamison when he disconnected the call a moment later. He'd offered nothing further from the conversation.

"I'm sorry?"

"You said before you thought we were conspiring with the FBI to get the diamonds. So what changed your mind? Why are you telling me all this now instead of . . . doing whatever with me?"

"Something didn't add up. If you were working with Vaughn, you would have brought the diamonds to him right away, not gone back to your condo. That is, of course, unless you were planning to meet up with him in the morning, say, because he had to arrive here from Columbia. But if that were the case, why did Jake suddenly leave the condo in the middle of the night, and particularly why alone? And why, after meeting up with Vaughn, did he leave again in Vaughn's vehicle, and why to go back to the condo?"

Rachel studied Jamison's eyes as he continued to talk. They seemed to be morphing, from kind and sincere to beady and accusatory. And yet, the change was so faintly perceptible that it could have just been the light.

"I could only think of one reason, and that's to vet Vaughn before handing over the diamonds. But if that were the case, he'd have left the diamonds with you, not taken them along as you claimed."

Rachel steadied her gaze. "You think I'm lying?"

Jamison pursed his lips, then slowly shook his head. "I do not. I think the most likely scenario is the one we contemplated for the last week, that you and your husband are who you say you are, regular people here on holiday who somehow got entangled in a mess you barely understand. You were duped by a crooked lawman into doing his dirty work, and now are just trying to make sense of all the conflicting information you're getting and find a way out of this mess."

His eyes were again kind and warm, and Rachel felt herself smiling. The accent probably didn't hurt any. She lifted her purse from over her shoulder, ducking her neck under the strap. She set it on the table and slid it forward.

"What's that for?"

"Frost was searching the apartment. I know she didn't find the diamonds there because they aren't there, and because you wouldn't be here talking to me if she had. Meaning either Jake has them or I have them, right?"

"It would seem so, yes."

She shrugged. "Have a look. I'd let you frisk me, but with my clothes stuck to my skin, it's pretty obvious I don't have millions in diamonds hidden in a pocket or anywhere else."

"You don't have to do this," Jamison said. "I do trust you."

"And I'm rewarding that trust by offering proof. Take a look."

He spent a moment very delicately checking her purse. He then zipped it up and slid it back. "I'm satisfied."

Rachel smiled as she took it back and set it on the booth beside her. "Now what?"

"Now, we try to find your husband and hope we aren't too late."

West was gone less than fifteen minutes. When he returned, he merely shook his head. He removed his wet jacket and sat down. "Mustang's gone. Nobody there."

Vaughn got up and paced.

"We can go back to the condo," West said.

"No, we stay put. We're attracting too much attention. And he can keep calling."

"For how long?"

Vaughn shook his head. "We know she has the diamonds. If she's been to the diner and got the car, we have to assume she knows we have her husband. She hasn't gone to the cops, so sooner or later, she'll contact us."

"How?" Jake asked. "I don't have a cell phone, and she doesn't know your number."

"She can contact the FBI field office in Columbia. They'll patch her through."

"So we wait?" West asked.

Vaughn's answer was to toss the phone to Jake. "Try her again."

Jake dialed the condo's number and waited through eight rings. He shook his head and extended the phone back to Vaughn.

He took it and nodded at West. "We wait."

The soft ding of the elevator stirred Rachel from a momentary daze. She walked down the hall to her and Jake's room, hoping that he might somehow be there. She punched in the code and expectantly entered the room.

The lights were on, which they hadn't been—save for the bedroom—when she left.

"Jake!" she called, closing the door behind her. She made sure it latched, then slid the deadbolt. "Jake?"

Nothing.

She quickly searched the condo, seeing no signs that he had returned. The blood was still on the floor by the bed, as was the penlight and the shards of glass. Rachel swept the condo again, returning to the bedroom. Avoiding the glass, she dropped onto the bed and put her head in her hands.

She had talked Jamison into letting her come back alone. She needed to think and emote in private, and she still wasn't one hundred percent sure she trusted him and Frost. Jamison had said he would check in with "Gabby" again, and they would see if they could use their resources to track down Jake or Special Agent Vaughn.

"I'll keep you updated," he'd said with more sincerity than the typical such law-enforcement promise delivered on TV.

"Thank you, Liam," Rachel said, finding herself once again believing the Englishman.

"Keep your chin up, Rachel. We will find him."

She smiled, and he nodded goodbye. They walked to their separate cars, and Rachel took her time getting in. She sat behind the wheel for a couple minutes, breathing deeply. Through the rearview mirror, she watched the headlights, then taillights, of Jamison's sedan drive past her. She turned her head out the side window, still streaked with rain. When she was sure Jamison was gone, she opened her door and got back out.

Already drenched, she had no qualms about getting down on her hands and knees on the wet pavement. She nearly had to prostrate herself on the asphalt to reach around the front left wheel. Her fingers scraped pavement, then something softer. She pawed at the item with several fingers, bringing it into range. She snatched the small, black pouch and sat back on her knees and heels, breathing a sigh of relief.

It had been a desperate plan, conceived in the split second after she'd fallen while running from Jamison. Her hands, feverishly digging in the purse for the Mustang's key, had come across the pouch with the diamonds. Not wanting it to fall into the wrong hands, and realizing it could possibly be a bargaining chip, she had pulled it from her purse and flicked it under the car, while at the same time reaching up for the door. She'd at first feared Jamison had seen her, but he'd never let on. And then, her gamble had paid off when she had been able to show Jamison her purse and "prove" she didn't have the diamonds.

She'd gotten back into the car, surveyed the parking lot and street to confirm she was still alone, and driven back to the condo. There had been no sign of Frost, Vaughn, or anyone else.

Choking back tears, Rachel stood. She wouldn't waste time crying. She had to think. And warm up.

She shed her wet clothes and put on the sweatpants and the shirt she'd worn earlier that night, along with the Iowa sweatshirt she'd worn their first night in Myrtle Beach, the night their condo had been broken into and they'd found that stupid PADL. While she dressed, Rachel recounted everything Jamison had told her and everything that had happened over the course of the last week. She had plenty of questions, but couldn't find any glaring discrepancies. It made sense that Jamison and Frost were with Interpol. But until she could talk to Jake and confirm what Jamison had told her about Vaughn, she wasn't convinced of anything.

She walked out onto the balcony to think some more. The rain had stopped, and the night air was warm in its wake. As orange lightning snaked across the eastern sky, the distant thunder echoing its light, Rachel debated whether or not to call the FBI and ask for Vaughn's cell phone number. If Jake was with him, it was the only way she could think of to contact him. But if Vaughn was indeed dirty, she wasn't sure she wanted to initiate contact.

What would Jake have told them? That she had the diamonds? Would he have tried to stall by claiming they were elsewhere? Had Vaughn called his bluff? What had he done then? And what would happen if and when Vaughn—by whatever method—learned that Rachel had the diamonds?

The shrill ring of the condo's phone interrupted Rachel's reverie. She looked back over her shoulder, through the sheer curtain, then hurried inside to answer the call.

Chapter Forty-Three

"Try again," Vaughn said, dropping his phone on the bed beside Jake. He noted the time on the phone as he tapped it to dial again: 3:39 a.m. It'd been just less than fifteen minutes. Vaughn was getting anxious, he concluded. That could be either good or bad.

As always, the phone was on speaker, and he listened to trills followed by silence. Two . . . Three . . . Fou—

"Hello?"

"Rachel?" Jake asked, relief flooding him like a hot wave.

"Jake, Honey, are you okay?"

"I'm fine, Babe. Are you?"

"I'm fine. Whe—"

Vaughn took the phone from Jake's hand. "Mrs. Taylor, this is Special Agent Vaughn. Is anyone else with you in the condo?"

Rachel hesitated before answering. "No."

"Good. Stay where you are. We'll be there in about five minutes."

"The diamonds aren't here."

Vaughn paused, his thumb hovering over the screen of his phone. "What did you say?"

"The diamonds aren't here. And if you come here, you won't find me. I'll be gone."

Vaughn looked at Jake, who shrugged. "What do you want?" Vaughn asked into the phone.

"You to let Jake go. When he calls me and tells me he's safe, I'll call you and tell you where the diamonds are."

Vaughn smiled, clearly not with pleasure. "I don't think you understand the gravity of this situation, Mrs. Taylor."

"I understand just fine, *Special Agent* Vaughn. You want the diamonds, I want my husband back. And as much as I love him, I have a feeling you're just as desperate to get your hands on the diamonds. And so is your pal *La Fantôme*."

Vaughn's face twisted. He bit down on his lip, pacing to the corner.

"And if we don't get what we want," Rachel continued, "if we can't strike a deal, your consolation prize is a network engineer and mine is a woman's best friend times seven, so I suggest we play by my terms."

Vaughn pointed at West, then zipped his finger toward the door.

Jake read a fellow man's signal just fine. "Rach, they're coming, get out of there!" he shouted.

Vaughn turned and swung a backhand at Jake, knocking him onto the bed. At the same time, West leaped forward, drawing his fist back.

Vaughn snapped his fingers and pointed at the door again.

"I'll call you in an hour," Rachel said. "Hurt Jake, and it'll be the last time you ever hear from me."

Her phone clicked off, and Vaughn slammed his hand down as if to spike the phone like a football. He didn't, instead unleashing a streak of profanity.

Jake hoped Rachel knew what she was doing, because he had no doubt from the look in Vaughn's eye that he would kill them both with pleasure.

Rachel frantically ran through the condo, simultaneously grabbing items she would need—her purse, better shoes this time, an extra shirt, her tablet, the diamonds!—and stuffing them into a backpack while changing clothes, plotting what else she should take—socks, if she was going to wear shoes—and doing math. Vaughn had said they'd be there in five minutes. Then Jake had told her to run. She'd issued her final ultimatum after that. Maybe thirty seconds had elapsed after Vaughn had sent someone after her. That left four and a half minutes.

She'd been running around the apartment for at least a minute. She stuck her second leg into a pair of jeans while flinging items into the backpack.

They'd brought it along in case of a day hike or a picnic. Now Rachel was stuffing it while prepping to negotiate a transfer of million-dollar diamonds for the life of her husband. Three minutes, max.

Backpack looped over one arm, purse in her hand, shoes in the other, Rachel made one last sweep of the apartment. She spotted the Mustang key on the dresser and looped it with a finger. She jerked open the door, dropping a shoe in the process. She stooped to grab it, stood, and ran barefoot into the hallway.

Whoever was coming—Jake had said "they're," meaning multiple people—could take either the stairs or the elevator. She doubted anyone would run up nineteen flights of stairs, but they might wait in the lobby for her.

The elevator was still on the nineteenth floor from when she'd returned to the apartment maybe half an hour ago. She stepped inside, pressed the L button, and jumped back out. She hoped that was a credible distraction. It seemed like the thing a spy would do.

Rachel burst into the stairwell, paying little attention to what sort of dirt and grime her feet were encountering on the concrete. She went down three flights, then stopped to listen. She heard nothing, such as the sound of Vaughn's henchmen climbing up toward her.

She set down the backpack and dug out her socks. She pulled them on, then stepped into her shoes and laced them tight, feeling her sore ankle for the first time in a while in the process. When she was done, she listened again. Nothing.

Rachel jammed her key into her jeans pocket, then stuffed her purse into the backpack along with everything else. Making sure it was zipped tightly, she shrugged it onto both shoulders. Then she descended a flight of stairs and paused to listen.

There was silence, and she repeated the procedure several times, stopping again when she reached the eighth floor. She stepped into the hallway and paused to think. There were three elevators in the building, and she'd sent one to the lobby. If someone was waiting, they would realize they'd been duped when it arrived. Unless they had called it and thought it came in response to that.

Rachel shook her head. Trying to manipulate this all perfectly was impossible since she didn't know how many people were coming for her or what their strategy would be. So she ducked back into the stairwell and repeated her descend a flight, pause, and listen routine. It brought her to the third floor safely.

She entered the third-floor hallway and crossed to the far side of the building, where she took that side's fire stairs down to the ground level and an emergency exit. She hesitated for a moment, knowing it was possible someone was covering the door. She concluded it wasn't likely, and her chances were much better exiting here than through the lobby. With a deep breath, she pushed through the door and into the night.

She was in a small driveway that served as a loading bay for deliveries, judging by the signage, and also housed the condo's dumpsters. But it was empty.

Rachel cautiously approached the sidewalk, peering around the edge of the building. She saw no one but reasoned if she crossed directly over to the parking garage, anyone hanging out in the lobby could see her.

So she turned north and walked for almost a block. The rain had stopped, but the street and sidewalk still glistened. Pausing in front of another high-rise, Rachel looked back. Still seeing no one, she crossed the street and started south. She entered the parking garage by a side entrance and combined a fast walk and a jog to the Mustang.

So as not to flash its lights, she didn't use the fob to beep it open. Instead, she extracted the metal key by pressing a release lever on the side of the fob. She used the metal key to unlock the door, then inserted it back into the fob, which functioned as the Mustang's ignition key. Rachel tossed the backpack onto the passenger seat, got in, and locked the doors.

Certain that every flit of her eyes, every glance in a mirror, was going to reveal a phony FBI agent coming at her with gun drawn, Rachel backed out of the stall and steered her way out of the garage. She turned south on Ocean, made the first right, then the first left, then the first right, followed by another right on Kings Highway. She drove for several blocks, then turned into a shopping center parking lot on her left.

It was vacant at four a.m., and she quickly navigated through it, exiting on a side street and continuing west for a block until she came to a stoplight. She turned left on North Oak Street, and followed it south until the next light, at 29th Avenue. Rachel hung a right and drove west for several blocks, eventually running into the four-lane Grissom Parkway.

As she made the left turn, she looked back in her rearview mirror one more time. She'd yet to spot a tail, although every pair of headlights behind her temporarily terrified her. Convinced that she had lost any possible pursuers, she drove south, past Broadway at the Beach, the minor league stadium of the Myrtle Beach Pelicans, and several strip malls. She turned right at an intersection that appeared to lead to a variety of commercial buildings. A few minutes later, she found what she was looking for, a twenty-four-hour Waffle House just across the street from a Dunkin' Donuts.

Remembering that Jamison had said he and Frost had tracked the Mustang, Rachel considered the possibility that an old-fashioned tail wasn't the only kind worth worrying about. She parked in the Dunkin' Donuts lot, grabbed the backpack, and hiked across the street. Looking like a cross between a runaway teen (more like the runaway teen's mom) and a homegrown terrorist, Rachel entered the Waffle House.

It was Rachel's first time at such an establishment, and she had no idea what she was doing. She'd thought it was fast food, but it wasn't. So she took a booth by the window, with the Mustang in view, and ordered a waffle and coffee (for the caffeine). When the waitress brought her food, Rachel asked if she knew the time. She was directed to a clock on the far wall. It was twenty after four.

"Thank you," Rachel said, then plowed into her waffle with relish. She felt guilty, with Jake in untold danger, but she had to fuel up. She also felt guilty, thinking back on all the things she had nitpicked and complained about in recent days. Now all she wanted was her imperfect, flawed, wonderful husband back.

She hadn't expected to have much of an appetite, but as the adrenaline that had carried her through the last hour and change wore off, she realized she was famished. She ordered a second waffle, and while she ate, tried to stop thinking about what could happen to Jake and focus on what to do.

She'd told Vaughn she'd call back in an hour, at roughly quarter to five. But what would she tell him? How would she ever arrange an "exchange" or "swap" where she and Jake came out unscathed? Her brain was dizzy with the where's and when's and how's and a thousand things that could go wrong. The issue, it seemed, was that at some point, either she would have to trust Vaughn—which she didn't—or he would have to trust her. She ate, drank coffee, watched the clock, and racked her brain for ideas.

As the large hand on the clock ticked past the 8, she still had nothing.

Chapter Forty-Four

West had returned in under half an hour. Rachel wasn't at the condo. The car wasn't in the garage. Jake wanted to plaster a smirk on his face but feared Vaughn would knock it off. And he knew they were far from out of the woods. They were just entering the woods, in fact. More like a forest.

"Why don't you go get us some breakfast," Vaughn said when West had reported out. "Could be a long morning."

He nodded and turned to go again.

"I'm partial to Taco Bell's Crunchwraps," Jake said. "Bacon, preferably."

West sneered, and Vaughn sent Jake a withering glare. Jake had no idea what was inspiring this flippant attitude, but he was resolved not to show fear and let Vaughn intimidate him. Somehow, he felt his and Rachel's lives depended on it.

West was gone twenty minutes this time, and returned with a sack full of sausage McMuffins and biscuits. No bacon. Not even Canadian bacon. Jake was still grateful and thanked Vaughn as he took an offered sandwich. Wordlessly, Vaughn set a coffee on the windowsill, within Jake's reach.

"Thanks."

They ate in silence for a few minutes, Vaughn watching the clock on the table between the beds. It's red letters glowed 4:42.

"Tell me something," Jake said.

Vaughn looked at him.

"Were Butler and Holmes in on this?"

Vaughn looked down, breaking off a piece of his biscuit with his fingers. He consumed it before answering. "No. They were doing what I told them to."

"And they're dead now because of it," Jake said.

"They're dead because Paul and Masters killed them," Vaughn said, clearly irritated.

Jake decided to keep pushing. "So who are they? Are they working for *La Fantôme* too?"

"There is no *La Fantôme*. He's exactly that, a ghost, a legend, a figment of people's imagination. They're probably working for another bidder."

"So who was Flynn working for and who gave us the PADL if not *La Fantôme*?"

Vaughn shrugged. "We saw the drop on security footage and decided to use you. But as for whose PADL it was, I don't know and I don't care."

"Don't you want to bring them to justice for killing your agents?"

"Why don't you shut up and eat?" West asked. He flipped a wrapped biscuit at Jake, then sat down. Vaughn looked back down at his sandwich, and Jake took the hint to quit asking questions. He didn't want to press too much and risk setting Vaughn off.

Jake had just finished his second sandwich, washing it down with a throat-searing gulp of coffee, when Vaughn's phone vibrated on the dresser. He quickly scooped it up. "Go for Vaughn."

Jake swallowed the lump in his throat, straining to hear Rachel's voice. With the phone not on speaker, he could barely hear her, much less discern what she said.

"And if I say no?" Vaughn asked. He listened for a moment. "Hello?" He pulled the phone back, then bit off a growl, which he followed with more profanity.

"What?" Jake asked.

"Your wife is a real piece of work," Vaughn said through gritted teeth. He flung the phone toward Jake's lap. "You'd better talk some sense into her."

Rachel's heart beat so hard that her ribs were in danger of cracking. She knew hanging up on Vaughn had been a risk, but she had to maintain control of the situation. And frankly, insisting that she talk to Jake to confirm he was okay didn't seem like a reach on her part.

She waited two minutes, making Vaughn sweat. She was in the restroom hallway of the Waffle House, having finished her meal and paid. The backpack with her meager possessions—and the Archibald Diamonds—was on her back. The Mustang still sat in the Dunkin' Donuts parking lot. Rachel had seen no one approach it.

She deposited another coin into the payphone and dialed again. She heard Vaughn's phone click on after only one ring.

"Hello?"

"Jake? Jake, is that you?"

"Yeah, I'm here."

"Are you okay?"

"I'm fine."

"Tell me where we went on our first date if you're really okay, and why you took me there. And if you're not, if they've hurt you, tell me some other place."

"Bold move, wouldn't you say, trusting me to remember something that long ago?"

"Jake! Not now."

She could almost hear the stupid grin in his voice.

"That depends if you count me jump-starting your car to be a first date or not. If not, I took you to Valentino's on 70th and A. I wanted to see if you could eat pizza without blotting it like a total girl."

Rachel blinked away the tears in her eyes. They streamed down her cheek anyhow. "Jake, Baby, we're going to get out of this."

"These guys mean business, Rach."

"I know it. So do I."

"Vaughn wants to talk to you."

"Put him on."

"We're on speaker," Jake said. "I love you, Babe."

"I love you too."

"Touching," Vaughn's voice came a moment later. "I trust you're satisfied, Mrs. Taylor?"

"I am. Here's how it plays out."

"You're done dictating terms."

Rachel slammed the receiver back onto the hook. She reminded herself to breathe. Her heartbeat shook her entire body, and she leaned against the wall for strength.

She waited another two minutes. She would have made it more, but she didn't know if the old thirty-second rule applied to tracing phone calls, or if it could be done even more quickly now. Or, for that matter, if Vaughn had the capability to trace the call at all. Was that something that still required fancy software, or was there an app for that? Either way, she didn't want to stay in one place too long.

"Vaughn," the FBI agent growled in answer the third time.

Rachel forced confidence and toughness that she didn't feel into her voice. "Here's how this plays out," she said slowly. "You bring Jake to Alligator Adventure at Barefoot Landing at five after ten this morning. Enter from the east," she said, referencing a map she and Jake had picked up on their visit and which she had subsequently stuffed in her purse. "Take the boardwalk past the exotic birds and Utan the crocodile and stop at the big curve overlooking the pond. I'll meet you there with the diamonds, and we'll make the exchange. Got it?"

"I got it."

"You come alone, and I come alone."

"No cops. No authorities. You call them, I'll know."

"Why would I need the cops? I'll have the FBI there," she said with as much snottiness as she could muster.

"That it?" Vaughn asked.

"That's it."

This time he hung up on her.

Rachel was quite possibly out of her mind.

To be fair, this was her first prisoner exchange. Her first interaction with a corrupt federal lawman. Her first foray into back-alley jewelry exchanges. Her first time trying to navigate a Food Lion.

She'd driven from the Dunkin' Donuts parking lot to an out of the way motel with parking in the rear, just in case. She'd paid cash for a room, signed in under her middle and maiden names, and set the alarm for seven a.m.

Although her brain had been going nonstop, her body had won out and shut down, and she'd slept for close to two hours. She'd then showered and driven to the nearest grocery store, where her basket held a box of Ziploc bags, a frozen Cornish game hen, a cheap wristwatch, and a box of oatmeal raisin granola bars.

Rachel was in a hurry as she headed for the checkout aisles. She'd had to leave the backpack in the car, albeit not the diamonds, which were in her purse. She feared Vaughn would use his FBI resources and traffic cameras or security footage to find her. She'd thought about taking the bus or calling for a taxi, but wanted the freedom of movement provided by having her own car.

She paid cash for her odd assortment of items and warily headed for the parking lot. The sun was up, peaking through low, scuttling clouds that trailed the storm of the night before. They gave every indication of breaking up and leaving a hot, humid day in their wake. Rachel hoped it would inspire the tourists to visit Alligator Adventure instead of sleeping in or seeking out a local church or brunch buffet.

The Mustang was untouched, and there were no signs of anyone observing her. Rachel got in and drove north, toward Barefoot Landing. She was early, but that was part of her strategy. She'd thought long and hard about her makeshift plan, hatched in the heat of the moment over the dregs of coffee at the Waffle House. She was convinced it was as good as could be conceived of on short notice and without any sort of "spy" experience. Even so, her entrance and (hopefully her and Jake's) exit strategy were still coming together.

She thought about consulting with Jamison and Frost, as she had several times throughout the morning. But Vaughn had said no authorities and, even though they might be able to help her, Rachel wasn't taking any chances. If she did solicit their help, they'd want to call the shots. And with Jake's life on the line, she wasn't ceding control to anyone she didn't fully trust. Right now, that group was pretty small.

Rachel prayed for wisdom and safety and munched granola bars as she drove. She wasn't terribly hungry after two waffles, but she knew she needed her strength and endurance. And her wits.

And quite possibly, a miracle.

Chapter Forty-Five

Rachel and Jake's pass to Alligator Adventure was good for a week, so she gained admittance to the park without having to pay a second time. She also gained admittance without having her backpack searched, which in a day and age of suicide bombers and wackos was a stroke of good luck.

She'd arrived at Barefoot Landing at twenty before nine and parked the Mustang in the northwest corner of the lot, between Greg Norman's Australian Grille and Castano's Italian Steakhouse. Double-checking that she had everything, Rachel had then walked through Barefoot Landing, most of its shops and eateries still closed, and crossed the lake in the middle of the complex via the westernmost of three footbridges. She'd walked past the empty T.I.G.E.R.S. Preservation Station, more closed shops and restaurants, and the Alabama Theater. Then she'd crossed the asphalt parking lot separating the theater from House of Blues, arriving at the end of the boardwalk leading to Alligator Adventure fifteen minutes after she'd left the car.

The sun had been high in the sky, beating down unhindered by clouds, and Rachel, having spent too much of her night soaked by the rain, had become soaked with sweat. She'd taken refuge in the shade of thick trees that crowded the parking lot, and spent the better part of an hour swatting at bugs, watching for snakes or wild gators, and wishing she'd thought to buy some bottled water. Watching the clock constantly, she'd waited until ten o'clock sharp. Then, after making sure she was all set and everything was in place, she'd walked up to the park entrance, hoping and praying some more that this cockamamie plan of hers would somehow work out.

After being admitted to the park, Rachel walked past the various crocodile and alligator pens she and Jake had visited a few days prior, then turned left, toward the feeding area. She kept a wary eye out, looking for Vaughn, anyone "official," or anyone or anything suspicious. The park was mostly empty, with a few families trying to beat the heat of the day and several staffers the only ones there.

She passed the pens housing the kangaroos and slowed as she reached the spot where the boardwalk through the swamp made a sharp turn to the right. It was the most isolated point in the park, with trees on the "inside" of the bend and a swampy pond on the "outside." It was also the farthest away from either entrance, which is why Rachel had selected it as the meeting point.

She stopped a dozen feet from the corner. Special Agent Simon Vaughn stood an equal distance away on the other side of the bend. He leaned against the railing, arms folded across his chest, sunglasses covering his eyes. He was alone. He was not armed, at least that Rachel could see. That didn't mean much, though.

They were the only two people in the area. Rachel had kept an eye out as she'd advanced on the boardwalk and spotted no one, and she saw nobody down the boardwalk behind Vaughn. To her right, the rest of the park was hidden from view by trees. To her left, House of Blues and an electrical transmission facility across the pond might as well have been miles away.

Rachel swallowed hard, looking at the murky, algae-covered water. She didn't immediately spot any alligators and wondered what their sleeping habits were like. And when the last feeding had taken place.

Vaughn pursed his lips and stepped to the middle of the boardwalk, like an Old West gunfighter striding to the middle of a dusty street. "You bring them?" he asked.

Rachel hoped her shaky knees weren't visible. "Where's Jake?"

Vaughn nodded back over his shoulder. "In the car."

"That's not the deal. Bring him out here. I want to see him."

Vaughn stared at her for a minute, then removed his sunglasses. He tapped them into the palm of his hand. "You know I could just shoot you and take them, right?"

"Not real easily. They're 'in the car.'"

Vaughn stuck his tongue in his cheek. Then he actually smiled. "I'm starting to like you, Rachel."

She said nothing.

He held out his palm, same as Jamison had in front of the diner several hours earlier—as he reached for his pocket. He lifted out a smartphone and tapped the screen once, then lifted one end of it to his mouth. Rachel was close enough to hear his single sentence.

"Bring Taylor."

"We agreed to come alone," Rachel said.

"I assumed you were talking to me and my partner."

She glared at him.

"Do you want your husband or not?"

Still glaring, Rachel nodded.

West lowered his phone and nodded at Jake, who sat beside him in the rear of the SUV. "All right, let's go. No funny business."

"No worries," Jake said. He opened his door and got out, squinting against the sun that reflected off a handful of other cars in the parking lot outside Alligator Adventure. He waited until West came around the SUV, then, at his urging, walked ahead of Vaughn's partner toward the entrance. West had a gun in a holster under his untucked shirt, but he couldn't hold it on Jake as they paid and entered the park. Nor was he likely to pull it once inside the park, which was of small consolation to Jake. Knowing it was there and that his wife could potentially be in the line of fire was not reassuring.

Side by side, they walked between the gift shop and a pool of baby alligators, then past several cages of exotic birds, desert turtles, and "Utan – King of the Crocs." From there, Jake and West's path followed a boardwalk out into the swamp, with an open pond on their right. Jake saw Vaughn up ahead, and then, as he took a few more steps, Rachel.

She wore an old pair of dark blue jeans and a white T-shirt with "Huskers" penned on the front in cursive. It was one of his favorites. Her hair was pulled back in a ponytail, but sweaty wisps had come undone. They weren't alone in being sweaty; her face and arms glistened in the morning sun.

She wore a backpack over her shoulders and stood with feet planted firmly, arms at her sides. She had never been more beautiful.

Rachel didn't move when she saw him, and Jake and West stopped beside Vaughn, standing three wide on the boardwalk, with Jake in the middle. For what it was worth, he smiled at Rachel.

"Jake. Are you okay?"

"Never better."

A thin smile broke onto her face.

"All right, he's here," Vaughn said. "The diamonds."

Rachel shrugged off the backpack, holding it in her right hand. With her left, she unzipped it, taking her time, keeping her eyes on Vaughn. With a little bit of a flourish, she lifted something out of the backpack, dropping the backpack as she did. Her right hand flicked a Ziploc bag away from the item in her left hand, which looked to Jake like a raw chicken. Rachel held it by a leg or a wing, and before Vaughn or West could react, she extended it out over the boardwalk railing.

"What's going on?" Vaughn asked, shooting a quick glance at West. If Jake read it right, he was telling him to keep his gun holstered. For now.

"I'm thinking of trying a new recipe: diamond-stuffed chicken. The pouch is inside. You make one wrong move, I so much as see a gun, I drop it, and your precious Archibald Diamonds will become gator food."

"You're crazy," Vaughn said. "You'll never do it."

Rachel turned and tapped the railing of the boardwalk with her free hand, same as the park staffer had done to summon the alligators and entice them to jump during the feeding demonstration a few days ago. Jake cut his eyes to the pond and saw several ripples as ridged, scaled spines slowly approached Rachel.

She turned her head to Vaughn and practically smirked. "Won't I?"

"You do, and your husband's dead."

"We already had this talk, Agent Vaughn. Now, do you want these diamonds or not?"

"You know I do."

"Then listen up. You let Jake walk over to me. When he gets here, I set the hen down on the boardwalk. We turn and walk away, and you walk to it. If there aren't any diamonds, we'll still be in range, and you can shoot us. If there are, you have what you want, and I have what I want, and we go our separate ways. Fair?"

Vaughn placed his tongue in his cheek again. "Fair enough."

"I don't want to see any guns until Jake's here."

"No guns." Vaughn turned to Jake. "Go ahead."

Jake nodded. "Don't spend it all in one place."

He made eye contact with Rachel, who still dangled the hen over the side of the railing. His eyes drifted to it, then to the pond, where four or five gators had approached, their tails swishing the water behind them. He looked back once at Vaughn and West. Vaughn stood with arms crossed. West had his hands on his hips, over his shirt, over his gun.

Jake neared Rachel. "You know what you're doing, Babe?" he whispered.

"We'll find out. Stand beside me."

He did, turning to face Vaughn and West. Out the corner of his eye, he saw Rachel swing the hen back over the boardwalk. West lifted his shirt over the holster, but didn't reach for his gun.

Without taking her eyes off Vaughn, Rachel set the hen down on the boardwalk. She held up both hands. "Okay, let's take this slow," she called to Vaughn. Then, to Jake, "Start backing away."

He did, one foot after the other, his eyes on Vaughn and West as they slowly approached the hen. When they were halfway there, Rachel nudged Jake's arm. She had turned around, now walking normally away from the hen, albeit looking over her shoulder. Jake did likewise.

"Can you run?" she breathed.

"What?"

"Can you?"

"Yeah."

"Get ready."

"Rach . . ."

Vaughn was to the hen. He bent down to lift it up. West stood beside him, eyes alternating between the hen and Jake and Rachel.

"Set . . ." Rachel whispered.

Vaughn stuck his hand inside the hen.

"Run!"

Jake turned his eyes from Vaughn and took off after Rachel, who was already sprinting down the boardwalk.

He'd taken no more than a few steps before the loud crack of a gunshot shattered the morning's stillness. A step in front of him, Rachel pitched forward and fell to the boardwalk deck.

Chapter Forty-Six

It sounded as if the gun had been right beside Rachel's ear, and she instinctively dove to the deck.

She had known it would be close. Using satellite footage on her tablet, she'd calculated how far she and Jake would have to run to get to safety, far enough around a gradual curve in the boardwalk to be out of gunshot range. It would depend, she had known, on where exactly she met Vaughn, how far apart they were when the exchange began, what side of the boardwalk the hen was on. She had purposely placed it as far to the "inside" of the elbow as possible without being obvious, trying to cut the angle a little. At best, she had known it would be tight, but she had still been surprised at how quickly the shot had sounded.

As she fell, Rachel scrambled forward, at the same time looking to see if Jake had been hit. He'd dropped beside her, but she couldn't tell why. She didn't see blood, but everything was happening a hundred miles per hour.

Another shot echoed through the morning, followed immediately by a third. Reverberating echoes were drowned out by distant screams that rang through the park. Rachel instinctively covered her head with her hands and arms, trying to burrow into the boardwalk.

Jake grabbed her arm and tried to lift her. "Rach, come on!"

She scrambled to her feet, her legs churning before she was upright. Jake held onto her arm, pulling her along. She couldn't help it; she looked back.

Vaughn lay crumpled in the bend of the boardwalk, the hen spinning on the wood beside his outstretched hand. West was staggered against the railing, facing away from them, gun drawn.

Another shot boomed. More screams followed.

Jake continued to pull Rachel, and she turned her eyes to him. Another shot bit into the railing to her right, sending splinters of wood toward her. She flailed her arm to block them while Jake pulled her to his side of the boardwalk. She stumbled but kept running.

No more shots sounded, and she didn't look back again.

Jake and Rachel were not alone as they made a mad dash for the exit of Alligator Adventure. Not knowing where the shots had come from, many people dove behind a building or just to the ground. But a handful of others dashed for the south exit and the boardwalk through the swamp that led to Barefoot Landing.

At some point, Jake released Rachel's arm. He looked back several times, but after they turned the corner past an enclosure housing albino alligators, he couldn't see where Vaughn and West had been. For all he knew, they were on his and Rachel's tail. He kept watching, balanced with looks ahead to find a clear path, but saw no signs of pursuit. He'd counted five total shots, but no more.

When they reached the exit, they were at the back of a cluster of five people who were half jogging, half looking back and murmuring. Short of shoving them out of the way, the only other option was to lag behind them. Jake didn't want to go at a slow pace across a largely open swamp, so when they came to the fork in the boardwalk, he pointed Rachel to the right, toward House of Blues. A few paces along, secluded by trees on both sides, and with nothing but swamp behind them, Jake stopped.

"What?" Rachel asked.

"Are you okay?"

"Yeah."

"You didn't get hit?"

"No, I'm okay. You?"

"Fine."

"You're bleeding," she said, pointing to his arm.

Jake inclined it to look and saw a scrape from diving on the boardwalk. "Not a bullet," he said.

"Did you see where the shooter was?" she asked.

"What do you mean? It was Vaughn and West."

"No. Somebody shot them."

"Shot them? Who?"

"I don't know."

Jake quickly looked all around. He felt for Rachel's hand. "Come on, let's get out of here."

"I'm parked way at the far end of the lot. Across the lake."

"Okay, back onto the main boardwalk," Jake said. He doubted that House of Blues was open yet, and if he remembered right, there wasn't much else for shelter that way, just a lot of open parking lot. If they could make it across the open expanse of the swamp and make a short dash across the parking lot, they could find concealment in the shops at Barefoot Landing while also putting more distance between them and the crime scene.

"Run for a beat of five, then walk for two, run for five."

"Modified Fartlek training?"

"If there's still a shooter, I don't want to give him a bead on us."

"Okay."

The boardwalk was clear enough that they could execute Jake's plan, twice dodging around slower movers. They reached the parking lot gasping for air, but Jake took Rachel's hand again and led her across the entrance drive and against the cream-colored wall of a restaurant. He bent over, taking deep breaths. Rachel put her hand on his back, and as he stood, wrapped her arms around his neck in a tight hug.

"I was so worried," she said.

"Me too. But we've gotta keep moving."

She stepped back and nodded.

Jake surveyed the area. "Around the corner of that next building," he said, pointing to a spot a little over one hundred feet away. "Then we blend in with the shoppers."

"Not again," Rachel said.

He forced a smile. "On three, you go first. One . . ."

"Two . . ." she said in the pattern they used when they "raced" on their bikes or when sprinting at the end of a joint run.

"Three," he said, and she took off. He started after her, just as an all-too-familiar black BMW rolled around the corner, accelerating to cut her off. Jake nearly collided with her as she debated between going around the front or the back of the car. At the same time, recognizing it, he reached to pull her behind himself. He was too late and watched in horror as the black driver's window rolled down.

He waited for the soft thup of a silenced pistol.

Rachel watched her reflection disappear in the dark window of the black car. It was replaced by the somewhat pale face of Liam Jamison.

"Are you both all right?" he asked.

Rachel stumbled out a, "Fine," while Jake pulled her around to his side and behind him.

"Quick, get in, we'll give you a lift," Jamison said.

"No."

Rachel squeezed Jake's arm. "They're with Interpol."

He shook his head. "We're not getting in a car with you."

"Okay, I get it. Look, get to your car as fast as you can and meet us across the highway at Cracker Barrel. It's a nice, open, public place. You'll be safe. And if you don't like what we have to say, you can walk away."

Jake still hesitated.

"Please, Mr. Taylor. I know you've had a rough couple of days, but give us a chance."

"Give us fifteen minutes."

"Thank you."

The window went up, and the car rolled away, making a gentle turn and heading for the exit. Jake watched it go, surveying the parking lot and boardwalk back to Alligator Adventure. Finally, he took Rachel's hand. "Come on."

"What are you thinking?" she asked.

"You said they're Interpol?"

"It's a long story."

"Walk and talk."

She did. They walked through the shops at Barefoot Landing, hand-in-hand as if they were midday shoppers unaware of the shooting a few hundred yards away. Jake kept his eyes roving, but otherwise listened attentively. Rachel explained how she had awakened to someone searching the condo, how she'd hit that person over the head with the hideous mermaid/wave statue, and how she'd discovered it was Frost. She recapped running through the rain to Peggy's Diner, being found by Jamison there, hiding the diamonds from him, and their talk where he had revealed that he and "Gabby" were with Interpol.

"He showed you his badge?" Jake asked. They had reached the T.I.G.E.R.S. Preservation Station and turned to one of three bridges crossing the lake.

"He did, but I suppose it could have been a fake. He explained that they saw Flynn give you the PADL at the airport. They surveilled us and concluded we were a proxy working for *La Fantôme*. He said when they questioned me at the auction, they were sure we weren't just a network engineer and a photographer, and they followed us hoping we'd lead them to *La Fantôme*. And they knew Vaughn was dirty. They thought we were working with him. But then when we didn't bring the diamonds to him last night, and you went to meet him, but I stayed behind . . . they realized we were who we are."

"The question is, are they?"

"I don't know. Nobody seems to be."

"What happened after you talked with him?" Jake asked.

"I wasn't sure if I believed him or not, so I came back to the condo, and he said he and Gabrielle would try to figure out where Vaughn had taken you. Then you called, I ran from the condo, and didn't stop running. I never called them because Vaughn said no cops. After that, I was so consumed with my plan to rescue you I didn't think much about them."

"I still can't decide if that was incredibly clever or just plain crazy," Jake said.

"It worked, didn't it?"

"Only because we got help. Which still doesn't sit well. Who else was shooting? Jamison and Frost?"

"Maybe. It would explain why they're here."

"If you didn't contact them, how'd they find us?"

"They've been tracking our car," Rachel said. "They planted a bug or something on it."

"Gabrielle," Jake muttered.

"What?"

"Our first day here, when I forgot my wallet at Beach House, I ran into her and she was admiring the Mustang, running her hands over the spoiler. She was planting the tracking device."

They had reached the parking lot and set out for the Mustang. Jake had stopped looking for shooters behind every bush, building, or bumper.

"How'd you know Vaughn and West wouldn't shoot once I got to you?" he asked. "Or once you put the—what was it, a chicken?"

"Cornish game hen."

"Once you put that down?"

"I figured if they had a way to get the diamonds without shooting, they'd take it. They wouldn't want the attention a gunshot would bring, and until they had the diamonds in their hands, they couldn't risk shooting me because I might be bluffing."

He shook his head. "Plain crazy, but well-thought-out at least."

"Thanks, I think."

Rachel reached into her pocket and tossed Jake her key.

"Thanks. Vaughn lifted mine."

She opened her door and leaned on it. "We going to meet them?"

"I don't know, Rach. I'm inclined to head straight for the airport and book the first flight out of here."

"Without any of our stuff?"

"We'll stop at the condo. Or buy new."

"And with all the potential legal matters unresolved?"

"We'll have our lawyer contact them when we get back to Omaha."

"We don't have a lawyer."

"We'll get one," he said, ducking into the car. Rachel slowly got into her seat.

"You trust them?" Jake asked, looking at her.

"I do. Maybe I'm just swayed by Liam's charming smile and manners, but yes. We can at least hear them out."

"Okay."

"Besides, there's a flaw with your drive-to-the-airport-and-fly-straight-home idea."

"What's that?" he asked with a quick glance at her as he started the car.

She picked her purse off the floor and reached into it. "We have to figure out what to do with these." She withdrew the pouch of diamonds and tossed it into his lap.

Chapter Forty-Seven

Jake studied his wife's mischievous, almost flirtatious eyes, then looked down at the black, velvet pouch in his lap. Back to Rachel's eyes, accompanied by a smirk tugging at the corner of her mouth, and back to the pouch. Then to her face once more.

"You were bluffing."

"Big time."

"You walked out onto that boardwalk with no diamonds."

"I did."

He shook his head. "You could have gotten us killed."

"I had a plan," she said, leaning toward him.

"A crazy plan," he said, also leaning.

"It worked."

"We got lucky."

She leaned the rest of the way and kissed him. "I wasn't about to give fifty million in diamonds to some crooked FBI agent running game on behalf of a criminal mastermind hiding behind some French nickname."

This time he kissed her. "I love you so much."

"You should. I saved your life." She winked and sat up straight.

Jake flipped the pouch back to her, and she returned it to her purse. "Let's hear what Jamison and Frost have to say," he said. "If they are legit, maybe they can straighten things out with the cops, the FBI, the NSA, DHS, *NCIS*, *NCIS: Los Angeles*, *Scorpion*, *Criminal Minds*, and whoever else might be in need of straightening."

She nodded.

"Besides, I'm hungry."

"And if they're not legit?"

"You knocked Frost out once. You can do it again, and I can surely take a skinny British bloke," he said in a bad accent.

Rachel rolled her eyes. "When this is over, we are so going to need a vacation."

"The first recorded history of the Archibald Diamonds," Frost said, "goes all the way back to the House of Savoy in Italy during the Renaissance. One of the many illegitimate children of Charles Emmanuel I—A.K.A. Charles the Great, Duke of Savoy—was Catherine Maria, daughter of Antonia Caterina Arcimboldi of Rome."

"Who's Antonia Caterina Arcimboldi?" Rachel asked.

"More or less the Marilyn Monroe of her day. Mistress to dukes, earls, and kings. Also a woman of immeasurable wealth. According to legend—and that's largely what it is this far back—she gave some of that wealth to her daughter by way of Charles the Great, Catherine Maria, in the form of diamonds. Seven of them, in fact. One, it is thought, for each of the Seven Hills of Rome."

"Where'd Antonia get them?" Jake asked.

"No one knows," Frost answered. "But from there, the diamonds crisscrossed Europe—being fought over and captured in various wars, stolen, paid as ransom, and cut somewhere along the line—until the mid-nineteenth century, when the diamonds were in the possession of a British duke named Kensington. On Christmas Eve, his home was broken into. He, his wife, and his three children were murdered, and the diamonds were taken by a gypsy woman named Vasilescu, who claimed to be the direct descendant of Catherine Maria. She was tried, convicted, and executed, as was her son when he assassinated a magistrate as retribution for her death. Somehow, the diamonds and all record of them were lost until they turned up at a museum in

Cairo in 1896. No one knows how they got to the museum or where they came from."

"Of course," Jake said.

"The museum was closed after Egyptian independence in 1922, but the diamonds showed up again a decade later in Algiers. It was thought that the Nazis captured them during their campaign in North Africa, but they were never recovered in post-war Germany. Then, in the 1960s, a Jewish Holocaust survivor by the name of Haber died, bequeathing all his possessions to his son, including the Archibald Diamonds. His son auctioned them off, claiming they were cursed, and they were bought by a man named Greenberg. In 1974, fire destroyed a bank in Zurich, including much of the vault. Investigators were able to identify the safety deposit box in which Greenberg had kept the diamonds, but they were gone."

Frost raised her eyebrows. "And that's the last time anyone saw or heard of them until now."

Jake leaned back, looking across the backseat of Jamison and Frost's BMW at Rachel. He wondered if she had been captivated by the tale, or if she—like him—was still too busy processing the morning's events to care about legend and lore.

Fifteen minutes ago, Jamison and Frost had been waiting on the porch at Cracker Barrel when the Taylors drove up. They'd waited for Jake and Rachel to park and walk to them, but had made no move to go inside the restaurant.

"We shouldn't linger," Jamison had said.

Jake looked from his stern face to Frost's. Despite a small Band-Aid mostly covered by hair beside her left eye, her face was as beautiful as ever. And yet equally stern.

"Why not?" Jake asked, turning back to Jamison.

"Because in the ten minutes since we've been here, I've already seen three police cars and two ambulances turn onto the road beside the park. There are two dead FBI agents, so before long, this area is going to be crawling with law enforcement officers."

"Like yourself, right?" Jake asked.

"Right. But Interpol isn't exactly high on the food chain when it comes to murdered federal agents on U.S. soil."

Jake shook his head. "How do you know there are two dead FBI agents even? And how do you know they were 'murdered'?"

"Because I'm the one who murdered them," Frost said as matter-of-factly as if discussing Cracker Barrel menu options.

"You?" Rachel asked.

"It wasn't murder but self-defense," Jamison said. "Defending you two. But that's not how it's going to look to the FBI, the police, and whatever other agencies coordinate on this investigation. Believe me, they will be swarming, trying to find the last two people to make contact with those FBI agents. If they're not already, your faces will be plastered everywhere. Suddenly people will start remembering seeing you on the Boardwalk or in one of the shops on Ocean Boulevard last night. You'll be halfway through ham and eggs and start noticing odd looks coming at you from people with phones out at other tables. You think that's crazy, but it's not. Believe me, I've been there. And your shiny red car, parked over there in the parking lot, doesn't exactly blend in. Just across the street from where all the action went down, how long do you think it will be until they find you?"

Jake looked at his wife. Her eyes gave him no indication of what she thought. Maybe because she had no idea what to think.

"So what, we go on the run for the rest of our lives?"

"The rest of your lives, no. The rest of the day, perhaps."

Jake shook his head again and started to speak.

Jamison beat him to it. "We can straighten things out."

"How?"

"I really don't have time to explain now. We need to be going. And I get that your head is spinning, but you really can't afford to hang around here. And neither can we. So Gabby and I are leaving. Come with us, and we can get you out of this mess. Stay here, and you're on your own."

"So you want us to get in your car and ride with you?"

"Yes."

"After you chased us across town last night, confronted my wife at a party, have been tabbed by the FBI as thieves."

"The crooked FBI," Frost said.

"Even so, all without the least explanation as to how you'll straighten things out for us?"

Jamison pursed his lips and looked to Frost.

"Our boss has a lot of pull," she said.

"So make a call. Why can't we have some breakfast while your boss pulls some strings?"

"Because it takes time," Jamison said. "And if you get pinched in the meantime, it will complicate matters significantly."

He sighed when Jake didn't respond.

"I had more rounds in my gun," Frost said. "If our intention was to hurt you . . ."

Jake looked at Rachel again. He was still hesitant to trust Jamison and Frost—or anyone, at this point—and wanted to believe if he could talk with a level-headed FBI agent or police detective, he could clear things up. But he was starting to doubt that too. Rachel's slight nod confirmed his decision.

"Okay."

They had followed the Interpol agents to their BMW and climbed in back. Jamison had taken a series of backroads and side streets, eventually meandering back to Kings Highway and heading north. As he drove, Frost had related the history of the Archibald Diamonds. After giving Jake and Rachel a moment to digest the story, she explained how she and Jamison had been assigned to retrieve them.

"About six months ago, Interpol was instrumental in the arrest of a highly targeted thief named Van Beek. He was subsequently locked away in a South African prison, but first, he taunted several law enforcement agencies by teasing about the 'Seven Archibalds.' At the time, the granddaughter of Greenberg hired a renowned Swiss P.I. named Sterling to investigate the fire at the bank, having long believed it to be an act of arson instead of the accident the authorities originally ruled it to be. Believing there might be something to the growing rumors that the Archibald Diamonds had popped to the surface, Interpol tasked us to pursue them. We've been on the trail since early this year, piecing together intelligence that ultimately led us here, where we hoped to recover the diamonds and their purveyors."

"How'd you find us this morning?" Jake asked, not all that interested, for the time being, in the diamonds' history. "Did you just follow Rachel around all morning and happen to show up in time to save the day?"

"We spent most of the morning trying to track you down," Frost said, turned halfway around in the passenger seat. They were zipping along now at forty-five miles per hour, past an endless string of small commercial properties and golf courses.

"We figured we'd have better luck working our typical channels than coordinating with a civilian," Jamison said, making eye contact with Rachel in a way that was—judging by her smile—completely inoffensive to her.

"We tried to reach her later this morning, but she didn't have a phone," Frost continued. "Then we got stuck in traffic following her, and by the time we found the car in the parking lot, she was gone."

"Fortunately," Jamison said, "we were able to use a series of Interpol, NSA, and FBI contacts to get a trace on Special Agent Vaughn's GMC Yukon. We tracked it to the theme park, concluded something was going down, and went into action, to cover you."

"I scaled the roof of House of Blues," Frost said, "and took up an overwatch position where I could see quite a lot of the park. Still, I was lucky. If you'd have been a few feet farther away, I wouldn't have had a line of sight." She shrugged. "When I saw Agent West reaching for his gun, I fired."

"How many shots?" Rachel asked.

"Three. Vaughn once, West twice. He got off at least one."

Rachel looked at Jake. "The one that exploded into the railing beside us."

"No, that doesn't make sense. That was the last shot." Jake looked at Frost. "If you killed him, how did he get off that final shot?"

"I saw him raising his gun as he went down. He wouldn't be the first to fire a shot in the throes of death."

"You didn't shoot him again?" Rachel asked.

"By the time I got my scope down to where he'd fallen, he wasn't moving and had dropped the gun."

"How do you know for sure he's dead?"

Frost cut her eyes to Rachel. "I know."

Jake took a deep breath. "Okay, so what now? How do we sort this all out?"

"That depends," Jamison said, "as it did last night. Do you have the diamonds?"

Rachel shook her head. She and Jake had agreed not to reveal to the alleged Interpol officers that they still had them. Call it a litmus test, Jake had said. If Jamison and Frost were corrupt or phony agents, they would lose interest in Jake and Rachel if they no longer had the diamonds. So Jake thought, at least.

"They were in the Cornish game hen," Rachel said.

"I beg your pardon?"

"I wasn't completely honest with you at the diner," she said. "Jake didn't have them. We stashed them, before getting back to the condo, in case we were caught with them."

"In a Cornish game hen?"

"Inside the gas cap of the Mustang. So I didn't have them, but neither did Jake. I'm sorry, I didn't know if I could trust you."

"I understand," he said with a trademark smile in the mirror. She returned it. "Now, about that hen?"

"I brought them to the park inside a Cornish game hen, which I hung over the alligator pen so Vaughn wouldn't try anything."

"I wondered what you were doing with that," Frost said.

"If he tried to trick me," Rachel said, "I'd drop the hen, and the diamonds would be snatched up by a gator."

"I'm not sure if that's brilliant or absurd," Jamison said.

"Join the club," Jake said.

"And then you set it down in exchange for Jake," Frost said.

Rachel nodded. "We ran, then kept running when we heard gunshots."

"So the diamonds . . ."

"Are baking on the boardwalk in a bloating, rotting, melting fowl," Jamison said. "Well, we can be sure no one touched it until the FBI or MBPD arrived to process the scene. And with Vaughn out of the picture, the diamonds should be in safe hands."

"Where does that leave us?" Rachel asked.

"I'm afraid, still in a bit of a wicket," Jamison said. "Unfortunately, the evidence could be construed against you. You were in possession of the PADL, you attended the auction and used it, you picked up the diamonds and possessed them, and the only people who can attest to your motives are dead."

"Butler, Holmes, and Vaughn," Jake said.

"Correct."

"Not to mention me almost killing Dane Paul and you being present when Spencer Flynn was killed," he said with a glance at Rachel.

"That too."

"But you can get us out of it?" Jake asked.

"We are just rather run of the mill Interpol officers," Jamison said. "Our boss, however, is not, and can likely clear things up. I believe the term you Yanks use is 'pull rank.'"

"So you'll make the call?" Jake asked.

"We'll do you one better. We'll arrange a face-to-face meeting."

"Where?"

"About five miles ahead."

"What? Your boss is here?" Jake asked.

Frost nodded for Jamison. Then narrowed her eyes as Jake and Rachel glanced nervously at each other. "What?"

"Nothing," Jake said. "It's just the last time a couple of law enforcement types asked us to come meet their boss, it turned out to be Simon Vaughn."

"Well, our boss is nothing like Agent Vaughn," Frost said. She smiled. "You meet, explain your side of things, and we'll vouch for you. By dinnertime, this will all be a bad dream."

Chapter Forty-Eight

Rachel held Jake's hand, in part because she was still a little nervous, but mostly because it felt good to do so after fearing she had lost or might lose him. While he studied Jamison and Frost's credentials (just to be thorough, he said) and asked questions about their boss (who had been in the area since Friday afternoon due to the "gravity of the situation" and was staying on a yacht docked at a marina in North Myrtle Beach, along the Intracoastal Waterway), Rachel watched the scenery out her window. She was shocked at the volume of seafood restaurants, stores selling beachwear, and resort properties.

The drive took maybe fifteen to twenty minutes total, and they arrived at a small marina in the shadow of a causeway leading to the mainland. Along with a brand new hotel, several eateries, a fishing charter company, and the marina office, there was space for forty or fifty boats. Most of the spaces were occupied, the crafts ranging from grimy, rusting fishing trawlers to sleek, stunning yachts. Maybe the grandest was a yacht parked at the far end of the marina from the parking lot. Jamison pointed it out as the group exited the car, then led the way onto the dock.

Rachel hadn't paid much attention since arriving at Alligator Adventure, but the heat of the day had intensified. Rolling cumulous clouds provided the hope of some shady relief, but they were few and far between. Nervous as she walked, she banked her hope on Jamison and Frost telling the truth, on their boss being able to clear her and Jake of any wrongdoings and sort out all legal matters. Then she and Jake could go out for a nice dinner, spend a quiet evening together, and still have a week of vacation left.

By Rachel's estimation, the yacht was close to seventy or eighty feet long, clearly the largest docked at the small marina. It was an elegant combination of white hull and black windows and looked as much like a racing vessel as one designed for luxurious leisure. Nagging at the back of Rachel's head was a question of what an Interpol officer—even a high-ranking one—would be doing on such a craft. But her mind didn't get the chance to ponder it for long. First, a grumbling diesel engine down the dock to her left startled her, then her eyes were caught by a pelican sitting on a pylon as the group turned the corner. From then on, all her attention was on the yacht itself.

A pair of Jet Skis bobbed in the water at the yacht's stern, to which they were attached. The yacht itself was too large to be affected by the pacific marina water, but Jamison nonetheless offered Rachel his hand as she stepped onto a small platform at the stern. Paneled in honey-colored wood, the platform matched dual staircases on either side of a central hatch. Jamison gestured to the one on the right side—starboard—and Rachel led the way up. Frost followed her, then Jake, and lastly Jamison.

Rachel looked at her reflection in a dark wall of glass ten feet in front of her. To its right, another staircase led up to a third level. Deck, Rachel was pretty sure. Left of the wall of glass, a sliding glass door was partially open, and the soft strains of classical music floated out. Beside the door was a small counter with a sink and built-in mini-fridge. Far left and right on the deck, narrow openings led to port and starboard walkways, respectively. And in the middle of the maybe ten-by-fourteen-foot space was a wood table, matching the grain of the deck, with seating for six, all in the shade of the deck above. So this was how the other half lived. And this was only the rear—stern, Rachel reminded herself, or was it aft?—deck.

"This way," Frost said, taking the lead. She opened the sliding door all the way. With a glance at Jake, trying to ask, "Is this really happening?" with her eyes, Rachel followed. They entered what was the nautical version of a living room (called a salon), complete with a plush sectional sofa and separate end chair that formed a U around a glass coffee table, a small entertainment console—with a hideaway TV—that blended perfectly with the free-flowing design, and port and starboard windows letting in plenty of light. The word that kept coming to Rachel's mind was sleek. From the light gray walls and cabinetry to the white sofa and chair to the way the entire room funneled toward a hallway that led—judging by the smell—to the kitchen, everything was refined and luxurious, right down to the graceful artwork on the walls and blue and peach satin throw pillows on the sofa.

Of all the places she and Jake had eaten in the last week, none of the aromas had begun to match that which wafted to Rachel's nose from the next compartment. She inhaled deeply, taking in the scents of garlic, onion, and basil as she followed Frost down the very short hallway into a kitchen—the galley—with marble countertops and cabinets to match those in the salon. More sunlight flowed through a starboard window as well as from a skylight over the dining area farther toward the bow. Soft recessed lighting also streamed down on an island counter that contained an electric stovetop and ample prep space. The stovetop was covered with pots and pans, the counter with measuring cups and small dishes filled with spices and chopped ham and tomatoes, a package of cheese and a grater, a bottle of olive oil, and two greenish-red and yellow mangos resting on a cutting board.

Behind the counter, facing the sink and window, was a dark-haired woman. She was approximately Rachel's height, with very tan skin revealed by a cream-colored baby doll blouse. As Frost, the Taylors, and Jamison stopped in the small walkway between the island counter and steps leading below deck, the woman turned around. She held half a glass of white wine in her left hand. Her face was sharp and taut, very beautiful, all channeling attention to vibrant brown eyes. Had it not been for slight creases around them and at the corners of her mouth, Rachel would have guessed the woman to be no older than thirty, maybe thirty-five. Instead, she estimated she was in her low forties. Now that she was facing forward, Rachel detected a very thin strand of hair near the front dyed a deep purplish red. Several gold chains—or maybe just one necklace with multiple strands—adorned her neck, and long earrings—also gold—dangled from her ears. She looked more like a chic runway model than a high-ranking officer in any law enforcement agency. Then again, maybe she was just the chef.

"Rachel, Jake," Frost said, "this is Tessa D'Angelo."

"A pleasure to meet you both," the woman said in a thick but not impeding Spanish or maybe Italian accent. "Welcome aboard. I apologize for the inconvenient method in which you had to arrive."

"Is this . . . your boat?" Jake asked.

"Yes."

"And you work for Interpol?"

She smiled as she said, "No," and took a drink of wine.

"What's—"

"We don't work *only* for Interpol," Jamison said as D'Angelo picked up an inch-and-a-half-thick chef's knife. She turned one of the mangos on its side and sliced off a third of it with a quiet swoosh.

"Then what—"

"We also do some private contracting, similar to how a police officer might work nights as a security guard or a bouncer at a club."

"Well, it's not exactly like that," Frost said with a smile, reaching for a slice of freshly cut mango. With lightning fast reflexes, D'Angelo swung the knife down on Frost's fingers before she could withdraw them.

Rachel gasped and watched for blood to start spurting. Frost emitted a quick yelp then shook her hand. D'Angelo swiped the dropped piece of mango back toward the pile with her knife and resumed cutting with a quick glance at Frost.

Rachel watched the quiet interplay wide-eyed, slowly realizing that D'Angelo had rotated the knife so as to rap Frost's knuckles with the dull side. All over a mango? She cast Jake a quick glance. Who was this woman?

"I am a collector and connoisseur," D'Angelo said in answer to Jake's earlier question. She worked quickly as she spoke, her knife making a repeated and quiet whoosh-clack-swipe sound as she diced the mango into perfect light-orange cubes. Nobody reached for any more. "I occasionally hire individuals to work for me. In this case, Gabby and Liam."

"And you're able to help us deal with the FBI and MBPD and clear our names?" Jake asked.

"Indeed. I have friends and contacts throughout the world, and am not bound by red tape or bureaucracy or protocol." D'Angelo scraped the diced mangos into a bowl. "I'll explain in detail as we eat, but first, you must taste the bruschetta," she said. She set down the knife and turned to the oven at her side. She opened it, and the aroma that had been tantalizing Rachel for several minutes intensified as D'Angelo removed a baking sheet lined with tiny slices of baguette covered in ham, tomatoes, cheese, and drizzled vinaigrette. She set the sheet on a waiting trivet on the counter behind her. Holding up a finger for patience, she reached for a wide spatula and slid it under several of the baguettes.

Rachel watched while glancing at Jake, Jamison, and then Frost with fascination. Was this really happening? Two hours ago, she'd feared for Jake's life. Then she'd faced down corrupt FBI agents on a boardwalk surrounded by alligators. After being shot at, she and Jake had run, been intercepted by Interpol officers who persuaded them to meet their boss, and were now standing in the galley of a luxury yacht being served bruschetta by a mystery woman who claimed she could make all of their problems go away. Was this a dream? Had she fallen asleep when Jake left to meet with Vaughn, and everything subsequent was some crazy machination of her subconscious?

No, the aromas were too robust.

"Please, try one," D'Angelo said, extending the spatula to them. "They will be warm."

Jamison reached first, and with a look at Rachel, Jake followed suit. Frost took one, then Rachel, leaving the last for D'Angelo, which she plucked off the spatula. She took a small bite off the end, immediately closing her eyes for a second and moaning softly. "Mmm, delicious, no?"

"Incredible," Frost said.

Rachel looked at Jake, who bit off half of the small baguette. She, still feeling the peculiarity of the moment, did likewise.

"I don't know how you do it," Frost said. "The same ingredients, and mine taste like tomato sauce on cardboard."

D'Angelo smiled.

"This is very good," Rachel said after swallowing. "Thank you." Peculiarity didn't mitigate manners, she figured.

"You're welcome."

"So, *Il Fantasma*," Jake said, referring to the name stenciled on the yacht's stern. "Is that Italian?" he asked as D'Angelo scooped several more pieces of bruschetta onto the spatula and extended it to him. "*The Fantasy* or *The Dream* or something like that?"

"You are half right," D'Angelo said as she reached for another baguette. Jamison did as well. "It is Italian, as am I. But the meaning is slightly different." Her brown eyes were like a churning sea. "*Il Fantasma* would most accurately be translated as *The Ghost*."

Chapter Forty-Nine

Jake felt his body slowly, very softly rocking. Not from side to side, but end to end. He was on a boat, a boat that wasn't moving. He moved his arms, banged an elbow, and blinked open his eyes.

He was looking up at an off-white ceiling, lit only from behind his head by what he presumed was a porthole. A wall was immediately to his right. A second wall extended from behind him to his shoulders on the left. Butting up against it was a small, built-in nightstand on which he'd bumped his elbow. An anxious wave of claustrophobia washed over him, but it passed.

Jake heard nothing. He had a dull ache at the base of his skull, dryness in his mouth, and lethargy over his entire body, similar to when he woke up in the middle of the night. But it wasn't the middle of the night, judging by the light coming in from the window. It was late afternoon or evening, or maybe mid-morning. He couldn't remember.

He was also cold. Lifting his head a fraction, he saw that he was wearing no pants. Or shirt. Just his underwear.

Jake sat all the way up, too quickly, feeling a rush of blood to his head. He held it in the heels of his hands for several seconds, then lifted his head, blinked a few times, and forced himself to breathe deeply.

He was sitting on a single bed that fit snugly between a wall at the foot and a sloping wall at the head. Into the head wall was built a small porthole, out which Jake saw nothing but sky. Across from him, almost touchable if he extended his legs, was another bed, built similarly into a symmetrical room.

The bed was empty.

Jake stood on wobbly legs. The headache pulsated but seemed to be fading. The lethargy and dry mouth not so much. He looked around, spotting a small flat screen TV mounted on the wall at the foot of his bed. A high-tech device that looked like a combination thermostat/smoke detector was affixed beside the narrow door between the beds. Opposite the door, in between the beds, was a tiny closet above the nightstand. Its door, Jake now noticed, was several inches ajar.

Rubbing his hand over his face and again noticing the dry clinginess of his tongue, Jake opened the door. A pair of brightly colored shorts and a white, sleeveless shirt hung on a pair of pegs. Pinned to the back of the closet was a handwritten note:

WEAR THESE

Jake looked around the room for signs that he was in some way being monitored. He saw none—no technology other than the TV and thermostat contraption. If there was a camera hidden somewhere, it was well concealed.

He climbed onto his bed, kneeling to look out the window. He saw deep blue water as far as the horizon stretched. A mostly cloudless pale blue sky complemented it. The sun was on the opposite side of the yacht, and low in the sky if the sky color and reflection off the water told him anything. Plus it just felt like evening, not morning. If so, that meant the boat was facing east or southeast and had clearly left the marina in North Myrtle Beach. But where were they now? How much time exactly had passed? And more importantly, where was Rachel?

Jake got down from the bed and, because the note said to, put on the shorts—actually swim trunks—and shirt. "Now what?" he asked himself, his voice muted for lack of saliva. It didn't take a genius to realize he was below deck on *Il Fantasma*, the yacht owned by Tessa D'Angelo. *Il Fantasma*—The Ghost. So she was *La Fantôme*—the Ghost Butler and Holmes had first mentioned? Or had that all been a fabrication? Vaughn had denied such a person existed. Was he lying? Ignorant? Somehow complicit? Jake's head was starting to hurt again.

He felt the handle on the door, found it unlocked, and swung it open. He stepped into a narrow corridor, with a wood floor like the decks above. The walls were the same patterned slate, cold like a prison, he thought.

There was a door directly across from his, two more on either side to the left—forward—and another at the end of the hall. All were closed. To the right—aft—the corridor curved to the right in a few feet, just on the other side of his room.

After spending a moment listening and hearing nothing, as well as looking for any signs that would tell him he was being monitored or show him where to go, Jake tried the knob across the hall. He was as delicate and quiet as he could be while still confirming it was locked. He turned to his left, facing forward. The door ahead on his right opened to a cramped three-piece bathroom. The door across the hall from it and the one at the end of the hall were both locked. He thought about knocking, about calling for Rachel. But if no one knew where he was or that he was awake yet, he didn't want to give that away. He decided to scout a little bit first.

He crept forward, hoping his feet wouldn't squeak on the wood. They didn't. He turned the corner and saw another closed door on the left and curving stairs ahead. He paused at the base of the stairs, listening. Still nothing.

Jake took the first few steps, peeking his head up. The stairs led to the galley, and Jake's mind flooded with his last memory. He and Rachel had met Tessa D'Angelo and eaten bruschetta while she translated the name of the yacht. He didn't remember anything else. Had they been drugged? But if so, how? Jamison, Frost, and D'Angelo herself had all eaten the bruschetta too. Had it been something else? How long had he been out? Where was everyone? Where was Rachel?

He climbed into the galley and found it empty. No people, no food on the counter, no dirty pots and pans, not even the faint hint of the aroma of the bruschetta. The dining area forward was also similarly vacant, as was the salon.

Jake squinted as he looked out the various windows. They were out in the open ocean, the yacht rocking gently and creaking quietly with the swells. Jake walked around the island counter and leaned over the sink. He peered out the window. Nothing but ocean until it bled into the sky in a thin strip of haze. He'd heard something about the curvature of the earth limiting vision at ground—or sea—level to thirteen or seventeen miles or something like that. It was not lost on him that International Waters started twelve miles from land, but what that meant for him and Rachel, he had no idea.

Looking around again—he was still alone—Jake decided to try to find a glass. But when he reached for a cupboard, he found it wouldn't open. He tried another with the same result. He tried one under the counter, but it wouldn't budge. What was going on? Where were all D'Angelo's utensils? Was this a separate yacht? Was this all a mirage, or a dream?

He took several deep breaths, realizing his mind was starting to play tricks on him, which was probably what somebody wanted. He tried the faucet and was somewhat surprised when a stream of water came out. He ducked his head under the faucet, taking several short drinks to at least wet his whistle. Then he stood again.

Where was D'Angelo? Where were Jamison and Frost? Where was Rachel? It felt for all the world like he was alone on the yacht, set adrift. Could that be? Was Rachel locked in a cabin down below? Was that how D'Angelo, Jamison, and Frost were getting rid of them, letting them drift out to sea? There had been a couple of Jet Skis off the back of the yacht. Had they taken them and made their escape? Surely they wouldn't cut Jake and Rachel loose in a million-dollar yacht? And not without the diamonds. Unless they—

Jake heard a very soft tinkle, like the sound of breaking glass. It was so quiet and distant that had it not been so out of place from the few nautical sounds he'd heard and were he not so highly tuned to anything out of the ordinary, it might not have registered. But it did, and Jake froze, trying to identify it as he listened again. He heard nothing more, just the creaks of a ship at sea. His mind tried to run wild with possibilities, and he concluded his best bet was to investigate. So he stole through the hall and salon and out onto the back deck, where he paused to listen again. Nothing. A gentle sea breeze ruffled his shirt, the sleeveless shirt that had been waiting for him in a closet with a pair of swimming trunks, reminding him how odd this was.

He turned for the stairs leading up to the top deck—the flybridge. Two-thirds of the way up he stopped, almost in shock.

Tessa D'Angelo stood between two padded wicker chaise lounge chairs. She had changed into white capris and a loose, maroon sleeveless top. Her dark-chocolate hair was tied in a low ponytail, the reddish streak in it flashing in the evening sunlight. She stood in front of an easel with a two-foot square canvas mounted on it. In her right hand was a thinly tapered paintbrush, and in her left a small palette with several dabs of paint—blues, greens, and one fiery red. A variety of brushes, several tubes of paint, and a bowl with wedges of pineapple sat on a small table beside one of the chaise lounges.

Jake's eyes quickly darted to the middle of the flybridge, where a couch and an L-shaped bar were shaded by a hardtop canopy, as was the helm beyond them. Jamison stood against the console of the helm, studying a folded-over magazine. He wore a shirt like Jake's, only blue, capris of his own, and crocs. He looked very European, and dorky. Frost leaned on the bar, on which was laid out a small spread of various cheeses, some crackers, vegetables, and fruit, along with several wine bottles and decanters, plus glasses to match the variety of drinks. She did not look dorky, wearing a pair of black beach shorts and a white button-down shirt, unbuttoned and knotted around her midriff over a blue bikini top. Her hair was fastened in a tight ponytail and she, like D'Angelo, was barefoot. She cradled a glass of red wine in her hand and looked up slowly from it at Jake as he climbed to the deck.

He cleared his throat, looking back to D'Angelo, who had turned from her canvas to him. "And here I thought I'd be underdressed," he said.

D'Angelo smiled as she set down her brush and turned around to place the palette on a covered grill at the near end of the U-shaped couch. "How are you feeling?"

"Like I was drugged. Where's Rachel?"

"I'm sorry about that," D'Angelo replied, her face failing to show compassion, the smile going nowhere. "But we were afraid you might make a commotion as we were leaving the marina and getting out to sea. I see you found the clothes we left for you."

Jake ignored questions about why he might have made a commotion and why the choice of apparel. Instead, he asked again, "Where's Rachel?"

Setting her glass on the bar, Frost walked to the end of it and stood in the sunlight. Her shorts did very little to conceal her long legs, and the golden sunlight was magical on her skin. Jake's mind was elsewhere, but he still noticed, and he wondered if that was the reason she had approached—to distract him.

"She's fine," D'Angelo said.

"That's not what I asked," Jake said, trying to keep calm. He and Rachel had been promised answers and the clearing of their names. Instead, they—or at least he—had been drugged and awakened to find everyone up top relaxing while dressed for a day at the beach. "Where is she?" he asked again.

"She's fine, Ja—"

"Where is she!" he yelled, swinging his hand at the canvas, knocking if off the easel onto one of the chaise lounges and tipping the easel over. It bumped the table, sending brushes and tubes of paint onto the deck and flipping the bowl of pineapple wedges onto the padded seat of another lounge chair.

D'Angelo merely looked at him. Frost maybe took a step closer. Jamison didn't even put down his magazine. D'Angelo continued to stare at Jake, her mouth slowly forming a smile. Then she reached up and undid the band restraining her hair, shaking it out, smiling all the while. The smile turned to a soft laugh, and then a hearty laugh. Frost grinned, and Jamison smirked from the helm as he turned the page in his magazine. Jake felt like he was in one of Gulliver's worlds.

D'Angelo stopped laughing and her smile faded. "I didn't much care for that painting anyhow," she said, eliciting a chuckle from Frost. D'Angelo grinned again briefly as the breeze ruffled her shirt and drifted loose hair around her face. She gently redirected it with a hand, and her eyes bored into Jake again. "Have you ever been Tased, Jake?"

"What?"

"Tased? Electroshock. A stun gun, like this?" She reached down to where her top was tight against her side. It made it easy for her to withdraw a tiny device from her waistband or rear pocket. It looked like a penlight, but Jake knew it wasn't.

"With the press of a button, this device will send fifty thousand volts of low-current electricity into your body." Somehow, her Spanish-sounding Italian accent added emphasis to her threat. "You will drop to the ground and convulse in great pain, followed by several minutes of neuromuscular incapacitation. That means you will have no control over your body. You will be powerless to resist or fight back."

For the first time, D'Angelo cut her eyes away from Jake, to Frost and Jamison. "Gabby and Liam have one as well and are more than capable of handling themselves in a physical altercation. So I strongly suggest you do not try anything stupid."

Jake exhaled, not willing to bring himself to apologizing to this quite possibly crazy woman. "Where is my wife?"

"For the moment, all you need to know is that she is fine."

"Is she on this boat?"

Instead of answering, D'Angelo reached down and picked up the painting, setting it against the cooler built under the grill. For the first time, Jake saw what was painted on the canvas. Two eyes peered out from a white background. They were dark, ominous, and D'Angelo had somehow created the illusion that the eyes emanated from deep within the white surrounding. They were the eyes of a ghost.

D'Angelo turned her shoulders toward the couch under the canopy, still looking at Jake. "Sit down, Mr. Taylor. We need to talk. When we are finished, I will answer any questions you still have."

Chapter Fifty

Rachel shivered awake. She sat upright, immediately regretting it. Her head felt like it weighed fifty pounds, and she quickly lowered it into the pillow.

Pillow. She was on a bed. Instantly more alert, she looked around. She was in a stateroom or cabin, on the yacht. Tessa D'Angelo's yacht.

Dual port windows looked out on her right, a closet was at the foot of the bed, across from a door in the left wall. A nightstand was right beside her, and the wall running from it to the door was home to a large watercolor seascape. Rachel studied it for a few seconds, letting the pressure in her head normalize and trying to remember how she had gotten where she was.

She remembered clearly bargaining with FBI Special Agent Vaughn, meeting at Alligator Adventure, running away while being shot at, and meeting with Jamison and Frost at Cracker Barrel—albeit as if it all had happened a week ago. Much hazier was their trip north from there, boarding *Il Fantasma*, and meeting D'Angelo. After that, nothing.

Rachel shivered again, and her eyes drifted downward. She startled. Her legs were bare. She'd been wearing jeans, socks, and tennis shoes. All were gone, and a heat wave washed over her. Had she taken them off? If so, why and where were they? She still wore the white Huskers shirt, still wore her bra, her underwear. She swallowed back the panic that tried to rise up in her. She was pretty sure she hadn't been sexually assaulted in any way. No, she was sure she hadn't.

So what was going on? She looked around, not spying her missing clothes anywhere. Nor her purse. She stood, gathered her equilibrium, and walked to the closet. She drew back the double doors and found several items hanging on pegs: a two-piece teal halter-top swimsuit, a loose-fitting coral tank top, and a note reading "WEAR THESE."

Rachel frowned. What was going on? Why had D'Angelo, Jamison, and Frost—presumably—taken her clothes and provided her with swimwear? She lifted them off the pegs. The tank top had huge, baggy armholes, and looked like something Jake would wear to the gym.

Jake. Where was he? Not with her. In another cabin?

Rachel hesitated, looking around her room. She spotted a flat screen TV and a device she at first thought was an intercom but realized was a high-tech thermostat with a touchpad and display panel. Rachel felt the doorknob. It was locked from the inside. Meaning she had locked it? Or the lock had been depressed and the door closed? Why?

She draped the swimsuit and the tank top on the edge of the bed and climbed onto it, peering out the portholes. She saw open water, meaning they had left the marina. The sun was bright and in her eyes, low on the horizon. They'd boarded the yacht around eleven. Had she been out all afternoon?

Unsure what to do, Rachel decided a change of clothes couldn't hurt. And maybe there was a good reason for all this?

She quickly changed, hanging her shirt and underwear in the closet, for lack of a better place. The swimsuit, although not the most comfortable ever, fit her well after a slight adjustment to the strap, and the tank top was loose by design. She felt awkward with no pants or shorts, but she was in a swimsuit and she was at sea on a yacht, so she supposed it was normal.

Her heart thudding, Rachel opened the door a fraction. She listened, hearing nothing. Then she crept into the hall. She was across a narrow, cold corridor from another room, this one with twin beds. One appeared to have been slept in—or rather, laid upon. By Jake?

Another door in the hallway led to a bathroom, and two others were locked. Same with a door at the other end of the corridor, beside the stairs. Rachel paused at the base of the stairs, listening, hearing nothing. She carefully crept up, arriving in the galley.

She processed the scene for a moment, noticing how sterile it was. No sign of D'Angelo's cooking. No sign of her, Jamison and Frost, or Jake. Rachel listened some more, only hearing the creak of the boat and the gentle lapping of waves against it. For the first time, her somewhat groggy brain processed that the yacht wasn't moving. What that meant, she had no idea. Was it possible she had been abandoned somewhere?

She noticed a hatch-like door on the starboard side, between the galley and dining room. Seeing no one, Rachel opened it and stepped out onto the walkway. She stopped, listening. She thought she caught voices up above, but with the open air and breeze, she couldn't make out what they were saying or even identify them.

Rachel chose to go forward, toward the bow, keeping close to the windows and looking up frequently. She also scanned the horizon, looking for any other ships or land, but saw neither. She came around to the bow, peeking up toward the bridge or helm or whatever it was called. She saw no one and questioned if the voices had been real or maybe transmitted over a radio or TV or something.

She saw a hatch in the floor as well as the anchor cable running through a hole in the point of the bow. Built in so that it abutted the dining room was a large bench seat where lovers could sit and watch the yacht cut through the waves. If only.

Rachel continued creeping around the port side of the yacht, pausing again as she heard voices. Now the breeze was against her, and she could hardly catch anything. She inched all the way to the stern, on the deck where they had first come aboard.

She paused. Down below was the boarding platform, with nowhere to go from it but through the doorway between the dual stairways. Else ride off on a Jet Ski, but to where? They were miles—or given the time elapsed, hundreds of miles—out to sea. To her left, stairs led to the top deck, from where she'd heard voices. She did some figuring. When she'd been down below, she'd been near the bow, and the stairs at the back end of the hallway had brought her up to the middle of the yacht. Meaning either the locked door beside the stairs led to a room that comprised the bottom of the yacht, or the hatch door off the stern platform led to it. Somewhere there had to be an engine room or some sort of mechanical room. That was always where prisoners were kept in the movies. Else in garages. Rachel decided to check it first, not wanting to expose herself to anyone until she had to. Maybe Jake was up top, having everything explained to him, and this would all turn out to be a crazy misadventure. Or maybe he'd woken up in the room across the hall, confronted D'Angelo, Jamison, and Frost, and had been chained to a bilge pipe in the engine room.

Cautious that anyone up above didn't see her, Rachel climbed down to the back platform of the boat, only a few feet wide. Being careful not to slip and fall, she tried the hatch door. Surprisingly, it opened, and with only a minimal squeak. Flitting her eyes up and seeing no one, Rachel pulled back the door and stepped inside.

Jake sat in the middle of the flattened-U couch. Jamison paced around the helm. Frost sat on one end of the couch, holding the same glass of wine, spinning it, eyeing Jake. Her long, tan legs and bare feet were propped onto the ottoman directly in front of him.

D'Angelo, meanwhile, stood between a pair of barstools, leaning against the bar, her hands outstretched to grip the edge of it. Her hair, caught between a crosswind and the funneled breeze created by the canopy's supports, blew behind her and to the side. Jake, despite the circumstances, couldn't help but think she looked like a European supermodel, a former Miss Italy, who had somehow defied the aging process.

"Tell me everything," she said in a voice that mirrored Penelope Cruz's, Jake determined. The Spanish and Italian languages were similar, so maybe the accents typically were too?

"Can't you tell me what's going on?" Jake asked. "Where's Rachel? Why are we anchored way out to sea? And why am I in a pair of swimming trunks from the mid-'90s?"

"All in good time. First, I want to hear your story. Start with your arrival in Myrtle Beach one week ago. Leave out nothing."

Jake wasn't sure what she was up to, and she had yet to tell him anything about Rachel other than a curt, "She's fine." But he was out of tantrums to throw, didn't feel like being Tased, and realized it was still possible—somehow—that D'Angelo would ultimately help him and Rachel. So he did as she asked, recounting their adventures. D'Angelo eventually sat on one of the barstools. Jamison just kept pacing. Frost watched Jake like a lonely woman at a bar just before closing time.

"We assumed Jam—Liam and Gabrielle were the ones to call the police about the auction, but we don't know," he said when he finished recounting his and Rachel's visit to Coral Manor.

"They were," D'Angelo said. "We thought you were working with Vaughn or another bidder. Sicking the police on you seemed like a good move. But you somehow avoided them."

"So you were behind this, pulling strings all the time?" Jake asked.

D'Angelo stared at him. It was the third or fourth time he'd interjected a question, each time met with just a stare.

"Right. We retrieved the diamonds from the beach," Jake said, and resumed the tale, taking her through the events of Saturday evening, overnight, and that morning. "Then I had a delicious piece of bruschetta, and the next thing I know, I'm mostly naked in a confined cabin while you three are playing like this is a cruise ship lido deck." He slapped his knees. "That's it."

D'Angelo eyed him for nearly a minute, then stood. "You forgot one thing."

"What's that?"

"Where are the diamonds?"

Jake shook his head, then looked to Frost and Jamison. "I told you," he said, his eyes back on D'Angelo, "they were in the chicken at the park."

D'Angelo surprised him with the quickness of her draw. Before he realized what was happening, he felt two pricks in his chest. He was distantly aware that he let out a violent scream, and then the jolting pain radiating through his body and the uncontrollable convulsions overwhelmed any other sensory perception.

Chapter Fifty-One

Even though Rachel couldn't see Jake's face, it was evident he was in pain.

He lay mostly on his back, but a little on his side and against the back of a short, wide sofa. His legs were bent so that he nearly hugged them, but the shaking of his limbs would make doing so impossible.

Rachel had been on the rear deck, having just climbed back up from below, when she'd heard a shriek. She'd recognized the voice as Jake's, even though it had made a sound she'd never heard from him before. She had quickly scrambled up to the flybridge, where D'Angelo stood by the bar, Frost sat outstretched on the couch, and Jamison practically lounged beside the yacht's steering wheel.

Rachel focused solely on Jake even as her eyes took in the layout of the upper deck and her mind processed the apparel changes by D'Angelo, Frost, and Jamison. She ran toward Jake, dropping to her knees by the couch. Jake's face was red and contorted, and she instinctively cupped her hands around it.

"Jake, Honey! Jake, I'm here," she said, choking back tears. She stroked his face, his eyes opening and focusing on her as his body continued to shake. "I'm here, I'm here," she said, draping her body on his chest in the hopes of stilling him. He was wearing a sleeveless shirt and swimming trunks; he must have been provided a change of clothes too.

Jake's convulsions lessened, and Rachel held him until they stopped. "Jake, Baby, I love you," she said, wiping tears on the back of her hand. She sniffed and whirled around. "What did you do to him?"

D'Angelo looked at Rachel calmly and emotionlessly.

"What did you do!" Rachel screamed.

D'Angelo didn't respond, and Rachel pushed herself up and lunged at the mysterious woman. From her knees, she drove her head toward D'Angelo's stomach. Rachel's momentum knocked D'Angelo off balance, but she not only looked young but also acted young. She took one step back, bracing herself against a barstool, stopping Rachel's push with a forearm. Before Rachel knew what was happening, she was yanked back by her hair, her arms clawing at D'Angelo, then at air.

With a scream, Rachel was thrown back to the deck, catching herself on her arms as she half crab-walked, half slid backward. She tried to sit up, ready to fight. She found Frost standing over her, a cold, menacing look on her face, and a small black cylinder in her hand. She pointed it at Rachel.

"No!"

It was Jake, a croaking plea.

"No," he murmured again.

"Wait."

This time it was D'Angelo. She stepped beside Frost and gently pushed her arm down. She took a few steps forward and crouched beside Rachel, too far to the side for Rachel to kick her and just out of reach of a fist, even if she were balanced enough to throw one.

"I used a stun gun on your husband," D'Angelo said calmly. "It delivers fifty thousand volts of electricity to his body, which creates immense pain and incapacitates him for several minutes."

Rachel felt her face flush with fury.

"But it has no lasting effects," D'Angelo said. "I tell you this so as to alleviate anger and incite fear. Because if you try anything like that again . . . I will shock him again."

Rachel swallowed.

D'Angelo smiled and extended a hand to Rachel. She was inclined to slap it away but took it instead. D'Angelo helped her to sit up, then stood upright and pulled Rachel to her feet. "Please have a seat beside your husband, Mrs. Taylor."

"What is going on?" Rachel asked.

D'Angelo nodded at the sofa, and Rachel sat down in the corner, helping Jake sit up. He was breathing heavily, but appeared to be coming back to form. Frost had retaken her seat on the couch. Jamison leaned on it behind her, and D'Angelo dropped again to a crouch on the other side of the ottoman.

"Now, as I was asking your husband, where are the diamonds?"

Rachel looked down at Jake, hoping for a cue. He just inhaled and exhaled.

"Do not bother telling me they are in a Cornish hen on a boardwalk at Alligator Adventure," D'Angelo said. "I know they are not. I know that you tricked Special Agent Vaughn. So please tell me, where are they?"

Rachel needed to buy time. "We left them in the car. When we got to Cracker Barrel, we weren't sure if we could trust them," she said with a nod in Frost and Jamison's direction.

D'Angelo actually smiled. "Where in the car?"

Rachel took a deep breath, hoping D'Angelo wasn't an expert at reading body language and didn't realize she was stalling. She couldn't say inside the gas cap again, as that's where she'd told Jamison before. Remembering something she'd seen on a documentary about drug smugglers Jake had been watching late one night, she said, "Inside the hubcap, rear passenger side."

D'Angelo nodded and stood.

Then she whipped a stun gun from her pocket and shot Jake with it.

Jake felt as if his chest was on fire. His body shuddered, but he could do nothing to stop it. The sensation, unreal and frightening as it was, paled in comparison to the pain.

He felt Rachel's arms around him, trying to hold him still. She said his name over and over, her voice breaking. Her hair draped over his face, and in that moment, with his body on fire, he couldn't help but think about how close they were to paradise, the two of them, in love, on vacation together. If only they'd never heard of the Archibald Diamonds!

Then he felt himself slipping out of Rachel's arms. He heard her scream. Frost and Jamison were both moving around, but his body was shaking too much for him to focus, and he had all he could do to keep his eyes open against the pain.

Jake heard Rachel yelling, "No!" and, "Get your hands off me!" He tried to sit up, but his body wouldn't respond to his brain's commands. He gritted his teeth and waited for the pain to subside and his body to function. When it did, he rolled to a sitting position, his arms folded over abdominal muscles that hurt from so much shaking.

Rachel lay on her stomach on one of the chaise lounges at the back of the deck. Jamison was attempting to bind her wrists, it appeared with duct tape, as Rachel squirmed to get loose. She wiggled out from under him, causing him to lose his balance against the railing. In the process, he tipped the lounge chair over, and Rachel's attempt to get to her feet was thwarted as the chair went out from under her and she fell beside Jamison. Scrambling, she made it halfway to her knees before Jamison fell on her legs. At the same time, Frost pounced on her back, and Rachel's body thudded into the deck as a moan/sob escaped her lips.

Jake tried to get up, but his legs weren't responding. He watched helplessly as Frost pushed Rachel's head against the deck, while Jamison sat across her upper legs and none-to-gently pulled her arms back and taped her wrists together. Frost stood, straightening the chaise lounge, and Jamison jerked Rachel to her feet like an angry cop would a violent perp. He shoved her down onto the chaise lounge and dropped a knee into her back. Rachel's breath came out in a crying gasp. All the while, D'Angelo stood at the end of the bar and watched.

"Wh . . ." Jake started. "What . . . are you doing?"

D'Angelo ignored him while pouring herself a glass of golden liquid. She plucked a grape off a plate and deposited it in her mouth. "We are getting answers," she said, then took a sip of her drink.

Jake willed his muscles to respond, at the same time struggling to comprehend this absurd reality and trying to find a way out of it for him and Rachel.

D'Angelo carried her glass to Rachel and crouched down in front of her, sweeping a loose strand of hair from in front of Rachel's eyes. She tried to jerk her head away, and Jamison used his leverage to push her into the chair.

"Rachel," D'Angelo said, waiting until she quit struggling. "I'm going to ask you again where the diamonds are, but before I do, I want you to know several things." She licked her lips, then nodded at Frost, who walked toward the bar. Kneeling on a stool, she reached over and around the small spread of food for something under the bar.

"Although I am not affiliated with any government agency, I do have friends and contacts with numerous agencies, including your FBI. I spoke to one of these contacts shortly before you arrived on my boat, and he informed me that the diamonds were not found anywhere at the Alligator Adventure park."

Frost straightened up and set something on the bar with a clank.

"I also hired a private detective in Myrtle Beach," D'Angelo continued, "and paid him handsomely for his services. Five minutes after you left the Cracker Barrel lot with Gabby and Liam, he searched your rented Ford Mustang, including looking behind the hubcaps."

Frost untied the knots of her shirt and removed it.

"He then went to your condominium on Ocean Boulevard," D'Angelo said. "To your room on the nineteenth floor."

Frost draped her shirt over the end of the sofa, casting a quick, blank look at Jake. He frowned, wondering if his brain was slowed by the two shocks and should be processing the obvious, other than thinking she was too warm.

"He turned the condo upside down, searching every nook and cranny."

Frost lifted the object off the bar, and Jake's eyes widened. It was a knife, similar to the one with which D'Angelo had been dicing mangos earlier.

"So you see, Rachel," D'Angelo said as Frost approached her. "I know where the diamonds are *not*. Now you are going to tell me where they are."

Chapter Fifty-Two

Rachel looked from D'Angelo to Frost. She held a large kitchen knife in her right hand, playing the flat part of the blade over the fingers of her left hand. The knife flashed as it caught the evening sunlight, and Frost lowered it to her waist as she raised her eyes to meet Rachel's. She had shed her white shirt, wearing just a swimsuit top and short shorts. She wasn't dressed that way because she was hot or to look sexy, Rachel realized. She was wearing minimal clothing so as not to get it messy.

"They weren't hidden in your clothes," D'Angelo said. "They weren't in your purse." She leaned forward and actually smiled. "So where are they, Rachel? Tell me, and this all ends."

"No," Rachel said. "You'll kill us."

"What I will do," Frost said, crouching in front of Rachel, "is slice the plica interdigitalis—the webbing—between your toes." She held up the knife, rotating the tip of the blade inches in front of Rachel. "It's terribly painful, very slow to heal, a major hassle as it does, and if scar tissue builds up, it can permanently disable movement. You'll struggle to even walk."

Rachel tried not to let the fear play in her eyes.

"Then, if you still haven't told us," Frost said, her voice soft, as if she was talking about her favorite piece of music instead of torture, "I'll move to your fingers. You may never take photographs again. You may not even be able to hold a camera." She smiled wickedly. "After that . . ." She lifted the knife and slid the flat part of the blade across Rachel's incredibly still cheek. "I'm sure we can find other things to cut."

D'Angelo leaned forward. "Rachel, just tell us where the diamonds are."

"I don't know," Rachel said.

D'Angelo smiled and sat back.

"No, I really don't!"

Jamison applied additional pressure to her back with his knee, holding her bound arms down with his hands.

"Please," Rachel said. "I don't have them."

Jake did. He'd been nervous before going to Cracker Barrel that Jamison and Frost might ask to search her purse. He'd kept them in his pocket, but now wasn't wearing his pants anymore. If the diamonds hadn't been in them . . .

"I don't have them," Rachel pleaded as Frost walked to the other end of the chair. Rachel turned her head, trying to see, but Jamison held her down. She looked instead to D'Angelo. "I'd tell you if I did."

D'Angelo said nothing, instead flitting her eyes toward Frost.

"Please," Rachel said, nearly in tears. Then she felt Frost grab her left ankle, and waited for the knife to tear her flesh.

⚓   ⚓   ⚓

Jake took several deep breaths and slowly lifted himself off the couch. His knee buckled, but he managed to stand by holding onto the arm of the couch. He couldn't believe his eyes.

While D'Angelo looked on with something akin to bored detachment and Jamison pinned Rachel to the chaise lounge chair, Frost advanced with the knife. She was prepared to torture his wife, on a yacht in the middle of the ocean. It was beyond surreal.

Frost raised the knife, and Jake found his voice. "Wait."

She angled the knife toward Rachel's foot.

"I have the diamonds."

"Wait." This time it was D'Angelo, her voice soft but firm. Frost lowered the knife, and Jake sighed with relief.

"Where are they?" D'Angelo asked, turning to face Jake.

"Just please . . . please let her go."

"When I have the diamonds."

"They're in the planter. In the kitchen."

"Of your condo?"

"The yacht," he said. "Under the TV."

Across the aisle from the island counter, mounted at eye height so that someone working in the galley could watch it, was a small flat screen TV. Beneath it, on a tiny counter, sat a faux flower arrangement. With uncertainty as to what was coming, Jake had deftly lifted the diamonds from his pocket and dropped them behind his back into the planter while D'Angelo had been removing the bruschetta from the oven. Rachel had been blocking Frost's view and Jamison had been standing half in front of Jake in the cramped galley at the time.

D'Angelo cut her eyes to Frost. "Check it out," she said. "If he's lying, cut her Achilles."

"They're there, I swear," Jake said.

Frost stood. "Sit down and sit back," she said, pointing with the knife. Jake obeyed, quelling the urge to vomit. His first priority was—somehow—to get Rachel out of this mess. His second was to make sure D'Angelo, Frost, and Jamison paid for what they were doing. Even so, he listened and sat down on the deck, his back against the cooler. Frost walked past him, still holding the knife, and took the steps down to the lower level. D'Angelo sipped her alcohol dispassionately.

Jake turned to Rachel, just able to see her eyes. "Baby, I'm so sorry."

She nodded her acceptance.

"We're going to get out of this. Somehow."

She nodded again, blinking away tears.

Frost's feet sounded on the steps in quick succession. She reached the flybridge, the knife no longer in her hands. Instead, she held a black velvet pouch.

Seeing it, D'Angelo stood. Frost handed her the pouch, and D'Angelo quickly untied the opening. She tipped the pouch and watched with a glowing smile as seven sparkling diamonds tumbled into her palm.

Rachel sat on the couch beside Jake, her arm laced with his, her hand in his. D'Angelo stood behind the bar, the diamonds arrayed on a purple velvet display tray she'd procured from under the bar. Rachel was surprised she wasn't wearing them already.

Frost, done playing torturer, had donned her white shirt again, leaving it open over the swimsuit as she sipped from a wine glass. She once again resembled a model on the shoot of a Nautica commercial.

Jamison leaned on one of two captain's chairs at the helm, his stun gun clenched in his palm. The message was clear, on top of a brief lecture from D'Angelo about the impact of repeated, short-term shocks on the human body. Jake had been stunned twice already.

"Who are you?" Rachel asked when D'Angelo looked up from the diamonds.

D'Angelo smiled, casting a last admiring glance at the stones. "I am exactly what I told you: a collector, a connoisseur." She came around the bar and stood in front of it, arms outstretched so her hands held the edge of the counter.

"If you're The Ghost," Jake said, "A.K.A. *Il Fantasma*, A.K.A. *La Fantôme*, then who was Vaughn working for?"

D'Angelo shrugged. "Another bidder, another collector? Any number of people were after the diamonds."

"Why you?" Jake asked. "You're clearly filthy rich. You can hire Interpol to do your bidding, have contacts everywhere, and this yacht must have cost, what, five or six mil?"

"Seven-four."

"This isn't just about money, is it?"

"No." She stood straight. "The Archibald Diamonds are mine."

"How do you figure?"

"My great, great grandmother—my father's father's mother's mother—was the niece of Maria Vasilescu, the last known Archibald to possess the diamonds."

"She that gypsy broad who killed an English duke and his family and stole the diamonds from him?"

"They rightfully belonged to the Archibald family."

"They switched hands a dozen times over the centuries," Jake said. "How can you possibly trace them that far back? Besides, there have to be a lot of people who can trace their ancestry back to Maria Vaseline. What gives you the right to them, any more than anyone else?"

D'Angelo smiled. "A lot of things. But how about this? Finders keepers."

Rachel sighed. "So now what?"

"Now, we sail for Bermuda."

"What's in Bermuda?"

"A reserved, secluded villa on the beach. It's a waypoint until the heat dies down."

"What are you going to do with us?"

"You will be set free on one of the Jet Skis."

"That's it?"

"That's it."

"You're letting us go?"

She nodded.

"Aren't you afraid we'll tell on you?" Jake asked.

"As you yourself said, I am *La Fantôme*. What exactly will you tell them? I have a dozen names in a dozen countries. I'll sell the yacht and buy another. Or change its name. Or deny your accusations for which you have no proof. Assuming, of course, you aren't arrested for stealing the diamonds and murdering several federal agents."

"What about them?" Rachel asked, nodding at Frost and Jamison.

"You mean the legitimate Interpol officers?" Frost asked. "Who are already considered thieves by your FBI? What will you do to us?"

"Nothing," Jake said. "Nothing at all. If it's all the same to you, we'll be on our way."

D'Angelo stood up straight and gestured toward the stern. "Your purse, wallet, keys, and other effects are in the under-seat compartment of the purple one."

"What about our clothes?" Rachel asked.

"The ones you have now are much more suitable for a ride on a Jet Ski, are they not?"

Rachel and Jake looked at each other. He took her hand, and she got the message. Let's get while the getting's good.

They stood, and Rachel followed Jake down the stairs, while D'Angelo, Frost, and Jamison watched from the top deck. The whole thing was so surreal, but surreal was becoming normal.

Rachel followed Jake again down to the stern platform, where the two Jet Skis bobbed in the water. Letting go of Rachel's hand, Jake untied the one on their left, then helped her onto the back of it. She straddled it and scooted back as Jake got on. She wrapped her arms loosely around his midsection as he pushed the starter button. He eased the Jet Ski back, away from the stern of *Il Fantasma*. Then, as Rachel cast a final look at the enigmatic Tessa D'Angelo and the two crooked Interpol agents, he turned away from the boat and accelerated toward the setting sun.

Chapter Fifty-Three

Jake's insides felt like jelly as he guided the Jet Ski through the swells of the open ocean. His engineer's brain was doing calculations of estimated miles per gallon and the likely size of a Jet Ski's gas tank. He came out with a pretty high number, one that should carry them over the horizon. The question was, how far over the horizon was land. Had *Il Fantasma* sailed just out of view of the South Carolina coast, or were they dozens upon dozens of miles out to sea? As in halfway to Bermuda?

To that end, his brain also tried to process the last hour. Had D'Angelo really let them go, or was she setting them adrift in the middle of the ocean, far from shipping lanes and air traffic? If they did make it back, what then? D'Angelo was right—he and Rachel were probably wanted for murder, amongst other crimes, now with no one to clear them.

He also couldn't help kicking himself for the way he had played things— hiding the diamonds, not giving them up immediately, his nearly letting Rachel get tortured. Somehow, he vowed, he would straighten things out with the authorities and get them to pursue D'Angelo, Frost, and Jamison. They would pay for what they had done.

Jake did not look back. He had no reason to. He wanted to put the yacht far behind him as quickly as possible. He also wanted to get as far west as he could before the sun set, he lost the light, and thus lost the ability to navigate.

Hopefully, by the time it was dark, there would be lights visible on the horizon to guide him.

The engine sputtered.

Jake's gelatinous stomach dropped.

The engine sputtered again, then quit, and the Jet Ski slowly coasted to a stop and began to rise and fall on the sea.

"What happened?" Rachel asked. "Are we out of gas?"

"Yeah." He sighed, looking into the setting sun. "So that's it, they set us adrift and sail off to Bermuda."

"I don't think they can."

"What?" He turned to look at Rachel.

"When I woke up, I was in a cabin down below."

"Yeah, me too."

"Before I came up and found you, I explored a little. The hatch at the back of the boat leads to the crew quarters and to the engine room. I picked the lock, thinking maybe you were in there tied to a pipe or something, like in *Titanic*."

He rotated his finger, telling her to speed up the narrative.

"I found two keys in switches just below gauges showing battery power. They were both turned to on, and I turned them off, then removed the keys."

"You removed the keys?"

"I didn't know what it would do. I hoped it would keep the boat from drawing battery power, and keep it from star—"

"What'd you do with them?"

She lifted up her tank top and reached into the waistband of her swimsuit bottoms. She pulled out two small, silver keys.

Jake looked at his wife incredulously, then lifted his eyes to *Il Fantasma*, no more than half a mile away. Back to his wife.

"I thought I could barter, have an ace up my sleeve, so to speak. When they told us to leave, I didn't know what to do with them. I thought if we could get away . . ."

Jake looked back to the yacht.

"You think they've noticed?" she asked.

"I don't think they planned to hang around long. If they haven't, they will soon."

"What do we do?"

He turned the Jet Ski off, then leaned forward and unscrewed the gas cap. He peered inside it, verifying it was indeed empty. "How'd you pick the lock?" he asked as he screwed it back on.

"Grant showed me that once, when I locked my keys in the car at work."

"I mean what'd you use?"

"The underwire from my swimsuit."

"What?"

She nodded.

"How'd you get it out?"

"Unhooked the vent cover and bent it to form a crude blade."

"Really? Wow, that's very innovative."

"Unfortunately I'm out of innovations, and, Jake . . ."

She pulled his shoulder, and he turned to look back at the yacht. He had to squint, but he spied two figures on the stern. Frost and Jamison, getting set to board the other Jet Ski. Jake doubted it would run out of gas before it reached its destination.

"What do we do?" Rachel asked.

"Stand up."

"What?"

"Stand up," Jake said. "We need to see what's in the compartment."

Rachel stood, trying to keep her balance as the Jet Ski rocked back and forth. Jake managed to turn around, and she steadied herself by leaning on his shoulder as he opened the compartment. D'Angelo had lied. No purse, wallet, or keys. Just a pliers, an exchangeable-head screwdriver, and a flare gun. He pulled out the gun, only to find it contained no flares. Nor were there any extra cartridges in the compartment.

"Anything?" Rachel asked, hoping he somehow could fashion a plan out of a few tools.

"No." He dropped the flare gun back into the compartment, closed it, and turned around. As he dug through another compartment in front of the handlebars, Rachel turned to look back at the yacht. Between swells, she saw that Frost sat on the other Jet Ski while Jamison appeared to be casting off. D'Angelo stood on the flybridge like a captain sending her crew off to battle.

"Babe, we've got to face reality, here. They never intended for us to live."

She looked Jake in the eyes as he leaned against the handlebars.

"The Jet Ski, the new clothes, no personal effects—I think they planned all along for it to look like we got lost at sea, if we were ever found."

Rachel swallowed and nodded.

"Now, I can't imagine they intend to leave us alive either. If we have the key, they'll take it and best-case scenario is we're stuck here with no way to get to shore or signal for help. If we ditch the key, they'll have no use for us and probably kill us right away."

"Okay, now for the good news," Rachel said with a nervous chuckle.

Jake grinned. "We fight. It's our only option."

"Do you have a plan?"

"Not much of one."

"Anything's better than nothing."

He nodded, then took her face in his hands. "Baby, I love you. I am so sorry about—"

"Not now, Jake. There isn't time. I love you too. Let's just try to get out of this, and we can spend the rest of our lives apologizing."

He kissed her on the forehead and dropped his hands. "Okay. You got anything else in your swimsuit?"

"Afraid not. The crew cabin was bare."

"Okay," he said again. He quickly took off his shirt, handing it to her. "Hold this. Take yours off too."

"What?"

"Twist it into a rope, as tight as you can."

"What are we doing?"

"Going out with a bang."

Rachel watched the Jet Ski bearing Frost and Jamison cut through the small rises and troughs of the ocean. Her heart pounded in her chest, a combination of fear of what would happen if she and Jake failed and anxious anticipation at attempting to execute Jake's harebrained plan. It was the sort of thing MacGyver would try, not the sort of thing that worked in real life. Yet this was fully real.

"Ready?" Jake asked. He'd just finished stuffing his shirt inside the gas tank, following it up with half of her tank top. The other half hung out onto the starboard running board, out of sight to Jamison and Frost as they approached. The Jet Ski's "hood" was propped open, presumably so Jake could check the sputtering engine. They were playing dumb, hoping the two Interpol agents bought it. In reality, he had found the machine's battery and removed it, placing it on the starboard running board. Also out of sight. For the second time that evening, Rachel had removed the underwire from her swimsuit, hoping the small perforation in the fabric wouldn't be noticeable. Jake had flexed the wire back and forth until it broke, creating two wires. He'd attached one end of each to the two terminals of the battery. The other two ends of wire were bent in such a way that they were less than an inch apart, just above where Rachel's wrinkled tank top fluttered in the breeze.

Frost and Jamison's Jet Ski whined as they cruised toward Rachel and Jake's. Frost turned the handlebars in a wide arc, timing her turn and her speed perfectly so that she came to a stop directly beside them, just a few feet off the port side. Both Frost and Jamison wore grim faces, and Jamison reinforced his by aiming a pistol at Rachel.

"Where are the keys?" he asked.

Per Jake's instruction, Rachel had put them back into her waistband. As a last resort, she would give them over, and they would take their chances adrift at sea. Assuming they were left alive. But that was the last resort.

"Did you know this was almost out of gas?" Jake asked innocently.

"You didn't really think we'd let you go, did you?" Frost asked.

"So what, we drift out here until we starve?"

"Or the sharks get adventurous."

"How far out are we?"

"The keys," Jamison said. "Where are they?"

"What keys?" Jake asked.

Jamison racked the gun's slide. "Don't make me ask again."

Jake raised the flare gun, which he'd held at his side, and pointed it at Frost's chest.

Jamison smirked. "It isn't loaded."

Jake had expected they would have known that but had banked on Jamison's instinct taking over. And it had. For just a moment, he'd swiveled his gun to Jake, at the same time briefly taking his eye off Rachel. That was her cue, and she extended her right leg, using her foot to nudge one of the two wires into the other. As she did, they sparked briefly. Her loose, silky tank top—which Jake had swirled around inside the gas tank—ignited.

Jake kept talking. "We didn't take your boat keys. You have the diamonds, and we have nothing."

Rachel, her arms already around Jake, squeezed slightly.

"Now how about you lower that gun," Jake said. "We'd be happy to come back and help you look for them in exchange for, say, a ride to the nearest English-speaking port."

Rachel didn't know how he did it—how he kept his cool. Out the corner of her eye, she saw smoke rising from her tank top. How long did it take a fire to reach the gas tank? What happened then? Did it just burn? Did it explode?

"I will give you one more chance," Jamison said. "Where are the keys?"

"I told you," Jake said. "We don't have them. But if you're stuck, signal for help."

He flipped the gun at Frost, who flinched momentarily. Jamison wavered, and in that instant, following their hastily created script, Rachel and Jake leaped over the starboard side of their Jet Ski. Her ankle gave as she tried to push off it, and she more fell than dove over the side, banging her other foot on the seat and then the running board in the process. But she dropped beneath the water without getting shot, and immediately stroked down and away.

They knew it was a long shot. Not just for their homemade, ad hoc "bomb" to blow, but for it to do so at just the right time. Rachel had watched *MacGyver*—both the '80s version and the modern reboot—with Jake. Mac could use a cigarette as a perfect fuse timer, counting on his explosion at just the right moment. In reality, her and Jake's margin for error was microscopic. If the fuse burned and ignited the gas fumes too quickly, the resulting explosion could kill them too. Too slowly, and Frost and Jamison could extinguish the fuse before it blew, or she and Jake might run out of air and have to surface in Jamison's line of fire. Or it might not even ignite at all. Long shot didn't begin to describe it.

The explosion was muffled underwater, and Rachel stopped swimming and turned. Beside her, Jake had also stopped. Both of them turned their gaze from where they had just come, the water turned into a frothy white as the sky above glowed orange and then black as the Jet Ski exploded into a ball of fire.

Chapter Fifty-Four

A quick glance at Rachel told Jake she was okay, so he stroked for the surface. The sea air was acrid with the smell of smoke and fuel, and small pieces of debris rained down in a circle around the charred, burning remains of the Jet Ski. It was maybe thirty feet away. Just beyond it, Frost and Jamison's sat rider-less. Jake swam toward it, careful to avoid any smoldering debris.

Jamison was floating face down in the water ten feet off the port bow of his and Frost's Jet Ski. She was nowhere to be seen. Jake swam toward Jamison, not sure if he should try to revive him or hold him under. Before he got to him, his eyes cut to the Jet Ski, and he saw a gun resting on the seat. He stopped. Had it somehow fallen there when Jamison was blown off the Jet Ski? Or had Frost placed it there as some sort of a trap?

Looking back to see that Rachel was treading water, he corrected his course and swam for the Jet Ski. Still seeing no sign of Frost, he pulled himself up onto it and reached for the gun. As he did, the water to his left parted, and Frost shot up out of it. She launched herself at Jake, flailing and missing. But in his haste to avoid her, Jake dropped the gun. It fell to the seat of the Jet Ski, then to the port running board.

Reorienting herself in the water, Frost surged up and reached for the gun again. Jake dove toward her, landing on her arms. Frost cried out as Jake's weight carried her off the Jet Ski and into the water, taking both of them beneath the surface.

Frost recovered quickly and looped her arm around Jake's neck. Just as it started to tighten, her grip released. Jake spun over and saw Rachel had charged into the fray from underwater, her momentum carrying Frost away. Jake followed after them, determined to protect his wife. For several seconds that felt like minutes, the three of them grappled like playful otters. Underwater, they were unable to generate much force with any of their punches or kicks. But as they floated to the surface, Frost's head butt caught Jake in the chin. It was not a powerful enough blow to knock him out, but it temporarily stunned him, and he fell back.

Frost took the opportunity to lunge for the gun. As she grabbed it, Rachel chopped her arm, pulling it loose and causing the gun to fall into the water.

With Jake still stunned, Frost grabbed Rachel, spinning her around into a headlock. They floundered and splashed in the water just off the bow of the Jet Ski for several seconds, but Rachel was unable to escape and Frost only tightened her hold.

Shaking away the cobwebs, Jake struck out for them. Before he could make much of a move, something rough and sandpapery brushed against his foot. The next second, Frost emitted an otherworldly shriek and fell back into the water, losing her grip on Rachel, who still submerged beneath the waves. Jake made several quick strokes, reaching Rachel just as she resurfaced. The water behind her had turned into a frothy, churning cauldron, and through the swells and spray, Jake caught a glimpse of a dark gray triangle. A fin. A shark!

Now fully lucid, he grabbed for the handle of the Jet Ski with one hand and for Rachel with the other. She took his hand, then hastily climbed over his back and shoulders onto the back of the Jet Ski, pulling him after her as he used the handlebars to leverage himself out of the water. They managed to get aboard without tipping it over, and Jake wasted no time firing up the Jet Ski. Ignoring Jamison, who floated aimlessly to starboard, and the reddish hue tinging the water to the left, Jake twisted the throttle and they lurched forward.

He sped straight ahead for some hundred yards before easing off the throttle and turning the craft around. There was no sign of Frost, and Jamison's body disappeared and reappeared on the swells, unmoving, still face down.

"Are you okay?" Jake panted, looking over his shoulder.

Rachel nodded, unable to speak.

He took several deep breaths, his eyes on the lookout for any more sharks. He couldn't remember, did they hunt in packs?

"It worked," Rachel finally said, wrapping her arms around him. She kissed his shoulder and squeezed again. "It worked."

"It worked," he said, eyes back on her.

"Why'd you stop?" she asked.

"We could be a hundred miles from land. Even if this has a full tank, we may not get close."

"You want to go back to the boat?"

"It's two against one."

"She has a Taser."

"I'm growing immune."

"Jake . . ."

"Seriously, Babe, I think it's our best option. South Carolina might be just over the horizon, or we might be closer to Bermuda." He gestured at the sun, now hovering just over the surface of the water, casting a blinding fiery reflection over the carnage of the Jet Ski. "Once it gets dark, we'll have no way to navigate. There's food on the yacht, water—"

"A psychopath."

"We can barter with her. Or try."

She grasped his turned head with both hands and kissed him hard. "Whatever you say, Jake. I trust you."

He nodded. Then looked around. No sign of sharks. Jamison hadn't moved, or been eaten. Jake started the Jet Ski.

"Do we just leave him?" Rachel asked.

"He's been face down in the water for several minutes."

"Still . . ."

"And there's a shark around, maybe more than one. I'm not risking your life to save his. Let's see what happens on the yacht. Then, if he's still alive after that . . ."

Rachel nodded, and Jake set a course for the yacht, being careful to give the shark's last known location a wide berth. As they zipped across the surface, he knew he should be thinking strategy, trying to figure out their approach and how they would deal with D'Angelo. Instead, he was in shock. Drugged. Tased. Abandoned. Attacked. Rescued by a shark. And it wasn't over yet.

Jake slowed the Jet Ski as they approached the yacht's stern platform. He didn't spot D'Angelo at the railing. She had to have heard the explosion if not seen it. Was she lying in wait? Down below furiously trying to override the battery switches? In the dining room eating caviar and toast points?

He tapped the stern with the front of the Jet Ski and reached for one of the ropes that had secured it, quickly tying it fast. A sick feeling pervaded his stomach as he stepped onto the platform and extended a hand to Rachel. He felt the same way he did when watching one of those TV shows where a character escaped from captivity only to realize they had to go back.

He just hoped this ended the way the TV shows always did, with the good guys winning.

Considering she and Jake had just blown up a Jet Ski and sentenced two people to a watery grave, Rachel was amazed at how still the evening had become. The sun was melting into the ocean, the last brilliant orange rays casting the west-oriented faces of the yacht in a burning white, and the rest in lifeless shades of gray. The air was still, the breeze having all but died. With her skin and hair wet, and clad in just the swimsuit, the air almost felt cool to her. And aside from the constant lapping of water against the hull of the boat and the Jet Ski, all was silent.

At first.

Then a distant, almost indiscernible sound reached Rachel's ears. Initially, it was drowned out by the water lapping against the hull, but as Rachel's ears acclimated to it, the noise grew louder. It was music.

"Do you hear that?" she whispered to Jake.

"Yeah," he breathed. He turned to face her. "If she has a stun gun, I'm going to rush her."

"No."

"She'll get me, but she won't be able to shoot you too. Take her out."

"With what?"

"Forearm to the neck worked pretty good last night."

"Let me take it. You've been Tased twice already. And you're stronger."

"No. I'm not letting that happen to you. No arguing," he said, silencing her. "Come on."

Things had been so hectic of late that Rachel hadn't found time to utter more than a quick "Help" in the way of prayer. Now, following Jake slowly up the steps to the main deck, she strung together a few words. She wondered, had God's hand been in any of this so far, keeping them safe, delivering them semi-miraculously from danger? How else to explain it?

Jake peeked through the open sliding glass door into the salon, toward the kitchen. He turned back, shaking his head. There were no lights on in either of the rooms, and as the sun disappeared over the horizon, the light was quickly growing faint.

Jake pointed up, Rachel nodded, and they climbed as quietly as possible to the flybridge, pausing partway up so that Jake, in the lead, could scan for D'Angelo.

The yacht looked abandoned. A bowl, wedges of pineapple, paintbrushes, tubes of paint, and an empty glass were scattered over the deck. An easel and a painting of two hideous eyes were both tipped against the far railing. Containers of alcohol and dishes of cheese and crackers and fruits and veggies were still on the bar. Absent, however, were the velvety display tray and the Archibald Diamonds. Also not present was Tessa D'Angelo.

"Where is she?" Rachel asked as a brief gust of breeze floated across the flybridge.

"I don't know."

"Down below?"

"Only place left."

"Why? Hiding?"

"I don't know," he said again.

She looked around, resisting a shiver. "I don't hear the music anymore."

"Coming from down below too." He lifted the painting, studying it for a moment. He dropped it on the grill cover with disgust. Rachel picked up the glass and set it on the bar.

"This is so weird," she said.

"Yeah. Let's get it over with."

There were no actual weapons on the bar—no sign of the knife Frost had been prepared to use on Rachel just minutes earlier. So Jake grabbed a half-full bottle of wine, because the evening wasn't weird enough yet. He raised his eyebrows at Rachel and nodded. "Come on."

Jake led the way back down to the main deck, through the salon and galley, and to the stairs leading to the cabins. He didn't spot the knife there either and wondered where Frost had disposed of it. He did hear music, growing slightly louder. Classical, yet not typical classical. More horns, more resonance. It was sweeping, building, unfamiliar but captivating. And distracting. And growing louder as they slowly descended the steps.

He felt Rachel's hand on his back as he reached the base of the stairs. The narrow hallway ran forward and was mostly dark. Soft light, and the music, emanated from the partially open door to his right. Tentatively, he inched forward. As the music reached a crescendo, he looked back at Rachel. Her wide eyes studied his as she shook her head, frowning.

Jake turned back to the door, gripping the wine bottle with one hand. He eased the door all the way open, revealing what was likely the master stateroom. A large bed dominated the room, decorated with colorful pillows and throws. Built into the wall behind it to either side were bookshelves and, lower down, nightstands. The one on the right flowed into a desk beneath a long horizontal window looking out at the dark water. The one on the left connected to a similar desk that more resembled a vanity. Plush carpet, vibrant colors, and warm lighting created an opulent, welcoming vibe.

None of it, however, captivated Jake's attention. That was drawn to his left.

Tessa D'Angelo stood in front of a full-length mirror attached to the bathroom door. Her hair was down, feathered, as it hung past large gold hoop earrings and onto bare shoulders. She wore a strapless purple gown that followed the contours of her body down to the floor. She looked resplendent even without the fifty million dollars' of diamonds adorning her neck. They shimmered in the light, clearly the focal point amid D'Angelo's beauty and in the luxurious stateroom.

The music peaked, and Jake was vaguely aware that Rachel stood beside him. He continued to stare at D'Angelo, smoothing the fabric at her sides while at the same time raising her chin so her hair trembled on her shoulders.

The strains of stringed instruments, a piano, and several horns faded into silence. As the song ended, D'Angelo flashed a perfect smile of pure joy. Her dark brown eyes roved from Jake to Rachel and back.

"So, how do I look?"

Chapter Fifty-Five

Rachel could feel the shock playing out on her face as she studied the Italian woman. Was this possible? After sending her and Jake off to their ultimate death, then dispatching Jamison and Frost to chase them down, she had gone down below and dressed for a formal dinner? And now she was admiring herself and the diamonds and looking for approval? Was she that mentally unbalanced? That obsessed with what she believed to be a family heirloom?

"They are stunning, no?" D'Angelo asked.

"Uh . . ." Jake said.

D'Angelo's grin widened as she turned back to the mirror, posing dramatically in front of it. "Where are Gabby and Liam?" she asked as if they had run to the store for milk.

"They're dead," Jake answered.

D'Angelo froze, then slowly turned as the next song began playing, Rachel still hadn't figured out from where. D'Angelo's head panned to Jake. "They're what?"

"Dead."

"How?" she asked softly.

"Well, Liam got blown up, and Gabby was eaten by a shark."

D'Angelo looked as if she had been slapped in the face. Her eyes sparked.

That's when Rachel saw the gun sitting on the middle shelf of the far nightstand. D'Angelo's head turned toward it as well. Her eyes cut back toward Rachel and Jake.

Rachel nudged her husband. "Jake."

Everyone moved at once. Rachel lunged toward D'Angelo. She, in turn, strode as fast as possible in a dress toward the nightstand. Jake dropped the wine bottle and leaped onto the bed. He bounced into the headboard, grabbing for the gun at the same time as D'Angelo reached for it. He got there first, and she clamped her hands on it and tried to wrest it from him. She had leverage, but he had strength, pulling her back onto the bed and on top of him. Rachel turned and dove into the fray as well, reaching her hands for D'Angelo's neck, either to strangle her or grab the diamonds and distract her.

D'Angelo let go of the gun and swung her hands at Rachel. She ducked under the blow, falling onto the bed. D'Angelo turned back to Jake, somehow driving a fist toward his groin. He dodged the punch, but in so doing, relaxed his grip and focus on the gun. D'Angelo reached for it but never got there. Rachel pushed up off the bed, grabbing D'Angelo's hair with one hand and the back of her gown with the other. She ripped her back, off Jake, and spun her down onto the floor with a move worthy of the WWE. She pounced, dropping her weight onto D'Angelo.

The Italian wriggled and struggled, flailing with her elbow and reaching a hand for Rachel's hair, pulling it hard enough that Rachel gasped. Then, suddenly, the pressure stopped. Rachel looked up to see Jake had gotten off the bed and knelt at the foot of it, the gun held firmly in both hands and pointed at D'Angelo's head.

"Just give me a reason," he growled.

Jake did not lose his temper often. Few things even made him mad. But Tessa D'Angelo, in numerous ways, had pushed him past his breaking point. He'd already taken a life that evening. The authorities in his home country—wherever that was in relation to their current position—likely believed him responsible for several more, and he had no idea how he and Rachel would ever straighten everything out with them. He'd been chased by spies, kidnapped by turncoat federal agents, had his wife threatened with torture and been tortured himself, and had been jerked around all day in a surreal experience that had led to this—his wife, soaking wet in a bikini, having wrestled an exotic and possibly crazy Italian woman in an evening gown to the floor of an opulent stateroom aboard a multi-million-dollar yacht. It was becoming too much to process, and he focused exclusively on his and Rachel's safety.

"Rach," he said calmly, "get up slowly, onto the bed."

She followed his directions while neither he nor D'Angelo moved.

"Okay," she said.

He stood and backed up. "Get up," he said to D'Angelo. "Slowly. One wrong move and you're shark food."

D'Angelo stood, her face registering no emotion.

"Hands on top of your head and interlace your fingers."

She again obeyed.

"Rach, stay where you are, then follow me." He turned to D'Angelo. "Walk, slowly, up the stairs. Drop your hands, and I shoot."

"What are you going to do, Jake?" Rachel asked.

"Give her a taste of her own medicine." He pushed the gun into the small of D'Angelo's back. "Tell me, Tessa, how much gas is in the other Jet Ski?"

"Jake, you can't just set her adrift. That's murder."

"We'll note the coordinates and send someone for her. She might catch sunstroke first, but she'll survive. That is if she can straddle a Jet Ski in a dress."

As she climbed the stairs behind Jake, Rachel realized just how exhausted she was. It wasn't just the physical strain she and Jake had been through in recent days. There was also the mental and emotional stress. Rachel so desperately wanted it all to be over, for her and Jake to be able to relax—no diamonds to protect, no crazy people chasing them, no fake FBI agents and foreign operatives, no legal problems.

They reached the galley, and Rachel was amazed at how dark it was. The western sky was still pale blue, tinged with orange at the bottom. But night was falling quickly over the ocean.

Jake marched D'Angelo through the salon and onto the aft deck. Just above the port stairway down to the platform where the Jet Ski was moored, she stopped.

"Keep going," Jake said.

"You are not serious, are you?"

"Dead serious."

"I can make it worth your while," she said, turning around.

"What, you'll part with 'the precious'?" he asked in a voice like Gollum from *The Lord of the Rings*. "Besides, we could just take them from you."

"You are not going to?"

Jake turned to Rachel, who stood to his left. He shook his head. "No. We've had enough trouble with them. Besides, when the Coast Guard or the Navy or Somali pirates find you drifting out here, your wearing them will be proof of our story."

"I will testify on your behalf. It is dark and—"

"Enough," Jake said. "You drugged us, stripped us, you practically electrocuted me, you were going to let Frost mutilate my wife! You're lucky I don't shoot you now."

"At least let me change my clothes," she said, taking a step back toward the salon.

"Forget it. You were th—"

D'Angelo had placed her hand on one of the chairs at the wood table, and she now shoved it between her and Jake. It knocked him slightly off balance and kept him from firing the gun. Not hesitating, D'Angelo stepped between the chair and the table. As she did, she swiped one of the candle jars off the table and flung it toward Jake. He was still off balance and couldn't duck in time, and the glass jar crashed against his forehead.

Rachel moved to cut D'Angelo off. But showing the quick moves of a jackrabbit, she planted her foot and cut left, causing Rachel to fall off balance and out of her path. That quickly, D'Angelo dashed into the dark salon.

Rachel rolled out of her fall and got to her feet. It didn't take long to see that Jake, although now bleeding from just above his eyebrow, was okay. Rachel didn't hesitate in taking off after D'Angelo.

The salon was dark, and Rachel didn't see that the large square ottoman had been moved into her path until it was too late. She banged her shin into it so hard it felt like it broke a bone, and also stubbed the toes of her right foot on the ottoman's foot. She cried out in pain as she tumbled to the floor.

Her emotions were turning from desperation and fear to anger. Practically growling, she got up, just as D'Angelo reached the stairs. She turned back, saw Rachel rising, and apparently thought better of retreating down below. D'Angelo turned around, to the door leading to the starboard walkway. Rachel ran through the hallway and dove around the island, lunging for D'Angelo as she reached for the door. Landing with a thud, Rachel grabbed onto the bottom of D'Angelo's gown and tugged her back, like a linebacker sacking a quarterback by the jersey. She felt as if she was yanking the fabric right off D'Angelo, but it held, pulling her away from the door. She tripped over Rachel and fell onto the U-shaped dining room bench seat. Her momentum carried her into the edge of the table, and she cracked her head and fell back onto the seat.

Rachel stood, ready to strangle the woman who had caused her and her husband so much pain. Before she could, D'Angelo swung with the only thing available to her, a throw pillow. It slowed Rachel and gave D'Angelo time to shove the glass table at her. Rachel staggered and fell, her backside bearing the brunt of the fall as her hands caught the table.

D'Angelo fled again, this time out the hatch door. Rachel lifted the table off herself and again gave chase. She turned her head fore then aft, not spotting her quarry in either direction. She assumed D'Angelo, having fled from the stern, wouldn't go back there, so she turned forward. The walkway was narrow, but Rachel hurried, bracing herself on the black glass exterior on her left and on the gunwale on her right. The walkway curved as the boat tapered, and she emerged to the open bow. The wide bench seat was to her left, the hatch and anchor directly ahead. D'Angelo stood as far forward as possible as if she had just realized she was out of options.

She turned and faced Rachel, a triangular bench seat extending from the gunwale on the right between them.

"It's over," Rachel said. "There's nowhere to run."

D'Angelo stared at her for a moment, then charged around the bench seat. Rachel met her halfway, and they collided and fell against the bench and railing in a mess of arms and legs and hair. Despite being constricted by the fabric of her dress, D'Angelo managed to gain the upper hand, looping her arm around Rachel's neck and pulling her into a chokehold. She spun her around, and Rachel saw why.

Jake had emerged from the port walkway, his gun drawn, aimed at D'Angelo and her human shield.

"Let her go."

"Drop your gun," D'Angelo said calmly.

He shook his head and moved slowly to his left. D'Angelo pivoted with him.

Under the guise of squirming against D'Angelo's grip, Rachel positioned her elbow in D'Angelo's solar plexus. She then made eye contact with Jake, hoping for once that he could read her signal as she winked.

He stopped moving.

Rachel drew her arm forward, then slammed her elbow back.

D'Angelo expelled a breath of air with a moan, and her hold on Rachel loosened. Rachel grabbed D'Angelo's arm with both of hers. She yanked it away from her neck and immediately ducked down. As she did, she heard Jake's gun discharge twice. Still holding D'Angelo's arm, Rachel felt her body shake as the bullets plugged into D'Angelo.

She staggered back, her arm sliding out of Rachel's grasp. Instinctively, Rachel turned, seeing two bullet holes in D'Angelo's chest, one just above her dress line and one just below it. Blood also trickled from her mouth, and she looked at Jake with a vacant gaze.

Her eyes turned to Rachel, and she reached out toward her.

Jake fired again, and D'Angelo's body reeled back against the railing. She flailed at Rachel as she began to topple backwards, and Rachel reached back in a reflexive effort to save her. Her fingers latched onto the first thing they touched, the diamonds.

The clasp of the necklace held D'Angelo's weight for an instant, just long enough for her to make wide-open eye contact with Rachel.

Then the clasp snapped, and D'Angelo pitched over the side and was captured by the sea.

Chapter Fifty-Six

Rachel had never felt more relaxed.

Each of her senses was flooding her with tranquility. She felt the comfortable linen of her dress swathing her skin, warm sand beneath her bare feet, the early evening sunshine caressing her skin. She heard the rhythmic, soothing waves lapping against the nearby shore and the quiet rustle of a gentle breeze in the palm trees around them. She tasted a delicious shrimp, mango, and jícama salad, along with plantain chips and refreshing iced tea. She smelled surrounding flowers—including an assortment of colorful lilies in a vase on the table—and caught a faint whiff of Jake's new cologne. And she saw beautiful pink sand, rich green foliage, bowed palms, and the cerulean ocean and its never-ending supply of foam-crested waves, all converging under a brilliant sky populated with tufts of white and gray.

Adding to her mood were memories of a day of total leisure—sleeping well into the morning, waking to the cadence of the ocean, brunch on their private patio, an afternoon stroll through the garden and along the beach, couples massages, and a nap in a hammock stretched between two palms with nothing in sight but the azure Atlantic. Considering the topsy-turvy few days that had preceded it, the serenity was magnified by comparison. The relief from physical pain, the lack of mental stress, and the absence of emotional anxiety over her and Jake's well-being all combined to enhance her feeling of comfort.

But more than anything, Rachel was relaxed in the knowledge that she and Jake were absolutely and utterly alone. Yes, there were other people at a handful of tables scattered along the private beach. There were dozens of other guests at their exclusive resort. There were waiters and waitresses and other resort staff. But not a one of them knew who the Taylors were, where they had come from, or what they had been through. Nobody who did know them had the faintest clue where they were. That, more than anything, provided Rachel a blanket of contentment that was almost indescribable.

Jake felt it too, she realized as she looked across the table at him. It wasn't in his smile, not even in his carefree posture as he dipped plantain chips into his salad. More than anything, it was in his eyes. They possessed—and had all day—a serenity that was a mixture of relief and happiness. Rachel couldn't stop staring at them. She'd always had a weakness for his caramel brown eyes, but now more so than ever. Rachel was continually drawn from the repetitive ebb and flow of the waves to Jake, to his eyes, to the drastic difference in them from seventy-two hours ago.

After shooting D'Angelo, Jake had dropped the gun and run to Rachel. She had melted into his embrace, letting a range of emotions she didn't even comprehend flow out of her in sobs. He had eventually stood back and held her face in his hands, brushing hair off her cheek with his thumb.

"We should get out of here," he'd said.

"Get out of here?"

"Away from . . . everything."

"Where will we go?"

"Just a few miles away. Then we can settle down and think."

Rachel didn't feel like she had the ability to think, so she decided to follow Jake. She nodded, then sagged onto the bench and against the railing, letting the diamonds fall from her hand onto the deck.

"Babe, are you okay?"

"Jake, I . . . I honestly have no idea." She pursed her lips to keep from crying.

Jake knelt in front of her. "I hear you, Hon. And we'll process this all, but we need to move. Are you physically up to it?"

She raised her eyes to his, drawing strength from them. "What do you need?"

"Just the keys from your swimsuit," he said with a thin grin. "You go turn on the batteries and meet me up top."

Fortunately, Rachel hadn't thought to lock the door to the engine room behind her and was able to get in without having to pick the lock again. She reinserted the keys, turned the switches back to on, and rejoined Jake at the helm. Three screens were built into the console, along with a host of switches and dials, a joystick, and radio. The steering wheel itself was just a clunky piece of metal, and the throttle beside it wasn't much different. Someone had left the key in the ignition, and Jake turned it, eliciting a low grumble from within the bowels of the yacht. The diesel engines caught and began humming smoothly. He gave them a minute to warm up, then took hold of the throttle. He inched it forward, and the yacht lurched and began to move, bouncing over a few swells and then cutting through them as he gave it a little more fuel.

Rachel leaned against the arm of the second captain's chair as Jake drove. The breeze lifted wet clumps of hair from her face and shoulders and chilled her in just a bikini. It was a constant reminder of how absurd this day had been. She tried to imagine a different scenario, where she and Jake were millionaires aboard such a yacht, cruising toward some romantic enclave at twilight, where they would frolic on the beach in slow motion like in those Sandals commercials. Instead, they had just survived a life-or-death struggle with two alleged Interpol officers and their crazy, eccentric, wealthy boss.

"Jake," she said after what she deemed a mile. "What are we gonna do?"

His eyes broke from the dark horizon to her. "I don't know, Babe."

"Are you going the right way?"

"Right way?"

"Toward shore."

"Which shore?" he asked.

She shook her head, not in the mood for wordplay.

"I was going to fire up the GPS when we're a little farther away, see where exactly we are."

"We're far enough, Jake. They're all dead."

He nodded and eased back the throttle, letting the boat coast to a stop. Then he took her in his arms again. For several long minutes, they just held onto each other. Eventually, her shivering made it impossible to hug him, and she stepped back. Jake suggested she go down below and find something of D'Angelo's to wear, but she glared at him. Then another idea hit her, and she said she was going to explore. He said he'd put a few more miles behind them and also see if he could figure out the GPS.

Somewhere, Rachel concluded, were the clothes she and Jake had been wearing that morning when they boarded the yacht. D'Angelo may have had them thrown overboard, but she doubted it. If nothing else, she knew where her own underwear and shirt were. So she made her way down below. After retrieving her clothes, she found a towel in the forward bathroom, dried off, and changed back into her underwear and shirt. Still without pants, she forced herself into D'Angelo's quarters. She found a full wardrobe in her closet and settled for a pair of sweats when she couldn't locate the rest of her and Jake's clothes. Shaking off the disgust of wearing the crazy Italian's pants, she tromped back up to the helm, where Jake stood in just the swim trunks, looking very much like a boat captain.

"Find anything?" she asked, placing a hand on his back.

He turned. "You found your clothes?"

"Just what they left me in. These are hers," she said, tugging on one of the legs of the sweatpants. "You know where we are?"

"If this is working," he said, nodding at one of the screens built into the console, "we are approximately due south of Cape Hatteras."

"How far is that from shore?"

"Hundred miles, give or take."

Rachel had sort of expected it, but the news still hit her like a shockwave. They would have drifted on the Jet Ski until . . .

"In other words, a quarter of the way to Bermuda," Jake said.

"So that really was the plan?"

"Seems so. The route's even charted into the computer."

"So are we near shipping lanes, or in radio range or something?"

He shrugged. "Haven't seen any signs of anyone else."

She leaned on the console and tipped her upper body in front of him. "Not to be a broken record, but what are we going to do, Jake?"

He sighed. "We have to figure out where we stand legally. Jamison and Frost made it sound like the dragnet was tightening around our necks, but I'm somewhat skeptical of their opinions."

"Fairly so."

"But, that doesn't mean they weren't telling the truth. Vaughn and West are dead."

"Who?"

"West, the guy with Vaughn. Whoever Jamison and Frost are, I'm guessing they didn't leave much of a trace at the park, which likely throws suspicion back on the two people known to have contact with Vaughn and West."

"Us."

"Right."

She blew out a breath of air. "Who knows we met with Vaughn?"

"Everyone at Alligator Adventure."

"Do they? Or did we just look like everyone else running from a shooting?"

Jake shrugged. "Maybe. But I'm guessing the authorities will piece together security cameras, get condo phone records, find out you purchased a Cornish hen, and put it all together. I don't want to take the chance that they have no clue it's us."

Rachel sighed again.

"Plus we have Butler and Holmes' deaths. Vaughn said they weren't dirty, that they were working for him without knowing what he was up to."

"Meaning?"

"I don't know, but I'm guessing knowledge of the operation wasn't contained with the three of them. When their deaths are investigated, there's a good chance our names come up since they were working with us. They had to have files on us, unless Vaughn had that all scrubbed and deleted any evidence. But I don't know when he would have had time to do that or would have known to do that. Plus there's the car with Butler's body and our prints inside, which I doubt got wiped away. And besides all that, we have no idea what evidence D'Angelo has stacked against us, on the off chance we survived or washed up on shore or whatever."

Rachel buried her head into his shoulder. "What a mess."

"Not to mention Masters and Paul, who at last check was in the hospital."

"And several dozen people saw me dart into traffic right in front of Spencer Flynn as he was killed," she said.

"I'd say we're persons of interest, to say the least."

She let her body go limp against his.

"And to make matters worse, this is all on top of the local cops knowing we're involved in something because of the break-in, the PADL I showed to Detective Robinson, and being at the auction where it was suspected something hinky was going down."

"So can't we come clean?" Rachel asked. "Just explain it all. Give them the truth?"

"We can," Jake said. "But I don't know that they'll buy the truth. And I don't know who 'they' are. If FBI Special Agent-in-Charge Vaughn was corrupt and two alleged Interpol officers were working for a crazy 'connoisseur' like D'Angelo, I don't know who we can trust."

"So what, Jake? We just sail to Charleston, book a flight back to Omaha, and hope this never happened?"

"We can't do that either. We don't know what happened to Paul and Masters. They could still be after us and the diamonds. Plus whoever originally hired us, since it wasn't *La Fantôme*, will want the diamonds."

"Nobody hired *us*."

"You know what I mean."

"So we give the diamonds back. You weren't thinking of keeping them, were you?" she asked, looking up at him.

"No, but it isn't that simple. Where are the diamonds by the way?"

"I dropped them up on the front deck."

"Shrewd move, grabbing them before she fell."

"It was instinct. I seriously wasn't thinking about saving them." She crossed her arms over her chest. "I wish I'd never seen them."

He raised an eyebrow in concession. "At any rate, even if we wanted to give them back, we don't know who to contact to make a drop. We can't just announce it because then we'll be complicit in this black market auction."

"We already are."

"But without the good old FBI to back us up."

She sighed for what felt like the tenth time. She looked up at Jake. "I just really want a hot bath, all these aches to go away, and for you to never have suggested we go to Myrtle Beach."

"Sorry," he said.

She reached up and kissed him. "I'm so glad you're okay."

"I think my pancreas might have been liquefied by all the Tasing, but relatively speaking." He pecked her back. "I'm glad you are too. I can't tell you how scared I was to see you in danger."

"You didn't show it."

"'Courage is being scared to death and saddling up anyway.'"

"John Wayne?"

"No other."

She raised her arms around his neck and kissed him again, slower and softer this time. "I always liked the Duke."

"Who wouldn't?"

"He was from Iowa, you know?"

"Is that right?"

"That's right," she said before he kissed her.

"What do you say we drift a few more miles and then . . ." He switched into a John Wayne impersonation. ". . . see about that bath, little lady?"

She smiled and pulled back from another kiss. "After you figure out where we're going."

"Actually," he said, releasing her, "I have a thought about that."

"You do?"

He nodded.

"Gonna share?"

He began humming. The Beach Boys, Rachel realized—"Kokomo."

"Bermuda?" she asked.

"It's in the GPS, and D'Angelo said they had a villa on the beach reserved."

"So?"

"So, they won't be using it."

"Jake."

"Look, Babe, this is clearly complicated, and we need some place to lay low for a while, while we figure things out. Somewhere off the grid, where nobody knows us or is looking for us. We can relax, recuperate, think. What better place than Bermuda?"

She opened her mouth and closed it. Twice. Then she shook her head. "How? You don't know how to sail. Do we have enough gas? What if she was lying? For crying out loud, we're in hurricane season. Jake, this is nuts."

"All I have to do is steer," he said calmly. "She wasn't lying because Bermuda was programmed into the GPS, which also means we do have enough gas, and if we're wrong, we can signal for help with the radio."

"And then what? We just lay around at a beach resort until inspiration hits?"

He smiled. "Yeah."

She shook her head again. "Jake, we'll get in trouble."

"For what? We've done nothing wrong."

"Except steal a yacht!"

"I doubt D'Angelo will press charges."

"And what about the diamonds? You think the FBI and everybody else will just forget them?"

"No. But they've been lost since 1974, so a few more days won't hurt anybody."

She sighed.

"Rach, Honey," he said, taking her hands. "You said you trusted me, trusted my leadership. Trust me now, one more time."

She looked up at him. "That's a lousy trump card."

"I'll throw in couples massages."

"Jake . . ."

"You said we needed a vacation after all this."

"*After* all this, Jake. *After*. It's not after yet."

"Almost, Babe. Almost."

"You keep saying that."

"Well," he said with a shrug, "sooner or later I oughta be right."

Chapter Fifty-Seven

Jake eyed Rachel as the waiter delivered key lime pie for dessert. Jake didn't lower his eyes when the waiter left, waiting instead for Rachel to take a drink of iced tea through her straw, then meet his gaze. It was true what he'd told her, that she had a natural beauty. She was cute in sweats or jeans and a T-shirt, right after waking up or with her hair just pinned up or tied back. But when she dressed up—say in an ankle-length lavender dress purchased the day before on a stroll through town—and took the added time to style her hair just so, she went from beautiful to . . . something else Jake didn't have words for.

"You're staring," she said.

He was. Watching the breeze play with loose wisps of her hair, even the ties of her halter-top dress. The backdrop of sand, rock, palms, ocean, and cloud-dotted sky created an ambiance—as did their table literally on the beach—that made him want to linger in the moment with her forever. But the truth was, they'd been putting off a conversation all day.

"I'm thinking," he said.

"About what we're going to do?"

He nodded.

Rachel leaned with her elbows on the table. "So what do you say?"

"I don't know," he said with a sigh. "I still don't know."

It had taken them the better part of thirty-six hours—once Jake had figured out the yacht's GPS, calculated the fuel rate to ensure they wouldn't run adrift in the middle of the Atlantic, and assuaged Rachel's remaining qualms—to sail to Bermuda. They'd used the time to decompress and process everything they'd been through, and also to contemplate and mull various ideas—everything from calling Detective Robinson and telling him every word of truth and hoping he could make it right to concocting an alternate story that would explain some of the less likely to be believed occurrences to anonymously leaving the diamonds somewhere with an explanatory note and returning home to Nebraska in the hopes that everything sorted itself out.

They had also cleaned up the yacht, wiping away (literally) every trace of evidence of what had taken place Sunday afternoon and evening. (Jake had taken exceptional pleasure in tossing D'Angelo's creepy ghost eyes picture overboard.) This after showering and changing into some of D'Angelo and Jamison's spare clothes. Rachel had found it more than a little creepy wearing a dead woman's apparel, showering in her bathroom, and cooking with her food—which they had only done after Jake found a switch that unlocked the magnetically sealed cabinets and cupboards throughout the yacht. They had also searched through all the trio's belongings, looking for evidence that would suggest more about their true identities. They'd found little, other than reservation details for the South Pointe Villas on the southern coast of Bermuda.

They had arrived under the cover of darkness, docked at an easily accessible marina at the northern tip of the island, hailed a cab, and checked into the villa under the name Andrea Fiore (one of D'Angelo's aliases, apparently) shortly before dawn on Tuesday. Exhausted (neither had gotten much sleep either night aboard the yacht), they'd slept most of the day away, spending their waking moments buying new clothes and checking the internet for word on what was going on in Myrtle Beach. Word had been pretty sparse. But at least there had been no evidence that they were wanted or that an international manhunt was underway.

Throughout the day Tuesday and Wednesday, Rachel and Jake had also weighed their legal options yet again. Jake had suggested calling a P.I. in the Myrtle Beach area to look into things for them. Rachel had suggested a lawyer who could broker a deal. Neither option particularly appealed to either of them. Rachel's responsible side and Jake's honest side kept bringing them back to calling the authorities and making a go of explaining things, which raised the same potential problems each time. And since money had theoretically changed hands between buyer and seller, the buyer would want the diamonds and the seller, possibly, full payment on delivery. If neither got what they wanted, Jake feared he and Rachel might still be in danger, no matter what the authorities said or did. Now, as Jake walked through everything again—taking a few pauses to account for their waiter bringing the check—they were as uncertain as ever.

"There's no good option, is there?" Rachel asked before sliding a bite of key lime pie off her fork.

"Not really," he said, taking a final swig of his post-dinner coffee.

She sighed and looked past him. Most of the other tables were now empty, adding to their solitude.

"You going to finish your pie?" he asked. His was long gone, and he craved more of the tart but sweet, smooth and airy dessert. It had been the perfect finish to a delicious meal of baked red snapper (freshly caught), steamed white rice, and spring veggies.

"Yes," she said, making a point of taking another bite. She swallowed and set her fork down, leaning on her hand, her elbow on the table. "Jake."

"Mmm."

"I'm behind you, whatever you decide."

"Are you weaseling out?"

"No. I just honestly don't know what to do. And it's like I said on the way to the auction—I trust your leadership. You haven't steered us wrong yet."

"Except maybe for getting in the car with Jamison and Frost."

"Okay, you haven't steered us wrong much."

"Leaving you behind with the diamonds while I went to meet Vaughn."

"So your decision making's terrible. I still trust you." She grinned as he took another swig of coffee. "But seriously, I have no idea what to do. And whatever you decide, I'm with you one hundred percent."

Jake smiled. "I appreciate that, Babe." He exhaled. "If only I knew what to do."

The moment was magical. That wasn't the way Jake thought, but it was how the commercials, travel magazines, and other vacationers would describe it.

He and Rachel had lingered at their table for over an hour as the sun sunk toward the ocean. Now it hovered just over the surface of the water, casting it in a resplendent glow while imbuing the small, puffy clouds above with decadent shades of pink, orange, and purple.

"This is so nice," Rachel said softly. They'd struck out along the beach, past the cobblestone path to their private villa, leaving the resort and even its moderate hustle and bustle behind. There was nothing around them but the ocean, the sloping beach, and the swaying palms. They were barely moving, arm-in-arm, her head against his shoulder. The breeze lifted tendrils of her hair against his face and neck. On a spring evening back in Omaha, watching *Watters' World*, that would be annoying. Here, it was a delightful ambiance.

"Mm-hmm," he said.

"But it's over, isn't it?"

He looked down. Rachel stopped walking and turned to look at him, half her face bathed in the orange glow of the setting sun and half cast in shadow.

"We have to go back," she said.

"Yeah."

"And probably sooner than later."

"Yeah."

Her sigh was audible.

Then absolute silence, minus the waves, as they strolled along.

"You think it worked?" he asked a few minutes later.

"What worked?"

"This vacation."

She looked up, frowning. "How do you mean?"

"I mean, we talked about lighting a fire with this trip, about getting out of the rut, about talking about issues, and spending time together doing more than just watching TV and eating dinner out. Well, mission accomplished. You can't tell me our relationship isn't stronger for what we've been through."

She just looked at him.

"I've never appreciated you more than I do now," he continued. "After all we went through, all the times you had my back, the way you kept going and never gave up despite it all. I wouldn't wish the last few days on anyone, but

I'm not sure I'd trade them either—not after all it's shown me about you and about us."

Rachel's face finally showed expression, a close-mouthed smile that surged to her eyes, animating and amplifying them into pools of darkened jade. She lunged up and drew him into a long, tender kiss. When she finally shrunk back, nestling against him, her voice was as soft as the breeze.

"I love you so much, Jake Taylor."

Eventually, they resumed walking, curving slightly around the beach. It was still deserted, the sky a myriad of colors as the sun reflected off scuttling clouds. It was more beautiful than any vista Jake had ever seen.

"You know," he said, letting his words trail into the breeze.

"Mmm?"

"There is one other option."

"What's that?" she asked without looking up at him.

"We could just take the diamonds and make a run for it. Fifty mil goes a long way."

She turned her head to him. The breeze blew a strand of hair across her face. She ignored it. "How you going to spend seven huge diamonds?"

"One at a time."

"I know, maybe we could hold a black market auction."

"That's good, Babe." He gently tugged the hair aside for her. "We'll trade that piece of scrap metal D'Angelo called a yacht in for a deluxe model, bounce around the Caribbean for a while—you know, island hop."

"You'll get bored."

"I've always wanted to do some sport fishing. Maybe scuba dive on old wrecks for gold doubloons and pieces of eight. I'll grow my hair out, my beard, it'll all turn gray, poke through the gap in my half-buttoned shirts. I'll wear torn shorts, never any shoes, and smoke cigars a lot. Maybe I'll even write a novel someday."

"Wonderful."

"I'll probably get a nickname like 'Graybeard' or 'the Captain.' And we will have to think of new names for ourselves."

"Mm-hmm. And what will I do while you channel your inner Hemingway, cook and clean the yacht?"

"Well, that and model skimpy bikinis for me."

"My dream come true."

"And you forgot cleaning my fish and editing my novel."

"I think I'll turn myself in to the FBI."

"You could take pictures of something other than weddings, high school seniors, and Nebraska sunsets."

"The photo ops would be amazing."

"Else we could become the next version of Jamison and Frost, crossing the world to buy and sell rare treasure and antiquities, slink around in alleys, dress in black leather, hold clandestine meetings in the rain, do other spy stuff. Only we'd be better looking."

"And far more suave."

"And we'd have our own boat."

"That settles it," she said, dropping his hand and wrapping her arm around his waist. She leaned into him as they walked, again letting the waves be the only sound.

"We could do it, Rach."

She stopped. Let go of him. "Are you serious?"

Jake shrugged.

"We'd be fugitives."

"Who'd committed no crime."

"Except stealing fifty-million-dollar diamonds."

"Stealing from who? There is no rightful owner."

"That doesn't make it us."

He shrugged again.

She resumed walking. "You're forgetting our families."

He took a few paces to catch up. "My parents are dead, and you seldom see or talk to yours."

"What about your brothers and my sister?"

"They each have kids, have their own families . . . I'm not saying we wouldn't miss them, but they aren't integral to our lives or us to theirs."

"And when we just disappear into thin air, you think they'll just move on and forget we ever existed? You know your brothers. We don't come back, and next thing you know, Nancy Grace will be doing remotes from Myrtle Beach looking for us. Tearful family interviews on *48 Hours* . . ."

"Is *48 Hours* even on anymore? Or Nancy Grace?"

"You know what I mean."

"I do. We'll send them a postcard from Turks and Caicos."

She craned her neck to look directly at him. "You're actually serious about this?"

"I'm saying before we make any decision, we should at least consider it."

"Consider island-hopping around the Caribbean for the rest of our lives, doing nothing but fishing and wearing a bikini, all after somehow hawking the Archibald Diamonds?"

He nodded. "Although, we wouldn't have to limit ourselves to the Caribbean."

"That's crazy. There are so many things you're not thinking of—our house, all our stuff, our jobs. You don't even know how to dock a boat."

"I managed."

"With the help of Felipe or whatever his name was."

"Just Philip. And I'll learn."

She shook her head. "Think of all the legal matters with us being declared dead or missing."

"Yeah."

"The hassle of maintaining aliases and true anonymity."

He sighed.

"It isn't realistic, Jake."

"I know. It was just nice to think about."

"Adapting to a new culture. Never watching your Huskers. We couldn't do it."

"I know."

"We just couldn't."

"I know."

He looped his arm over her shoulders, watching the sun melt into the Atlantic. It disappeared and seemed to send a fresh breeze their way as a result.

Rachel stopped, a crooked frown-turned-grin on her face. "Could we?"

Author's Note

In the summer of 2015, my wife and I took a "tenth anniversary" trip to Myrtle Beach and fell in love with the place. It was on the Grand Strand, drawing inspiration from the pounding surf, flapping palm fronds, and rows of brightly colored hotels (and from the Clive Cussler novel I carried with me), that I latched upon the idea for *Fire & Ice* and the *Last Resort* series.

My goal, in addition to telling what I hoped was a compelling story, was to immerse my reader in the environment—to take them to Myrtle Beach. I have several more novels planned in the series and, in each, the setting will be a character all its own, playing an integral part in the story. After all, we go to fiction to be entertained, to escape from everyday life. A destination-based novel seemed to me like the best of both worlds.

As always, I relied closely on my wife, Sierra, for feedback and critique. My parents, Doug and Jean, aided in the proofing process, as did my wife's aunt, Chris. Without them, this would be an impossible venture. As always, any mistakes that still exist are mine.

To that end, I depicted Myrtle Beach as precisely as possible from memory. Where I erred—or took artistic license for the sake of plot—I hope the good people of the Palmetto State will forgive me. Or better yet, invite me back so I can more accurately and intimately acquaint myself with the Grand Strand!

Also by Nathan Birr

Overnight Delivery – The Douglas Files: Book One
Three's a Crowd – The Douglas Files: Book Two
All an Illusion – The Douglas Files: Book Three
Shot List – The Douglas Files: Book Four
Chasing the Wind – The Douglas Files: Book Five
Blood and Treasure – The Douglas Files: Book Six

Black Male – A Douglas Files Short
WinterKill – A Douglas Files Short

God, Girls, Golf & the Gridiron
(Not Always in That Order) . . .
A Love Story

All is Calm? – A Christmas Novella

The Book of Levi

www.nathanbirr.com

www.ingramcontent.com/pod-product-compliance
Lightning Source LLC
Chambersburg PA
CBHW020931020726
47495CB00002B/448